NEW STORIES FROM THE MIDWEST
2018

NEW STORIES FROM THE MIDWEST 2018

ANTONYA NELSON
Guest Editor

JASON LEE BROWN AND SHANIE LATHAM
Series Editors

newamericanpress

Milwaukee, Wis.

n e w a m e r i c a n p r e s s

www.NewAmericanPress.com

Printed in the United States of America
ISBN 978-1-941561-18-8

Book design by Shanie Latham
Cover image © 2014 by Julie Blackmon

For ordering information, please contact:
Ingram Book Group
One Ingram Blvd.
La Vergne, TN 37086
(800) 937-8000
orders@ingrambook.com

All stories reprinted by permission of the individual authors and/or publishing companies. Grateful acknowledgment is made to the journals, magazines, and books where these stories first appeared:

"Prairie Fire, 1899" © 2017 by Mike Alberti. First published in *One Story* issue no. 226 (March 2017). Reprinted by permission of the author.

"Neck Bones" © 2015 by Ron A. Austin. First published in *Ninth Letter* 12.1 (spring/summer 2015). Reprinted by permission of the author.

"Abu the Water Carrier" © 2017 by Abby Bardi. First published in *Bellingham Review* vol. XL issue 74 (April 2017), winner of the 2016 Tobias Wolff Award for Fiction. Reprinted by permission of the author.

"A Good Breath" © 2017 by Michael Byers. First published in *Missouri Review* 40.2 "Mischief Makers" (Summer 2017). Reprinted by permission of the author.

"Girls Like Her" © 2017 by Alison Clement. First published in *The Sun* (March 2017). Reprinted by permission of the author.

"Where I Was Before" © 2015 by Robert Day. First published in *New Letters* vol. 81 no. 1 (January 2015). Reprinted by permission of the author.

"Wraiths in Swelter" © 2015 by Steve De Jarnatt. First published in *New England Review* vol. 36 no. 2. Reprinted by permission of the author.

"The Inevitable" © 2015 by Daniel A. Hoyt. First published in *The Sun* (December 2015). Reprinted by permission of the author.

for Jay

CONTENTS

* Winner of the 2018 Jay Prefontaine Fiction Prize

EDITORS' NOTE

New Stories from the Midwest 2018 showcases twenty stories set in the Midwest by midwestern and non-midwestern authors. The goals of *New Stories from the Midwest* are to celebrate an American region that is often ignored in discussions about distinctive regional literature and to demonstrate how the quality of fiction from and about the Midwest (Illinois, Indiana, Iowa, Kansas, Michigan, Minnesota, Missouri, Nebraska, North Dakota, Ohio, South Dakota, and Wisconsin) rivals that of any other region. To collect the stories, editors put out an open call via Submittable for nominations from both editors and writers and also solicited nominations from more than 300 magazines, literary journals, and small presses. We received more than 540 stories from more than 175 publications, editors, and writers. *New Stories from the Midwest 2018* contains stories published in 2015, 2016, and 2017, and by pure numbers was the most competitive volume to date. Editorial readers narrowed nominations to fifty-five finalists, which were passed on to guest editor Antonya Nelson, who chose twenty stories for inclusion. The thirty-five finalist stories are listed in the back of the book.

We are pleased to announce that Susan Perabo has chosen Cady Vishniac's story "Girls Girls Girls" as winner of the 2018 Jay Prefontaine Fiction Prize. The prize was named after writer Jay Prefontaine, who co-edited the first volume of *New Stories from the Midwest*.

Perabo said this about the winning selection, which first appeared in *Salamander*: "'Girls Girls Girls' is dark and smart and funny. It's a story that by all rights should be really, really sad, but ultimately it's not because you love everyone in it, every damaged and vulnerable and flawed soul that lights up the page. In that way it's pretty much exactly like life."

Susan Perabo is author of two collections of short stories, *Who I Was Supposed to Be* and *Why They Run the Way They Do*, and the novels *The Broken Places* and *The Fall of Lisa Bellow*.

— **Jason Lee Brown and Shanie Latham**
Series Editors

INTRODUCTION

EVERY TIME SOMEBODY MENTIONS THE MIDWEST, a debate ensues. What is the Midwest, anyway? The "middle" of the "west" would be, ostensibly, Nevada. But Nevada's a no-go. So who qualifies? When I asked this series's editor Jason which of the United States were in, he provided a list.

"Oklahoma's out," I told my husband.

"Good riddance," said he.

But beyond geography (you can google "Midwest" and see the official list; that hurdle was the simplest to surmount), these stories feel authentic. And I don't mean strictly realistic, because there are plenty of surreal and magical moments herein. These characters and their troubles feel true, if not factual, and they are engaging, if not always "likable," folks. They are plucky and pathetic and hilarious and doomed; they are desperate and baffled and despicable and guilty and aware of their luck, be it bad or good.

I appreciate the way weather and animals populate these stories, the way the natural world operates forcefully upon the fates of their people. The big emptiness of the landscape plays a role, that large expanse the coasts label "flyover" but which the locals know to cross via the inevitable highway that cuts through it, in the car upon the road, with its driver and passengers facing the possibility of meditation, escape, sojourn, and mishap. Beyond the car, the relentless presence of terra incognita, distant horizons, impending acts of God. Outposts of civilization appear in the forms of religious fervor and comfort food; there are surprises everywhere.

And the pleasure, for me personally, in reading these stories is that they celebrate (or at least take seriously) my homeland. I grew up in Kansas, in Wichita, in the geographical center of the (lower)

United States, famous for its farthest distance from either ocean or international border. Airplane manufacturing was first located there so as to be less vulnerable to foreign interference. I have been an avid reader since I learned how to do it, and my parents were English professors, so our house was full of books. Yet I don't recall many of them written by local authors nor set in my neck of the woods. I was always pleased, inordinately so, to discover one or the other; I was named for Willa Cather's *My Antonia*, a favorite of my father (for who can read "There was nothing but land; not a country at all, but the material out of which countries are made" without immediately recognizing the Midwest?) And how lucky I've been, to have a location I know well mostly under-represented in stories or novels; it has been so singularly my turf.

Though I also remember how glad I was to meet another Wichita native who also wrote fiction, Janet Peery, how giddy we both seemed, finding a kindred spirit among the wheatfields and stockyards and grain silos; that certainly isn't the way somewhere like Brooklyn works, right? Where you can't swing a laptop cord without hitting another writer. Where you aren't the only writer in your zip code (maybe even your building). Where writers are a dime a dozen. Still, it seemed wonderful to know that somebody else was on my team. That's how these stories strike me: written by comrades, honoring a much-maligned or, perhaps worse, ignored terrain, and gathered here to share with the wider world.

— **Antonya Nelson**
Guest Editor

PRAIRIE FIRE, 1899

Mike Alberti

FIRST THERE WAS NOTHING, just the silent, empty prairie and the darkness lying heavy over it.

Then there was the train, the great black engine that had steamed out of Fargo and hurled itself west across the plains, making speed because its cars were empty of freight and because every hour the engineer yelled back to the stoker to keep the fire roaring. Boiling, furious, the train heaved through the night and through the liquid predawn glow, and as the sun floated up over the eastern rim of the world, the train was still churning west and towing that blazing globe behind it, pulling it up out of the dark. Midmorning, the train stopped in the coal town of Sims, North Dakota, where it took on four cars of brown lignite and then went on, aimed at Tacoma. Ten miles outside of Sims, the stoker cleared the ash pan, tossed the white-hot clinker out of the engine into the vacant prairie, where the wheatgrass and bluestem were October-brown and bending with a western breeze.

That breeze blew back to Sims, where it was Sunday, Sabbath. After the hopper cars had been loaded, the workweek was over and the forty-three men employed by the Northern Pacific Coal Company lined up to get their pay. Colonel Bly—the mine manager—sat at the table he set up every week on the platform at the depot, smoking his cigar and scrawling his signature across the bottom of the company scrip. At his right elbow stood his foreman—a tall, glowering Swede named Knutson—who looked up each miner's name in his ledger as they approached and saw there what weight of coal had been logged for the week and calculated the man's pay in his head to tell Colonel Bly, who wrote it out on the scrip and signed. After that weekly sacrament, the men were free until first shift started the next morning. Some attended services at one of the three churches in town—Catholic, Lutheran, Presbyterian—which were postponed every Sunday until after the train had been loaded. Others, homesteaders, went to buy provisions for the week at the general store before starting the long walk out to their sod houses and farms. The rest made their way to the saloons, where they would spend a good part of their wages and where, later, some commotion—bets, challenges, insults, fistfights—could be expected.

Those short, bright hours after being paid, when their time was their own and they were free to do what they pleased, were the sweetest part of the week. These were men who had been underground, breathing the black dust, crawling on their knees through the cold catacombs they had blown open with dynamite, checking the flames of their lamps to make sure they did not burn green from the poison gas that was the earth's dank breath. And now, aboveground, they could breathe the free air in daylight and smell the crisp breeze that came from the west.

By noon that breeze already carried the smell of smoke, though faintly, feebly. Norma Goodwin caught a hint of it as she crossed Main Street to visit her friend Joanne Crocker, who was sick with fever. Norma paused and lifted her nose to the west, but she couldn't locate the smell. It was stronger an hour later, when the congregation of the Sims Evangelical Lutheran Church trickled into the street. They all smelled it, but no warning was raised: it could have been anything, a trash fire or the usual output of a dozen stoves all warming Sunday dinner. Irvin Olin, who worked for the railroad overseeing the depot, was playing cards with August Weinrich, Jr., when they caught the smell in the air. They were sitting on the porch of the depot out on the edge of town, and when he smelled it, Olin stood up and breathed and looked off to the west from beneath the brim of his hat, but he didn't see anything, just sky and prairie, both yawning empty.

The first to see the smoke was old William Crump, known locally as Uncle Willy. In the war he had fought under General Sherman, at Shiloh, at Vicksburg, at Chattanooga, Atlanta, Savannah, Columbia, and afterward he had come west to Dakota Territory and worked for the railroad before his homestead section came through: one hundred acres of flat grassland where Crump tried to live and raise grain for five years. At all times he carried in his belt a pistol he had recovered from a dead Confederate officer in 1865. He had taken a ball in the right shoulder at Vicksburg, and he could still feel it in the mornings, the shoulder stiff, aching, and throughout the day he brought his left hand unthinkingly to that place. Out there alone on the prairie his mind had turned back to the war and he had begun to live simultaneously in both times: while running a team across his field he was riding slowly through the Georgia swamp; while shooting antelope he was aiming at a Confederate position entrenched in the rocks along a stream. When it became too much for him out there alone, he moved back to town. On Sundays he bought a bottle of whiskey and drank it on the roof of the grain elevator, the highest place around, where he could see for miles and project his memory out into that blank open space and overlook the past from the high ground. To the passerby in the street below he seemed a lonely watchman, scanning the western plains, waiting for something to come up over the long line of sky. And indeed, that day, when Uncle Willy saw that low, gray smear along the western horizon, he rose slowly to his feet and squinted for several minutes until he was sure, and then he shouted, Hey! Hey! Fire! Fire!

But down below, the only people in the street were Jonas Herbet, a miner whose hearing had been blown out the year before when a charge of dynamite had exploded prematurely, and Norma Goodwin, who was now returning home from her visit with Joanne Crocker. Norma heard Uncle Willy's gruff voice and she looked up to where he stood on the elevator, pointing west. Although he was such a fixture on the elevator on Sundays that she hardly noticed him anymore, he'd always been silent, and so the sound of his voice gave her pause. But because she was preoccupied with her friend's illness, and because she was in a rush to begin cooking Sunday dinner, and because Uncle Willy's words were smudged in the wind, she put him out of mind and hurried on her way home.

Uncle Willy saw her hurry. Proud, vindicated, he took a drink from his bottle and raised his left hand to his shoulder, to the scar that was there beneath his shirt.

Nearly an hour later, Thorsten Larsen burst into the Mineshaft Saloon, yelling in Norwegian, Fire! Fire! Larsen homesteaded a plot three miles outside of town and was generally considered odd: at harvesttime each year he refused to help with the threshing because he claimed the work would stiffen his fingers, which he wanted to keep limber for his Hardanger fiddle. He had brought the violin with him from Norway in 1891 and often displayed it, but no one had ever heard him play. It was now packed along with the other things Larsen had managed to salvage in his cart just outside the saloon, where his wife, Laura, sat holding a rescued shoat in her arms. Because Larsen was shouting in his native tongue, the gathered miners did not register what he said for some minutes, until like a wave the news spread through the barroom, and then in a great rush the men hurried through the door to see for themselves.

There it was, now: that gray smear along the western horizon.

For a moment the men looked out in silence, stunned. Then their shock thawed into panic. Three men were sent into town to raise the alarm. The others—about a dozen in total—ran to the general store, where they told Sam Fletcher what was happening: a mile out, maybe; wind's blowing straight in; be here in a few hours. There were several shovels in the store, and the men took them out past the depot and began digging a trench there, carving up the dry grass around the town. They all knew what was necessary: to cut a scar into the prairie along the western perimeter of Sims, an arc long enough that it would divert the fire from the town like a windbreak, and wide enough that the flames couldn't sail over to the other side.

Just as they began to dig, the bells from the Lutheran Church rang out—one of the messengers had thought of that—and the sound was so incongruous at that quiet time of the Sabbath as to call people from their homes. Soon a small crowd had gathered in the middle of the main street. As the news circulated, their voices grew louder and more frantic: Should we leave? Sure it's coming this way? What about the children?

Rosa Anderson stepped up onto the porch of the post office and raised her voice above the others. Rosa was married to George Anderson, the baker, but before that she had been an opera singer in Chicago. She had stood on stage at Crosby's Opera House and thrown her voice into the teeming crowd: Rossini, Bellini, Donizetti, Verdi. She had been a rising star, billed the Belle Canto of Chicago, until the great fire razed Crosby's and most of downtown. Rosa had planned to go east after that, but in the spring she had come down with a bad bout of pneumonia that collapsed part of her lung and ruined her career for good, and when she was finally able to leave her bed, she married the man who had visited her every day in the hospital and filled her ears with his dreams of going west: sad, sweet George Anderson. Now, nearly thirty years later, Rosa filled her lungs with air and bellowed from the porch: All right! All right! Now, friends, what we have here is an emergency. We're going to need to act quickly. No time to waste. We've all helped to build this town and now we're all going to have to help save it.

Under Rosa's direction it was decided that the children should be taken to the only building in town that was not made of wood: the new brick schoolhouse, just completed that summer. Simon Lewis, who operated the telegraph, ran to the depot to send messages to all neighboring towns and request help from the village of Glen Ullin, which had a fire department. The townswomen dispersed to see to their children and their homes; their husbands were dispatched to the edge of town to help the others dig.

Out at the trench, the scrape and churn of the shovels had fallen into a steady rhythm. The sound of the digging floated up to a sparsely furnished bedroom on the second floor of the Mineshaft

Saloon, where Fannie Hall sat brushing her hair in front of her dressing mirror. When she heard it, Hall rose and went to the room's small window and opened it and stuck her head out and saw the men digging there below and called out, Hey! What're you all doing digging in the dirt down there? My girls are trying to sleep!

It's a prairie fire! Jay Knowles shouted back. Better get your girls waked up!

Fire! Hall said. Well damn.

She shut the window and sat down heavily at the dressing table. Hall was the madam of the small bordello that operated above the bar. Before coming to Sims she had worked in a brothel in Minot, where she had met and married a man named Joseph Blackburn, who had staked a mining claim three miles south of Sims and died a year later when the entrance to the shaft collapsed, burying him alive. That same spring, Hall changed her name and opened her own house of ill fame and now was one of Sims's wealthiest citizens. After thinking for a few moments, she took a long pull on her cigarette and then rose again and went out of the room and walked down the hallway, banging on each of the doors and shouting, Wake up! Wake up!

One by one, the three sleepy-eyed women opened their doors and peeked their heads out into the hallway. What is it, Fannie? It's just three o'clock.

It's a damn fire, Hall yelled. Heading this way. You all hurry up and get yourselves dressed and ready to get digging!

Half an hour later the four women had dressed and tied their hair back and joined the men at the trench, where they dug with whatever tools were at hand—picks and a rusty ax—and by then other men worked alongside with scythes, cutting down the tall grass and raking it away. Two plows were hitched and their iron blades carved beneath the sod and turned it over, leaving a ragged gouge in the prairie.

Great flocks of birds were flying overhead and soon the animals began to appear—antelope, deer, coyotes, running alone or in pairs; and even some fugitive farm animals: horses, pigs, a few sheep—

all fleeing, panting, tongues lolling out of their mouths. More homesteaders were riding into town with their carts packed high, and like grim harbingers they delivered the news: it was moving fast, due east; a mile west of town the very sky was made of smoke. Some of the farmers stopped to help, but others, less hopeful, drove on, headed for Sims Creek on the eastern side of town.

By four o'clock, the sky had dimmed and the setting sun was veiled by smoke, a pale disc gleaming through a gray curtain. Still, looking west over the low swell of the land, the men saw nothing, just the ceaseless sway of grass. From his perch on top of the grain elevator, Uncle Willy watched and waited, and when he saw the horizon light up as though a second sun were rising in the west, he turned his eyes to the line of men and women digging along the edge of town, and his old, rough-hewn face cracked into a crooked, satisfied smirk.

A quarter of an hour later, E. J. Burke drove his wagon into town, yelling for a doctor. Charley Mato was pulled from the line of diggers and hurried to the wagon. Lying in the bed was Burke's daughter, Stella, a girl of twelve. She was still alive, he saw; her chest rose and fell. But half her face was black, charred, the skin peeling away from her skull. Her eyes looked up blankly at nothing. Doctor Mato was a Mandan Indian and he had been educated at Carlisle before coming back to North Dakota to work for the mine. In that work he had seen miners blown apart by dynamite, treated miners whose legs had been crushed in a tunnel collapse, watched miners cough up dark, powdery blood. He understood that there was damage that could not be undone, things so broken they could not be fixed. Doctor Mato forced himself to meet Burke's eye and then he shook his head silently. The girl, he knew, was beyond hearing, but he could not bring himself to say any words. Likewise silent, Burke looked back, slack-jawed and red-eyed, and after a moment he lifted his hands, loose at the wrist, and Doctor Mato saw that they were also badly burned. Burke said, She went back into the barn for her calf. It was all afire but she went back in, and when she come out she was all afire, too. I put her out myself. I put her out with my hands. Seeing those hands, Doctor Mato could foresee the pain that Burke would soon be in. He looked back at the girl in the wagon. She was dead. Still wordless, he took Burke's elbow and led him into town, to the clinic, where he put salve on his hands and wrapped them in bandages. They left the girl in the wagon, where she lay like some terrible portent in the street, her sightless eyes still open, aimed up at the sky, which was slowly dimming.

Colonel Bly, the mine manager, was looking at that same sky, standing on the porch of his house and rubbing his eyes. A moment before, he had woken from his afternoon rest to the smell of the smoke and now he looked out blinking, waiting for comprehension to jolt him fully out of sleep. His house was a half mile outside of town, near the mine, and looking west past the drab, gray mine buildings—the office and warehouse squatting in the foreground and the hoist house and tipple towering thirty feet high above—he could see the new red glow along the skyline. He saw that flushed undersky and felt his guts go liquid and he bolted off the porch and ran toward town. He was a large bewhiskered man with a huge belly and gout in his feet and by the time he reached the line of diggers he was winded and could not take a breath to speak. The miners, so accustomed to taking his orders, stopped digging for a moment and waited for him to say something, but he stood crouched and panting for so long that they resumed their work. When he finally regained his breath, the colonel bellowed: The mine! You damn idiots! The mine! You have to save the mine!

The men stopped digging again and looked out to the northwest where the mine buildings stood in dark silhouette against the purpling sky. They looked at the mine like their serf ancestors might have looked upon the lord's manor at dusk, with a mixture of awe and fear and nerve-taut hatred. The colonel's exhortation hung in the air until Lawrence Wilkes, a young miner from Chicago, said, It's too late, Colonel. We got to do our best to save the town.

There's no town without the mine, you son of a bitch! The town is the mine! Jesus! Where's Knutson?

The men looked around but the Swede was not among them. The colonel swore and turned and set off running again, this time toward the mine, and the men stood for a moment watching his lonely figure recede. Then they went back to work.

When he reached the mine, Colonel Bly thought his lungs might burst. He tore into the office and found it already in disarray. The door hung open and inside papers were scattered around the wood floor. The steel safe was gone from its place in the corner, and with it five thousand dollars' worth of twenty-dollar bills issued by the First National Bank in Williston. The Northern Pacific Coal Company was owned by the colonel's cousin, Terrence Bly, who had secured his position for him in exchange for a large investment of capital funds. Gone.

Winded, sapped of strength, the colonel sat down heavily in his chair. Knutson, he thought. It must have been the Swede. From his desk drawer he pulled two bottles: one of laudanum, which he took for his gout, and one of Kentucky bourbon. He took a long drink of the first and followed it with a long drink of the second. Then he turned toward the small grimy window, through which he generally surveyed the comings and goings at the mine, but through which he now watched the approaching line of fire as it swelled red against the gathering dark.

At that moment Knutson was already four miles away, riding through that dusk in the stolen wagon with the stolen safe. By daybreak he would be in Mandan and by the next night Bismarck and then gone, swallowed up by the teeming country: Minneapolis, Chicago, St. Louis, New Orleans. Or perhaps east, Boston, New York, Philadelphia, Baltimore; or west, Denver, Seattle, San Francisco. Swallowed up. Gone. He just had to decide where.

And so in Sims, as the light leaked out of the day and the fire loomed, the residents dug their trench wider, and others emptied their houses into carts, heaped their valuables there in preparation for flight, and the children huddled in the brick schoolhouse where their teacher, Miss Evelyn Crawford, led them through every song she knew, and then again, the children's fearful faces looking up at her in the light of the lantern, singing, my country 'tis of thee, sweet land of liberty, of thee I sing.

Soon the fire was close enough to be heard, roaring and whooshing and spitting, gnashing its teeth. The flames like forked tongues rose high as two men and the smoke billowed into town and down the throats of the residents, acrid, scorching. The diggers tied handkerchiefs across their faces and went on working.

At six-thirty the mine caught. The blaze shot up the tipple like an eruption, the wood of that tower coated with flammable coal dust, and the flame rose thirty feet above the prairie and waved there like a giant red flag. Anyone in town with a sightline stopped to watch. Soon they heard the explosive sounds that were the other buildings catching fire, the windows breaking from the heat.

All eyes that watched that terrible blaze had seen other fires before it, and those antecessors hung before their vision like conflagrant ghosts. Many of the trench-line men had worked in the city factories, where the giant steel forges were like red mouths gaping, insatiable in their hunger for the coal that the filthy, sweating men shoveled into them without end. Irving Olin had spent time working oil rigs in Pennsylvania, where he had seen a fresh gush of oil ignite from a lamp and spout into the air like blood from the earth's black veins. The pastor of the Presbyterian church was reminded of a picture he showed the children in catechism: four huge horsemen riding across the plains and revealing God's awful wrath in their fiery wake. Uncle Willy, still watching from his post on the grain elevator, saw in the burning mine the spirit of Columbia, where he had danced drunk in the street with the other soldiers while the city consumed itself around them. As the tipple began to collapse in a shower of sparks and flaming wood, he rose unsteadily to his feet and, stepping back, he pulled the Confederate revolver from his belt and fired six shots aimlessly into the blazing night.

During the Great Fire of Chicago, Rosa Anderson had fled through the swarming streets, the air choked by cinders and smoke and ashes falling around them like snow. Down Dearborn Street to the edge of Lake Michigan where thousands were waiting, surrounded by what they could save, and some of them swimming out in the freezing lake to get as far away from the fire as they could. She had sat on her trunk on the beach and watched the fire for hours through her scorched eyes, watched it come right up to the shore and stop there, menacing. Rosa saw the mine collapse and, like a commanding general, raised her voice again to the crowd assembled at the edge of town: The creek! The creek! Fall back to the creek!

Except for a few men who stayed behind to work, they left the town then. They collected their children from the schoolhouse, and carrying their things and pulling their carts and riding in their wagons with their animals in tow like a line of penitents, they made their way east through the prairie to Sims Creek and in a slow file crossed the narrow wooden railroad bridge to the far bank, where others had already gathered. From that vantage they watched the fire approach and waited to see if the trench would hold.

And for a time it seemed that it would. The few men who stayed behind backed away from the blaze, the heat intolerable, the great wall of fire hovering at the border, coming right up to the line they had dug, looming, but not proceeding. Halted, the high flames bent forward in the wind like reaching arms. The trench was wide and curved around the whole western part of town, and when he saw that the fire was stopped, E. J. Macally clapped the shoulder of Jay Knowles in celebration, said, Hooo-ahh, we goddamn did it!

Then the jackrabbits appeared, running out of the blaze, disturbed from their tunnels beneath the prairie and risen to escape but too late, so that they ignited as they fled and became small fireballs barreling across the trench and into the dry grass on the other side.

When they realized what was happening, the men began swinging their shovels like mallets, stopping the flaming rodents and stomping them out. But there were dozens, then hundreds. The rabbits stampeded out of the fire like a plague and the men could not keep up and small fires began burning on the town-side of the trench and soon the porch of the depot caught fire. The men rushed to put it out, filled tubs of water from the pump there and threw them at the burning porch, but the fire was too hot and they could not get close enough. Jay Knowles said, I'll get closer and you all throw water on me so I don't catch fire, too. They fought the fire that way for a quarter of an hour, but soon it reached the roof of the porch and caught the shingles there and the ashes and cinders blew in the wind and landed in the livery, in the dry hay of the stables. And that hay caught and the cinders from that fire began to fly, as well, and the rabbits kept coming as if from some endless supply and the men were so tired they could barely walk, and finally they fell back, stumbled down to the creek, where along with the others, they watched the town begin to burn.

They were all there, watching. Norma Goodwin and Irvin Olin and August Weinrich, Jr. and Thorsten Larsen and his wife, Laura, and Sam Fletcher and Fannie Hall and Doctor Mato and Lawrence Wilkes and Jay Knowles and Evelyn Crawford and E. J. Burke and E. J. Macally and Simon Lewis and Rosa Anderson and sad, sweet George Anderson, who was weeping quietly into his handkerchief, and all the residents of Sims and of the homesteads that stretched for ten miles across the prairie, one hundred and thirty people gathered in the dark along the river.

Not all, though. Not E. J. Burke's daughter Stella, dead. Not Knutson the Swede, escaped. Not Colonel Bly, dead. Not Uncle Willy Crump, who had fallen from the water tower and lay broken and cruciform in the street. Not Joanne Crocker, forgotten, sick with fever, very soon to burn alive in the bedroom of her house.

From that safe distance the rest of them watched their town burn and they breathed a silent eulogy.

They had all had dreams and those dreams had driven them west. West to America. West to Dakota. They had come on the train or on horseback or in wagons, led by their belief that beyond the western horizon their bright future lay crouched and waiting.

But those dreams had been heavy, too, and they had carried them while they worked, while they sweated in the factories and busted sod and lay on their backs in the mine as their lungs blackened, paid a pittance in company scrip while their children were hungry and sick. They had slept with the dreams perched on their chests in their dirty bunks and miserable sod houses. They had seen violence done in service of those dreams and many had done violence themselves.

Let us watch them, now, as they stand on the riverbank, watching the fire. Let us watch them watching and imagine their best dreams burning off like fog. Let us imagine that at that moment they abandoned their ideas of progress, of destiny. That they took the train back east and stayed.

And so a strange exuberance spread among them, tired as they were, and as they watched the buildings catch fire, one by one, their exuberance grew into a kind of joy. They were wretched. They were poor. They understood that at any time a fire could raze their dreams to nothing, or if not a fire then a drought or plague or tornado or quake or flood would wash away whatever paltry progress they had made, and that each such cataclysm was trivial, just a sneer across the earth's ageless face, and that in the face of that fire and all other fires and all other forces of the world they were but nothing. And in that knowledge let us imagine that they felt relief and joy and fellowship.

E. J. Macally turned to Jay Knowles and smiled slightly and said, Well, I'll be damned. I never thought of those rabbits.

Then he began to laugh, and Knowles joined him, and others, and soon there were many laughing together. In the morning they would wake and sift through the burned wreckage of their lives and face their blank, uncertain futures, but now they were laughing and touching one another's arms and hands and washing one another's soot-blackened faces and lifting their children high in their arms to watch the fire burn in the inky night. Laughing and talking in jovial voices until one voice rose above them all: the beautiful clear soprano of Rosa Anderson. For what seemed like minutes she sang out one long, unwavering note which floated up from her lungs and spread over that crowd and beyond it across the empty prairie, the hymn of their longing and their renunciation and their bittersweet goodbye.

At that moment, as if to punctuate the song that followed, distant explosions thundered across the prairie, and they could see spouts of sparks rise high into the air beyond the town. It was dynamite, stored in casks in the cellar of the mine warehouse, exploding belatedly like fireworks, and with each new blast a cheer went up.

Let us imagine, finally, that some of those citizens dropped to their knees and sent silent prayers to their God, thanking Him for this unburdening. Let us imagine that their God was listening. And indeed he might have been, because that fire burned strong and luminous on the dark prairie, burned long into the morning, and it was quite a spectacle, bright enough to catch even the oldest and most tired eyes.

If God was looking down upon Sims that night, as its citizens stood on the far edge of the river, on the far edge of the century, in the middle of those great plains, in the middle of this vast continent, he would have seen them laughing and singing and slaughtering goats for a midnight feast under the star-blown sky, and he would have seen Thorsten Larsen take out his Hardanger fiddle and, with limber, practiced fingers, begin to tighten the strings.

NECK BONES

Ron A. Austin

I HID OUT IN THE BASEMENT, thumbed through Grandma's recipe book, and waited for the fight to end. Mom's voice sawed through the basement ceiling. *Danielle, what is this?* Yell mumbled something. Mom jabbed back *unh-unh. If it's in my house, it is my business.*

I could picture bad temper ruining their straightened hair, strands curling in feral spangles, hard sweat on their foreheads, polished nails cracking inside smooth fists, lipstick-embellished snarls. Mom hollered *nobody is playing with you, little girl.*

Shame on me, but I wished they'd just kill each other and be done with it. Shouting thumped against the walls, belligerent and frantic as a trapped animal. I refocused on the recipe book. Bizarre cartoons complemented Grandma's recipes. Dapper, cigar-smoking razor-backed boars in tuxes strutted margins. Roosters worked cast-iron skillets next to the secret ingredients for dirty fried chicken, wings flapping, cockscombs slicked. A fat-lipped trout luxuriated in a pot of roiling stock and celery. Keep that recipe book close, and you could learn everything about bouillabaisse, whipped mashed potatoes with beef gravy, liver and onions, headcheese, all that classic, down-home goodness.

Grandma's precise and pretty handwriting even detailed how to debone rabbits and French racks of lamb. Her handwriting was the only thing boldly feminine about Grandma, how it curved and swooped deceptively. With hands calloused and hard as a gravedigger's, she swung mallets, wielded skewers and knives, hocked *motherfuckers* and *whores* at anyone who stepped inside her general store and failed to buy a hot plate and show proper respect. Upstairs Mom and Yell volleyed FUCKYOU's back and forth. In my head I heard Grandma's specter hollering AWWWW SHUT THE HELL UP!

Grandma could diffuse their fights with a few mean words and a good meal. She would tell Mom something like *Go shove your fat head in the icebox. You might learn some sense.* She'd hit Yell with *You bad, but you ain't grown—keep on, and I'll cut you down to a stump, sho'll will.* Then she'd lure them into the kitchen and throw leftovers on the stove, greens and ham hocks, cornbread, pork chops pan-fried in bacon grease, neck bones.

Every time Mom or Yell parted their lips to hurl another blame, Grandma would spoon broth in their mouths, put forks in their fists, and tell them to go on and eat before all that good food got cold.

I figured Grandma spiked her food with mood elevators because after a small plate or two, Mom and Yell's bickering became secondary to slow chewing, lip-smacking and, eventually, cautious laughter. I wished I had Grandma's matter-of-fact grace, but I had no such easy charm.

A door slammed upstairs. Mom wailed, "Avvvveer-ree! Avery! You better come get this little girl!" Once Mom and Yell's fights got physical, it was more pro-wrestling than anything serious, grandstanding, figure-four leg locks, loud, echoing slaps to the chest. If I let one kill the other, drown her in a sink, contuse her with a hot comb, it'd be completely my fault.

In those days, I was nothing but a trifling sixteen-year-old dork who wore the same musty Teenage Mutant Ninja Turtle boxer shorts for days in a row and pissed in tea jugs when the bathroom felt too distant. I had no business mediating the affairs of grown women.

I trudged upstairs and found them in the hallway, bullying each other in rough kickboxing clenches, hands on throats, nails in hair. At least no blouses had ripped; no skirts had flipped up to reveal intimate and unsettling seams of satin and lace. One time, I accidently grabbed a boob trying to break them up. My hand felt contaminated for days. I scrubbed and scrubbed my palm raw, but it still felt soiled.

"I'm right here!" I shouted and forced myself between them, jamming the points of my elbows into their chests. Hands whipped overhead like hawks, tore out chunks of hair and scalp. Scabs and regrets would harden by morning. Mom was the first to relent. She stepped back, put her hands on her knees, spoke slowly.

"Avery, you need to get this know-nothing bitch out of my house." She straightened up, gulped a breath.

Sincere worry broke across her face. "I'll kill her. Swear I will."

I nodded, turned to Yell like a tough guy, deepened my voice, and told her, "Yell. You need to leave."

Yell folded her arms and said, "No."

So I pleaded, "Please just leave."

She razed me with a hateful glare. "And who the fuck are you?"

"Yell—"

"—Avery, I said no. And if you touch me—"

I snatched her shoulders and pushed hard. She was bird-boned yet surprisingly heavy, as if her resentments had condensed, become rocks in her belly. She cussed me the whole way out the door—*you pussy, you punk, you bitch*—the gravel in her breath scraping my face. On the porch she pouted and asked me, very seriously, "When are you gonna get off the titty?"

Yell had it in her head that I was the favorite, but that just wasn't true. Mom considered me a lazy fool, and I considered her a bully—we just never got to swinging about it. Foul words fumed in my chest like noxious gas, but I couldn't call Yell anything nasty. Didn't want to spit diesel on the flame. "Forget you" was the best I had.

She told me to gobble a fat dick and skulked off down the block to shake fifth graders for lunch money and hitch rides with bad dudes—whatever it is grimy girls do.

Mom was inside using an antique hand mirror to try to get a good look at the fresh, raw bald spots on the back of her head. She cut me a worried glance and asked, "It doesn't look bad, now does it?" Her bald spots were red and shameful, but I told her what she wanted to hear.

It was just Mom and me later that night, eating freezer-burned TV dinners in separate rooms. That processed mush was no better than charbroiled socks smothered in onion gravy. Mom couldn't cook. I suspected she never liked to anyway. Even when Dad was around she over-salted meat, overlooked tiny bones. She always burned the butter.

That TV dinner was unsatisfying, left me wanting real food. I looked inside the refrigerator, found nothing promising, lunchmeat slimy like the skin of some sightless, cave-dwelling creature, squishy red potatoes shaped like grubby feet, toes and all.

Saltines and tomato soup, bricks of ramen lined the cupboards. I settled on a stale Hostess cupcake hidden behind the microwave. I ate half of it and flipped through Grandma's recipe book.

I wanted mounds of salmon croquettes and dirty fried corn, hunks of fork-tender pot roast with crisp rinds. I stopped at Grandma's recipe for goat stew, struck by the cartoon, a witless lamb, roller skates on his hooves, careening into an incinerator's mouth, flame and smoke spewing. I only had that stew once, and truth be told, the goat brought for the slaughter wasn't that carefree.

Tethered to a post out back of the corner store, the goat was shaking, bleating, and shitting all over the asphalt. Grandma and Granddad were debating on the best means of quickly and efficiently killing it

Grandma flipped a wickedly sharp knife and said, "You slit his throat. Nothing fancy. Nothing to it."

Granddad spun the loaded chamber of his revolver—*TAT-TAT-TAT*—slapped it closed then tapped the barrel on that goat's head. "N'all. You blow his brains out—what's quicker than that?"

"And ruin the meat? You crazy as Hell, just want to make a mess. See here," she picked up a loose, red brick, "might as well clap him with this."

This was nothing but fun to Grandma and Granddad. They were transplants from the country, scrabbling through the city. If they wanted greens, they'd grow them. If they wanted goat, they'd kill it—simple as that.

Granddad pointed his revolver at the goat and asked me, "Boy, what do you think?"

I was nine, and my underdeveloped brain couldn't decode this complex multiple choice question:

HOW DO YOU SLAUGHTER A GOAT?
A. Knife   B. Gun   C. Brick

"Well, boy," Grandma said, "Which is it?" Her teeth and the paring knife flashed in tandem. I crushed moths and water bugs beneath my sneakers, but I hadn't worked up to this level of necessary violence, hadn't killed anything with skin and a heartbeat. I put my hands up and shook my head.

Granddad twirled his revolver and said, "C'mon, boy, let me lay him on out real smooth. In fact, I'll let you pull the trigger—how you like the sound of that?"

I didn't like the sound of that at all. My bladder was suddenly hard and heavy.

Grandma objected to Granddad's fast play and hollered, "N'all!" She flipped her knife up in the air, caught it, and pointed at me, "If you want to see it done right, you'll choose this knife. Ain't two ways about it."

"You'll choose this gun, if you know what's what," Granddad said.

"This boy don't know his ass from a hole in the ground," Grandma said.

They sniped at each other like that for a few minutes. Then Grandma grabbed the brick and raised it overhead. The goat bleated and trotted in a slow, frantic circle, succeeding only in wrapping himself around the pole, no escaping this back lot butcher shop. The reaper had come for him in a faded sundress and slippers. "Let me get him done."

Grandma brought the brick down. Hit the goat once, twice—

WHOP! WHOP!—clapped him easy. His skull cracked and syrupy blood oozed from the wound.

Grandma smiled with carnal satisfaction. "There," she said. "Nothing to it. Can't make a meal without a little blood on the floor." Granddad took Grandma's knife, got a length of rope, and field-dressed the goat right there. He slit the goat from the rooter to the tooter and hung him from the limbs of an apple tree. Blood pooled on the asphalt.

Stunned silent, I placed both hands over my crotch and hung my head. Grandma smacked my shoulder and told me, "Watch. You better learn."

Granddad tore out the goat's guts, easy. He pitched the heart, liver, and kidneys into the alley. Cats gathered and ate, lapped viscera off the cobblestones. Granddad said, "Might as well let them have their fill. They don't get this often."

Seeing the goat shiver and bleed had soured my appetite but didn't bother my folks any. After the goat was butchered, processed, and stewed, Mom and Yell came over for dinner. They sat down at the table, draped paper napkins over their laps, dug right in. Not one nasty word was spoken over that meal.

After Grandma and Granddad died, we no longer enjoyed that kind of simple peace.

Of course Mom and Yell wouldn't reconcile over stale cupcakes and gross TV dinners. I couldn't kill a goat, but I could cook a meal, sauté and roast soup bones, make a new covenant at the dinner table.

Determining the exact duration of petty grudges between Mom and Yell was a mystical art. I referenced star charts and lunar revolutions and concluded Yell would come back home in three days, enough time for me to gather equipment and ingredients, devise a tantalizing meal that'd make Satan spit-shine his horns and take supper with the holy ghost. I skimmed the recipe book and settled on St. Louis's Best Pork Tenderloin for the main course. Only an idiot with two left hands could fuck that up.

First I needed good cooking instruments. Our everyday utensils were ruined, fork tines snapped, serving spoons battered, butter knives that couldn't cut butter. I imagined the quality silverware and single set of china we never used were hidden under Mom's bed, guarded by rat traps. So I went downstairs and searched boxes inside Grandma and Granddad's old room, careful not to disturb the gloomy peace.

Boxes and boxes of junk crowded that space, as if summoned by a revenant pain that preferred to hide, fester, and grow in potency. A fat, green spider dangled overhead while I rummaged through rusted wrenches and screws, empty tobacco tins, glossy doo-wop wigs that reeked of Grandma's sweat—goddamn—smelled just like her, that bitter tang of constant toil.

Before long I found graters and tongs and scoops and sharp, sharp knives. Blades glowed softly in the midday light. I'd written a report on Japanese culture for school once, and holding those utensils, Grandma's most trusted tools, I was reminded of Tsukumogami—household objects that attain life after a hundred years and become tricksters who waste sentience on nasty pranks or worse.

I couldn't tell if my hands were trembling or if it was the knives themselves, plotting to slip and slice my fingers. I got the hell out of there before that revenant pain could spend any more time touching my thoughts, making me weird.

Clattering down the hall, I was afraid Mom would find me out, but she was too busy tossing Yell's room, scrutinizing Polaroid pictures with a sleuth's roving eye, popping heart-shaped locks off those old middle-school diaries, pitching thongs and short-shorts in a trash bag as HOW'S and WHY'S conspired in her head and offered this flat, confounding equation:

$$\frac{\text{shaming}^{\text{nth}}}{\text{new clothes}\sqrt{\frac{\text{private}}{\text{school}}}} + \frac{(\text{ballet}) \times \left(\substack{\text{piano} \\ \text{lessons}}\right)^{2}}{\text{ass-whoopings}^{10}} \neq \substack{\text{perfect} \\ \text{daughter}}$$

She muttered and calculated, but none of it added up to her. I moved on quickly, not wanting to see the calculus she had on me.

Next, I took my last, soggy twenty-dollar bill to shop for ingredients at the small, Arab-owned grocery store. The place smelled gamey and metallic. I shuffled through aisles of canned meat and passed a circle of Morlocks who guzzled Kool-Aid Bursts and smacked their gums. Inside the butcher's display case, liver and Braunschweiger sweated clear goop, honeycomb tripe flared translucent ridges. Chicken gizzards gleamed dark ruby.

The butcher thumped a mallet on the counter and asked me, "What you like?"

I was feeling ambitious, so I ordered the pork tenderloin, the gizzards, and one gauzy sheath of tripe. He wrapped up the meat and asked me, "You cook?"

"Trying to," I told him.

He nodded gravely then pointed at a bright red bucket of chitlins sitting in crushed ice. "You cook this?"

Grandma, Mom, and Yell used to cook chitlins for Thanksgivings. All I could think of was their quiet teamwork, Grandma scrubbing the stuff against a washboard, Yell rinsing it in cold water, Mom wearing plastic gloves and a surgical mask, holding the pale strands of flesh up to the light and pinching off any mysterious, dark flecks with a pair of tweezers, that barnyard funk when it got to boiling and rolling, looking like swamp snakes dueling in the broth. Believe it or not, it wasn't so bad served with hot sauce, mustard, fresh onion, and potato salad—melted in your mouth.

So I told him, "Sure, I can handle them."

I eyed up a pyramid of canned greens on my way out, but figured I would do better scrounging through what was left of Grandma's garden. After hiding my goods in the basement deep freezer back at home, I grabbed a pair of shears and set out for the ruins.

After Granddad got whopped by that stroke and couldn't work anymore, Grandma thought she could revive his body and spirit with a testament to hard labor. During that summer of agony and woe, me, Grandma, and a sturdy team of men remolded the general store's back lot into a garden.

It flourished for a while—it did—fat tomatoes and waxy bell peppers, all the flowers you could ever want. There were even designs on a peach tree, but we'd never see it. Try as we might, no miracles took root in that rocky soil. God's right hand closed over Granddad, crumpled him up like paper. Six months after he passed, God's left hand closed over Grandma, smothering the fire in her breast, reducing that lick of bright flame she called a tongue to a crackle inside my head.

Nobody knew what to do with the junk left behind, those barrel drum smokers, buckets of salt, and sacks of weevil-infested flour. Nobody knew the blood magic behind snoot sandwiches, or how to sew a life out of throw-away parts. So the corner store sat sagging and stagnant.

I had been avoiding that block where the corner store stood. I wouldn't even turn down that street. I couldn't. I don't know why. I don't know what I expected to see there: a crater, a black hole. I expected to find anything except for volunteers tending Grandma's garden.

A colorful sign that read BACON STREET COMMUNITY GARDEN had been erected in front of Grandma's rose arch. Grandma had wanted that rose arch to represent her children and grandchildren, each blossom a pulse. She would've gutted any fool staking claim to what she had built. Even though those volunteers willed spinach and hot peppers out of scarred earth, nurtured celosia into lashes of flame, I couldn't stop believing Grandma and Granddad's half-buried corpses fed that soil, phantasms sundered from flesh, thick roots gripping rib cages, pelvic bones. I couldn't stop seeing phlox surging out of their skulls, blooms studding eye sockets and gaps between coffee-stained teeth.

As I approached the garden, a white lady in a floppy wicker hat waved a trowel overhead and lectured a group of bored little kids. Little boys dueled with copper pipes or dozed, hugging shovels taller than them. Little girls compared and catalogued braid styles, whacked each other with slap bracelets, giggled madly. The lady croaked louder, thrusting her trowel, trying to intimidate and tame. Nobody listened.

I snuck to the back row of the garden where raised beds of collard greens grew. A rich vegetal musk rose as I snipped their stems and chlorophyll ran cool across my palms, highlighting life and love lines.

The lady approached and said, "Excuse me." She pulled that floppy hat tighter over her knobby head.

"Exactly what are you doing?"

The little kids *awwwwww*'ed and whooped like sirens. At least they'd have entertainment.

I played it slick, kept gathering, and said, "Nothing at all. Just picking greens for dinner."

"I'm sorry, but you can't do that." She wrinkled her nose as if I stank—I probably did. That bone deep summer heat and handling pounds of rank offal did me no favors. "This is a community garden. Anyone is more than welcome to the harvest if they put in their fair share, but I'm not sure I've ever seen you." She shook her head gently and tried to offer a pitying frown, but it crinkled into a tired scowl.

So I told her my name and where I lived and about Grandma and Granddad and a bunch of stuff about the corner store.

Her scowl flipped into the type of smile that cracks under pressure. "How nice!" She eased the Ziploc bag of greens out of my hands and sidled herself between me and the garden. "Let's make a deal: why don't you come back on Friday in clothes you don't mind getting a little dirty? We have plenty of alfalfa and cardoon to plant. It would be wonderful having a man who knows his way around this land."

I wanted to tell her the crop of greens I harvested were probably ones I had planted, grown wild and strong, and there was a red brick etched with my full name and birthdate somewhere near the alley, and I wanted to tell her about the fearsome growl of a chainsaw as it revved in my sweaty grip, the scream and whine of dead limbs, wood pulp in my eyes, and about how dull hatchets bust against tough tree stumps, and about the scars on my hands and knees, bleeding all over brambles.

I wanted to tell her about Grandma's hair, white and thin as milk-pod fluff, how she shriveled and sagged like rotten fruit, moaned and saw ghosts on her deathbed. I wanted to tell her I knew nothing about botany, but a drop of warm blood could feed spring blossoms through winters and winters and winters—goddamn—I wanted to tell her don't play with my intelligence. I wanted to tell her to get the fuck out my face. But I didn't know her like that. So I just shrugged.

The lady nodded approval. Those little kids sniggered, pointed at me. I loped away with my head hung low. I schemed. No barbwire fences protected the garden. No motes, no guard towers. I would come back at night, infiltrate Bacon Street Community Garden, take what was rightfully mine.

The moon hung overhead, slight and yellow. Heat lightning sizzled inside streetlights. Moths wobbled drunkenly through swampy air, collecting what nectar they could. Residual heat pumped off the concrete and steamed the soles of my ratty sneakers as I stalked inside the community garden, fearing a gruff voice would holler *FREEZE!* I'd spend the rest of that night in a cell with a deadly felon asking me *what you in for, lil' homie?* And I'd have to tell him *rutabagas. I stole rutabagas and collard greens.* Dude would be like *oh, for real? Nigga, you cold-blooded.*

I collected greens as dumbass rabbits darted underfoot, their furry rumps bounding across the garden. They romped with acrobatic grace then suddenly stopped and flattened out in the grass. The shadows loosed a stray dog, clawed feet beating, kicking up clods of dust. Those dumb rabbits juked and jived, scattered over a hill and vanished. That fool dog lunged after them, his long, red tongue flying like a war banner.

I yanked up a few beets, just to be ornery, and before leaving I searched for that brick with my name on it, wondering if it might contain a critical piece of my backbone. I picked through rubble and wiped away dust with my T-shirt but found nothing. A high-pitch shriek sliced the viscous night. I caught a tang of iron on the stale, oily breeze. I scattered too, not wanting to be the next kill.

My lunar charts proved correct. Yell was back in her room when I returned home with a fistful of greens and soil. I could hear her spitting mean whispers into the cordless phone. I snuck across the floorboards, squatted in front of her door, and spied on her through the keyhole. She ate those slimy flaps of turkey meat and chalky saltines. Between bites, she nodded her head and said *right. If you ain't feeding me, fucking me, funding me, what good is you? Nah—I can't tell her that. I can't tell her nothing. Right.*

The next night I set out the good linen tablecloth. It rolled like a sea of cream in soft candlelight. Polished forks and plates and glasses floated atop lavish, milky waves. Daylight from the window drained and my shadow began to loom monstrous against the kitchen wall. I toiled over the stove, scanned Grandma's note cards for methods of damage control. I read Grandma's recipes thrice, followed them to the exact letter—I did, I swear I did—but the greens were brown, and the cornbread stony, and that tripe still looked hideous—like tripe—and the gizzards were hard as plum pits.

And then there were those chitlins.

Those awful, goddamned, evil-assed chitlins. I scrubbed and washed and rinsed, scrubbed and washed and rinsed, but once they started boiling, it stank like donkey-butt soup. So much worse than barnyard funk. Only an exorcism can rid a house of that stink.

I had confused desire with ability. Grandma's cooking was a dark and necessary form of alchemy. Her blood thickened the gravy. Her fat fried the fish. She ground her bones to flour, rolled biscuits with her marrow. Grandma's devotion was ascetic. How foolish could I be, trying to conjure her miracles in one manic night?

Frantic, I tried lifting the pot of chitlins off the burner with bare hands, blistered my palms, dropped it back in place. I was yowling when Mom tromped in with a rag over her nose. Yell followed a hot minute later. My failure had summoned them like a bell.

Mom and Yell were stunned by that foul odor. Once they made eye contact, their stances widened automatically. Nothing had been settled. Yell tied her hair into a tight ponytail, plucked out her earrings. Mom clenched her jaw, kicked off her flats. My body coiled, readied to spring between them. But that reek smothered all will to fight.

"Avery," Mom said. "What in the world is that stink?"

Yell grimaced and asked, "What died?"

I stammered the answer. "Chitlins."

Mom and Yell shook their heads, eyes dazzling with grim wonder. They lifted lids and adjusted burners, studying that food cautiously. Mom came to a hypothesis first, "Avery, please don't tell me you called yourself cooking dinner."

Yell smirked and said, "Oh my God. Boy, you could at least open a window." She rolled her eyes and relaxed. "That funk is making my hair frizz."

Mom broke a mean smile and said, "That stink is peeling my nail polish."

The oven timer beeped and Yell said, "Don't worry, y'all—I'll get this one." She couldn't hide her glee as she whipped on oven mitts and pulled out that pork tenderloin. It smoked and looked more like the mummified shank of a forgotten king than the Best of Anything.

Yell guffawed, and Mom said, "Oh Lord, please help us."

Mom and Yell chewed and spat out the greens, crushed cornbread in fists, told jokes: *Who taught him to cook, Wolfgang Yuck? Boy, you're bout the only one who'd get fired from a soup kitchen. Shoot, a bum couldn't eat this—that's cruel and unusual. Now, does this count as an act of terrorism? We don't need feds kicking down the door. Won't somebody please open a window? I am so serious—the damn drapes are burning.* Their contempt and mean jokes were good as cleavers against my throat. You can't make a meal or reconcile a feud without a little blood on the floor.

I snatched the oven mitts from Yell, hefted that pot of chitlins overhead, trudged out to the alley, and pitched them all over the cobblestones.

Pigeons fell out of the sky like rocks and cats slinked between chain-link fences. They fought over the best cuts, feasted on that mess. Looking over at the kitchen window, I could see Mom and Yell laughing their heads off, snapping tongs at each other, giddy as fifth-grade girls. I was mad enough to cry. But I knew they didn't enjoy this kind of sisterhood often. Might as well let them have their fill.

ABU THE WATER CARRIER

Abby Bardi

MY UNCLE IS ASLEEP ON THE COUCH. I sneak past. If he wakes up, he'll say good morning to me in his language, and I don't want to hear it. He'll run to the kitchen and brew me a cup of black tea, and I'll be late to work because I'll have to stand there while he jabbers at me. I won't be able to understand anything until I hear my supervisor say, "You're late again, Richie" in English, the only language I want to know. My dad watched a lot of TV to learn English when he first came to the US, and yes, I am named for the guy on *Happy Days*.

I'm almost past my uncle when he opens one eye. "Go back to sleep," I say. "Goodbye. I am going now." My uncle sits up in bed. He's wearing striped cotton pajamas that my father bought him at Marshall's. There's a Pierre Cardin monogram on the pocket but I think it's fake. The stripes make him look like an old-fashioned prisoner.

My uncle says something to me but I don't understand. I say, smiling, "I wish you'd take your sorry ass out of here." He smiles back.

After work, I go to Henry's house. He shares a townhouse in Capitol Hill with some other guys. We sit on his couch and put our arms around each other, and he licks my ear. "I don't get it," he says. "Why don't you just move in with me?"

"It's complicated."

"It's not complicated. You just make it complicated. It's easy. You just pack up your shit and move in. Done deal."

"I don't even have any shit. I have a dresser, that's it."

"You could put it right in this corner."

"You don't understand."

"What don't I understand?"

"How we do things. My father needs me there."

"Why does he need you? He's got Abu the Water Carrier."

"Don't call him that."

"You're the one that started calling him that."

"I know, but it's mean."

"Well, we wouldn't want to be mean, would we?" He kisses my neck.

When I get home, my father is washing the dishes. "Where were you?" he asks. His face is lined and leathery, like a mask on the wall of a museum. "You missed dinner."

"I had dinner with Henry."

My father purses his lips and doesn't say anything. Where he comes from, it's fine for men to have dinner with other men, but maybe he senses that this is different. Then he says, "You need to help Chachi with his homework."

My brother is at the small table next to the kitchen, pretending to read a trigonometry book. I can tell he is really listening to the TV in the next room, where my uncle is on the couch watching *Seinfeld*.

"I hate this shit," Chachi says. "It don't make no sense."

"That's where you start," I tell him. "You know it doesn't make sense. That gives you the advantage."

"Man, you a freak," he says, punching me on the arm. I'm tempted to correct his grammar, but instead I grab him in a hammerlock and we wrestle.

I'm on the couch next to my uncle. We're watching *The Tonight Show*. My uncle could not possibly understand a thing Jay Leno is saying, but he laughs through the whole show, sometimes in the right places. My uncle looks a lot like my father, even though they are not related—he is my mother's brother. He and my father both have long, tired faces and tall heads, like their brains are too big. They have wide, sad eyes. My uncle has a long scar on his cheek. The skin is puckered like it healed the wrong way, and there are white dots where crude stitches must have been. When he laughs, you can see he's missing a bunch of teeth on the same side as the scar. Just after midnight, his eyes start to droop. I push him over until he's horizontal, throw a blanket over him, and turn off the TV. Then I call Henry.

"How's Abu?"

"He's asleep in front of the TV. He sleeps whenever he feels like it."

"Must be nice. Has your father told him to go get a job?"

"Why are you so interested?"

"Duh, Richie. If your uncle was bringing in some bucks, you could move in with me. You wouldn't have to be everyone's sugar daddy."

"My father works." Sometimes Henry annoys me.

"I know he works, baby, but he doesn't make enough."

"It's not like I'm Donald Trump either."

"But I make plenty of money. Enough for both of us. If your uncle got a job, you could move in with me."

"Just stop," I say. "Henry, I love you, but stop."

As I weave through traffic, I think about my uncle. It's not like I could just give him a brochure on any chosen career. I can't even tell him what time it is or how I want my eggs. I ride my moped up on the sidewalk and nearly run over some women in long dresses and running shoes.

"What did he do back home?" Henry asked me months ago, when my uncle first got here.

"I don't know. I think he was a water carrier."

"A what?"

"They have a shortage of water. That's why they move around so much. At least, they used to before the fighting started. So I think my uncle was the person who found the new wells and made sure everyone got water. If the well ran dry, they moved on."

"So what you're saying is he had a fairly important position."

"I guess so. I don't know—my father didn't tell me much about him. I guess my uncle doesn't like to talk about it. It was very upsetting for him. I think they hanged his son in the public square."

"His son? That would be your cousin."

"Yeah."

"I'm so sorry, honey."

"Well, it's not like I knew him or anything."

"But still. It scares me to think about it."

"You mean because it could have been me?"

"Don't be sarcastic."

"I'm not. It's just that I can't imagine it. Living there. Being like my uncle. He's so weird, Henry. He eats with his hands."

"Of course he does, baby, that's what they do over there. I'm sure he thinks we're weird, too."

"I don't know what he thinks. That's the scary thing about him. He's always smiling, like he's always in good mood, like he just doesn't understand that his life sucks."

I leave my moped by the curb and take the elevator to the tenth floor. I hand the receptionist the package. She doesn't look at me. That was how I met Henry—I was delivering something to the congressman he works for. He started talking to me about the weather, then my job, then he asked me to lunch. At first I couldn't figure out why he was bothering with me at all, but he told me later that he fell in love with my eyes. He said my eyes looked hopeful, like I thought I was about to win the lottery, I just needed to be patient. I told him I'm not really all that damn hopeful, in fact I'm pretty cynical when you get down to it. But he said no, baby, eyes don't lie.

When I get home, my uncle is in the kitchen, wearing a flowered apron that belonged to my mother. My father has taught him how to make hamburgers. A plate of raw burgers sits in front of him, the patties molded into big, awkward blobs. When he cooks them, they're always raw in the middle, and sometimes, if the meat has been frozen, ice cold. My uncle smiles when he eats a burger, like he thinks it's just too damn funny. I think my father intends this burger-making thing to be some kind of vocational training. "Dad, he's got to learn English first," I told him a few weeks ago. "He can't even say 'Do you want fries with that?'"

"He will learn," my father said, scowling. "I learned English in three weeks."

When he says this, I never tell him I don't believe him. "Dad, he's been here for almost six months and he doesn't even know how to say hello. He can't even answer the phone right. He picks up the phone and says 'Phone' into it. Then he just hands it to me. He doesn't even know who it is. He doesn't care!"

"He will be ready soon," my father said. "What is your big hurry?"

"No hurry," I said, thinking of Henry and his townhouse and how convenient it would be to drive to work from there instead of riding my moped five miles through city traffic, always afraid someone's going to hit me on the head at a stoplight and steal it. Without that moped, I'll be at a 7-11 in one of those green jackets with my name on the pocket.

"Hamabugga," my uncle says, holding up a deformed-looking beef patty. He looks proud, like he has just recited the Gettysburg Address.

No one says anything during dinner. Chachi is at basketball practice, so it's just me, my father, and my uncle. My uncle is still wearing that flowered apron.

"Why is he living with you?" Henry asked me when my uncle first came. "Doesn't he have any other relatives?"

"It's some kind of custom, I guess. The wife's brother can live with you if he gives you some cattle."

"Did he bring you cattle?"

"No. I don't think he has any. I don't think he has anything. He didn't even have a suitcase. Just a little Nike bag."

"They have Nike over there?"

"I guess so. Anyway, my father would never turn away a relative. Isn't that how they do things in your family?"

"I can't imagine any of my relatives dropping in without calling first. Let alone just showing up at the airport like that."

"In my family, just showing up is OK."

"I don't know if I could handle that." He laughed, and I felt weird for a second, like he was laughing at me.

"Don't you have any strange family customs?"

"Red wine with fish. That's basically it."

"Truth is, I think my uncle reminds my father of my mother. I think he likes having him around. He misses my mother."

"Do you miss her?"

"I don't remember her." A few dim memories of her sometimes surface for a second, then flicker out.

"That's sad, honey." He stroked my cheek.

I wasn't sure I liked all that pity. "It's OK, dude. You don't have to feel sorry for me or anything. It's just the way things are."

"I guess that's the big difference between us, Richie. You can accept the way things are. I always want them to be different."

This is not true—I do want things to be different—but I don't bother to correct him.

My uncle sees that I have finished my hamburger. Before I'm even done chewing, he whips another one onto my plate. "Thanks," I say, though I really don't want it. In fact, I didn't really want the first one.

"You wedcome," he says, beaming at me.

"Hey, that's pretty good," I say to my father. "If he keeps this up, he'll be saying 'Merry Christmas' in a hundred years."

My father doesn't respond. He's a heavy man, and when he chews, he makes a little groaning sound, like his jaw is tired. He's on his third burger now; he probably doesn't want to offend my uncle by not eating them all. There are still eight patties on the plate, some blackened on the sides. I guess my father is going to sit here all night eating them one by one until they're gone.

"I've got to get out of here," I say to Henry on the phone. "They're driving me nuts. When Chachi isn't here, no one says anything to me. My father talks to my uncle in their weird language, and I can't understand anything."

"I thought you spoke your father's language."

"They're speaking my mother's language. My mother never spoke her language to me. I think my father wouldn't let her. He thought it was low class."

"How can a language be low class? A language is a language."

"I don't know. How can anything be low class? It just is."

"Maybe if your father quit speaking it and just talked English to him, your uncle would learn English."

"Maybe so."

"Maybe your uncle doesn't really want to learn English."

"Why wouldn't he?"

"Maybe he's afraid it would change him somehow."

"How?"

"He'd start thinking in English. Then he'd be like you, Richie."

"How am I?"

"There's this difference between what you are and what you say. Maybe your uncle isn't like that. Maybe he's just pure being."

"That's pretty patronizing, isn't it?" This is a word I learned from Henry.

"I guess so. Sorry. I'll try not to patronize you." He says it flirtatiously.

"You're not patronizing me. You're patronizing him."

"You're defending him. That's sweet. It really is."

"Shut the fuck up, Henry," I say. I picture him on the other end of the line, light curly hair and wire-rimmed glasses, gentle blue eyes. He's fragile and kind, and it's hard to be mad at him. "Just shut the fuck up." He can tell I'm smiling.

The noise from the TV is keeping me awake. It's some late-night talk show, a bunch of guys talking in monotones about politics, and their voices lull me, but every time I start to drop off, a loud commercial comes on and I hear my uncle laugh. He seems to love commercials. One time when I came in the room, I caught him dancing to the theme song for Payless Shoes. I roll over and put the pillow over my head, but I can't sleep. My pillow smells bad, like those little strips you put in the dryer. My uncle has been doing the laundry, and he puts in ten strips at a time. He seems to love doing laundry. He sits in the laundromat and watches the clothes spin like he's watching TV. I see job possibilities for him in this, but I don't want to think about that right now. Right now I want to be asleep. Henry told me to try counting backward from one hundred by threes, and I start to, but by the time I'm in the seventies I find that I'm angry. Who is this guy in my living room? Why does he sit there watching TV all goddamn night every night while normal people, people with jobs, have to try to sleep? Why can't he speak English like everyone else? Why is he watching a talk show he can't understand and laughing like it's some kind of fucking sitcom?

I sit up in bed and throw the pillow across the room, then stomp over to the door and open it. "Hey, turn that shit off," I yell at him. "I'm trying to sleep."

He stares up at me, his smile gone for once. His eyes are big and sad, and this just makes me madder.

"I said turn it off. Turn that goddamn thing off. I can't stand it any more. You're driving me crazy."

He just sits there. I stomp over to the TV and turn it off, then stomp back into my room, slamming the door behind me.

In the morning, he is still asleep on the couch. His face still looks sad, even in sleep, and that just makes me mad all over again.

When I get to the dispatch office, I find that I have to deliver a package in Henry's office building. When this happens, I take it as a sign that it's going to be a good day. I'm still feeling this kind of sick, hungover feeling from yelling and then not sleeping well, but as I ride over to the Hill, I cheer up. It's a beautiful spring day, and the cherry blossoms are blooming. The air smells good, like perfume and money. I park my moped in front of the building and go through the metal detector, showing my ID to the guard. I saunter down the marble hall as if I belong there, drop off the package on the first floor, and take the stairs up to Henry's office. I open the door and am about to sneak up behind him—his desk faces the wall—but he's not there. "Do you know where Henry is?" I ask the tall woman standing there. She's Mary, his office mate, and I happen to know she's a bitch on wheels.

Mary squints at me.

"Henry—do you know where he is?"

"And you are—"

"Richie. His friend."

"You're his friend?"

"Yes."

"And you haven't heard?"

"Heard what?"

"Henry's in the hospital. He got mugged last night."

"Oh my God." I lean against the desk. I feel like I'm about to pass out. "Is he all right?"

"Yes, he's fine. A few broken ribs and some bruises. They're keeping him in for observation just in case some organs were involved." She is still looking at me with suspicion, but it's obvious I am really upset. She softens a little and says, "I can give him a message for you if you like."

"I have to go see him. What hospital is it?"

"I'm not sure if he—"

"What hospital? Tell me this instant." I had no idea I could talk to someone in this tone of voice. Maybe my ancestors were royalty.

"I'm afraid I can't—"

"It's GW, isn't it," I say. Henry is on the GW Health Plan. He always says that if only the laws changed so we could get married, I could have health insurance, too.

"It's—yes," she says, probably hoping I won't punch her and break a few of her ribs. "How did you get in here?"

I'm out the door before she can call security.

Outside the hospital, I fling my moped down on the sidewalk and dash into the main entrance. A security guard at the information desk tells me Henry's room number. He tells me visiting hours aren't until later and asks if I'm family. I tell him yes.

I was too young to visit my mother when she died, but my father always said it happened in the hospital, and the way he said it made it sound like they'd killed her. For years I thought hospitals were places people went to die; I didn't know anyone ever came out again. They still scare me, and I try to avoid them. But here I am sneaking around, looking for Henry's room. I find his name written in blue marker on a white board, and I stroll up and down, reading the charts on each door. I have to say that while I am afraid, there is something interesting about this place, about how everyone has some kind of problem that landed them in the hospital. It would be nice to be able to help them, to give them the right medicine and get them out of here. I'm worried sick about Henry, sure, but suddenly I am also seeing myself as some type of healthcare practitioner, maybe even a doctor. I am still having this fantasy of me in a white coat with a stethoscope around my neck when I find Henry's door.

I see his feet at the end of the bed. I'd know them anywhere: his toes are short and fat, like piggies. I walk into the room and am about to hurl myself at him, carefully so I don't hurt him, when I see a man and woman standing next to him. The woman is thin, with the same shade of colorless blonde hair as Henry's, the same blue eyes, only hers are like ice crystals. She's wearing an expensive raincoat and pearl earrings, like she has just come from a party. The man is stocky and balding, with wire-rimmed glasses like Henry's.

"Richie," Henry says, seeing me. There's a strange note in his voice. He doesn't sound as happy as I expected.

"Henry, are you OK?" I want to rush to his bedside but I am frozen in the doorway.

"Sure, I'm fine. Just a few ribs. I was lucky."

"What happened?"

"I was mugged. It was my fault, I shouldn't have been out after dark. Bad neighborhood, right?"

"I guess."

He turns to his parents. "I'm sorry, Mom, Dad, this is my friend Richie. He's one of my roommates."

"Oh, hello, Richie," Mom says, reaching out to shake my hand. She has a thin, cold hand; it feels like a chicken's foot. Dad just nods at me.

"Yes," I say, giving Henry a weird look. "I'm one of Henry's roommates. I live in the townhouse. The charming little townhouse Henry lives in."

"Thanks for coming," Henry says, making pleading eyes at me.

"You're quite welcome. I'm so happy to see that you're well. Lovely to meet you both," I say to the parents, and I back out of the room, bowing.

"Your roommate?" I hiss into the phone. My father and my uncle are in the next room playing checkers.

"I can't really talk now," Henry says. "Mom and Dad are here again. Thank you for calling. Richie, call me later, OK?"

"Maybe I will. I don't know, Henry. Do you want me to?"

"Of course I do."

"I don't think you do."

"Of course I do."

"You know what I think? I think you're ashamed of me. You don't want your parents to know you've been slumming, and your boyfriend is a low-rent little foreigner who never went to college and eats with his hands." This last part isn't true, but the rest is, I can feel it in my stomach. I am trembling.

"Please, Richie. It's not like that at all. This just isn't a good time." His voice has a chill, a formality I have never heard before. "Thanks so much for calling." Click.

Slowly, I put the receiver back in its cradle. I walk over to the couch and sit. From the couch, I see my father and my uncle framed by the arch between rooms as they sit at the table. They look like a painting of two weird middle-aged men, one in a blue terry-cloth bathrobe and one in a gray security guard uniform, the checkerboard between them. I sag against the arm of the couch. My father looks up. "What's the matter?" he says in his language.

"Nothing," I say in English, wiping my eyes.

"Something bad happen?"

"No. It's nothing."

"It is your friend Henry?"

"Yes."

"He is OK?"

"He's fine."

"Did he say something to pain you?"

"My heart is sad," I say in his language. It's not the kind of thing you can say in English. "It is hurting me."

My father says something to my uncle in the language I don't understand. My uncle regards me with what is obviously great concern. He says something back to my father and my father says something back to him. My uncle makes a clucking sound in his throat. He stands up and comes closer to me, looking at my face as if inspecting me. Then he goes into the kitchen and comes out carrying a glass of water. I'm afraid maybe he's going to throw it in my face, but he holds it out and offers it to me. I take the glass from him and drink all of it. Water gushes down my throat. Then I put the empty glass down on the table. He sits on the couch beside me and puts his arms around me. I lay my head on his shoulder and cry.

A GOOD BREATH

Michael Byers

OH, HE WAS A LOUSY FIFTH-GRADE TEACHER, certainly worse than any of his own teachers had been with the possible exception of Mrs. Davis, she of the pear bottom and mustache, and he having volunteered himself to teach only because he had no skills and no direction after college aside from the fanciful notion of going home to Seattle and somehow working for a newspaper, which was never anything but an idea, and because his girlfriend Antonia was signing up, and because he sometimes enjoyed her company and she enjoyed his, and he had no better opportunities. Then by the middle of his second year he and Antonia were barely tolerating one another and living with their blond housemate Chrissy Cox in the town of Fort Destry, Texas, all of them working at José Cultivar Elementary School three miles down the split-lane highway along the Destry River, which was sludgy and full of rotting reeds, the school sprawled at the edge of Fort Destry itself beneath a platoon of power lines that hummed as though full of marching demons. The flag was raised and saluted every morning, they unconstitutionally prayed before all-school assemblies, they ate lunch in the stinking lunchmeat lunchroom with the students, they worked through the math folders and the required reading, they made their way. He was not helping the world in any obvious sense aside from providing cheap instruction to a set of children who needed something better, something more dedicated, but who thanks to budgetary realities were getting him, Paul Lake.

He had actually enjoyed the previous year, when he and

Antonia had been posted in the far northern Panhandle where they had lived in what now seemed bliss in an ancient clapboard house on the edge of a stream near the mouth of a canyon, from whose echoing halls they could hear coyotes all night as the wind moved through the mesquite and the radio picked up stations from Denver and St. Louis and the stars were legendary. Then that post had ended and they had been transferred here. He could not wait to be done and gone, and Antonia had already been admitted to a linguistics program in Chicago and he had decided to head home to Seattle and to prepare his own PhD applications in classics, he had to do something with his life that was more satisfying than this, and at the same time he was preparing, in fact, to go to the clinic and to get some probably bad news about what had been happening to him lately, which was this terrible shortness of breath that had begun plaguing him in January, on a run, when he had suddenly been unable to breathe, as though someone had inserted a barrier in his chest so he could get air into only the top third or so of his lungs. He told nobody about this for weeks and weeks until finally he confessed to Antonia who observed him collapsed on the couch and said, "Well go see the doctor, dummy."

But he didn't, because he didn't want to know what was wrong with him, because he was afraid of the news, he had never been to doctors growing up (his father a doctor) and also because he was sure that he was going to be told he was dying, that he had a mass pressing on his sternum from behind, that he would have to call his mother and father and tell them so, and his brother, and that he was going to learn that just when he hoped to be done with what now appeared a mistaken period of his life, teaching elementary school, living with Antonia, being in Destry, Texas, he was going to be told that he was done before he'd even really started his life, that he was almost out of time.

A list of his failures as a teacher was no doubt being kept somewhere in a file folder and some set of administrators was surely every week sighing and checking calendars and deciding that it was easier to keep him on for the rest of the year than to fire him now. The year before had been better, the desperate poverty of the students having genuinely shocked him, almost all of them Kiowa Indians from the Pennholtz Reservation, troubled and sweet in turns, his and Antonia's favorite being a tiny slip of a boy named Albert Fee, who lived in a trailer with his painfully young parents and his eight siblings and who coveted Paul's and Antonia's fast-food wrappers, wanting them in order to wallpaper the interior of his trailer's walls. Paul had not failed Albert Fee, not exactly, except in the way the whole world had failed Albert Fee, by failing to give him a warm bed and good food and parents who had gone beyond the fifth grade.

But he was decidedly failing the students at José Cultivar, some of whom were the children of migrant farmworkers and so appeared and disappeared within weeks, and some of whom were the children of settled families of Mexican ancestry, and about half of whom were military children from Fort Destry itself, most better-traveled than Paul and also presenting a rotating group, arriving from Korea before going on to Germany, following their fathers and mothers in their postings. It could be argued, and Paul argued to himself sometimes, that his failures here did not matter as much, that these students by and large would be all right, but this did not account, for example, for his calling Gordon Jacobson "Bullet-Head" or Tina Lopez "Disgustina" or for tossing over an empty desk when the class wouldn't quiet, striking Felicity Green in the shin, at which she widened her eyes in offense and declared, "I want to talk to the principal." He was reprimanded for this, also for teaching a Raymond Carver story with the line "He howled when he entered her," although he had taken care to block this out with black crayon (which someone's mother had scraped away), and for screening Mel Gibson's *Hamlet* without watching it first (he knew he was in trouble when Chico asked, "What is he *doing*?" during the Gertrude scene, the rest of the class transfixed in delighted shock). Some of this was laziness and some was just disinterest and some was real cruelty, and he despised himself for all of it but especially for the cruelties, for example when he didn't listen to Márquez's mixtape though it was only four songs long, or when after having read *Bridge to Terabithia* aloud to the class and having choked up with the rest of them when Leslie drowned, and after the class in a spasm of need and sorrow had written letters to Katherine Paterson, he, unable to figure out where to send the letters, had simply thrown them away. "I guess she just didn't write back," he shrugged. Or when he rolled his eyes and groaned when poor Inez failed, again, to grasp the associative property of multiplication, then celebrated aloud when her paperwork at last came through and she was assigned to the special-ed class, or for example when one day after Maria-Vera complained about his bad breath, and he leaned down, placed his face in hers, and exhaled, saying, "My *what*? My *what*?"

She recoiled and said, "I'm sorry, Mr. Lake, it's just terrible."

And at this a stroke of fear went through him: she was smelling some rot coming up from his dying lungs, he supposed. By then it was May, and the students were all eyeing him with suspicion and contempt, and he was struggling to get even a single good breath as the day went on. His terror and despair had surely leaked into his life here in the classroom, giving rise to some of his behavior. He estimated he would live long enough to finish the last month of the school year (unless he just fell down dead in front of the class), and either way Antonia could go to Chicago to start her PhD, and if he lived long enough he would make his way back to Seattle, make his announcement to his family, and wither away, clutching the blankets to his chest and wishing he had done something differently a long time ago, way back when it had still been possible.

His final cruelty was so strange, and so embarrassing, that he never told anybody about it. Every six weeks or so their housemate Chrissy's itinerant surfer boyfriend Cal would make one of his swings through the state, driving over from the Gulf of Mexico for a week to lounge, shirtless, on their thready white sofa, the length of his lean torso like a cut from some ridgy beast. Paul envied Cal's thoughtless health and the ease with which he seemed to move through the world, although he was also supposedly rich, which probably had something to do with it. On the other hand he drove a shitty listing old Datsun with his canary-striped surfboard lashed to the roof and wore the same clothes at all times, a pair of army green cutoff shorts and a loose white button-down shirt and Vans, and he drank only green tea and ate mostly big servings of brown dusty stuff from jars, spooned over yogurt. He believed uncritically in the idea of "energy" and its power to direct fate and more than once he had described the sensation of knowing the ocean was thinking about him. "It notices you," he said, "after a while, and then there's a little while where you've got its attention, and then, you know, it moves on." He was ridiculous but perfectly at peace and Paul would have traded places with him in a second.

As usual for the first day Cal and Chrissy vanished as they took to her bed but eventually Cal took Paul by the shoulder and directed him to his leaning car. "I want to show you something," Cal said. He thumbed open the hatchback. The car smelled of straw and some dry hippie perfume. In the trunk was a cardboard box. Cal lifted the lid. Inside was a long spotted lizard resting on some pebbly orange sand.

"What is it?"

"It's a Gila monster," Cal whispered. "They're basically free in Mexico."

Cal had imagined the Gila monster to be excellent for Chrissy's first graders but it grossed her out. Also it was technically venomous.

"So, finders keepers, if you want him," Cal said.

The school year was almost over but it struck Paul that a Gila monster would be a way to rescue the last few weeks, anyway he could leave things on a positive note, and after he was dead they would remember that at the last minute he had done this for them despite having been terminally ill, in secret, and they would consider his brave stoicism and forgive him everything.

"Cool," he said.

"I was just going to set him free," Cal admitted, "but I'm trying to be more responsible with things."

With his salt-hardened fingernail Cal scratched the lizard between the eyes.

So Paul brought the box to school the next day, parading a little self-consciously through the halls, balancing it like a waiter's tray while he unlocked his classroom. But the interest he had hoped for did not materialize, maybe because in fact the arrival of a Gila monster seemed transparently designed to make amends, and nobody was interested in amends from Mr. Lake. Offers of lettuce and lunchmeat were made by fat Chico, but after a week when the lizard did nothing but lie around, once a day or so scratching at its sand and producing a wrinkled tube of excrement, it was ignored by everyone. It was Texas; people had seen Gila monsters before, so what if he had brought one in?

So one afternoon after school he carried the box up the hot dry hill behind the school and prodded the lizard out onto the soil and watched the thing paddle listlessly away into the cactus.

It was only Chico who noticed, nice silly fat Chico whom he had alarmed with Mel Gibson's thrusting. "Where'd he *go*?" Chico inquired.

"Oh, he died yesterday," Paul found himself saying.

Not that he had set it free, but that it was dead. Why?

"Aw," Chico said.

"Who died?" the class now inquired.

"The lizard, man," Chico said.

There was a small stir as the class recalled that there had been a Gila monster in the corner, in a cardboard box.

"*I'm* dying, actually," Paul said. "I'm going to be dead in a year at most."

Someone laughed. "What you dying from?"

"I can't breathe," he said. "My lungs are failing."

"*You* ain't dying," someone decided, into the silence.

He had shocked them, anyway. "You'll regret saying that," he sighed, working to get the pity, the forgiveness, into his voice. "You'll think back, and you'll regret that."

*

In fact in the last weeks of the school year he found himself plunging awake in the darkened bedroom, grasping his chest and sucking at the humid air while Antonia slept on beside him. Then he would take himself out to the sofa and read, creeping back to bed only when he had become so exhausted he could tumble into sleep in a moment. Yet he did live long enough to finish the year, so six weeks later, after the last day of school finally ended, after report cards went out and he cleaned out his classroom, trashing heaps of ungraded papers and makeup exams and ripping his gradebook into tiny, tiny squares, after Cal came back again and took Chrissy away to Florida, where it turned out Cal's family had an island, after Paul and Antonia divided their books and mailed them to their next destinations, after he and Antonia drove out of sweltering, chicken-factory-smelling Destry for the last time, north to Chicago, after he felt so dizzy in Arkansas he exited the freeway to let Antonia take the wheel, after he gasped as he carried her things up the three flights to the small studio at the back of her brick building in Lincoln Square, after he spent the night on a blanket on the kitchen floor and hugged her quickly the next morning, and after she said, "Well, goodbye, then," with a shrug, and after he drove in a speckled dream across the sandy summery plains, over the mountains, down into the green coast—after he made an appearance before his parents, neither of whom noticed anything wrong, happy to have him back in town, pleased to hear about his plans of grad school, after he counted his meager savings and settled himself in a rented room behind Husky Stadium, and arranged his Thucydides and Polybius and Xenophon along a scarred windowsill—

After all this he had nothing to do but to get ready, and to wait, to die.

So obviously it becomes a little difficult to account for Paul here. He does not make much sense to an outside observer, or the sense he does make is of a dreary, unsurprising sort. Clearly he is having panic attacks, or at least he's suffering from some chronic species of anxiety disorder. He is probably depressed. He is certainly suffering. He is inflicting suffering on others. Yet he does nothing to make it stop. And even if he's really sick, if he really does have some mass behind his breastbone, as it so vividly seems to him—what kind of person thinks such a thing and does nothing about it?

Anyway, this is where he found himself. PhD applications were due in December. It was June. He could live in this well-lit lousy rented room with these anonymous housemates and read everything and live off his small savings. His first plan was to review Thucydides and to map out all the troop movements and battles, so he would really know them, and then he would do the same for the *Anabasis*, and so know everything about the Peloponnesian War. It was fusty old stuff and Antonia had always suspected him of being a sort of show-off but in fact the deep history appealed to him in powerful ways. If Sthenelaidas had not been such a prick in the Spartan *Gerousia* the war with Athens would never have been waged, and the Golden Age could have matured into something unimaginable, steam engines having already been invented, and what would civilization look like in that case? It was interesting to think about. Or if Pericles had not been such a waffler, if the plague had not struck just at the height of the Spartan invasion, if the Athenian general Demosthenes had not made his unwise raids on Sicily—it was that the course of the world wasn't set, maybe, or that it could change radically on these small hinges. For the first month in his rented room on 38th Avenue, behind University Village, he had reason to consider these matters. Why this? Why this of all worlds? Now this tightness in his chest, this gasping reach for breath, studying his face in the mirror, the incipient blue smudges beneath his eyes, the weird pulse of weakness when he stirred in the morning, the exploding watery shits, the slumping desire in the middle of the afternoon to return to bed—

It was all this, and loneliness, that led him to call Hillary Tanner. Their first meeting was at a café down the street from her apartment. They had been in touch off and on, mostly off, since they'd been together in high school, since prom and the weeks after. Over the first two years of college they had exchanged batches of letters, Hillary's enthusiastic swooping pages full of blue pencil while he sent her in return his painstaking letters on fussy, starchy white paper, black ink. And what a beauty she was, actually, now. A sweet rounded chin and clear blue eyes and a shapely nose, her brown hair thin but prettily kept under a white band.

"So how do I know you're not just going to disappear on me like you did before?" she asked.

She wore two silver bracelets on her right wrist. She removed them when she was at the piano or played the violin. But otherwise ran them up and down. She had interestingly hairy forearms, which he had forgotten.

"I'm here now," he said.

"You just stopped writing me letters for no reason."

Antonia had wanted him to stop, actually, so he'd stopped.

"And anyway you're going off to grad school next year."

"Possibly. Also, that's a long time," he said.

Maybe she was flattered by the persistence of his interest in her. But she wouldn't need flattering, she was beautiful. Maybe she liked him, despite everything. Or was just bored with her life. Or she had suffered too, and so she was vulnerable to anyone, maybe, who had once been fond of her. At any rate within a week they were in bed. Naked she rolled under him, curves and heat. Her apartment had a view of Lake Union where the seaplanes landed, and some afternoons when she was off practicing, or at one of her jobs (she accompanied for voice lessons and recitals, she played the organ at three separate churches, she taught at a piano camp, she was always doing something) he would bring a book to her apartment and lay himself naked in the big plates of sun that fell over the carpet. The seaplanes could get a good look if they cared to.

He did not quite mention to Hillary the fact that he couldn't breathe. Once he admitted to her that there was a feeling of tension in his chest. If she found him dead in the morning one day she would have had some kind of warning, she could think back and remember. But he wanted not to poison this, whatever it was, however temporary.

Before long, he didn't want to be away from her. He began going with her on her jobs. He sat in the last row of folding chairs at a voice recital for which she played piano, a trio of lieder by Schubert, her sweet round chin bobbing. He was the only one watching her as the girl singing was a tall creamy redhead with hefty tits but at certain points during the performance Hillary cracked a secret smile seemingly at some extravagance of phrasing. "That was funny," was all she said afterward, rolling a shoulder into him in the front seat of her rounded old Volvo. He climbed with her into the creaking organ lofts and sat on a step, out of sight of the congregation, while she stomped and yanked and the old pipes heaved and hooted. This was his favorite way of watching her, hidden, unacknowledged, herself hidden and unacknowledged, her face glowing from the effort of the instrument as its wooden and metal workings thudded and clicked around them.

And now something new began for him, in which vivid memories of his sins as a teacher enlarged themselves, pushed themselves to the center of his vision. How awful he had been at it! How pained and full of misery and fear. And how grotesquely he had taken it out on his students.

What a monster he had been.

He burned with shame.

When he thought of what he'd done he would grunt and recoil.

"What?" Hillary asked.

"Nothing," he said. "Just what a shitty teacher I was."

"You weren't."

"I was! I was horrible."

"Horrible how?"

"I don't know," he said. "I was mean to those poor kids."

"I'm sure you weren't mean."

"I was *mean*," he insisted.

"Well," she said, "that's not an easy job."

"Nobody *else* did what I did."

Like what, she wanted to know.

"Ech," he said, and waved it away. "I don't want to tell you."

So, really, she didn't believe him. And he didn't want to give her the details, of course, they were so shameful. She knew an earlier, kinder version of him.

Then it was September and for the first time in memory he was not in a classroom, and as the fall mellowed he had the sensation of being detached from time, let loose into a new world.

The days grew gray and drizzly, the welcome weather of his childhood. He bought a new sweater.

He made dinner, having done the grocery shopping while Hillary was out.

He moved his books and things in. He read all day while the seaplanes drifted overhead. He was still dying, but not as quickly as he had feared. He could still get a good breath once in a while.

She had begun taking him to concerts, things in which she was not herself performing. She laced her arm in his and leaned in, using his shoulder in the dark, and sometimes her sweet little laugh would flutter to life. (He could never guess what had been funny, and she couldn't explain it.) Now and then they would have a plate of pasta at Café Septième where the red wine came in short scratched tumblers.

How was it that after he had failed so badly his life was better, sweeter, richer?

And what would be wrong with staying here, with making a way with Hillary for as long as he could, with just deciding that very good was good enough?

These were not questions he would ask himself until years later.

Then in October she took him to an event at her old music college: a children's concert. Some of her students were performing.

"I don't know," he said, "turns out I'm not so good with kids."

"I bet they're not the same ones *precisely*," she said, taking his arm.

Always she had found him funny and kind, and then he had stopped writing her without explanation or apology, and still she had accepted him back again. And now he was preparing to leave her once more, wasn't he? He was, he was. He'd already written his essays, he was applying to schools in Los Angeles, in New Jersey, San Francisco.

The stage was bare and bright.

He was expecting nothing. Or something through which he would have to force a polite interest. And for a while that was what he did, as brittle Asian girls played their violins and hearty, round-shouldered girls whacked away at their cellos and flop-haired boys played piano, hiding their faces, and Paul grimaced in sympathy when they flubbed and winced a little at the effort they all made and the ambition they all possessed, it reminded him, of course of his sad kids in Destry, and from his high seat in the balcony he could see the distance between there and here, this place of privilege and accomplishment. And how little he had helped.

Eventually a very fat boy came out, his shirt untucked. He carried no instrument. A girl sat down at the piano.

The boy walked to the front of the stage and stood in a pool of light and set his hands at his waist and began to sing, and immediately Paul was caught. It was a beautiful song, a lullaby, and the fat boy sang it with a sweet, embracing tenderness. The boy had a high clear tenor and lifted his voice without effort into the corners of the hall, an Irish song, very simple and plain, four notes up, four notes sideways, four notes up, three notes down, but the thing that caught him was this, that the boy who did it stood in the light with his eyes closed as though he were just dreaming the music, and he didn't care that he looked so stupid, he just sang.

Hillary grasped Paul's arm in the dark, and he grasped her back. The notes rose, shifted, rose, fell. This was a benediction, and it was meant for him. It was meant for him. Because if a huge slobby fat kid like that could go up and belt it out, could stand in front of a bunch of strangers and sing his heart out and not give a shit, then how could Paul be ashamed of anything he'd ever done?

So maybe he needed to think that, in the moment. We use whatever we can use. But of course he was wrong, he was all wrong. He was right to be ashamed. He had behaved horribly. He was right to feel he had no one to apologize to, but only because all his victims were children thousands of miles away, and he would never see them again.

Ah, he was all wrong.

No, what he should have taken from it was, just, goddammit—look, Paul, it's not that hard. Just—be kind, and take care of yourself, and then, if you're lucky, you'll one day lift your head and you'll get to notice all this beauty. Because it's everywhere. It's just sitting around everywhere, like gold in the streets. It's the kingdom of heaven come. That's where you are right now, pal. It's where you've always been. That dark old house in Destry with sour Antonia, and that mushy gully of the river, and the buzzing power lines, and it's you and silly Cal and your poor students and the Gila monster finding its way into the scrub and everybody. And now! Now especially—look at lucky you, there in those high seats with that nice, nice girl, what's-her-name, Hillary, a girl who means you no harm, who despite everything holds you dear, who has taken you in for no reason you can fathom—it's where you could have stayed, despite yourself, and if you'd been better at this, if you yourself had been kinder, if you'd been brave enough to take care of yourself, you would have come to your senses at just around this point and you'd have opened your eyes and seen it for yourself, and taken a deep full breath and felt it, the great clear air you wouldn't otherwise know for years.

She's right there. So are you.

Ach, it's hard to love this guy. It's hard to love this Paul. It's hard to forgive him being such a goddamned dumbass for so goddamned long.

Give him time, is all you can say. He's lucky. He'll have it, despite what he thinks. He'll have plenty of time.

GIRLS LIKE HER

Alison Clement

I GOT THE CALL IN THE MIDDLE OF THE NIGHT. I dressed fast, expecting Parker to wake up any minute and make me come back, but he didn't. It was summer, and the air warm even at two a.m. I made a cup of coffee and walked down the long driveway to the road. Julie was giving me a ride, but she'd never been to my house before. Nobody ever came there to see me. I walked down the drive, drinking coffee. I had brought the flashlight, but the moon was out, so I didn't need it. I could see the neighbors' black-and-white cows in the field next to me—or, at least, I could see the white part. I pretended, just for a moment, that I was never coming back, that I had never lived here in the first place. I was just a woman walking down a country lane. I didn't have any before or after. It felt good.

The main highway wasn't far from our house: just down the feeder road and past the Farm & Fleet. If you headed north on that highway, you could get to Chicago in less than two hours. A lot of times I'd think about standing there and putting my thumb out. If you're a girl or a woman, you'll get a ride fast. Parker said girls who did that deserved what they got, that they should have known better. The first time I heard him say something like that, I was surprised, but I got used to it eventually.

At the end of the road I waited and looked back at the house. When you live in the country, even just three miles from town, you always know about the moon: if it's full or crescent, waxing or waning. It's a presence. I liked that part of living there. From where I stood, I could just make out the shape of the house. There were trees around it. Burr oaks. There was an old barn, too, and a brick silo built to store corn but empty and falling apart now. I liked to go in there and sit in that round, quiet place, the blue sky a perfect circle above where the roof used to be. Parker grew up in the country and did not find it romantic. He didn't especially like the cows or the garden or the moon or any of it. He didn't form attachments.

Parker had a little boy in town, but he didn't visit him, and he didn't give the mother any money, either. "How do I know he's mine?" he would say, but anybody could see that the boy looked just like him. The same sweet mouth and blue eyes. I only saw the child once, so I can't speak for later. But that's the way he started out, with those kind blue eyes.

I saw him when Parker and I went to his mother's apartment. She looked at me and said, "Jailbait," but I was nineteen by then. Parker said later she was jealous, which I doubt. He'd come there to argue about money. The baby was in one of those wind-up swings, rocking back and forth. Some babies fall straight asleep in a wind-up swing, but he just sat very still, with his father's blue eyes and his father's lips. It was too bad he didn't look like his mother. Women like that sometimes, for the baby to look like them, especially if the father is someone like Parker. If I were that baby's mother, I wouldn't have wanted to be reminded of Parker every time I turned around. I wouldn't have wanted Parker's face looking at me. So that was unlucky for the boy.

I sat next to him while they argued. Parker said he didn't have any money to give her, even if he was inclined to, which he wasn't. "Hey, baby," I said to the boy. Every time the swing came forward, I touched his tiny, naked foot. For days after that visit, I loved Parker again, just a little bit. But it only lasted so long, and it wasn't enough.

That boy would be almost three years old now, I thought as I stood waiting for Julie. He'd be one of those skinny, anxious, doomed children you see sometimes. Or maybe not. Maybe he'd turned out different. It seemed unlikely, but maybe his mother had managed to love him anyway, despite his father, while it still mattered.

Finally I saw the headlights.

Julie never knew how to talk to me. During volunteer training, we'd learned that, once or twice, mentally disturbed women had volunteered. Maybe Julie thought I was one of them. I got in the car and sat looking out, wondering this myself.

"Follow my lead," she said. "When we get there. I'll talk, and you listen. The first time out, you mostly observe how it's done."

"Right," I said.

I wished I had taken a drink before I'd left. Just one. Not enough to be drunk but enough to keep me calm. They say if you drink vodka, nobody will smell it. I wasn't sure that was true, and vodka sounded terrible just then, which probably meant I wasn't an alcoholic.

"Where are we going?" I asked.

"The police station."

"Not the hospital?" In training they'd said we would usually go to the hospital.

"They already did the hospital," said Julie. "They should have called us then, but they didn't."

We were out on the highway now, headed toward town. I could see Parker's and my house. It looked OK in the dark. I'd planted flowers all around the front: coreopsis, sunflowers, Shasta daisies, freesia. I was partial to yellow flowers that year. Earlier I had gone through a red phase. I never did like a white flower. Sunflowers are still my favorite: ridiculously cheerful and as tall as a human being.

I'd left a note for Parker, hadn't I? I'd left it on the table in clear view. And I had told him about volunteering, and he hadn't objected, although he could change his mind.

Julie turned on the radio, then turned it off again.

I tried to think of something to say to put her at ease, but everything I thought of seemed phony. Anyhow, I didn't care what kind of job Julie had, or how long she'd lived in town, or how long she'd been a volunteer, or why she'd volunteered in the first place, which was a touchy subject for a lot of women. I looked at her feet. It was two in the morning, but Julie had thought to wear good shoes, shiny with low heels. She wore a navy-blue skirt and a tasteful white blouse. Her pocketbook on the seat between us was the same color as her shoes. My own shoes were scuffed and muddy. I was leaving dirt in her car. I had just thrown on whatever clothes were handy: blue jeans and a T-shirt. They hadn't mentioned in the training that we should dress up. They hadn't said: low heels, skirt, tasteful blouse. Julie wore lipstick. She must have gotten the call and then gone into the bathroom, stood in front of the mirror, and put on her lipstick while somewhere a girl sat waiting for us. Julie had picked out shoes to match her pocketbook. She was not sitting here now wondering if she had left a note for her husband, and would he find it, and would that be OK? She was not wondering that. She was probably wondering about me.

"It's a nice night anyway," I said, and Julie agreed. Then I questioned my use of the word *anyway*. Why had I chosen it? To imply that, even though this terrible thing happened to someone, it was still a nice night? I'd once known how to talk to people but not so much anymore. At one time I would have been completely at ease with someone like Julie.

"How old is she?" I asked. That was a question I really wanted an answer to.

"Fifteen."

The number hung in the air. Too young. Not that any age is all right. Fifteen. A kid, but without the benefit or the forgiveness we give little kids. It seemed exactly the wrong age. I shouldn't have come, I thought. I had the wrong shoes, the wrong thoughts, the wrong history, the wrong life. I was all wrong. I was not someone you would call for help. I was the one who needed help. I needed somebody driving through the night to get to me, somebody trained who knew what to do.

"You'll do fine," said Julie, as if she sensed my insecurity.

When we got there, the girl was sitting in a waiting room. She said her name was Tracy.

"That's my name, too," I said.

"Mine's with two ee's. T-r-a-c-e-e."

She was a skinny girl with long hair and blue jeans and flip-flops. She had a *People* magazine on her lap, but she didn't look at it. Some movie star in a bikini was on the cover. Tracee rolled the magazine up as if to swat somebody, then unrolled it again. Her fingers were pale. She had chewed the nails down past the quick. I let Julie take the lead, like she'd said, and she filled Tracee in on what would happen. Then a cop came in, and Julie got up to talk to him.

Tracee had a small round bruise on her neck. "You OK?" I asked.

She nodded. "My granny gave me something."

"Something?"

"A pill."

"To make you feel better?"

"That's right."

"That's good." I looked over at Julie and tried to remember what they'd said we should do in training. I had written it all down in a spiral notebook.

"You got a mom?" I asked. This was not in my notebook. This was nosy.

She shook her head. "I live with my granny."

"OK then." I wondered whether her mother didn't know how to spell Tracy, or if she thought she was giving her child something special: a name that sounded normal but was spelled different, like it was French, maybe.

"If you want to talk," I said, "you can."

"I already told them."

"You know, whatever somebody does to you, no matter what, there is some part of you they can't get at. They might want to, but they can't. Some special, secret part that nobody can get to."

She looked right at me for the first time. "You believe that?"

"I know it." This was not in my notes. I was not supposed to offer opinions or reassurance to the victims—no, that was the wrong word. They were not victims. They were some other word I couldn't think of. Not client. That would be totally wrong.

"I just wanted to go for a ride on his motorcycle," she said.

If it weren't for the framed pictures of cops on the walls, this might have been anyone's waiting room: a doctor's, a dentist's, a high-school principal's. A man in wrinkled khaki pants walked past carrying two styrofoam cups.

I excused myself and went to the bathroom and washed my hands and face. They always tell girls not to take a bath afterward, but just thinking of it made me feel dirty. I looked at my face in the mirror. I combed my fingers through my hair and rinsed my mouth out and used a paper towel to wipe my teeth. Once, when I was hitchhiking, I'd taken a whole sponge bath in a bathroom sink.

I was pulling my hair back in a ponytail when Julie came in. "In a minute, he'll take her statement," she said. She went into one of the stalls and shut the door. "She's kind of loopy, don't you think?"

"She's OK," I said.

"If you say so."

"She took a downer."

"A what?" I could hear Julie lifting her skirt.

"A tranquilizer or something."

"She told you that?"

I could see Julie's shiny shoes under the door. The cop would take Tracee's statement soon. In the training we were told that people needed to put their experience into a story with a beginning, middle, and end, so they could begin to fit it into the bigger narrative of their lives. The trauma. How to fit it.

"I'm glad you can talk to her," Julie said. "Because . . ." She hesitated. "Between you and me, I'm having a hard time relating to that girl."

I didn't answer. Maybe if I stayed quiet, she would think I hadn't heard her. Who's to say I had? Or maybe I thought she was just talking to herself in there. I opened the door and slipped out.

A few minutes later we were all sitting in the detective's office. He sat at his desk with a pad of paper and a pen, ready to take the girl's statement. We huddled close together under the fluorescent lights, our knees almost touching.

For a moment I had the irrational sense that it was my statement he was taking; that any minute I'd be expected to tell a story with a beginning, middle, and end. It would have to make sense and could not contradict itself. It would have to be logical. It was logical, of course, if you thought about it. If you went step by step, each one small, almost innocent, until finally you've gone too far and can't get out.

She took a ride on his motorcycle, she said. His name was Ray. She didn't know his last name. "We went out in the country. There was a farmhouse, but nobody lived in it. We pulled in the driveway." Tracee leaned closer to the detective to watch him write. "And there was this other guy there."

"How old?" the detective asked.

She shrugged. "I don't know. Your age maybe?"

"Thirty?" said the detective.

"Something like that." She stopped talking until he had written it all down. "Wait. The other guy showed up later."

The detective stopped writing and looked at her. "He was there, or he came later?"

"I just wanted a ride on Ray's motorcycle." Her face was calm, but she twisted her fingers in her lap while she spoke.

"So tell me what happened."

The first time she told us the details, it was shocking, even though I'd already imagined what she would say. Maybe there are small variations, but it's all the same. There was nothing new or original about it, and yet . . . The second time she told it was better. I mean, it wasn't so hard to hear. And then, when she had to say it a third time, I felt like we were stuck in some kind of hell, like we'd have to sit and listen forever, and I thought they shouldn't have so much power, those men who'd done this to her, that we had to listen again and again and imagine what they'd done again and again and they kept doing it forever. Even though I knew they were the weak ones—that this crime revealed something about them, something pitiful and contemptible—still I couldn't deny there was a kind of power in it, a power that had brought us there in the middle of the night to listen to this story.

By the middle of the third time, she thought she had it straight. The second man had pulled in the drive about fifteen minutes after she had arrived with Ray. This would not look good in court, if the case ever went to court: her uncertainty about the sequence of events, which was the fault of the tranquilizer, maybe, muddying things up. Why should we be expected to remember everything, I thought, and what did it matter which came first? Tracee was not impatient with the questions. If she had to say something three times, she would.

The second man—he was related to Ray, she thought—drove a motorcycle, too. A Harley. His "hog," she called it. And that's when the little alarm went off in my head, but distant, like it was in the next room, or downstairs, or far away.

"Was his name Gary?" I asked.

Julie shot me a look. We were there to offer support, not to ask questions.

"Yeah," Tracee said. "That was his name."

I sat back in my chair. I thought of the baby, three years old now, and his tiny feet, his ears like little seashells. Ray and Gary were Parker's friends. They had been to my house. They'd sat in my living room. I knew Ray's wife. Sometimes I took care of their kids, Dee Dee and Little Ray. They were always kind to me—much kinder than Parker. I had thought that helping other girls might be the beginning of a way out, but it had only taken me deeper. I could feel Julie watching me.

"Ray Campbell and Gary Chisholm," I said. I spelled their names and waited for the detective to finish writing. "They're cousins."

Their names wouldn't help, I feared, even if she got her story straight. They would get to her. She would go home and be alone, no cops around. Or she would go out somewhere. She would walk down the street or an alley or be in a car—anywhere—and there was nothing we could do, because Tracee was not like Gary and Ray, and she was not like the cop, and she was not like Julie, who wanted to help but was having a hard time relating to a girl like this, a working-class girl, a girl who lived with her grandmother, a girl who was slightly high because her grandmother had given her a pill, a girl who hung out with the wrong kind of guys, a girl who'd walked straight into a trap, a girl who should have known better.

WHERE I WAS BEFORE

Robert Day

The Harvest Moon

I WORKED ON A SMALL RANCH north of Hays, Kansas, in Buckeye Township—above the Saline River and the breaks that run into it. Some days I taught school as a substitute. I lived in that country ten years. I did not marry.

One Friday, toward the end of summer, the ranch owner got a call from the banker who had loaned him money to buy heifers. We had hopes of breeding them and selling the calves for a fat profit. But the price of money was going higher, and the price of beef was going lower. That's when the phone rang. I told the banker that the owner was outside, but I would get him.

I will use Ward for his name, but that was not his name. I am superstitious about some things, and writing about the dead and using their names is one.

"Hello," Ward said when he got on the phone. He had been walking toward the house when I called him. Long, even strides. He was a tall man with big hands. The phone vanished into his fist. He listened and frowned.

"I don't have that kind of money unless I sell the herd, which I won't," Ward said. "They're just bred. And the price is piss-poor." He was shaking his head back and forth. That usually meant he was about to swear. He was gifted at it, and the more he shook his head before he got started, the richer the gift—and the better it gave.

"Tell those pig fuckers on your board that's what they get for lending money at fourteen percent." Hanging up, he said: "You guys are lower than snake shit at the bottom of a posthole."

It wasn't funny, but later that night when we poured ourselves Black Jack. It got us laughing as we retold the story more than once, back and forth, adding something with each version. Not about bankers being lower than snake shit at the bottom of a posthole: That was for real.

There were just the two of us working the place in those days. Ellen, Ward's wife, had died a few years before. He had a son not to be found. Later, there was Patsy, whom we hired from Hays to help with the chores around the Home-House and make a garden in exchange for her wage and meals—and for the comfort of our company.

We were good company, and not hard to please with what she fixed: stews and soups in winter at noon, what is called "dinner" in that country. Chicken or pig for supper in the evening. Buffalo steaks from a bull Patsy's hippie nephew and his girlfriend won in a lottery and had us kill. Fish out of the pond. Ducks we shot. Pheasants. A deer in winter. Cold beet and vegetable soups from Patsy's garden in summer. Salads as well for what Patsy called our "cesspool system."

Patsy was no rose. Not even a shriveled flower at the stem's end. Mostly thorns—especially if you crossed her. And given to Jesus-God. That was her word: Jesus-God. Also, we didn't live in Buckeye Township, Ellis County; we lived in West Jesus Land, Kansas. Every place else was The Rest of America.

If Patsy had a dress, we never saw it. Well, I did: once. Summer or winter she'd wear blue-striped bib overalls and work boots. In winter she layered shirts and sweaters. In spring and early fall she'd wear T-shirts, and in summer when it got past "Hell's low-roast number" (100), she'd wear nothing but her bib outfit and sockless boots.

"The way her knockers show out the sides of these overalls, she'll get sunburned on both the east and west of them," Ward said.

"She might be naked underneath," I said to Ward one day.

"There are some things best not to picture."

In the side straps and pockets, Patsy carried pliers, gloves, a beer opener (bottle or can), baling twine, a snub-nosed .22 revolver, golf balls she'd put in the hen's nests to fool them into sitting, a small cloth bag for eggs and, always hanging at her side, a hatchet for beheading chickens and snapping turtles on the cottonwood stump by her garden. Breakfast, dinner, or supper, she'd take her meals with all her "armament attached," as Ward would say. Patsy was built like her overalls, tools included.

I had in those days a girlfriend in Lawrence who would drive out Fridays from teaching grade school and stay through Sundays. In summers she'd live with us weeks at a time. Monique was a rose: tall, trim. Short hair. No thorns. A pail of fresh milk. And blonde nearly to cream.

We had known each other at the university but got separated the way you do when you are young: she went on a student exchange to France; I took a job teaching school in western Kansas. Before we found each other again, there had been another woman in my life. Very crazy. There had been a man in Monique's life. Not that she talked about him much. His name was Bruno. That was his real name.

Ward's ranch was small, but good grass. No plow land. Springs that flowed into the draws, deepwater wells, one big pond and a few smaller ponds in the horse back pastures. We had windmills that fed the stock tanks, and there were limestone outbuildings from an abandoned homestead on the northwest quarter. Good fences, good gates with deep-buried dead men to hold both posts straight. Stout corrals. Rattlesnake quarters with rock outcroppings and soap weed down to the river.

The Friday the banker called about the loan for the cattle, Ward and I stayed in the kitchen waiting for Patsy, drinking coffee and chewing the fat over bankers and women.

I've never known what to think about women. Not about Monique or Patsy, but women in general. Ward had a theory that it was better not to think about women or bankers by yourself because it would lead to *confusion and certitude*. Better to talk about them with someone there to say "good thinking" or "bad thinking." Those were two of Ward's favorite sayings. *Good thinking. Bad thinking.* Not that the world was black and white to him, but some of it was.

"Talk is ventilation for the brain," Ward said. "Just like you need to open the vents and damper on the Woodsman now and then to keep it from smoldering and getting creosote in the flue pipe. You don't want smoke in your head."

"What else is there but 'certitude and confusion?'" I asked. "It seems to me, if you have one, you don't have the other."

"They're opposite sides of the same silver dollar," said Ward. "Especially, when it comes to women and bankers. You get confused and then to clear your head, you think you need to get certain. But that's bad thinking. Nothing is certain." Because he was not given to clichés, he stopped there. About that time we heard Patsy drive up. She'd check for eggs before she came in.

"We were just talking about women," Ward said when Patsy opened the door. He liked to get her started.

"If I spent as much time talking about men as you do women," she said, "you'd be eating the oil cloth off this table instead of breakfast. And bindweed instead of carrots—which at least would do your cesspool some good."

"Just about as much time as you talk to Jesus-God," I said.

"Jesus-God is worth it," Patsy said. "I talk to Him when I'm doing dishes. You don't mind doing dishes or cleaning house if you and Jesus-God are talking. You come to Jesus-God or you'll get barbecued in Hell," she said, putting away her eggs.

"Well, at least that would be the end of it," said Ward. "Not so," said Patsy. "You're never dead in Hell. The Devil barbecues your body parts for different evils. Curse Jesus-God and your tongue gets cut off and barbecued. Every body part that has offended Him gets barbecued."

"What about . . . ?" I asked.

"That too," she said, "if you've had a propensity to whore-fuck. What's left gets tossed to the three-headed wolves to scarf down.

Demonically 13:23." Like Thomas Jefferson, Patsy had her own version of the Bible.

"I see," I said.

"Black snake ate my golf ball," Patsy said, as she poured herself coffee and joined us at the table. "But I got it back. Chopped his head off. I'll curl him down around one of my tomato plants for fertilizer. Waste not, want nothing."

Then she took our picture with the Polaroid that was usually on the kitchen table and that Ellen had bought for the ranch when they moved out from Hays.

"Better to start a worm farm with us than stuff a coffin," Ward said. "Or toss us in the pond to feed the turtles."

"Not me," said Patsy. "I'm flying to Jesus-God when The Rapture comes."

While Patsy finished her coffee, we ventilated our brains on Jesus-God, bankers, The Rapture, and whether turtle food or worm farms were a better way to go. Then Ward and I headed out to check cattle, but not before I took a picture of Patsy.

Our herd was about two hundred. First-calf heifers. They had been bought cheaper that way, even though we'd have trouble calving them—which we planned to do in January so we could beat the late summer market at the sale barn when everybody was bringing in their cattle before the grass dried up and winter came on. Supply and demand. But with the cattle market, it's mostly luck.

One day we lost two heifers on the Saline when they got into quicksand. I found them up to their bellies, dead, the water going around them, making eddies. Maybe one wasn't dead, but trying to rescue her was foolish. My horse got his front hooves stuck at the edge of the river, and I had to rear him up and spin around to firm ground. Across the river was Mencken Cody's place, so when I got back I told Ward he might give Mencken a call about the quicksand, should he have any cattle near Saline. It was Mencken's Gomer bull we were using to breed the herd.

A week later when Ward and I rode back to check our fences, the two heifers were mostly skin and bones. Both heads were on the carcasses. Eyes gone.

"At least someone got to eat," Ward said. "What goes around and comes around isn't bad thinking." We rode back to the Home-House, and when we got there Patsy was ringing the yard bell for dinner.

The ranch had been in Ward's family for two generations; however, Ward and Ellen had lived most of their lives in Hays. When their hired man died, they sold the Hays house and moved to the ranch. Ellen died a few years after. I was at school when her accident happened.

I lived in a Sears and Roebuck cabin to the north of Ward. There were lodgepole pine fences around both houses, and the larger yard of about five acres was fenced with barbed wire. In that yard were tool sheds, calving pens, horse stalls, and a Butler Building where we worked on trucks and parked equipment. To the north, west, and south ran a WPA shelterbelt of shrubs and trees, leaving the east side open.

Everywhere were chickens scratching and hens running to hide their eggs from Patsy—plus rabbits and squirrels and cats mixed in for good measure.

One year we found a beehive in a dead cottonwood tree below the dam. We let it get started until the following year, then every year after that I'd put on a long sleeve shirt, gloves, and a winter stocking hat with eye holes and a mouth cut out to dig out a few combs with a small trowel. From the honey, Patsy made syrup and oatcakes.

At the beginning there was Milky, who was past her prime but now and then I'd give her a try. I thought it might please the old cow to be of use, the ranch cats gathered under her, milling and meowing.

"You get in some good thinking putting your head into the side of a cow," Ward said when he saw me going into the barn with a bucket.

The first summer Monique stayed with me, she put her head into the side of Milky as much for what I'd told her Ward had said as for the cats.

"It works," she said.

"Good thinking?" I asked.

"Yes," she said.

"What do you think about?"

"Us."

I went to get the Polaroid.

Later that summer, Milky died one night and it was Monique who found her in the morning. Ward hooked up the backhoe to the tractor and dug a burial pit south of the Home-House where, after we hired Patsy a year or so later, she planted her first garden, never knowing why it came on so well from the beginning and for all the years afterward. It seemed a pleasure to keep the secret.

The evening we buried Milky, Monique sang a version of "The Night They Drove Old Dixie Down," with the chorus as "The Night Old Milky Died," and there was no irony in her version, only sadness—even though she had not known Milky but that summer. Nor did Monique use her guitar, but sang *a cappella*.

"She's a fine woman," Ward said to me the next morning when we were alone over coffee. "A pail of fresh milk to be sure, but more than that." As with Monique's song, there was no irony in what Ward said.

We had Amos, a black lab dog of mine, and later, Murphy, a mutt Monique found abandoned at a truck stop. There was Moshe Dayan, a one-eyed tomcat that Patsy brought out to catch mice but whose specialty was not mice, but anything bigger than himself: chickens, box turtles, in addition to the pheasants, ducks, turkeys, and the deer we'd hang in the well-house behind my cabin.

Moshe would get to the game with a leap and a hiss—and hang on. I'd find him chewing as best he could on a shot mallard until he fell off and went to look for a yard rabbit. Without Milky and with the arrival of Moshe, the other cats hit the dusty trail.

One blizzard night Patsy brought Moshe into the house and fed him grocery store cat food.

"You know what that is?" Ward said, pointing at Moshe.

"A cat," said Patsy.

"That's the only animal in the world that can turn money into cat shit." It was Monique who had given Moshe his name.

Sometimes you'd see rattlesnakes. Two owls: Dame and Monsieur, *Pas Blanche*, as Monique named them. Doves coming in and out of the shelter belt. The summer he got snake bit in the shelter belt, Moshe took himself into the heat of the south pasture to die.

"Leave him be," said Patsy when Monique thought she might drive him to the vet. "Leave him to himself. He knows what he's doing. When he's gone, the fire ants will finish him."

The day the bank called, Monique was to come out, leaving Friday after a teacher's workshop to stay a week or so until school started. Saturday was Patsy's birthday and the plan was to fix her a meal in the Whorehouse Room. That's what we called the big room in the Home-House with the Woodsman stove and ceiling fans. We had let Patsy decorate it after she started cooking and cleaning for us.

"She wants to buy red wall paper," I had said to Ward. "It's furry with gold gilt in it. And paint the window trim red." There were two windows on the north side of the room, one on either side of the Woodsman stove.

"Let her," he said.

"And hang framed mirrors." I had gone to Hays with Patsy to look at what she wanted.

"Just as long as she doesn't get scared away for seeing herself."

"And chandeliers," I said. "When she's done, it will look like a whorehouse."

"Good thinking."

Patsy had us put down a purple shag carpet on top of which she laid the hide we got for shooting the hippies' buffalo. She covered the chairs with deerskins, and the couch with a large bedspread that had a stag's head in the middle. We weren't allowed in with our work boots.

I bought a player piano from the Woodcutter's Widow in Bly who was selling out piece by piece. The deal came with fifty rolls of old-time songs—all of them in good shape. Even though Monique could play the piano (and a guitar that she'd leave so she didn't have to bring it out each time), she'd pump the pedals and we'd all sing along: *You are my sunshine, my only sunshine, you make me happy when skies are gray, you'll never know, dear, how much I love you, please don't take that sunshine away.* Patsy would join in.

"She can't carry a tune in a pickup," Ward said. But after we went goodbye with a stout glass of Black Jack, we didn't much care.

The year after I bought the piano, Ward and Patsy bought Monique a French horn we also kept in the Whorehouse Room.

"I don't know how to play it," Monique said when they gave it to her.

"Well, it's French and on sale," said Patsy, "and I know how you like France, so . . ."

"I can learn. And thank you," Monique said. "Both of you." I suspect she knew it was Patsy's idea and Ward's money.

The next time out, Monique brought an enlarged photograph of the Dodge City Cowboy Band from the 1900s. It showed twenty or so bug-eyed and half-drunk cowboys with their instruments, some men lounging on the floor toward the front, others on risers leading up to a lone woman, young to be sure, but not a pail of fresh milk, sitting on a set of very large long-horns. There were tubas and trumpets and tambourines. Drums and clarinets. But no French horn. One man was holding a pistol.

"For the Whorehouse Room," Monique said when she gave the picture to Patsy. It was framed in barn wood.

"I like the men with the tubas," said Patsy.

"They are upright E-flat altos," said Ward. "Not tubas."

"How did you know that?" Monique said.

"I used to play one in the high school band," Ward said.

"Then you can play my French horn."

"I only play upright E-flat altos," said Ward.

"I'd like 'The Red River Valley,'" said Patsy, when she saw that Monique had brought a book of French horn instructions and sheet music. For my part, I had bought a music stand from the Widow Bly.

"I'll try," said Monique.

Over time we'd hear Monique doing what she could with the French horn, and when she was not around, we'd find Patsy giving it a polish.

"Jesus-God told me to keep it shiny for Monique," she said.

I must say, to Patsy's credit, the Whorehouse Room was always clean and looked as if a High Dollar Dodge City dove of low moral character might leave her perch on the long horns and join us at the player piano to sing "The Red River Valley." And, as it turned out, the Whorehouse Room was where we had our Black Jack every night after work—but not before we had showered, tended to cuts and bruises, combed our hair (Patsy was big on combed hair) and put on clean clothes.

"'Be clean and combed for Jesus-God once a day.' Evaticus 7:3."

"Goodbye," Ward would say by way of a toast when he tipped his whiskey glass. Goodbye, so said we all as the pain of work began to fade. Patsy drank long-necked Coors.

After our Black Jack we'd usually go into the kitchen for supper. On Saturdays and Sundays we stayed in the Whorehouse Room and Patsy (and Monique, if she were there) would bring the food to the big wooden trestle table that dead-ended on the west side just below where we'd hung the picture of the Dodge City Cowboy Band.

The table had a long rough scar down the middle. Ward said the scar was a mystery, but he wouldn't say much more, and so we'd take turns telling stories of how the table got its flesh wound and why. Sometimes Ward would tell a version, and if it were the real story or not, he never said. It was a routine we liked. No matter how we sat at the table, it was understood no one sat at the far end under the picture of the Cowboy Band, and how we understood that was our custom was not talked about.

*

When hunting season began, the Ranch Doctor would drive out from Lawrence with Monique. In exchange for taking him shooting, he'd give us physicals, and his last time out, he became part of Monique's *Whorehouse Room colloquy*. As did we all.

Sometimes I'd cook for Patsy. She'd sit in the sunshine on the south side of the house by her garden, pulling on a long-necked Coors. She liked being called to dinner or supper instead of ringing the bell for the calling. Not always, but for a break. Small luxuries are better than big ones if you live in the country. And I liked fixing the meal. Even setting the table and washing up.

Ward didn't cook. Only slabs of venison on the pit grill when we shot a deer. Patsy knew how to make jerky, and we had a hand-crank meat grinder for everything but the good cuts. A buck could feed us through to spring if we portioned it out: steaks, ground meat for chili, a couple of roasts, jerky for the truck when we were windshield ranching. Patsy would mix the ground deer with the ground buffalo and call it "two beast burger" that she'd use for meatloaf, chili, or hamburgers. We tanned and tacked hides on the south side of my cabin to cure.

Patsy grew hot peppers she'd string and hang in the kitchen to dry for the chili. And braid onions and hang those in the well house. Keep carrots and potatoes covered with straw so sometimes we'd have them into December. She planted sweet corn and tomatoes and green and red salad peppers. One year she had me bring sand up from the Saline and mix in it on the south edge of the garden where she grew watermelon. The garden got better until it became "abundant." It was a word Ward had once used and Patsy borrowed.

"The abundance of Jesus-God," Patsy would say when looking over the garden. Most anything good in those days was "abundant" to her. Patsy liked words. We all liked words. *Propensity* was a favorite.

"She's an *abundance* of Jesus, that's for sure," Ward would say after Patsy had gone off on one of her religious benders.

"With a *propensity* for hell," I said.

"That too," said Ward.

"Have you decided to tell her about Milky?" I asked.

"No. Let her have Jesus-God as the tomato deity, and we'll worship the old cow."

Patsy had me build a "moat"—a small wire fence—around her garden so she could keep a dozen or so chickens there to eat the grasshoppers before they got to her plants. The other chickens ran in the yard, but Patsy thought the best ones for cooking came from the moat because of the grasshoppers they ate. The yard chickens were for soup or stir-fries. And eggs.

"When Jesus-God made Himself a chicken, He was thinking of women," Patsy used to say. "You take a chicken and a woman who knows how to pick it, and she can feed all of West Jesus Land, Kansas, half of The Rest of America, and be pleased to do so."

Well, we had horses to work the pastures down along the river; two old four-wheel-drive pickups with granny gears; a John Deere 4010 for ground we leased west of us to grow oats for the horses, a square baler (that was always breaking down) for the prairie hay when we could get a cutting and for a small alfalfa patch in a creek bottom leading to the Saline. All of it mortgaged to the bank. Not the horses. Not the Home-House or my cabin. Not Milky. They can't take what you ride or where you live. Or what's dead.

It was good while it lasted, and to be fair to the fates, it lasted quite a while. Even with Ellen's death partway into it. And even after we were broke. There's a lot you can do without much money if you put your mind to it, and it's not a bad use of your mind. In this way, we ate well and lived well, being careful. For a long time nobody got hurt or sick. When the end finally came, it was Patsy who helped me bury the dogs, two months apart, in the shelterbelt west of my cabin, their name tags nailed to trees. I took her picture next to the graves, then we went to town where Patsy put on her dress for the service, what there was of it, the two of us standing by the flat stone marker with no name on it. Then we went back out to the ranch where Patsy packed up her paintings, pots and pans, stuff, the French horn, books and took three live chickens to town. I helped her move.

It was much later that Mencken Cody wrote to say Patsy'd come back out and they found her half-crazed in the heat and the wind of a bad August, tearing down the chicken moat around her garden and shooting her pistol shots into the sky at the Anti-Christ. Mencken took her to Blaze where she lives with her sister.

The Friday before Patsy's birthday, Monique got to the ranch at sunset just as Ward rode up on Canyon Snip from checking cattle. Patsy had gone to town, so we were on our own for supper, but I knew Monique would have something. And a meal for the next day—not that Patsy knew we had learned it was her birthday.

"What's the moon?" said Ward, still sitting in the saddle and looking east.

"The Harvest Moon," said Monique.

"Very good," said Ward.

"You want to ride?" said Ward, taking his foot out of the left stirrup. "Double. It will be like riding bareback."

"With a man in the moonlight not my lover?" she said. "Sure. And I've never ridden bareback."

"I'm not harmless," Ward said. "But I'm not dangerous, either."

"Supper is in the truck," Monique said, as she swung in behind Ward and off they went into the east pasture, while I took a box of food and wine into the Home-House.

Monique had brought one of her homemade pizzas and several bottles of Chianti. I had made a salad from Patsy's garden. There was apple pie. And two rounds of cheese, both Italian.

As I was getting supper ready, I looked outside and saw them coming up to the yard; Monique swung off, patted Canyon Snip on the nose, opened the gate, then headed for the house while Ward went to the tack room.

"How was it?" I said. "Double with a tall handsome cowboy and bareback to boot."

"I'm going to recommend bareback to my daughters," she said.

We ate that night at the Scar Table and instead of telling stories, we talked about food and wine, horses and moons. Ventilation for the brain.

The next day we put Monique to work fencing. We had taken old wire off a mile or so of posts and were putting up new wire. You can pull it tight with fencing pliers if you're not running the wire along more than half a dozen posts. Doing it that way, you hear the creak of the wire, and the sound of the hammer when you tap in a new staple. But this morning our run was long; Monique drove the truck ahead of us so we wouldn't have to walk back to get it. Then before we got to her, she'd drive farther down, leaving a can of staples. It doesn't sound like much for work, but it made the job quicker and that pleased her to do it.

"Leo, you going to marry Monique?" Ward asked as we made our way up the fencerow toward the truck. I could see her sitting on the tailgate. She was watching us. When she saw us looking her way she waved.

"We haven't talked about it."

"She will."

When we finished our fencing we went back to Ward's, where Monique began preparing Patsy's dinner while I set the Scar Table. For a present, Monique brought an autographed book of paintings by Robert Sudlow, the Kansas painter of the prairie. We had signed it earlier that day, each of us adding "a bit of affection"—as Monique asked us to do.

"I know him," Monique said, "and I had it autographed: *To Patsy of West Jesus Land, Kansas, Robert Sudlow.*"

The book was wrapped and put at the head of the table where Ward usually sat but where Patsy would sit for the evening. Supper was a French meal: *Poule au pot.*

"It means chicken in a pot," Monique said. "Henry the Fourth thought all his subjects should have *Poule au pot* each and every Sunday."

I was in the kitchen with her slicing and dicing as she began putting the meal together, using some ingredients we had but more she had brought: garlic, celery, parsley, bay leaves, juniper berries, leeks, small turnips, new potatoes—but not carrots, which were still coming on in Patsy's garden.

Earlier in the week, I had killed and plucked a chicken and kept it in my refrigerator. Also in my cabin, Monique had put two bottles of Bordeaux wine and a Roquefort cheese.

"Instead of a birthday cake," she said to me, "I am going to make a chocolate soufflé. Since Patsy is not here, it is up to you, *tú*," she said blowing me a kiss, "to find a dozen eggs."

"Moi?"

"Ah oui," she said. "And bring the wine."

I met Ward coming toward the house and roped him into helping me look for the eggs; it took a while, but we got a dozen together; Ward took them into the house while I got the wine. Then we stayed in the kitchen to help as we could. Ward thought to have everything ready to surprise Patsy.

"If you had told her," Monique said, "she would have gotten dressed up. Women don't like being surprised as much as men do. They like better getting ready."

"How about we tell her next time around?" I said. "A year to look forward to it."

"That's a long time getting ready," Ward said. "And the future is not always that far off."

"She'd be pleased," Monique said.

Just then Patsy drove up and Monique handed Ward the wine and I took the food. Candles had been in various places around the room. Monique got the French horn and when Patsy walked in she played a rough version of "Happy Birthday."

Patsy was bewildered and for a moment joined in the song, singing as badly as ever, until it dawned on her maybe it was her birthday she was singing about.

"I didn't bring a present," she said, still confused.

"We took care of that," Monique said. And here Ward got the book and handed it to her. Standing, she unwrapped it, looked at the cover with its celebrated *For the Villages, a Kansas Landscape* snowy painting and turned it over and over, then opened it to see our tributes and Sudlow's dedication—all of which she read aloud, thinking to my ear that she liked Monique's comment the best: *To the greater woman of the ranch, from the lesser one.*

"I'll put it with my Bible. For later," she said.

Then she looked at dinner all set out and the lighted candles around the room and shook her head saying nothing as she took the tools from her bib overalls: pliers, pistol, gloves, beer can opener, baling twine, golf balls, the hatchet, and, putting them with the silverware at her place, sat down smiling.

"Hello," said Ward, raising his wine glass by way of a toast. Hello, so said we all—even Patsy.

As we ate, each of us told a Scar Table story, mine being that Ward had caught a thief trying to steal his World War II souvenir Samurai sword and, using his Winchester model 70 30-06 deer rifle (he had been out hunting, which I did not include because our Scar Table stories never had much exposition to them), fired off a round from his hip, the bullet passing along the top of the table leaving the scar. Where it went from there (into the body of the thief or into the wall now covered with Patsy's wall paper) I did not tell, nor what happened to the thief, it also being our custom not to advance the plot from one of our stories to the next. Or even to continue the story we had started. Or weave it into the stories of other authors.

As for Patsy, she said it was not a bullet at all but a bolt of lightning from the end of Jesus-God's finger (Monique had once brought out an art book with Michelangelo's Sistine Chapel in it) that was a warning to get right with the Lord or get zapped with gravediggers going horizontal like Jesus-God would when he flew east to west not long from now. In the end we'd have arrows of lightning all over our bodies just like the heathens did to Jesus.

When it came Ward's turn, he said he did not have a Japanese's Samurai sword and never did have one, but now that he had shot a thief trying to steal it, he'd see what he could do about getting one from the Widow Bly, given that her husband had traded for many things over the years and she was now selling out. Either that or he only wounded the thief, who fled through the kitchen with the sword that Ward never had in the first place, and maybe he was dead in a back pasture by now and we'd find him skin and bones like the quicksand-trapped heifers, but still holding the Samurai sword that we'd bring back to go with the story about how the thief got shot trying to steal it.

Beyond this, Ward said nothing, and none of us asked if he'd like to tell a story of his own, which apparently he did not. I remembered two he had already told about how the scar came to be. However, both of those were before Patsy and Monique, as were two I had told. And we did not retell them, that also being our custom.

When it was Monique's turn, she said it was not Jesus who had been shot with arrows but San Sebastian, as depicted in a number of paintings from the Renaissance. As for the scar, she said a woman made it with her wrath.

"What about her wrath?" asked Ward.

"Well," said Monique, "The Woman got pissed and scanned her eye down the table and the fierceness of her glare was white hot, and it burned the scar into the table from one end to the other, causing all the food and drinks that had been set out for dinner by her to boil and burn, and Lo! The men could neither drink nor eat until the Woman's wrath was calmed, now and forever more: Hermitica 6:22." Here she winked at Patsy, who said, yes, that was in fact Hermitica 6:22.

After Monique's story, we began to eat, although Ward suggested we would be wise to test our food should it burn our lips. Nobody asked why the Woman had become pissed, that too being left out of the narrative. Or how her wrath was calmed—if it was.

At the end of supper, Ward went over to the couch and from behind it got another present, not wrapped. It was a copy of Frederic Remington's *The Fall of the Cowboy*, and, like the Dodge City Cowboy Band photograph, it was framed in barn wood.

"What's that?" asked Patsy, thinking, I supposed, she might be getting another present.

"It's my birthday as well," said Ward, "and I got this for myself."

"Is that true?" said Monique, to which there was no answer as Ward turned to Patsy and said,

"For your room upstairs. I'll hang it tonight and you might as well stay after we clean up." Patsy agreed and stood and gave Ward a Paris cheek kiss, asking Monique if she'd done it right, which she had.

It was later that night that Patsy came to my cabin to say Ward had walked out into the night and had not returned and what did I think we should do? This was past midnight. I got dressed, as did Monique, and we walked into the yard. His truck was there. The horses were standing by the outer fence, all but Ward's horse, Canyon Snip.

"Has he gone for a ride?" Monique said.

"Yes," I said.

"Where?"

"Maybe nowhere. Maybe somewhere."

Then we saw him coming out of the night with the moon on his shoulders and Canyon Snip holding his head up against the bit as he always did, even if Ward was not pulling it into his mouth.

"He hasn't seen us," I said. "Let's go back inside."

"Do you think it is his birthday?" Monique asked. I said I did not know.

The big pond in the north pasture was fenced off so cattle couldn't get into it. There was a pipe through the dam into the stock tanks below. Early on, I built a raft of oil barrels and wide board blanks and floated it to the middle, where I anchored it with an old engine block. Every once in a while, I would pull the engine block up to let the raft drift with the breeze from one part of the pond to the other, then re-anchor it.

Sometimes in summer, if we had worked the horses hard, Ward and I would take them to the pond for a swim. We'd unsaddle and ride into the water bareback and, slipping off to the side, get a swim for ourselves. When she was out, Monique would ride and swim as well, but not off the horses.

Springs fed the pond from draws to the west and east, and from the bottom. The ones from the bottom made for cold patches. When Monique would feel one, she'd do a surface dive down into it. Her legs would come up for a moment and then slip away. She could hold her breath a long time—and she never came up where she went under; sometimes she'd resurface halfway across the pond. I'd be treading water looking for her.

"Here, over here." If no one were around she'd swim nude. We both would.

"How did his wife die?" Monique asked me one day on the raft.

"A grain truck from the feed lot ran a stop sign on the Seven Hills Road and hit her broadside."

"Did she live long?"

"Too long."

Monique was quiet.

"Someday I'd like to have a picnic on the raft," she said.

"Sure," I said. I thought she might be buying time to say something else.

"Does it have a name?"

"The raft?"

"Yes. Did you name it?"

"We didn't think to do that," I said.

"Could we name it for her?"

"Ask Ward," I said.

Monique didn't ask Ward about naming the raft. But between us we named it for Ellen—but it was not "Ellen," as I have written before. The next time we had a picnic on the raft, Monique christened it with a champagne toast.

Patsy and Monique liked to fish the pond for the large-mouth bass and the big white-meat channel cat, and snappers we'd put in a rain barrel by the garden and fatten with scraps, and milk to sweeten the taste. When they got big enough, Patsy would put a broom handle into the barrel and, after the snapper hit it, haul him to the chopping block to "cleave his parts apart."

"Most of what's a turtle is in his head," she'd say, as its body ran around the yard until it stopped, the head still snapping elsewhere. If Moshe were around he'd go for the body.

"Where'd you learn about turtles?" Monique asked.

"When he's done snapping," Patsy said, "toss him in the garden unless Moshe wants him," not answering Monique's question.

"Where'd Patsy learn to clean snapping turtles?" Monique asked Ward.

"With some women, the cleaning of snapping turtles is a genetic memory," Ward said. "What comes around, comes around." As with other pronouncements of Ward's, I could never be sure the manner of mirth intended. If any.

"Transmigration," I said.

"What's that?" Ward asked.

"What comes around, comes around."

"Good thinking."

Patsy had an apartment in town, and although we knew where it was, we had never been inside. But we had been in her room at the Home-House.

Patsy would bring pictures she had painted and hang them on the walls. There was no perspective. Her sense of color was poor. All of them were scenes at the ranch: views of her garden. The yard. The pastures. Portraits of Moshe, Murphy, and Amos. The horses. There was one of a windmill that pumped water for the stock tanks looking south and west. She never seemed to have her paints, and we never saw her make sketches, so she must have done the paintings from memory. Every now and then she would take some back to Hays and bring others out. When she'd leave, we'd go upstairs to see what was new.

Under her bed she kept a portrait of Ward that I suspected she'd hang when she stayed over and take down when she left. I knew about it because one day I hid a present for Monique there. I never told Ward.

"That's looking west," said Ward one day in the room. "How

come the trail road doesn't go to the stock tank like it should? It's more up in the air than on the ground."

"She's not that kind of painter," I said.

"What's Monique think?" Ward asked.

Monique wasn't a painter, but she had majored in art history and her talk with us was "salted"—that was Ward's word—with references to paintings. The pond was right out of Corot. Patsy could have been painted by Toulouse-Lautrec. Ward by John Curry. She told me her hope was to teach American art history in France. Her French was good enough, she thought. She wanted to teach the French about the American painters: Sloan, Hopper, Bingham. They knew about Mary Cassatt because she was one of theirs. Also Whistler.

"The French can be provincial," she had said. "And proud of it."

Monique brought out her art books and showed us the paintings she was talking about, and when she did, she'd let Patsy keep the books until she returned. You could see Patsy looking at them on the Scar Table. She was very careful.

"I wash my hands before I touch the Bible or Monique's books," Patsy said. "And not in dishwater." Later, this was true for her Sudlow birthday book as well.

When we showed Monique Patsy's paintings, she said they were vignettes in the American primitive tradition. For me a *vignette* was a small story.

"It's paintings as well," Monique said. "See how there are no edges or frames on her landscapes, how they fade off the canvas as if there is a mystery beyond the edge? That's what makes them a vignette. Not that she knows, which is what makes her an American primitive."

In summers Monique would spend weeks at a time with us before going back to Lawrence for a few days to water her plants and check her mail. I'd send her a postcard before she left so she'd have something besides bills. I wouldn't tell her and after awhile she came to expect them, but it still pleased her. We lived this way, back and forth, for six years.

"I think I want to get married," Monique said. We were on the raft.

"Why?" I said.

"It's something I'd like to do," she said. "Do you want to get married?"

"I don't know," I said. She was quiet for a moment. The cottonwoods around the pond were just starting to drop their leaves. When they do that, they flip in the breeze, first one side out then the other. I could see Monique looking at them.

She got up and dove into the water. She was naked and we'd just been lovers. This time she swam on the surface, doing a head-out-of-the-water breaststroke. Once I saw her shudder.

"Hit a cold patch?" I said.

She did not answer. She swam in widening circles around the raft, and then when she got close to the bank, she stood up. She was one of those women who is beautiful, even far away. It was only later that I felt the weight in my mind of what I had said. And not said. It is now, even now, that I do not fully understand what happened between us. But I'm gaining on it.

She did a shallow dive into the water and swam the crawl back to the raft.

After our swim, Monique and I went back to the Home-House. Patsy had arrived, and while she cooked, Monique set the table. Ward and I took the truck into the pastures to check the heifers then drove to Hays to get supplies for various repairs. When we got back I helped Ward unload before I went to my cabin for a shower, while he tended to the horses.

Earlier than usual I heard the bell ring, and when I walked out it was not Patsy ringing it but Monique.

"It's not time yet," she said. "I just wanted you out of the cabin so I could put on something nice for supper without you seeing it first."

"Good thinking," I said as we crossed paths. She had a yellow dress she'd bought after she'd read a story of mine where the character says yellow is his favorite color. When she came back, that's what she was wearing, but neither of us said anything about how it was special. Or about what had happened on the raft. In the meantime there was the bustle of Patsy who ran us outside so as not to be in the way. Ward was at the east edge of the yard.

"What's he doing?" said Monique.

"Talking to the horses."

He had cattle cubes in his pocket and was feeding them. Duke was a chowhound; he'd whinny to be fed. I could see Ward scratch the white arrow on his forehead. He seemed a horse who understood affection. Rare in the breed. Angel had her ears back, which meant she was "pissed about being pleased," as Ward would say.

There was a slight rise east of where Ward stood, beyond which you could see the top of a windmill that we had not disconnected from a water-well pump. Some of the other wells we had put on small gasoline engines to run water into the tanks for cattle.

That pasture was where we kept our horses, and they could get water either at the edge of the yard from a small stock tank or at the windmill. Now they were up close. We had five: Angel, Canyon Snip, Charlene, Duke; and my horse, Chief Lightfoot. We'd take turns riding all of them but Charlene, a mare that had been Ellen's. She had bred her once, using Mencken Cody's stallion, the foal Duke coming just before Ellen died. All had kind eyes but Angel. Chief and Canyon Snip could be stubborn, but not angry about it.

If you don't ride a horse now and then, they can become difficult. Patsy didn't ride: "Anything a woman wraps her legs around is going to give her trouble," is what she'd say when asked about it. Nothing more, even though Ward once asked if she'd ever been married, and all she'd say was that her sister Testy had been.

"He was ugly as a bucket of assholes and smelled twice as bad." Nothing more about that, either.

Monique liked Angel best, but she was a small American saddle horse with an independent streak and Monique was not a confident rider. Sometimes I'd use Angel to check cattle, and in that way she'd get ridden in advance of Monique coming out. Once, when I got in the saddle, Angel reared, and I put my fist to the top of her head hard, which would usually bring her down. But this time she flipped onto her back. I pitched off to the left and hit the ground. I looked to the right and watched the saddle horn dig into the dirt. Ward had seen it all.

"An inch to the north with that saddle horn and I've got dead help," he said when he came over. "Dead help is bad thinking." Angel got up and was about to bolt, but Ward grabbed her reins.

"My father was killed by a horse," he said as he walked Angel in figure eights. I got back in the saddle.

"I didn't know that," I said.

"Best let Monique ride Charlene," he said. "I'll take her out to settle her down. It's past time she gets ridden. Maybe even bred again. I'll ask Mencken."

Ward opened the gate to the north pastures, and I headed out on Angel to check the cattle. Later that day and a few times that week, I'd see Ward on Charlene but said nothing about it. Thinking back over those years, what went unsaid seemed natural. Even what I have promised not to write.

That night we took the meal to the Scar Table, and instead of a story, Ward told Monique how I was almost killed by Angel and that she could use Charlene if she liked.

Later, back at my cabin, Monique asked why I hadn't told her what happened, and I said I didn't want to frighten her but that it was also Ward's way of letting her ride Charlene.

"She was Ellen's horse," I said.

As we went to bed, I sensed Monique wanted to say something but did not. In the night I got up and went outside to look at the moon, now high above us. My leaving did not wake Monique.

I have kept her postcard all these years. First as a bookmark, then later by itself on whatever desk of mine. In the cabin I had a small table and over it I put a plate of glass, under which I arranged our Polaroids: Me and Ward at the kitchen table. Patsy with a big watermelon. Ellen on Charlene. Ward. Moshe with the good-sized rat. A headless snapping turtle. Chief Lightfoot. Monique and Milky. Monique. A basket of eggs. The French horn. Monique.

For a while I'd keep it script-side up, then down, the picture of *Pont des Arts* up. That's the way I left it when I left. That's where it was when I returned years later to get it before I left to find her. I have it now.

"Maybe her family will tell you where she is," Ward said.

But after that, he didn't say anything more—nor did I.

The Hunter's Moon

It stayed warm for all of September and into early October when we caught a small snow, and then it warmed into a long, soft Indian summer. The Ranch Doctor decided to come out to shoot doves and ducks instead of waiting for pheasant season, and that meant we'd move up the colloquy.

The Friday of the October snow, the bank had called again, but Ward just hung up, refusing them even the gift of profanity.

"It has snowed in Kansas every month except August," Ward said when we finished our coffee before we went out to check on the heifers.

"Good thinking," said Patsy, who had stayed over and was fixing us breakfast.

It was a soft, wet snow. It hadn't been that cold but the wind had been hard all night and into the early morning. There were drifts into the draws, but the ground was warm and you could see water running through the snow.

We spotted Mencken Cody's Gomer bull before we found the herd. He was still marking and that meant we'd have to bring the heifers up to the corrals for insemination. You had a few days after you saw the blue patch. We could have inseminated them ourselves, but we weren't set up for it, so we called the vet when we had half a dozen or so ready.

Over the next rise and down into a big cutout below the dam to the pond was the herd. They had found a place out of the wind. And grass as well. It was their first snow, but they knew what to do. Bunched up like they had not been all summer and into the fall, it was a sight. Bawling and milling. I spotted three new ones for breeding. Ward saw a fourth.

A coyote hustled over the hill toward the river. As they do, it stopped to look back. Sometimes there were deer along a line of cottonwoods to the west and north of where the herd was, but not this morning. Wild turkeys, though. I could have taken one, but the shot would have spooked the heifers.

In the pickup were the cattle cubes. I climbed into the bed with a scoop shovel, and Ward drove along slowly while I laid down a line. We had fed the heifers cattle cubes a few times before so they'd know what they were—and to follow the truck if we needed to move them. Now we were just trying to pour energy to them. They'd need more in the evening.

"You want to horseback the marked heifers up?" Ward asked as we drove to the Home-House.

"Sure."

"I'll drop you off to get saddled," he said. "There is something I want to do."

"Yes," I said. I knew where he was going. The next day was the date of Ellen's death.

Ward and I had scattered Ellen's ashes in places she especially liked: the line of cottonwoods where we had just found the heifers; among the old homestead of limestone buildings that was abandoned by the time Ward and Ellen bought the quarter; onto the waters of the pond, standing on the east side that day because of the wind; some at the top of the breaks that ran into the Saline. And one place Ward kept to himself, taking the last of her ashes with him.

We had driven the pickup far into the west pasture where there wasn't much but grass and a few rills. No trees. A small tank of a pond that was dry most years. Beyond the tank we'd use horses to work cattle. It had been warm during the days, but at night—and it was getting to be evening when Ward had me drop him off—it could get brisk quickly. There might be more wind in the air by sundown. Where he got out would be two miles from the Home-House.

"I can come back to get you," I had said out the cab window.

"I'll walk," he said.

An hour later, just as the butane yard light started its slow glow, he came into the house. That night he made his Black Jack toast for the first time. We had chicken from a Crock-Pot. This was before Patsy.

"What are we going to do about the bank?" I said when I came into the house after bringing up the heifers. Ward had passed me in the truck and was sitting in the kitchen. Outside, it was warming up. It wouldn't melt all the snow, but most of it.

"Let them figure out what they're going to do about us, first." Ward said. "Sometimes it is best not to talk about troubles when they are on your back." What we didn't know was that the bank was trying not to go broke by trying to take us down.

"Monique coming out this weekend?" said Ward. We could hear Patsy in the Whorehouse Room, cleaning.

"That's the plan. Tonight after school, if they didn't get snow east of us, like the radio says."

"Does she know about Saturday?"

"I told her."

"There were some teal on the pond this morning," he said.

"I saw them."

"Do you think she'd eat teal?"

"I think she would. Would you rather have a turkey? They'll be back below the dam later today."

"Teal," Ward said. "How about that wine she brings?"

"What about it?"

"Maybe she'd bring something special for the teal."

"I'll call and ask. You want me to shoot the teal?"

"Let's both go," he said. "But we need to get the vet out for the heifers."

"Fine by me," I said.

After the vet came, we drove into Hays for errands. By the time we got back, there was no snow on the roads, only in the bar ditches, and that was melting fast. I found myself thinking that in an hour or two Monique would be on the highway, and four hours later she'd be at the ranch. It would be dark, but we'd wait supper for her. I'd left a message at the school about the wine.

"You want to take the teal now or tomorrow morning?" I said as we were coming up the lane.

"Now," said Ward. "Let's feed the heifers while we're at it."

We shot the teal not long before Monique arrived. They came in at sundown. Ward shot two as they made a pass by our blind, and I shot two more when they came back a second time. We'd gutted them and hung them from the cross pole in the front yard with the dinner bell.

Monique got to the ranch just after sunset. We had a good-sized moon to the east when she drove in. I had been standing in the yard looking for her lights. She drove a secondhand pickup with a spotlight through the roof, and when she'd make the turn off the highway onto the Buckeye Road, she'd flip on the spotlight. From two miles away you could see her coming.

A smoke signal, she called her light. Ten minutes later she'd be up the lane and in the yard.

Driving in at night, she'd put the spotlight on me then turn it on and off, so I'd be in the dark for a moment then in bright light.

"Sing," she'd say when she got out of the truck. "When the spotlight's on, you're supposed to sing."

Like Patsy, I can't sing; only in my case, I know it. Monique could sing. A lovely voice: Maria Muldaur lyrics. *We worked so hard, we died standing up. Midnight at the oasis put your camel to bed.* Run a song through once, and she had the tune and the words. Even from the radio.

"The man at the liquor store in Topeka didn't know what kind of wine went with teal," Monique said, "but he suggested Cold Duck."

"Sounds reasonable," said Ward who had come out.

Ward knew nothing about wine, and I had learned what I knew years before when Monique and I split a case in college from money we earned collecting mistletoe out of the trees along the Wakarusa and selling it to the university faculty for Christmas. I would shoot into the branches with a .22 and Monique would collect the splintered mistletoe. Back at her apartment she would tie the mistletoe with ribbons into bunches. I had an old Studebaker, and we'd drive around to the professors' houses. Monique would go up and make the sale. She was good at it. A dollar a bunch. Two dollars for three. This was before she went to France, but not before she wanted to go. It was also the year I got rabbit fever and almost died of it. Had it not been for Monique, I might have.

"I brought us a better wine," Monique said and smiled. Then she gave Ward her Paris-Cheek-Kiss, brushing her cheek against Ward's, first on one side then on the other. Ward had to bend over for Monique, which he did with ease.

In those days we grew beards for winter, and Ward's was just coming out, as was mine. In the spring we'd choose the date to shave them off. One year, mine was in honor of A. B. Guthrie, whose novels I was just then reading. Another year it was on the birthday of the playwright William Inge, who was ahead of me at the university. When *Picnic* came to Hays, it was Patsy who said that all the men were watching Kim Novak during the dance scene while—and here Monique finished Patsy's sentence—*all the women were watching William Holden.*

Ward picked the defeat of Custer the year I picked Inge. The next year he chose June 17, the date the Bonus Army bill was defeated in Congress, and he stayed with those two, Custer on even-numbered years, the Bonus Army on odd-numbered one.

"My dad was in that march to Hooverville," Ward had said. "He wasn't hurt, but he had a friend who was killed." Like other observations, Ward would not expand, and you got the sense he didn't want to. Much went unsaid after what was said at the start.

"Pretty soon you'll look like Curry's John Brown," said Monique to Ward as we walked toward the Home-House. "Just don't let bugs get in your beard, otherwise I'll have to shake hands when we meet."

"Everybody's got to have a place to live," Ward said as he scratched his cheek.

"Good moon," said Monique, turning to look east at its climbing.

"Do you know this moon?" said Ward.

"I do not," said Monique.

"It's going to be the Hunter's Moon when it gets full," said Ward, as he pointed at the teal.

"My heroes," said Monique and gave Ward another Paris-Cheek-Kiss and me one as well. "What's a summer moon called?"

"Ellen called them Lamplighter Moons," said Ward. "By their brightness, you could find what you'd lost in the yard." He paused and looked east. "One night we walked into this pasture to search for a bullwhip of mine that had come loose from Canyon Snip earlier that day. We could have waited until morning but. . . ." Here he stopped.

I picked up Monique's bag and took it to my cabin as she went into the Home-House with Ward.

Patsy was still there and had made buffalo meatloaf for supper, the kind where you get whole hard-boiled eggs in it so that each slice might have a slice of egg in the middle, like a yellow eye. That's what we called it: *yellow-eye buffalo meatloaf.*

Patsy would also make one-eyed Jacks: slices of bread with the middle cut out into which she'd crack an egg and fry it in the Griswald. Sometimes she put in a ring of link sausage and bring the frying pan to the table where we served ourselves. Other times she cut a slice of cheese over the egg-eye. We'd get these for either breakfast or dinner. *Enough to feed Coxey's Army*, Ward would say.

"Stay," Monique said to Patsy when she saw she was getting ready to leave for Hays. "I brought you some French beer."

"I didn't know the French made beer," said Ward.

"Very good beer," said Monique. "Do stay," she said to Patsy.

"I think you two got better things to do than sit around with me after supper," she said looking at me.

"Oh, he can wait," said Monique and helped Patsy out of her coat. I could have taken it badly, but we were not like that with one another. And whatever had happened on the raft between us seemed to have faded.

We went into the Whorehouse Room where Ward poured himself a Black Jack and said his traditional good-bye, even though it hadn't been all that bad a day. Monique opened a bottle of the wine she'd brought and a bottle of beer for Patsy.

"*La Belle Dame sans Merci*," said Monique, as she turned the beer bottle toward Patsy so she could read the label. "It means 'the beautiful woman without mercy.'"

"Well, half that's me," said Patsy and took a pull from the bottle even though Monique had put out a glass.

We drank and talked a bit: about the snow that had come through and how quickly it had melted. About Monique's drive out. French beer. Our beards and what date we had selected in the spring to shave and why. How soon the Ranch Doctor would come and Monique could have her colloquy. That kind of talk until we went into the kitchen for the buffalo meatloaf and baked potatoes, after which Patsy cleaned up and Monique and I went to my cabin.

At times like this Ward might go back to the Whorehouse Room where he'd read. In the morning I'd find him there, not asleep in a chair with a book in his lap as you might expect, or on the couch near the wood stove, but sacked out on an old army cot he kept there for what reason he never said.

"He doesn't want to get into their bed alone," Monique said when I told her about it. "A memory of her."

"From something he's been reading?" I said.

"Maybe," she said. "Was he with her when she died?"

"Yes." But I didn't say anything more, not about what the doctors had said or what had happened in the hospital.

When we got up the next morning, Monique and I stayed in my cabin past noon. There was a small window at the head of our bed in the loft where we slept.

"I don't think we can get out," Monique would say each time she'd open it. What she was really saying is that she could probably squeeze through but that I was too big. In those days I had half a grain-sack belly from eating too much of Patsy's food.

"Let's try."

"Me first," she'd say. And out she'd go and down the ladder. But I always had some excuse not to follow. We came to call it the *Thin Man Window*.

I had made a pot of soup a couple of days before. A mason jar of tomatoes, onions, chicken broth Patsy had given me. Chicken as well. Frozen corn we'd put up from the garden. Peas. Bits of leftover rabbit and pheasant we shot and froze the year before. Monique had brought soup of her own. She mixed our soups together and we had it for lunch; then she put it on the woodstove with a trivet underneath.

"Soupe éternalle," she said "It's what the French call it when you keep it going." She also had brought bread as well—a hard-crust dark bread that she'd make herself and Ward liked but Patsy did not—although she would use it for her one-eyed Jacks.

"Not gooey enough," Patsy would say and bring out a loaf of Wonder Bread. She was also fond of Velveeta cheese.

"I don't see how a woman who cooks so well and grows her own garden, cleans fish and snapping turtles, can like Wonder Bread and Velveeta cheese," Monique said to me one day.

"And Spam."

"No!"

"Yes."

As we were heading over to Ward's, Monique said: "Do you remember the time Moshe came to the door with a large rat? For once he'd caught something he could handle and seemed proud of it."

It was the first time we'd talked about Moshe since he'd died; not even Patsy had said anything about him. I was about to say something about Milky and our first summer together but did not. In these ways we had learned to leave some things unsaid.

"Does Patsy know about today?" said Monique.

"Yes."

Sometimes Patsy would come out on Saturdays but sometimes not. For sure she never came on Sundays. She'd go over to Blaze where Testy held prayer meetings in the Pool Room Tavern. Sometimes there were only the two of them; other times a few folk from around Blaze and Bly would show up, more for stories to tell than for religious instruction.

According to Patsy and Testy, when the End Time came Jesus-God was going to fly over Kansas east to west at thirty-thousand feet, arms spread for wings, legs apart like a wishbone. As He flew, the holy power of His body would suck up the Believers and leave the rest of us to roast. A Believer could choose the place on Jesus where he or she wanted to be attached.

"Like ticks," said Ward. "The best way to get them out is with the hot end of a burned match. That way you don't leave the head."

"Testy wants an earlobe," said Patsy, ignoring Ward. "She won't tell why. Not even to me. You guys are going to get burned black like you were cooked on that ground pit you use for deer steaks unless you get right with the Lord. Hell is going to bubble up from the innards of earth and catch it on fire, topsoil, cattle, pheasants, soap weed and all. Even that pond will be burning. Not just boiling. Burning. 'Water will be damned and turn to a lake of flame.' Jehovah 4:36."

The week we had the prairie fires Patsy was sure she'd see Jesus coming across the sky and so she started for Blaze to be with Testy. Not to be together on an earlobe, though. Patsy was undecided between the scar on Jesus' right palm or the scar on His left foot.

"You get right with the Lord before the devil roasts you like a hotdog on a stick," she said before she drove down the lane, the smoke getting thick to the north of us.

"Has she decided between the hand and the foot?" Ward said as Patsy drove off.

"I didn't ask," I said.

"Good thinking," said Ward.

It wasn't long before Patsy had to come back. Because of the smoke and fire, they'd blocked off the road. She stood in the yard looking in the sky for Jesus.

"Could you see the fire on the ground?" Ward asked.

"Yes," Patsy said. "It was over by Mencken Cody's place. Coming our way."

"Was it jumping the roads?"

"The cow turds were," Patsy said.

"On fire?"

"Yes." All this time she was looking at the sky.

"That's the way it spreads," Ward said to me. "The cow flops catch fire and sail on ahead with the wind."

"Flying flaming Frisbees of shit," Patsy said. "It's the way the world is going to end. In a blizzard of flaming Frisbees of shit."

"Is that what it says in the Bible?" Ward said.

"Ravitics 3:26," said Patsy and walked into the house to fix dinner.

"How does she know about Frisbees?" I asked Ward.

"Her hippie nephew and his girlfriend," said Ward. "They throw the Frisbee back and forth across the Saline. Naked."

"I never saw that," I said.

"I wish I hadn't," Ward said.

We went inside where we got a sermon: It turns out that while the real Jesus is going east to west, a fake Jesus is going west to east, and if, as you are roasting away in pasture ponds of fire or getting pelted by flaming flying Frisbees of shit, you try to repent at the last moment, Jesus-God knows you're a fake and up you go to the West-to-East Jesus where you get sucked into his blood stream, which is full of AIDS, and there you live all covered with blood and sores forever and ever and ever. Better to stay in Buckeye Township and get cooked.

"Her version of Job," Ward said.

Patsy came out the Saturday anniversary of Ellen's death and cooked the teal so that each of us got a duck. She'd wrapped them in bacon and served them with carrots and potatoes from her garden that was still producing, even given the recent snow. At dinner Ward raised his glass but did not say "good-bye," instead saying something to himself. I had seen him do this before but could not lip-read to know what it was.

Over dinner we laid plans for the colloquy. Monique wanted us each to pick a topic. She had picked "The Fall of the Cowboy" by Remington, since Ward had it framed on the wall. The Ranch Doctor had told her he'd talk about an organ but had not decided which one. He'd bring illustrations. That left me, Ward, and Patsy. I said I'd talk about Andy Adams's *The Log of a Cowboy* because I was in debt to it for something I had written and, as I had extra copies, I'd pass them around for all to read.

"I'll do pagans," Ward said.

"Pagans?" I didn't remember Ward ever saying anything about pagans. "What do you know about pagans?"

"I am one. That counts." Then he gave a short preface to his presentation, talking about Irish Druids and how pagans don't have songs that go *Onward pagan soldiers, marching on to war, with the shells of turtles, going on before.*

"Is there something we should read about pagans?" I asked. I didn't get an answer because Patsy said she was going to talk about how Judas didn't hang himself from the Judas tree but got such a bad stomachache from having betrayed Jesus that his belly split open and he spilled his guts into his vegetable garden where they got plowed under and for forty years afterward it was known as the Blood Garden because it grew very fine tomatoes. "Acts 18 to 20."

When we were back in my cabin, Monique said that for once Patsy had the Bible more-or-less right.

The next morning, Patsy fixed us one-eyed Jacks early because Monique had to leave before noon in order to get home before dark and Patsy wanted to get to Blaze.

"We are going to read the passages from Acts," said Patsy, "where they are communists, and if you try to hide money from God that should go to the poor you get shot." Monique said later that Patsy had gotten that right as well.

When Monique drove down the lane, she turned her spotlight around so that it was aimed backward toward us. At the gate, before making a left on the Buckeye Road she switched the light on and off a number of times until she reached the highway. It was her usual way of saying goodbye. Patsy followed her to the highway, and Monique turned south, and Patsy north. We were getting some wind from the east as they left.

"Three days of wind from the east," Ward said, looking after Monique's and Patsy's going down the Buckeye, "and we get rain. The guy who ran Half-Vast Ranch believed he could hear his dead wife's voice coming out of the verbena that grew down by the gate to the place. Crazy old goat. He thought he was Prince of Goa, whoever that is. He's pushing up soap weed now but I admired his madness. He was the last of the Prairie Populists. We need more like him in this country. Maybe I'll hear Ellen's voice in the rain if it comes from the east," he said, as in fact it would in three days. Then walking to the kitchen, he asked how I thought I'd die.

"In my sleep," I said.

"'Death's second self that seals up all in rest,'" Ward said.

"Yes." I had left a copy of the Shakespeare book we were using at school in the Home-House and apparently Ward had been reading it. He was a big reader but never of junk. Whatever I'd bring back from the Hays library, or some of the books I'd buy, he'd ask to read. And it wouldn't be long afterward that he'd find some use in our talk for what he'd read. Sometimes it would be weeks or months later, but it would crop up. This time it was pretty recent.

In fact, I had never thought about my death. It was a cliché answer. Ward called such answers "white bread."

"The reason they make white flour is because rats won't eat it," he'd say when Patsy would serve us her Wonder Bread sandwiches. He looked forward to Monique's bread.

"Do you think you'll go anywhere?" Ward asked.

"After I'm dead?"

"Yes."

"Transmigration," I said.

"You coming back around as yourself? Or coming back as a horse?"

"More like when Dorothy goes to Technicolor Oz and meets the folk from black-and-white Kansas, including that witch of an aunt of hers."

Coming into the house I asked: "How about you?"

"Ellen always thought she'd die on horseback," he said. I noticed once again he had not answered the question I asked, but answered one I did not ask. That happens.

"Get thrown?"

"No. She thought she'd be riding in the back pastures beyond the tank on Charlene one day and just die. She thought she'd be old. But not too old to ride. She said she'd know in advance when the time would come but wouldn't tell me."

"I never saw that kind of thinking in her," I said.

"I didn't either," Ward said. Sitting down at the kitchen table there was a pause between us, broken when Ward asked if I was going to write about us like I had once before. When I didn't answer, he said he'd learned from one of my schoolbooks that an elegy was poetry for the dead and a eulogy was prose.

"That's true." And nothing more was said. That night he skipped his toast before supper. Nor did we tell a story of the scar except Ward asking if I had one, and I said it could wait.

The following week it got warm. The snow melted in the pastures quickly and for far into November the sky was clear. The Gomer was still marking the heifers. Some days you'd see three or four. Other days only one. You couldn't drive just one heifer, so if the herd was close to the yard, we'd rope her and lead her up to the corrals until there were others ready for the vet. Farther away, we'd hog-tie her in the bed of the pickup.

By the time the Ranch Doctor came out and we had our colloquy, all that were going to get bred were bred, and we took the ones that weren't to the sale barn and returned the Gomer to Mencken.

After we loaded him into the stock trailer, I thought to untie the breeding collar. Over the summer it had lost its color, and we were finished with him in any case.

"Don't bother," said Ward.

I was reaching through the opening on the side of the trailer near the front and almost had it off. That's when he rattled his horns. I took a hit in my right hand.

"Damn it," I said. I wasn't as gifted at swearing as Ward.

"You OK?"

"I think so." I looked at my hand: It was not punctured, but the Gomer's horn had knocked it against the side of the stock trailer. I was skinned raw on the backside, but that was about all. It would be black and blue by morning.

"Best to leave bent-peckered bulls alone," said Ward. "All bulls for that matter."

"Good thinking," I said.

We took the Gomer over to Cody's where we off-loaded him into a corral.

"How'd he do for you, Ward?" said Mencken.

"Only three didn't get bred. We lost two in the Saline from quicksand."

"Thanks for calling about that," Mencken said. "It's a bad way to go."

"Know any good ways?" said Ward.

The Waning Moon

The following Friday, the Ranch Doctor came out from Kansas City, picking up Monique in Lawrence, where he had a community holistic clinic. They arrived late, but Patsy had waited supper: buffalo chili over twice-baked potatoes and a big salad. The next morning we had our physicals, rudimentary to be sure, but at least the Ranch Doctor put a stethoscope on us, hit our knees with the little arrow-headed hammer, pounded us on the back and chest with two fingers, looked in our ears and down our throats and—very important—grabbed our livers. Patsy had made it clear he couldn't pry into her privates "where the moon don't shine."

All was pretty much the same except I noticed that the Ranch Doctor did not as usual advise Ward to quit smoking, the advice being a routine joke between them because Ward had stopped years before. Monique had gotten her physical at the Ranch Doctor's clinic in Lawrence, which was why they were late.

We had supper in the Whorehouse Room and the Ranch Doctor

told his version of the Scar, it being that it was like the life line on your palm, but in the case of the Scar, you could see your fate by running your eye along it from Ward's end to where nobody sat just below the picture of the Dodge City Cowboy Band, and somewhere along the line you'd feel the power of life start to give out, and somewhere just past that you'd blink, and that was your fate.

I could have taken it the way I took Patsy's vision of the End Time, but I did not. I noticed only Ward seemed to be running his eye down the table toward the empty chair. I looked away so as not to see if he blinked.

After supper we had our colloquy: First, Patsy made a cheerful presentation of the End Time with all her grim details of the world on fire from flying Frisbees of shit, barbecued body parts, the Anti-Christ going the wrong way, but finally the joy of joining the real Jesus-God on his body at last, the only change from her previous predictions was that at the last minute she was going to grab me, Ward, and Monique by the hair and haul us along with her. The Ranch Doctor would have to fend for himself.

Monique took *The Fall of the Cowboy* off the wall and propped it on the music stand. Patsy wanted to know why it was called *The Fall of the Cowboy*, because the man standing by his horse had clearly not fallen off but gotten off. Monique asked Ward if he knew the answer, and in this way Monique did not have to do much explaining of the painting but only ask us questions to which we gave answers, the first being from Ward: that its title was exactly right because the man had gotten off his horse to open a gate, and in this way the West was now fenced off. From that point on, we all talked about the painting, with Monique getting us to understand perspective and how cold the painting was because of the pigments Remington had used.

After about half an hour, Ward said we needed a break, and we all poured ourselves another drink, mine being to stay with wine as did Monique, the Ranch Doctor going back to whiskey along with Ward. Patsy got a bottle of *La Belle Dame Sans Merci* she had been saving. Before the Ranch Doctor and Ward made their presentations,

Monique played the piano, singing a version of *I ride an old paint, I lead an old dan, I'm going to Montana for to throw a Hulihan*.

When it came his turn, the Ranch Doctor told us more than we wanted to know about lungs, saying that when he was a young man he had first been a medical illustrator and lungs were his favorite organ.

Somehow he had no ability to make lungs interesting even though he knew more about his subject than the rest us of knew about ours, mine being *The Log of a Cowboy* that I thought was nonfiction until Adams had his cattle drive from Texas to Montana go through a bog in western Kansas, just about the location of Ward's ranch—where there was no bog.

Finally, it was Ward's turn:

"To be a pagan means what comes around goes around. Life is eternal but to my mind not the way Patsy thinks it is. You feed yourself to the birds in the sky through a tree in the air or grass going to seed on the ground, or you feed yourself to fishes and the turtles in the pond and you're part of life everlasting—even if it isn't yours. I don't see what difference it makes whose life it is, just as long as it's life. The fire ants got Moshe and that was fine by Moshe when he was dead and fine by the fire ants when they were alive. Milky is growing tomatoes and lettuce and carrots and potatoes in Patsy's garden and that is fine by us when we have salads or stews, and it is fine by Milky, who died for a good cause the way she lived for one. And that will be fine by me when I get past blinking down the Scar. Just like Uncle Sol who started a worm farm in one of Leo's poetry books he left around here when he was teaching school."

Here Ward raised his glass and observed that goodbye has two syllables and so two meanings. Patsy asked who Milky was.

Later that night I woke and realized that Monique was not in bed with me, so I put on my clothes and walked over to Ward's. Patsy had gone back to Hays, and the Ranch Doctor was going to stay over in her room. Through the window into the Whorehouse Room I could see Monique and Ward talking to the Ranch Doctor.

I decided not to go in but went back to my cabin where I could not sleep until Monique returned, and then I pretended I was asleep.

The next day they left for Lawrence and Kansas City. That morning Monique and I had not talked about much. Nor, without her truck, could she flash her spotlight goodbye. Still, I had sent her a postcard two days before.

"The television is calling for snow," Patsy said. We were into early January.

Monique had spent Thanksgiving with her parents in Kansas City and then went to Paris over Christmas and New Year's to visit the family where she had stayed when she was a student. She invited me to go along, but I needed to be with Ward and the herd. It would have been my first trip outside the United States. And her invitation seemed tentative.

"How much snow?" said Ward.

"Ten inches and wind."

"You want to stay?" I asked Patsy.

We were standing outside. Ward started walking toward the cut through the shelterbelt on the northwest side. From there you could see over the breaks into the Saline and beyond. You could see the northern sky and the western one as well. This time of year the snow came from the north; early ones, like the one in October came from the southwest. As did spring blizzards. Patsy and I walked behind Ward, and when we came out of the cut-through we saw a line of low clouds.

"How much?" said Ward again.

"Ten," Patsy said. "Maybe twenty."

"Cold?"

"The television said about the snow and wind; I didn't hear about the cold," Patsy said.

"It looks to be cold. You better get to Hays if you're going," Ward said to Patsy.

"I'm staying."

*

That was the blizzard where we didn't get out for a month, except near the end to horseback Patsy to the highway, me on Chief leading Patsy on Charlene.

At the start, the wind took the phone lines down; the roads were drifted in after two days; we lost our electricity after the third day. It was a week after Patsy left before we got any mail, in my case the *Pont des Arts* postcard.

"What you got, Leo?" Mencken Cody said when he saw me and Patsy off our horses on the edge of highway. The road was clear but packed, and the most trouble we had was getting through the snow the state had plowed into a drift. Mencken was the first one to come along.

"Patsy needs to get to town. And I need some food. You just get out?"

"Yes," Mencken said.

I tied the horses to a stop sign and we went to Hays, after which Mencken gave me a ride back and Patsy stayed at her place until we could get the lane cleared.

"Any whiskey in those gunnysacks?" Mencken said as he let me off coming back.

"Only buttermilk," I said, tying two sacks over Charlene's saddle and one to my horn.

"I'll believe that when Testy's Jesus-God comes flying by," Mencken said.

I followed my trail through the snow home, ponying Charlene. It was getting dark. And it had started to snow and blow again. I was blue-steel cold when I got there.

"Goodbye," I said to Ward as I tipped my Black Jack toward him.

"Blood's not meant for anti-freeze," he said.

A Dénouement of Moons

Here's what happened:

The heifers started calving in the blizzard, and we had to bring them up to stalls when we could; some of the calves froze when the heifers dropped them in the snow. Some of the heifers died as well.

Others we didn't find until the spring thaw deep into the horse back pasture where sometimes we find a calf or two, but those were "cold burnt" and would never put on any weight. There were days when the snow was too thick and the wind too hard for me and Ward to keep track of each other. After getting badly separated toward one evening and taking an hour to find one another, then another half an hour to get back to the yard, Ward got out his father's .45 Army Colt and Patsy let me use her .22. In this way we would fire off a round to signal where we were. Up in the yard, Patsy would blast away with my shotgun every hour on the hour so we knew where she was. In this way we worked for weeks.

Once I ran a heifer and her calf ahead of me toward the yard and then could only see the heifer and went back and found the calf and roped her. I hoisted her over the front of the saddle and rode back that way, following Ward's pistol shots.

Patsy ran a rope line from the Home-House to the calving stall so we could get back and forth without losing our way. We kept the horses up with the calves, all except Angel who could not be caught and was not found later no matter where I looked when spring came, only Mencken Cody saying he'd seen her in the snow down near Blaze first running with the wind, then into it, kicking up her heels and whinnying like something possessed. Nor was Ward to be found the summer that followed the blizzard.

It was early February by the time we got Patsy back out to the ranch, and it was that week, too, that we began to count the dead in the herd. Given what we'd brought up to the yard and calved out, we'd lost half of everything. Some nights I thought I could hear a heifer bawling in the distance, mostly north of the yard, but when I'd ride out the next day, I'd find no tracks. *Ghost cattle*, Ward would say, confessing he'd hear the same thing. It was the Ides of March before there was more ground to see in the pastures than snow. A Robert Sudlow painting. Even given our troubles, *Maybe her family knows where she is* was always on my mind. But as I would learn, they would not know themselves for many years, and by the time I got there she was gone.

Vignettes in Search of a Lamplighter Moon

Coming out of Ward's one summer day to ask Patsy if she needed anything in town, I saw her lying on her back in the chicken moat. Her eyes were closed; chickens were walking around and flapping themselves over her. She was talking to herself. Not gibberish. Her hatchet was in her right hand and, as I watched, she raised it, the blade pointed first south, then west, then east, then north, all the time her talking. Finally, she turned the blade to the sky and shook it, still talking. As she is alive, and might some day recover enough to read this, I am not going to write what I heard her say, except that it was a benediction for all of us I have included here.

Late in March we caught an ice storm, then snow on top of the ice, then a rain that froze on top of the snow so that the pastures were crusted. Ward and I stood at the north edge of the shelterbelt from where we could see down toward the pond. We had moved what was left of the herd into the big yard where the heifers (now cows) and their calves were milling among the houses and the sheds.

The sun was out. It was getting to be a warm afternoon. To the west was higher ground and the pastures there ran downhill toward the pond. In some places there were small waterways, and it was from those waterways that we heard the sound, faint to be sure, but distinct. Farther down we could see water emerge from beneath the snow, breaking into the open for a stretch, then flowing again under the crust.

We stood there listening and watching the sun lower itself, tossing shadows from the distant trees in the west toward Patsy's trail road and stock tank painted in the air, the edges becoming a mystery of their own making.

Instead of ringing the bell for supper, Patsy joined us, and the three of us watched the shelves of ice and snow collapse into the small streams they themselves had created. For no special reason we could name, we ate at the Scar Table that night but said little.

*

Monique's first winter at the ranch, Ward said the pond was frozen solid and Monique and I might like to skate on it, which we did, after awhile going to the raft and sitting there for a rest, Monique teaching me the French for snow (*neige*), pond (*l'étang*), ice (*glacé*), and the name for the small bottle of liquor she had by *bonne chance* brought out that weekend and which we now drank.

It was June before I thought to check the pond to see how the raft had made it through the winter. Sometimes the ice would twist it and in so doing buckle the planks that made the top. One time it had lost a barrel. Instead of either driving down or riding Chief, I walked. Now and then that was what Monique and I had done, walk, and on the way back she would pick prairie flowers for a bouquet.

When I got to the pond I saw the south wind had blown the raft north and beached it on the slope of the dam. I wondered how this could have happened because the engine block I used for an anchor was connected to the raft by a log chain that we secured to the raft by running it through a large U-bolt Ward had salvaged from a dead tractor. When I got to the raft there was no log chain, no engine block, and the U-bolt was attached and sturdy.

Where I Am Now

The last of the tanned hides are on the south wall of my cabin. There are rabbits. Sleeping over, I heard the owls. It is summer. *The Thin Man Window* is open. My second morning I go through it and down the ladder.

Mencken Cody has stopped by to see who is here. He tells me he took the horses before the bank could get them. Charlene dropped a foal, a mare he named for Ward's wife. Angel is with the hippies on the Saline but cannot be ridden; Mencken has my saddle and Ward's as well. He knows to leave me be, and heads for Blaze.

Volunteer tomatoes have come up in Patsy's garden among the

weeds. Milky, I think. The ranch is in some kind of legal limbo; the grass looks good, and with no cattle or horses, it is thick and high. I walk the shelterbelt to where Patsy and I buried Amos and Murphy and then over to the cut where we stood that winter day looking north. *How much snow? Ten to twenty with wind.*

I go into the Home-House and sit at the Scar Table and talk to myself for all of us. *I can come back to get you. She's not that kind of painter. Sing. Jesus-God. Good thinking. Demonically 13:23. Here, over here. I don't know. She's not expected to live or die.*

Following the line of the scar from one end to the other, I do not blink. Instead, my mind's eye makes pictures: Ward in the moonlight on Canyon Snip. Monique swimming. The heifers that first morning of the snow. A turtle head snapping in the dust of the yard. Me with Ward one day on horseback when he asked what it felt like to miss Monique, and after what I said, nothing more was said. Nor can I write it here.

The pictures fray at the edges and fade in the background: Moshe taking himself into the pasture. Butane stars coming on. Ward and Ellen walking together on a summer's night, looking for a bullwhip. A yellow dress of yours and mine.

I wonder what has become of me for not finding you.

WRAITHS IN SWELTER

Steve De Jarnatt

Prithee Do Not Tarry

IT WILL NEVER LEAVE HER—seven hundred screams melting to a single cry above the roar of combustion. When you've been to hell as a child, you'll always hold some brimstone.

What was little Winnie thinking that crisp Sunday morning, the last of 1903, as she slipped on her rose crinoline? She'd tried other dresses too, but always came back to the pinkish one. Seven times. Because it was beautiful—and because a numerical demon inside her craved that digit, compelling most everything to be done in sevens.

Her family had wealth, she was fairly certain. Perhaps an inordinate amount. There was a packing plant, a school, and two parks in Chicago named for the Gillespie family. The best steakhouse in ten states. So her clothes were of the finest silk from Siam.

Off to the matinee premiere of *Bluebeard* with her aunts, six cousins, and Robbie Temple, the regal nanny who'd raised Winnie since her father left to set up the mines in Bolivia after her mother perished from a bout of influenza. (In truth—a long scourge of laudanum abuse). Robbie, of Cape Verdean Creole heritage, whalers from New Bedford, spoke nine tongues, and she taught Winnie how to use a slide rule from Uncle Isaac's factory in Sheboygan as well as all the standard dictums of "finishing" a proper young lady. Robbie, so proud of her new custom-built Crestomobile Runabout, third off the line and gaudy red as a baboon's ass. As it pulled up, the crowd murmured, assuming she was some exotic potentate, layered in her multi-hued finery; hair a grand nimbus of intricate graying curls. Something to behold. The crowd parted as they made their way in through the crowded rococo lobby, down the sloping aisle of the parquet level of this five-story cultural cathedral built to shame all others in the city. Winnie brought her best friend, Sabatha, who'd been loved so dearly, stuffing poked from every seam.

Seventh row. Seventh seat from center. Seventh Heaven it would be, she thought. Waiting with a tingle of anticipation for the rest of the relatives to arrive and the show to begin, and as they all found the Gillespie row and settled in, the star of the play, Eddie Foy, squeezed his boyish face through the curtains, revealing a smear of hubbub behind him and a little blur of smoke leaked out. He began to calmly announce that there would be a brief delay in the matinee schedule—then something cracked and fell somewhere, and a red dragon of flame ate a hole in the billowing curtain in two bites. The audience, witness to utter chaos backstage, begat their own with a collective gasp and in an instant ferocious movement flowed toward the lobby.

Because the doors opened inward, they were doomed. Because the bascule locks of the exits were fixed tight from being painted over, they were doomed. Because the new fangled *fire proof* asbestos curtain failed to descend when its designated stagehand fled; because the Kilfyre containers were half empty (though it would not have mattered by then)—they were doomed. But mostly fate was sealed as the crowd, reacting to the most primal of stimuli, became a hive mind, limbic and merciless.

The room brightened orange with an explosion of flame from the stage, then just as quickly began to dim from obsidian smoke. Robbie poured tea from her thermos across a hankie telling Winnie to drop to her knees and breathe through it. Both were trampled—first by the cousins, then again by dancers leaping from the stage. The aisles jammed quickly; even those scrambling over seatbacks could not move another inch. The stampede stalled sudden as it began, squeezing itself into one cruel mass as leaping fire grew everywhere. With her last strength, Robbie was able to heft Winnie up above the cooked smash of bodies, which had begun to melt, flesh into flesh. Robbie gave a prayer and a push to usher her young charge on toward the transom above the lobby doors where arms were waving in a shaft of light. A walk of fifty feet to saving air.

"Forty-nine steps to get there! Seven times seven little one!"

Winnie froze after taking just a few, till Robbie began to sing: "Skip to my Lou, skip to my Lou my darling—"

Winnie squinted back, lucky that smoke obscured Robbie's great head of hair aflame. The little one could still hear the straining melody through the din and hurried on—as if heads were lily pads and she were a dancing frog. At forty-seven she was yanked upward Rapture-like into oxygen and coolness. A return to the realm of life.

Surgeons all over the Prairie State were called in to delicately sever best they could the ghastly mass of charred remains for individual burial. (A wicked secret few were privy to—twenty-seven butchers, the best in the city, had done the same) A week of closed casket wakes and impotent blame, the likes not seen since the O'Leary bovine took the rap for burning the Windy City back down to the sod a score and a half ago.

The *Tribune* caricature artist, Franklin Meeks, fallen back on the sauce again, his cynicism spiking, wielded vengeance against civic fools who'd skimped on safety, against the rich in general, but saved his most acid vilification for a privileged girl. His front-page sketch was reprinted in most every paper in America, prime fodder for a Roman appetite of the grotesque. It depicted a gussied-up brat, doll swung in hand, as she blithely skipped her way to impossible survival along the tops of human heads—the worst of Bosch and Dore all around her, writhing just below her feet. Smiling all the while with a carefree *let-them-eat-cake-whilst-they-burn* air. Some victims knowing they will perish are reaching up, trying to pull the little imp down to join them in gruesome death. Envy of the greenest hue.

Her name for years to come would engender abnormal scorn. Little Winnie Gillespie—damned to infamy.

Sisyphean Nights

The call has come again from a well-known location, aborting Rahman's knight-to-bishop move. I race my partner to the rack for gear, pulling on an EMS jacket labeled *Buddy Rawlson*, though that is not my true born name. We mount the chariot and roar away from Station 43—off through the Chicago summer night.

"Your queen would have been taken in two moves," Rah assures me as the reds are run down Rockwell.

"It certainly would. Laying the Spielman Trap, my friend—The Art of Sacrifice," I tell him, and he expels a self-loathing lungful of air. But of course.

It is comforting to know that waiting for us on Windsomer Avenue there will be little unknown to be dealt with. A junkie will either be alive or dead. Or somewhere in between. If still breathing, one of us will pump Narcan in their heart and yank them back across the River Styx. If dead, we'll call homicide, cart the corpse and drown in paperwork the rest of the shift, chalking up another death by misadventure.

First half of 1995, we've taken this same call a dozen times now. Over thirty times the last two years. We spew cherry light south, blurring east, then wail up the hill to park at the base of the old Reinhold Arms Building, a stellar exhibit of Prairie Renaissance splendor fallen to SRO squalor and decay. (One of the few structures in this part of the city to have survived the Great Fire of 1871). I stop to pluck a handful of red mutant roses from an untended garden, stash them in my bag, then methodically trot the seven flights up. (Otis—deceased since '92).

Rahman's tongue clucks as we rattle/squeak the gurney down the bile green hall. Wheels were greased again last night but have wills of their own and persist to yelp like violated chipmunks. Faces poke from chained doorways, all the same visage—*not again!*

"Why not let their God take them? You can only tempt him so many times," Rahman ponders, lungs heaving from the climb.

"Took an oath, remember?"

"Then it is we who play God."

"We play Cook County EMS. So says our checks. We do what we can. Go home. Do it again tomorrow."

Mascara melts over mountain range acne on a once-pretty waif standing in the doorway at the end of the hall, waving us to hurry.

"Ice'd him in the tub like they said," she shout-whispers, fevered and shivering at the same time, itching furiously at the crook of her elbow. The door swings wide and out roll the unventilated ethers of those who've lost their shame. Sickly yellow light leaks from windows taped with old *Tribunes*, peeling in pentimento. Dribbled red caked on the floor from the missing of veins, emptied sugarcrap and copper wire scraps scattered everywhere. A couple bodies barely breathing. Rahman and I will check them all before we leave, offer ignored advice, and drive away. The slothful monsters we battle here are human will and inertia. They are powerful foes.

Rah maintains scuttlebutt he's heard, that the whole building is owned by Lionel Workman, the bluish occupant we find in a tub of ice. He's held opiate court here for four years now. The last dregs of a once plump trust fund going up his arm.

"Precisely why you never let your children have a single thing they have not earned," Rahman mutters. "Their most certain ruination."

The Narcan injects—Lionel bolts alive like a jump-started corpse in a James Whale film. His body wrought in soul-deep ache as the waif hard squeezes him with love, nearly back to death again. He nods to her to offer us a tip of soiled money from a cache hidden beneath a rug. We shake our heads no as we always have before, but Rahman gives an odd glance and we both seem to consider it this time. Why the hell not? Next one perhaps. (As Rah prepped the dose, I'd pilfered what was left of a dime bag from a nodding junkie's palm).

I've been cursed to return again and again to the place my Ruby died and take this all as penance deserved. Rahman, my partner of two plus years, doesn't know she was lost in this very apartment. She'd gone to score and never returned. I'd made the Reinhold call three times before putting it all together, such was the state of my life not so long ago. I could harshly judge these addicts, try to exact some hollow Hollywood retribution, but that would not bring Ruby back. She chose the life long before she met me, and I walked it with her for a while. In the half-light and fetid air, I've often thought I've heard her speak my name, turning to witness something shimmering just beyond peripheral view. There—not there. If some limbo-realm could exist on earth, the Reinhold would surely be the place.

In the repetition of this OD run, an ornate door, the only one on the northern side, became a fascination. One could imagine the stellar view this massive suite must have all the way down Pershing to the Lake. Sometimes a face appeared. At first, just shadow behind the eye peep, but I began to make a point of whistling along with the scratchy 78s bleeding from the mahogany walls. "In the Good Ole Summer Time" or "Shine on Harvest Moon." Noticed delicate footsteps and soft breathing behind the door. One day, a harmonized humming returned the favor. I came to believe that upon hearing our siren's slow fade downstairs, the elderly denizen here would be expecting me. Despite Rahman's irritation, I'd often pause to hear the rattle of the chain, the soft click of several locks, and there would be a sliver of translucent skin and cornflower blue eyes, shy and glistening. A once great beauty, hair oddly coiffed in youthful style from some distant decade. Smiles were exchanged, sometimes innocuous chats were had. She seemed to enjoy my gentlemanly flirting. The stillness of her room always kept fifteen degrees below the temp of the hallway, an eerie essence seeping out.

She never lets me in.

It became a hobby learning all I could about her. The Workman rumor was dead wrong, though I never told Rah; Winifred Sabel Gillespie owned the Reinhold Arms, as well as six other apartment buildings. She once had a certain notoriety and rarely has left the premises in the entirety of a ninety-nine-year life. Probably a hoarder, say the select few who provide her service. None allowed beyond the parlor. The Super told me there are three redundant AC systems dedicated to her private wing, her cool comfort being one of many obsessions. He gave me clippings—the same perennial rehash article some city rag runs every dozen years or so, speculating about the little survivor of a gruesome Chicago tragedy.

As another emergency call comes in—I knock seven times and leave seven flowers outside the door. (Having learned of her numerical affliction). I do not turn back to witness her reaching out with a walking stick to fetch them. That would be rude, but wrestling the gurney back down the stairwell, a whiff of sweet pollen is sensed and I know somehow her nose is deep in roses. A small joy.

Any health-fucked soul getting Wagon 19 on their 411 out of 43s should consider themselves a very lucky bastard. Rahman was a full-fledged MD back in Bangladesh. A surgeon, so he says, though he misses pneumothorax enough for me to doubt this, but he knows his street damage and battle wounds in a masterful way, having used Army Med Corp to snag a green, then his bonafide US Cit. Rah has a special feel for the limbo just before the flesh gives way unto death, as only one who has walked halfway down that tunnel themselves can possess. In childhood a congenital heart defect stilled his blood repeatedly, till a Catholic missionary group gifted him an operation. It takes every shred of Bangla will each day for Rahman not to exceed his sanctioned limit as a lowly EMT here in Illinois.

Few know I quit two months short of adding *Dr.* before my real name not that long ago. From Johns fucking Hop no less. None know the real story. I've told Rah only that I dropped out first month of a nameless med school. Just didn't have the stuff and couldn't hack it, not that I'd been on the verge of *first in class* from a top five school. But he suspects what I've hidden; few things escape him.

Crazy Hazy Kisses

It had taken only one night veering from the destined tracks for me to annihilate all my parent's dreams. In my previous incarnation—

Hubert "Buddy" Kahn—I'd aced everything in life—SATS and MCATS, a Phi Beta Kappa Ivy grad at twenty. Just waiting out the fait accompli of the next crowning achievement. A five-star banquet of life was lain before me—but I went out for a street taco to feed some parasite of self-loathing I had no clue was coiled within me, ready to hijack my will.

Flat Duo Jets were playing Ottobar. Having heard them for the first time, just a random thirty-second snippet on the radio, I went to check their wild groove that night—on whim. I didn't do whim back then. I paid dearly for the deviation.

I met Ruby coming out a men's room stall. A girl unlike all others I'd ever known back in Barstow. *Barstow—the poor man's Bakersfield.* That was another life. Two dentists in the raw Mojave living through their sole progeny—small town golden boy, class Prexy, two sport league MVP—full ride to Princeton. I'd dated Queens of Prom and Harvest there, then courted a few daughters of world industry while a Tiger in New Jersey. None ever sunk the hook like Ruby. She fit none of the folks' criteria for a lady friend. That was precisely the attraction.

She needed a bass player for a gig, the last one, sadly, fresh in the grave. I'd never even heard of a Fender Precision, let alone held one, but I'd been first chair cello up through college. (Same genus I thought, why not give it a try). It weighed heavy on my neck, and as it throbbed on, crackling out from their stolen Ampeg—my bones awoke. Sine waves surged through my pelvis and rattled thunder in my skull. Her band had attempted rehearsal twice before, but by the second song I was already leaps and bounds better than them all, striving to keep tempo and key. (Which proved pointless). Batting smiles back and forth with incandescent Ruby, I turned my fingers loose, fucked it up, and felt the purity and joy of neophyte rock 'n' roll.

I'd never touched a tatoo'd back. Never lay down with hot inked skin impaled with metal, so ready for whatever. She relished my corruption.

"No rules of desire. Wallow with me Buddha-Kahn."

Beasts we became. Her in heat and I, slave to scent and primal purpose.

I cried when I came. And I came like I'd been birthed again. She laughed at me so sweetly—drinking, toking, hoovering rails of this and that, then Sunday morning—saying *Church*—she brought it out. The needle. So petrified of that spike violating my blue quivering vein. Refused even a skin pop. Mind racing—HIV, embolism, staph. Relenting, I chose to chase the dragon—let an evil wind fill a shallow soul. Possessed that very moment. By the end of the month I followed Ruby to Chi-town as would a yellow chick a mother hen, full well knowing the absolute betrayal being done. Numbed to consequence. So I deserved the hell of '95.

Neither Rahman nor I do angel work just for the money. We do it for some purpose, so the collapsing balloon of our lives won't seem quite as null. Rahman is a quiet man. The only time he trips loquacious is when we pass one of the creations of his countryman, the Great Fazlur Khan—*Einstein of structural engineering.*

"Chicago is monument to him. There shall always be the Sears Tower—no matter what devil should purchase and try to change its name!"

Rahman has poured through Khan's archives at the Ryerson and Burnum Library. Quotes from memory Fazlur's favorite poet, Rabindranath Tagore: *Death is not extinguishing the light; it is only putting out the lamp because the dawn has come—Let us not pray to be sheltered from dangers, but to be fearless when facing them.*

His extended family dwells on the entire third floor of a brownstone on Devon. They took down half the walls between units. A bit chancy since they do not own it, but the deed is held by a family who share a business with relatives in Dhaka.

Rahman's social circles and mine hardly overlap, but I've been to his mosque twice, his home thrice. And he brought his daughter Yasmine to see my new band, stayed for two songs, and only barely mentioned it a week later. The frenzy of the pit disturbed him more than the speed chording and one-note screaming.

"Not important if we're any good or not. It's catharsis, not even music really," I explained.

"Some cleansing ritual then?"

"If you will."

"And the girl you chased from Baltimore—she no longer plays such music?"

Rahman doesn't know that Ruby died at the Reinhold three months after I hit town. That I curled fetal for weeks, trying to stop my heart, but it kept on beating. My lungs would not cease just because I wished them to. The sun rose again and again, despite my damning of the light. When I finally emerged from that necrotic womb of depression and chose to be human again—the EMS trials and tests were a snap. I possessed superior knowledge of the flesh and still had the organic strength of a blue chip athlete. What better way to pay the rent, as well as procure certain elixirs necessary to remain benumbed, yet highly functioning, when I needed to be.

Khan/Kahn. Would Rahman love the anagrammatical rhyme of that? Would the coincidence offend him? Or only that I'd lied? I appropriated my nom de plume from an old Spike Jones ditty my Grampa sang. Only thing I can remember of him. *Hut-sut rawlson on the rillah-rah and the brawla brawla soo-it.* A staple on the set list of every band I've had. At 180 BPS.

Another serendipity I hold secret from Rahman—Ruby Owings was the black ewe of a founding family of the Great Khan's firm, Skidmore, Owings and Merrill. They'd allowed the brilliant immigrant's radical "tubular" design to prevail in building the world's tallest building here in the big-shouldered town.

Rahman knows he pushed his eldest son too hard to emulate the Great Kahn. Not just the naming of him Fazlur. Nothing short of *Fountainhead*-like prowess in the field of architecture was going to suffice, and Faz was failing, falling further behind each quarter at SAIC. A dowry-sized bribe helped procure a diploma. Another, an internship at SOM.

On his twenty-fifth birthday, Fazlur took his father up to the skeletal top floors of a skyscraper the firm was working on. He pointed up through the naked steel beams to show him the flag stand edifice he'd been part of the design team on. Had, the operative word—the young man was let go earlier that day. Faz knew he would never measure up to his namesake or even a portion of the grand expectations—that he should be designing long-range plans for the Burj Halifa in Dubai or some other noble dream. He noted the limit of his father's patient smile; the sigh in realizing Faz was merely a flagpole designer. As Rahman began yet another lecture about dedication in the land of plenty, his son took steps toward the east, towards Mecca, where no girder existed but on blueprint and screamed—*Forgive me*—forty-nine stories down.

Rahman never speaks of this. Only that he lost a beloved eldest son to disease. But I know at least five variants of the story. As he knows at least three of mine and Ruby's. Those in the urban fray—cops, fire, and emergency—hold no real secrets from one another; a rumor always will out someday. And it's never quite the exact story, but it's still—every word true.

The Hearth of July

Seventh day of the seventh month—an elephantine weather system ambled in and sat on the toddling town. The wind had vanished somewhere, driven underground perhaps. Slow, infernal suffocation began. *Cook* County apropos. Calls were ceaseless once the oven came.

Those who summer somewhere flew the coop to milder climes, cabins, and second homes. Others with lesser means took transpo the hell outa town to stay with cousins and friends, anywhere beyond the red molten lines of the meteorological map. The poor holed up right where they dwelled and waited. As if there were any other choice. Sleeping on rooftops, packed sardines in every library and lobby. Toward the end, the day of the killer crux, the enormous power drain of 24/7 AC usage shut down the grid, and it was no longer the twentieth century.

I'd been dreaming of heat after a spring of damp night shifts and was heading west as it began—a quick jaunt out and back via

Route 66 burning unused sick days before expiration. The stated goal—to spit off the Santa Monica Pier and return post haste. Perhaps an excuse to find myself passing through Barstow on the way and rationalize a making of whatever amends might be possible. It should have been in a Corvette, like Milner and Maharis, but it was a Chevy Citation, which broke down before I hit OKC. Made it back on Greyhound to find the station empty. All of 43s were out on calls around the clock, meals taken on the fly. Not being pegged on the board for duty and with authority so taxed, no one could even take the time to tell me where the hell to go. I helped awhile with the incoming phone jam but quickly reached my limit of uselessness and commandeered a Wheeled Coach with a broken muffler from Motor Pool Repair, pilfered supplies, and set out to do some fucking good.

Rahman was sleeping the day away after OT on three night shifts. He'd already heard word of the stolen vehicle I was driving but said nothing, just hopped in. There was no beating anyone to calls, no predatory tow truck attitude. Jurisdiction meant squat as the city baked. Life moved in molasses. We could not see the burning forest for the ailing tree or two we aided. Less aware of the whole of the event than the millions huddled at the tube, fed the intravenous fear drip round the clock. The news just can't help itself.

If the Reinhold Arms call had chimed, we would not have taken it. There were more pressing needs. But I thought of her the whole time. Winnie Gillespie—all alone in Room 777.

After another thirty straight, Rah became delirious. The plum wine he'd often swig from beneath his seat when he thought I wasn't looking had pulled the water from his cells. He was as high of a functioning alcoholic as I was a weekend dragon monkey and could hide it just as well. But not in this heat—which broke every deceit upon its anvil.

"It's coming—only miles away now—the great Bhola Cyclone," he babbled, believing he was seventeen again and back in East Pakistan.

"Will George Harrison be singing?" I chided him.

He wanted to take a kid with a compound fracture to the Royal Empress Hospital on the banks of the Buriganga. It was overwhelming to see such a proud friend come unglued. He looked into me with a Father's eyes—at his lost son.

"I'm so sorry—to the depths of my soul. It is I who should have leapt, not you Fazlur—" he stammered then, eyes clenched, manically quoted his poet till he fell to slumber.

I dropped him home to the anemone of his family's waiting arms, all chattering Bengali, in dire need of patriarchal comfort. Took an ice bath, ate his wife's *maach bhuna* and *sabzi*, then went back out into the broasting night.

Solo in the Noonday Sun

I can relive that peak day as if it were right now anytime temperature and humidity rise toward the century mark. Dormant, folded back in some deep brain recess, easy to rekindle. Eyelids droop and the day of the crux, when the city broke, waits for me, moment by moment. I am there again———

Temperature 106 degrees. Humidity 93%. All emergency rooms on bypass status. All morgues full. There is nowhere left to go. The belly of my vehicle holds what I believe is perhaps a Kurdish mother, her three heat prostrated children, unconscious grandfather in renal failure, and two deceased neighbors from Nicaragua.

"Do you know their names?" I ask the living of the dead.

"Always argue. Scream day and night—fuck you hey-zus! Fuck you mah-ree!" the mother spits, unable to conceal contempt. The oldest child, a green-eyed teen, pulls her mask away, wanting to defend them.

"But the next day—(gestures hands into a vase)—always flowers."

"Stolen from a neighbor's garden!"

"Then the tears. A squeaking bed."

"And shouting again! Like a clockwork moon, the wax and wane. Madness."

We're crawling through Cicero looking for an underground free clinic I've heard about where one can procure Canuck scrips and such. Perhaps they can take this fragile cargo.

The road ahead is slick with mirage, rippling in heat warp. Someone in a bathrobe stands in the road to block the path, waving a wimple in the air. A nun half-clad in slumber wear. Her body stunted, trapped in juvenile form, though she must be in her sixties. Sharpei wrinkles looking like a mask, a life of too much sun.

I decide not to run her over.

"A woman upstairs," she pants at the window when I crack it; the hands of Fahrenheit reaching in for my throat.

"Already beyond capacity. Sorry."

"She's going with you," the nun tells me, mouth caked white, fingers affixed round the rear view so tight I'd have to pry them with a Halligan tool to leave. I offer the last of my water. She waves it off.

"You will drink. And I will take them."

She accepts the bottle; plastic adhering to her tiny trembling hands as she draws a languorous sip of the warm liquid, clouds of my backwashed snot-spit floating there.

"I'm Sister Lucy."

I've heard there are fires now that cannot be put out. Too many hydrants open. This moment I don't care. I crack open one more. In the shade of a distant skyscraper. There's a limp upsurge of a dozen feet, an ever-changing shape, back-lit and glowing. If I squint, a glimpse of human form quivers within it. Today I believe in water sprites.

The wagon pulls beneath the fountain, crashing mercy across the roof. Metal steams. A staccato beat tattooing, repetition a calming thing. I yank the gurney from the back and roll off to find another half-baked beast for my ark.

Soul-less jackals come to pick the ambulance clean of drugs— Sister Lucy pulls her wimple on, the rest of her body still in PJs, feet in bunny slippers, hiding behind the front end of the ambulance. When the carrion seem ready to assert their way, she pulls out a snub-nosed .38 and they retreat. She wishes she'd kept the bullets, in case it comes to more, but couldn't pull the trigger if it did.

Sister Lucy asks the family if they would like her prayers. They tell her they are Zoroastrian, but they will take what words she will give them. The Sister kneels and gives last rites to the dead Nicaraguans—that they may find a final peace together and never fight again in the next life. The green-eyed child has one more request.

"Can you marry them?" she asks. "They never got around to it. Engaged and broke apart, then planned again, but never enough time between the fights. Could you please?"

"Of course," Sister Lucy sighs, "And let us hope it will bring *Armaiti* as they approach the Bridge of the Requiter. May we all seek *kvarenah*—in this life, in the next—unto the last."

The family is nearly turned to stone, astonished by her cursory knowledge of their beliefs. Lucy wishes to ask them if lore of their burial rituals is true—that their heaven or hell is all left to nature's chance. The first vulture landing upon an open-air funeral pyre will always peck first the eyes. If it chooses the right, there is salvation of sorts. The left leaves damnation. The totality of life's good works not factored in. Only a buzzard's whim. Such is eternal fate.

Four flights up in another SRO warehouse of sorrow, a 400-pound woman from Alabam lays face down on broken tile in the communal bathroom. I tilt her head to expunge vomitus so she won't *Jimi* out, then strap a mask from a small go tank, which blesses her with the minimum O2 to keep her this side of the Pearly Gates for awhile. Neighbors help heft the woman. No one knows her true name. They call her Namu. She's dropped eight times, but with their assistance we get her to the street.

There's not even barely half the room for her in back, but she's wedged in somehow, this nameless one. The children must sit atop her now, riding like cowpokes.

Sister Lucy kept thieves at bay for a while, but a sneak thief cracked the front window in while their crew distracted. The fountain has drenched the seats and dash. The radio is gone. As are my cigs and wallet—and worse, my petty stash from the glove compartment. The smidgeon of monkey repellant I'll need to make it through the day.

"Will you come with us?" I ask the Sister.

"Still much to do here."

"Can't even find out where next we can't go."

Sister Lucy scribbles on a page and rips it from her Bible.

"Scripture won't help us now."

"Only paper. My friend hangs meat at McLemore's. Out where the stockyards used to be. Its black market, so make sure they know you come from me."

"Guess that's a plan."

"A good one. I'll gather the old and infirm from over there," she says pointing to a derelict building that would make Cabrini wince.

"I'll be back. When I can. If I can."

I am strangely compelled to tell her my real name instead of the Rawlson ruse and give her Rahman's number, asking a favor—that if one or both of them could pay a visit to the Reinhold to check on Winnie. The way I speak of her, Lucy seems to think she must be a nine-year old girl. I do nothing to change her mind.

Out on the western outskirts, I stop to check the map against Lucy's scribbles. In the back, the dead have their final say. Expulsion of infernal vapor from orifices. First the Nicaraguan man, then his mate, then the man again. Back and forth, sounding like a string of words, some last whispered conversation. The mother thinks—*We know now—we know*—was said. The daughter heard—*she shows how—in shadows—the toll, the truth.*" But it is an unknowable ill wind. And I pretend I didn't hear Ruby saying—*see you soon Buddha-kahn.*

Despite AC barely keeping a livable 88 degrees inside the wagon, I crack windows to expel the unbearable stench and heat seizes all within. Those who do not throw up, faint.

Up ahead, a cinderblock building glows in the dying red light of sunset, painted gorgeous from the palette of a hundred fires. Nothing marked on any walls, until I park and walk near enough to find scrawled just above the nipple of a buzzer—*This is McLemore's. You better know us. If you don't—you still have time to run.*

I laugh reading it. How could I not?   A camera watches and I nod its way, brace myself and breathe deep. Heavy footsteps approach inside, then a rattle of locks and a door swings wide as sweet winter rolls out. A stout old man with an unlit cigar sniffs me over.

"Sister Lucy sent us."

He makes sure I see the handle of his belt-tucked gun.

"Mercy. That's all I got," I tell him.

The man looks out at the ambulance packed to the gills.

"Tough times I guess. Ok."

I drive in under a roll top metal gate, which drops back down as soon as I pass. Everywhere swaying carcasses and red-smeared butcher paper packages stacked to the hilt. My flesh, on the verge of collapse all week is cured of every cellular ill within minutes. As lush a welcome as any fix.

The Zoroastrians make a nest in the corner. Huddle and pray.

"All Gods are one tonight. May they listen for once."

Miss Alabam lays in the soiled truck, nursing another oxygen tank empty. All will help wash and carry her before I head back out into the night.

The stout man helps me with the perished ones. Together we wrap them several times in plastic, then build an igloo of ice around them.

"Names?" asks the stout man.

"Marie and Jesus."

"Serious?"

"What I heard. Gonna be a lot of dying without knowing who these days."

"Lucy sent you? She alright?"

"Right in her wheelhouse. Made for such times," I tell him, sharing a look of deep admiration.

"We were common law seven years till she took up the cloth again. Lucky to have those, being an unrepentant sinner and all.

We ran a niteclub for Momo if you can believe that. Twelve years older'n me. Lapsed nun she was then. Then got herself unlapsed. The things she's seen. Calcutta—those favelas down there in Brazil. A year in the heat vents of Ulan Bator with feral kids. God knows how many other hell holes."

"She knew your worth man. Sent us here with faith in you."

I put an arm around him as he breaks down. A festival of tears and quaking. *May I bring more of the lost and stricken?* He laughs and waves his hands in gesture I take for consent and leave.

The Night Cannot Breathe Another Breath

Most of the county grid shuts down after five more loads are brought back to the meat locker. It will stay cool in the blackness two more days despite the little campfire the stout man keeps going in the corner of his office. Every block of ice I load going out, melts in minutes. Not until I leave for the last time do I notice the ancient faded signage on another condemned building on the lot— Gillespie & Gillespie Meat Company.

The last trip to Cicero, the vehicle is only half-filled and for once, no other criticals waiting. I come upon an incongruous sight: six humbled gang members, all too weak to stand, being IV'd by Lucy and Rahman. Both of them say I look like I'm about to drop.

"Not 'til the temperature does. Back in a jiffy."

"What is this jiffy?" Rahman asks Lucy.

"You know—three shakes of a dead lamb's tail," Lucy says just to stump him with more quaint Americana.

After staring for a long confused moment, Rahman breaks out in gut bust laughter. We all do, the gang kids too. At nothing. Because this moment we all need it as much as oxygen. When ribs have ceased throbbing and our faces melt from the rictus of involuntary grinning, I try to convince them that Winnie's AC might be just the saving grace for those in the ambulance and any more we might yet find. I tell them the electricity at McLemore's, like two-thirds the city, is on the blink now.

They won't let me leave on my own to go check up on things at the Reinhold Arms. Both squeeze in front. I will not let Rahman drive.

"This is all on me," I insist. "You were never here, ok?"

The chariot slinks sans siren and crimson all the way to Winsomer, an echo of all the other times haunting as we pull up for the last one and park where the flowers have died.

Lucy and Rahman begin to comb the lower floors, seeking more of the overcome, as I hike up through the dark stairwell. Extra batteries in my pocket, a webbing sling if needed to haul down Winnie's brittle bones. The air is oppressive, like water on the bottom of the sea at some ungodly pressure per square inch.

The junkie door stands open. A knowing silence. No life here. They are gone, one way or another, all of them. My demon half wants to pillage every inch inside for some portion of a discarded gram. I am dope sick, in early stage heat prostration and on the verge of diabetic coma. Left foot inches inward—but my weight and better angels pull me back with the right one. Something smolders in the kitchen, then fire erupts in full, but I pull the door tight.

Let it all fucking burn!

My Halligan tool jacks the door from its hinges and light sweeps through Winnie Gillespie's suite. Vast and dark, mist hugging the floor, a chill intact as back up diesel generators pump out a cool 46 degrees. I call out and am unanswered. Decades dust upon every cluttered object. What appears to be silver bullion, stacked ten feet high and tarnished to a dull filthy hue. Robbie Lee's Crestomoble, dismantled and reassembled seven stories up. The deepest red I've ever seen. Hundreds, maybe thousands of slide rules in a wanton pile like Pick Up Stix.

I approach a tiny portrait in a gilded frame. Young Winnie in a pink dress. Stylized and heroic, doll in hand—faceless human forms elongated in the chiaroscuro darkness behind her. I cannot stop staring at the damaged grace of this perfect child. Reaching out to touch it, a voice calls—and I turn. *Buddha-Kahn!* Only Ruby ever called me that.

Tattoos writhe on someone who appears before me. Ribbie and Roobarb—defunct Comiskey Park mascots who never quite caught on. In the midst of a lewd act. These are her tats, but it is not my dead Ex, but some glowing alabaster thing with obsidian eyes, playing cards with a little girl. All dealt from a Tarot Deck, each one The Reaper. They smile my way and wave for me to join them.

"We need a third for Hearts," they chime in unison.

I have begun to slowly dissolve—out of Chicago and into this room. I want to join the game, I want to sleep forever in the cool bliss here but tell them a better game is underway and they should follow me down to the street.

"You can play in the hydrant with a water sprite!" I promise.

The slide rule in her hand flashes into a syringe and the wraith is a fully cackling Ruby now. Little Winnie's eyes reflect a roaring fire, but she smiles and the flames are extinguished. She stands and with each step she takes across the dusted floor to the wall of the portrait—she grows and ages five years, all the while, her face skewered by a sliver of light across it, as if through a barely opened door. She tells me how a young Thomas Benton Hart was commissioned to paint it during his two-year stint at the Art Institute of Chicago. The Gillespie family paid for a full-page print to be published every year on her birthday in the Tribune after they bought the paper and fired Franklin Meeks. Great sums were spent to procure every last copy of the infamous sketch of the privileged brat who skipped upon skulls to safety in the theater fire. 100-year-old Winnie pulls the last existing one from a pocket on the back of the frame. She unfolds the brittle pulp, which crumbles to dust in her hand, then hands me the painting and the few remaining cloth remnants of Sabatha, her ancient Bru doll. A solitary eye-bead dangling.

"For my only friend."

I slip them into the folds of the webbing sling. Smokes begins to fill the room, fighting the mist for obfuscation, as voices call my name from down the bile green hall. The familiar squeak of gurney wheels.

Knees buckle and the floor rises to meet my face.

*

My parents had come to visit while I was comatose. They'd left my favorite home-cooked foods, a simple card they bought in the gift shop along with a *Buddy Bear*. But they did not stay until I woke. Perhaps hoped I never would—the concrete truth in front of them worse than all the dark possibility I'd made them endure by the incommunicado years. A junkie EMT. Their benign imaginations had me happy somewhere, a struggling creative sort, a convert to some religious cult at worst.

Rahman had met them and declared I was indeed a fine young man. He defended me—as a son. Astonished they were not proud. Furious they would leave before I woke. He'd smiled oddly telling me all this—a twinkle in his eye. A concealment. I will not find out for two more years when I come down off the mountain and return for a visit that he nearly left his family for Lucy and she nearly left the church again. They counsel immigrants and the aged together in Cicero where Lucy grew up, the great grandniece of one Alphonse Capone. Both kept their vows in the end. What bond they have is more than enough to satisfy what they need from one another. As I'd hoped, Rahman indeed feels the divine at work with the Khan/Kahn connection. What more he told me, I refused to believe.

Winnie Gillespie died seven weeks before the heat wave.

Homewood

I was late to the service on the outer edge of the metropolis. I came to pay something—respect, more penance. Not for Winnie (who indeed had been buried in the family plot in Sheboygan), but for three hundred unclaimed souls laid out in serpentine trenches of worm wriggling loam. Caskets like runes strewn or the spine of some plesiosaur. Cheap boxes of repurposed wood and cement nails.

Is this Rwanda? Kosova or Cambodia? The shame! People choose Chicago because there is a machine here that gets things done. Snow falls and is salted away while you dream or an Alderman gets the boot. A hard, simple town. But fair, always fair. Not this time.

The dead here outlived everyone they knew, or were abandoned by them. More than half are nameless. Left this earth with not a single other soul in their lives. The wind stops to remember. Even leaves are moved to silence. Though the heat has crested, it's still balmy and uncomfortable. Shirtless youths begin to toss the gesture of dirt on top of the coffins, echoing a dull thud down the line. Heavy machinery grinds on, standing by to fill the ground whole.

I watch a scrawny Dalmation weave down the trench, following its snout, in search of its perished owner. Panting heavily, slobber dribbling in great foaming gobs. Miles from wherever home had been, growling at anyone who would halt his mission. The dog finds a particular casket near me and sniffs in circles, building a low moan into a high-pitched crescendo howl filled with such sorrow that all work halts a moment. The old dog paws at the wood, whimpering, digging furiously, then finally in acceptance or exhaustion—curls up upon it.

The Reaper isn't any fearsome wraith; Death is only slow, relentless attrition, a breaking down on the cellular level and the civic. Atrophy of oxygen, of compassion, of companionship. In the aftermath, as everyone threw blame like monkeys with their excrement, I was an easy target—the rogue healer gone off the reservation. *Rawlson lied about his name and many things, broke protocol, turned his radio off. Illegally borrowed and did not return the vehicle to the motor pool. Ralston used supplies unauthorized and perhaps OD'd on some of them.*

The aberration of the 1995 heat wave brought a brief light to bear on the plight of those who outlive their people. A tiny clot of media came to newsbyte the sadness of it all, the harsh truth that almost no one showed to mourn these dead. My photo was taken—head hanging, tears streaming, still in my CC EMS windbreaker, bringing that dog a bowl of water. I became a minor iconic figure for a week or two. The over-worked Joe who cared. My own *Fifteen Minutes*—for empathy, not infamy. The Department hated me even more for that. Rahman sent copies out to Barstow.

I left Illinois with a single duffle bag and the dog who mourned a nameless master.

Licking Wounds on the Roof of the World

I've gone as far away from that Chicago summer as I possibly could. In centigrade and longitude, in attitude and altitude. I supervise a clinic in Nepal during spring and summer with a couple Gurkahs and their wives. I'm the doctor when the doctor is not here, which is often. The rest of the year I live humbly in Lumbini and help other volunteers rebuild the water works. The vague plan is to stay here 'til I turn 29—then walk down and join the world again. Worked ok for Gautama.

Winnie left most of her holdings to the U of Chi and other charities, but some were parceled out to staff and distant relatives. And an undeserved portion to me. I set up a scholarship at SOM in Fazlur's name. Paid my parents mortgage off and some other such gifting.

I live penniless as possible in a cinderblock abode with a wood-burning stove. The Dalmation, now named Homewood (*Homey*) always at my hip. That Thomas Hart Benton the only treasure I possess. A tiny rouge island on the ocean gray wall—exactly opposite a small window with a universe-class view of Kanchenjunga. Storm clouds roiling endlessly across the Himalayas. They are significant creatures up here, the breath of Gods. I have order and simplicity—the needs of others keeps me occupied from my own. I sleep well from good exhaustion. In dreams though, haunted still by lust, chaos and regret.

Time to time I'll read from some dog-eared paperback I brought (Stuart Dybek stories mostly) and wonder what's the what back in the Second City. Ponder deep dish and Ditka, all that's good about the humble berg. And every useless jag off I ever met as well. Part of my soul will always be there. Some still at Princeton and in Baltimore, and way too much left back in County Kern. My dream now—to be of some new place. Another me with better memories, looking back on a life yet to be lived.

On occasion, I stoke a fire with extra fuel, boil water to steam the room, bundling up in layers of fleece till a lather of sweat (and a small chew of the local *wolsbane*) brings back the veil of madness. *Some cleansing ritual—if you will.* Every once and awhile, I'm sure Ruby can be glimpsed in the serpentine shadows behind Winnie in the portrait. That *why not* smile. Flames crackle and I hear her tender, wicked laugh beckon once more.

Two daughters of privilege—one who embraced oblivion in league with another who lived long beyond a destined fate. It all stirs a maelstrom within me. Sometimes Robbie Lee calms things with a song.

Can this be a bit of true magic, conjured by ordeal, artistry and alchemy into century old paint somehow—or only the trick of thin air, heat and my synapses dying—one—by—one?

THE INEVITABLE

Daniel A. Hoyt

A BIRD HITS THE WINDSHIELD, boom, but the windshield doesn't care, and then I check the rearview, and the little corpse appears on the asphalt. These sparrows are intent on killing themselves. They cross the road from one cornfield to the other (like there will be a difference), and there's me driving along at seventy miles per hour, trunk full of guitars, and conk, no more bird.

All of my thoughts have these interjections, these exclamations. Conk. Boom. I'm touring the Midwest folk-music circuit alone, and I need to create my own imaginary noise, the way I create my own imaginary throat trouble that will end my singing career. I'm good at that: I can create imaginary cancer. I can create imaginary problems back at home, though if anything happens, Drew will work it out with the girls. He's a good husband. My daughters and I were lucky to acquire him. He plays stand-up bass with me when I get paid enough to tour with an acoustic trio. And when the pay sucks, he stays home with the girls, thirteen, eleven, and five: all prime numbers, and they all have blond hair, and two of the three have the same father, the other man I married. The youngest, Gracie, is the spawn of a certain folksinger who is widely known among men who can braid their own hair. One of his songs is in a car commercial. When it comes on at our house, we change the channel.

In addition to the three blond girls, I have sheep and chickens and a cat and two dogs (who have an unsteady alliance) and Drew, who is unflappable. Me, I'm flappable.

I don't want to do this Kansas show that I'm driving to and will not enjoy it, but I've learned that you can grit your teeth so that it looks like a smile. You can be nice to folks. You can be self-deprecating. You can make sure you play the three songs people know. You can play a clever cover tune, but never anything written by the man who has a song in a car commercial. You can pretend to be flirtatious. I used to have a reputation for raising a little hell. It was really such minor hell—barely even heck—but folks still want that. They want to see me guzzling from a bottle of Jack, sitting in a stranger's lap, kissing someone on the lips. Drew understands. It's part of the show. Easier than singing.

Sometimes I wonder if the true me is the one kissing strangers or the one sitting here, all alone in the bird-death mobile. I kill a lot of bugs, too. So many I can barely see through their yellow guts and have to scrub them away at the self-service gas pump.

Halfway through the set—which is going sort of kind of maybe pretty good—I think about that kid in the town in Missouri that I'd never heard of before, Ferguson. Right before I went on, I saw it on the TV in the egg-yolk-yellow green room: a cop killed a black teen named Michael Brown. The sound was off, but I saw police with assault rifles. I saw tear gas. I saw black people with their hands in the air.

Here at this arts center, one state away, the crowd's all white, like me.

Between songs I mention the trouble in Missouri. Only half joking, I say, "If I knew that rap song, I'd play it right now." I pause. "You know, the one that goes 'Fuck the police.'"

Some people laugh, and a few clap, but one guy, yells, "Fuck you!"

"No, no," I say. "Fuck the police." And then I start playing to get myself out of that shitstorm.

After the encore, I sit at a card table in the lobby and talk to people and sell copies of my new CD and sign things and say somewhat earnestly, "I remember you from the last time I played here." I like this part more than the performance itself. I like the human exchange—and I don't just mean when someone buys a CD.

Maybe fifteen people are lined up, and I can guess which one is the fuck-you-er. He's handsome (maybe a little too much chin though) and rigid, almost as if he's holding his breath. He looks like a cop, his black hair short, like a buzz cut that's grown out. He's standing with a woman, but they aren't talking. She keeps turning away from him. I can tell she doesn't want to be in line. She wants to go home.

I sell six CDs. I smile a lot. I say, "Thank you kindly." Then they're standing in front of me.

"She wanted to come see you," the fuck-you-er says, and he shoves his chin out at the woman, probably his wife; she wears a plain gold band on her left hand.

"I wish we hadn't," she says quietly.

"Fuck the police huh?" he says to me.

"No," I say, "fuck you."

He gets up close to the table and leans across until his face almost touches mine. He smells good actually: cologne with a hint of smoke.

"What did you say?" he asks.

"I told you to fuck off." I don't know if my voice shakes, but I'm guessing it does.

"He's a cop," the woman says.

"Was," the man says, and then he gasps, and he begins to cry.

"Fuck her," the woman says. She turns to me. "Fuck you." The guy is blubbering quietly. The woman says it again, louder: "Fuck you!" She's doing it for him. I can tell. I almost admire it.

The kindly gray-haired woman who runs the arts center finally arrives. I can't remember her name.

"Is there some kind of problem?" she asks.

"I was just telling these people to go fuck themselves," I say pleasantly.

The wife doesn't comfort her husband, the former cop. She shoves the card table toward me. She's shorter than I am and skinny.

I think I could take her if I had to, though I haven't fought anyone since high school, when I ripped a hank of hair out of Gretchen Jenks's head. I smile thinking about it.

"What the fuck are you laughing about?" the wife says.

"Oh, honey," I say, and then she tries to flip the table over. I hold it in place, but a few of my CDs clatter to the floor.

When I look into her eyes, she's crying, too. "Why'd you have to ruin everything?" she says to me.

"Call the cops," I say to the kindly woman. Martha, her name is Martha. "The real cops."

Martha just stands there.

"Call the police, Martha!" I say.

Martha scurries off, presumably to find a phone.

"Honey," the wife says. "Honey, call the station."

He sniffles and pulls out his phone. He must still have the station on speed-dial, because within a few seconds he is saying, "This is Jake. You're going to get a call to come to the arts center. It's fine. Don't come." He pauses. Then he says, "I know." Pause. "You too." Then he hangs up. "They're not coming," he says. "I still have some juice."

"He is the cops!" the woman says to me.

"Would you like a copy of my new CD?" I ask her.

"I think we'd better go," the ex-cop says to his wife, and they walk away. He even totters a bit, as if his world has been kicked off kilter. Sometimes I wonder why we don't all wobble.

The couple of people who were in line behind the fuck-you-er have split. Can't blame them, but I really could have used another CD sale or two—for gas money.

Martha reappears and locks the big front door. "Just in case," she says to me.

I could collapse right now like this card table. My limbs could fold right up.

Shit.

Lacey, my tall, blonde, newly Christian thirteen-year-old, believes that anything that happens to me will end up on the Internet and will embarrass her in front of the entire planet. "It's inevitable," she says every time she uncovers a maternal infraction on the Web. I think of her as "the Inevitable," even though I shouldn't.

I don't know if anyone pulled out their phone and filmed the scene with the ex-cop, but it's probably coming. Somehow this will matter to Lacey.

The ex-cop sounded like he took it personally, but someone telling you to fuck off isn't personal anymore. Maybe it was once. Maybe it summoned images of the actual act, but now the word is dead and wooden. For me, it's mainly a punch line.

Yup, pretty funny.

I've got a couple of guitars to put in cases and haul out to the car, some cords to unplug and coil. I get my check and load up, and when I turn around and see my name up on the arts-center marquee, I think, Show's over. Get that down.

I drive as fast as seems prudent, then faster. Speeding used to feel more dangerous. The whole point of driving fast is to court danger, but in a newish, somewhat decent car in the twenty-first century, there's no rattle, no threat. On a good road, ninety doesn't feel like ninety anymore.

Out of my fucking way, sparrows!

I didn't think until now about what could have happened back there. The ex-cop could have been waiting for me in the parking lot. He could have said, Hands up. No, that's not it. He would have rushed me, and then, when I reacted, he would have shot me and claimed self-defense. The angle of the bullet—probably bullets—would have indicated my possible aggression. I think they can argue that. He's an ex-cop. He would know the angles.

I don't even know if Kansas has "stand your ground," or whatever it is that allows you to shoot people in Florida. But they've got paranoia here. I can smell it.

I'm speeding just for the adrenaline rush. It's one of the few thrills I have left. I try not to drink because I get awful hangovers now (imaginary brain cancer!), and I'd never fuck around on Drew, and hard drugs scare me too much. So these days I have to depend on the chemicals my body makes all on its lonesome.

But this highway screams straight through the state. Speed does nothing for me here except get me home to Iowa sooner.

Shit, fuck. I almost forgot about the show in Lincoln, Nebraska.

I seek shelter at a hotel and then, after a few hours of Web surfing and bad cable, my mind finally shuts down and I sleep. In the morning, I grab a muffin and toast at the fruit-less continental breakfast. (No continent would claim this meal.) Then I'm back on the road.

Drew calls me on my cellphone.

"You shouldn't be driving and talking," he says, and I say I'm not, and he says, "I can hear the engine. Oil needs changing," and I think there's no way he can tell the oil needs changing because of the sound. No way.

But maybe he can.

"Any crises I should be aware of?" I ask, and he says, "Not that I'm aware of," by which he means it's a mess there, but he'll take care of it. We're starting to have Christian boys hanging around to see Lacey, who's already striking in a frightening way. The boys don't even do anything; they just want to look at her. But they need to be watched, and the girls need to have their self-esteem boosted—or crushed, depending—and the dogs need to be fed, and those love-stricken boys eventually need to be run off.

I don't mention that I almost totally forgot the Lincoln show. I don't mention the cop—the ex-cop.

"I'm going to sing that new song," I say, and Drew says, "Great. Mellow out the chorus, and they'll love it." By "they" he means the twenty people there. By "love" he means they'll clap for me.

"The chorus is all you," I say because he wrote it, and he says, "Shucks," and I say, "I'd better go," and he says, "All the love," and I say it back. It doesn't make the sun shine brighter, but it doesn't hurt. That's my motto: If something doesn't hurt, you can probably keep doing it.

I'm driving to a folk-music outpost, one of the last settlements of Nerdbraska. Usually there will be fifteen people who will sing along with every song, and I'm grateful for them. The temptation always boils up just to let them sing. If only one of them could play guitar! I'm planning my own obsolescence. I dream of it. Doesn't everyone? But if I die, who would make sure Bones and Slobber got three walks a day, and who would keep the girls from becoming cheerleaders, and who would sing a cover of Tom Kimmel's "Blue Train" that makes people weepy, and who would fuck Drew until he's content? Somebody else could do some of those things, but only I can do them all.

Before, during, and after the show, I'm offered drinks, and each demurral takes more energy than the last. That energy's got to run out sometime. I'm on my last wisps of self-control. At least I don't say the word fuck in proximity to the word police. In fact, I studiously avoid both words: I'm still learning.

Post-show I drive my own car to the bar we're all going to—me, the nice hippie couple who organize the shows here, and a handful of fans from the audience. (One woman I've known forever. Whenever I play here, she'll be in the crowd. We hug hello, and we hug goodbye, and I have no idea what her name is. She knows mine. That's the easy part.) I could bail on them. I'm following the hippie couple's red Toyota, but I could take the next right, and it would lead me to the interstate.

Instead the red Toyota tugs me along like a magnet. This is supposed to be fun, I know. They've been looking forward to it, and my job is to pretend that it's not a chore. I make a list of topics I will not talk about: global climate change, fracking, Michael Brown, the Affordable Care Act, or any kind of catastrophe anywhere. America is the great grizzled god of denial, and I accept this. I won't be cynical tonight. But my eyes in the rearview are cynical and tired and puffy. I've got three to five years of still being pretty for a certain age. And that's not cynical. That's optimistic.

The bar's parking lot is nearly empty: I see a Prius and a pickup, plus our little caravan of despair.

I try to kill my cynicism before I go in, but, oof, it's tough. It can survive a shiv to the kidney. It's got a big old will to live. I pull out my phone and point it to the sky and say to the nice hippie couple, "I've got to make a quick call home. Meet you inside." Then my brain performs a miracle: Their names are Reggie and Bill! She's Reggie. They smile and nod and go into the bar, and then I don't call anyone. I just hold the phone to my ear in case anyone looks outside. It's OK to be a liar, but not OK to be outed as one.

When I go inside, I find a greasy dive with a beautiful old bar— probably solid maple—but it's dead quiet, so I stomp right over to the jukebox. "Music!" I say, and I skip the country and veer toward classic rock. Led Zeppelin riffs fill the room.

The true sign of friendship is when we allow each other the illusion of being cool. So I reach over with my thumb to remove a smudge of lipstick from Reggie's cheek, and when she looks at me, I say, "I just wanted to touch you," even though that wasn't it at all, and she gets kind of soft and glimmery, so I kiss her on the lips (no tongue), and then I kiss her husband the same way, and then I kiss her again, and someone in the bar claps and hollers.

For a minute the air feels charged. We've let the idea of sex into the room, but it's only a phantom. They can bring the idea of me into their bed with them tonight. That's the point: Let them have the dream; the real me can drive home.

My oldest, the Inevitable, the newly minted Christian, does everything electronic: She blogs. She texts. She Tweets. I can't tell if she's really good or really bad at it. I feel like it has to be one or the other. I don't think there's a middle ground.

I'm drinking coffee at a rest stop and looking at my little phone, and I guess Lacey's up late and looking at her little phone, too, because here's her latest Tweet, posted seconds ago:

Lacey Christian Soldier @laceybug43—34 seconds
A world of hurt just needs a big bandaid from Jesus.

I can't tell if she's proselytizing or doing some form of stand-up. I imagine her curled on the couch, pale-skinned and elegant. She takes up two-thirds of the couch this way, which means that if both her sisters are in the room, one is relegated to the floor. Lacey likes to relegate. Or maybe she's alone, out in the backyard, in the dark. She likes to sit under the only tree. I watch her sometimes during the day. She sits in the shade, and her fingers move furiously. If you didn't know she had a phone in her hand—from a distance you can't see it—you would think she had some muscular degenerative disorder.

Wherever she found Jesus, it wasn't at our house. It happened sometime over the last year. She entered teenhood, and I was all ready to get her on the pill and confiscate Miller Lite from her bedroom. Instead she went to church with one of her friends. She brought home a Bible. She brought home a purity ring.

We fought over the purity ring, which she got for vowing not to have sex before marriage. I don't think you should vow anything at thirteen. She vows, she Tweets, she blogs, she prays.

She has a terrific voice that she wastes in church.

It's not that I don't believe in god (lowercase g). I do think there's something bigger than us. I just suspect that it's our collective sense of ourselves, all 7 billion of us. But I drive Lacey to church, to church socials, to choir practice. I am her vehicle unto Jesus. If that's not a mother's love, I don't know what is.

I sleep just a few hours in a Motel 6 and get home early in the morning. Drew's the only one up.

"I kissed Reggie and Bill," I say.

"Both of them?" Drew asks.

"Yup," I say.

"How are they doing anyway?"

"Good," I say. "They say hi."

"What did Bill say about the farm?"

"Um, nothing really."

Drew would have talked to Bill about his organic carrots and what Bill does to eliminate squishtoe bugs, or whatever. He probably doesn't eliminate them at all. He probably finds them nicer homes. He makes them squishtoe-bug mansions.

"Good show in Lincoln?" he asks.

"Good enough. Sold twelve CDs."

He nods. He's all Drew, all the time, which is really hard to pull off. I've never been fully myself for more than three or four minutes at a whack. He also has nice triceps. I'd never really appreciated triceps until he took me to bed.

Drew's better with the girls than their fathers are. He says things like, "If you brush your teeth, we'll let you stay up an hour later," and "Good stuff will happen tomorrow. You'll want clean teeth for it. Feet, too." He's so calm sometimes I think he can shut off his brain. Most of us can't do that—we outsmart ourselves.

I don't want to talk to Drew about the ex-cop yet. I want to talk to Lacey first, as a form of penance. She might already know. She Googles me all the time. She follows all the folk-circuit blogs, keeps track of my sins.

Around noon, the Inevitable comes into the kitchen, where I'm slicing carrots into matchsticks for a stir-fry. (When I'm around, I cook healthy lunches.) I can tell she wants to make an announcement.

"What is it, honey?" I say. I keep chopping. There's something therapeutic about it.

"You kissed some girl up in Lincoln," she says. "In public and everything."

And I didn't even think those kisses were worth noticing, let alone capturing on a phone.

"It's true," I say, and she says, "Drew!" the way she does, and I say, "He knows."

I don't add that I kissed a boy, too.

"Do you want me to kiss people?" she says. "Do you?"

Maybe Lacey hasn't kissed anyone yet. It's possible. "Sure," I say. "If you're ready to kiss someone, and you want to, why not?"

"I don't even want to kiss anyone!" she says.

Well, don't then, I think, and I continue chopping.

"Mom!" she says.

"Honey," I say, "it was nothing."

She's picking at the edge of the countertop with a fingernail. A loose piece of linoleum comes up. We've glued it down before, but it never stays. She doesn't understand what I'm saying. I could say, Hoo boy, I used to do much, much worse things. I've got a doozy of a story from when I was pregnant with you, but I don't think that will supply the necessary salve for her wound.

She thinks this is some form of betrayal or family tragedy, and she has a right to her opinion, to the wonderful umbrage of childhood. I haven't been that sure of anything since the mid-1980s. She will outgrow it: that feeling of certainty.

"No one listens to your music," she says.

She wants it to hurt—and it does, a little—and I say, "Plus, I got into it with a cop. Well, a former cop, I guess."

"Mom!" she says.

"Don't you 'mom' me," I say, but I knew she would. I wanted this one. It felt good.

"What happened?" she says.

"Nothing really. We just yelled at each other."

"I'm Googling it," she says. "I'm Googling it right now."

When I was about Lacey's age, I huffed gas fumes. Way out behind one of the outbuildings at the Johnsons' farm. I think it was propane, but maybe not. It pops you with this burst of cold, like snorting winter, and then, in seconds, your brain flips, and your legs turn jammy, and the sky is just this immense joke, and people love you, and you love people.

A hit of that lasted a long time, but not forever.

Even now, when I see a propane tank hooked up to someone's supersize gas grill, I think that I could easily sneak out there in the dark of night and blast myself. I'll never be fourteen again, but maybe I'll get to feel like it.

It wasn't propane. At least, I don't think so. I've Googled it now to try to figure out what I did to myself, to my neurons. Who knows what deficits I have? Who knows what kind of higher intellectual functioning I've lost? I can't even balance a checkbook. Well, I probably could, but there's no point to it now. You can check your statements online.

Maybe writing songs only uses lower intellectual functioning. Medium, maybe.

Or maybe my brain is one tough bitch.

Later, little Gracie and Agnes, my middle child, help me make cookies. Gracie likes to measure. She likes to smooth off the flour—packed in its tin cup—with the flat edge of a butter knife. Agnes likes to eat dollops of batter.

"Don't eat too much," I say, and she sticks another gob in her mouth and replies, "I won't."

I'll be the first to admit that "too much" is difficult to estimate. I've erred before.

When the cookies are done baking, Gracie and I pull out the first sheet. She wants to eat one now.

"Let 'em cool a bit, sweetie," I say.

"Gracie," she corrects me.

"Sweet Gracie," I say, and that's good enough for her. She understands negotiation.

Drew comes in with a layer of sawdust on his left sleeve, and he pops a whole hot cookie into his mouth. I watch him chew around the heat of it. He never lets anything cool down.

"What are you building, Daddy?" Gracie asks, and he says, "Secret project," and he winks at her. She tries to wink back, but it's more of a blink.

"Still hot out there?" I ask, because it's another scorcher. Even in the air conditioning, you move slowly and under duress. Drew nods and pops another in his mouth.

"Can you even taste them?" I ask, and he says, "All over," and then the girls ask if they can each have one, too. I say yes and join them. We put ours on plates because we're dainty like that.

When I stick my head into her bedroom, Lacey's hunched over her laptop on the floor. She looks beautiful, slightly pallid, and crooked. My diagnosis is temporary computer-assisted scoliosis.

"Hey, baby," I say.

"I know: 'When you die, you'll look back and cherish all this time you spent on the Internet,' " she says in a weird, strangled voice. It takes me a second to figure out she's imitating me.

"It's really nice to see you, too," I say.

"What happened?" she says.

"What happened where?"

"With the cop," she says, and she points at the screen of her laptop. "It's inevitable."

I walk over, and there's a big old picture, with shitty focus, of me yelling at the ex-cop. Our mouths are both open. He looks like he's about to cry. The wife's just standing there—though, honestly, she yelled the most.

"Where did you find it?" I ask.

"Somebody's Tumblr."

"Whose?"

She shrugs. "There's only one post," she says. "What happened?" she asks again.

"I don't think it's any of your business," I say. "What happens on the road . . ." I stop.

"What happens on the road—what?" she says.

"Honey," I say, "that guy was a dick. He heckled me, but, to be honest, I feel bad for him."

She waits for me to continue.

"He told me to fuck off, but I pushed his buttons first," I say. "I own it. I did it. I didn't know I was doing it, but I did it."

Lacey starts clicking and opening bookmarks: There are all kinds of YouTube videos of me and also ones on Vimeo. We watch a long take of me telling a convoluted joke onstage, and to my left, Drew holds his stand-up bass and winces at the punch line.

There are lots of me singing, and sometimes I sound great. There's even one of me saying, "What happens on the road, stays on the road."

"Baby," I ask, "why are you digging around in my dirty laundry?"

"I don't know," she says, and she picks at one of her thumbnails with the other thumbnail. Her voice isn't really sad, but someone else might think it was if they overheard it.

"I saved some cookies for you," I say, and I go get them. When I come back, Lacey breaks one in half and nibbles at it.

"Do you want to go drive fast in the car with me?" I ask, and she says, "Not really," and I say, "Come on, sister."

She shakes her head and looks up at me with the eyes of Bambi, the mouth of a guppy, and the brand-new breasts that announce, I'm here! Those eyes will stun the boys, and then her beauty will incinerate them, and then she'll tell those poor souls about Jesus.

"What happens on the road is bullshit," Lacey says. She's right: It doesn't stay on the road. It follows you home. It stays forever.

She likes the cookies though.

Gracie has leg warmers on under her dress, and I say, "Sweetie, it's a billion degrees out." She doesn't care. I admire this about her.

"Come here, baby," I say, and she climbs up in my lap. She's not too big for this yet.

"Is Lacey mad at you?" she asks.

"Yeah," I say.

"Are you mad at her?" she asks.

"Not at all," I say, and it's true. Lacey's working out some kind of identity for herself. She wants to be my opposite: the square to my pentagram.

Gracie likes thick, fuzzy blankets that approximate the pelts of wild animals. In this house we turn the AC up to Ice Age so we can still snuggle under the covers all summer. I know, I know. We're killing some small percentage of the planet in order to cuddle comfortably. Gracie's hair needs to be washed, but she smells good: a mixture of child and lavender and oil.

Sometimes I think of Gracie's folksinger father, and I actively hate him a bit, and then I smell his daughter for a good long while.

While I was gone, Drew and the girls acquired a new cat named Mumps to go with the old one named Measles.

"I draw the line at Rubella," Drew says, and I laugh, and then I say, "Guess how many assholes I met out on the road?"

Drew's mouth is poised at an odd angle, ready to laugh or chide me, whichever's necessary. "I'm guessing a bunch," he says.

"Two," I say.

"Yeah?" he says.

Perhaps I should mention that we're naked and pressed up against each other in bed.

"This asshole talk's pretty sexy, huh?" I ask.

He laughs, and I tell him the story about the ex-cop, even though it's a sure mood-killer.

"Face it," he says, "you're an asshole magnet."

"It actually makes me a little sad," I say, and I guess it does.

"You do know how to get on people's bad side," Drew says with a smile, and he pulls me closer, and I wrap my hand around his penis.

Out of bed and in the middle of the night, I Google the photos of Michael Brown, and I try to imagine Lacey taking his place, dead in the street. It's unthinkable, but I try to think of it anyway. I should be grateful. A mother in Missouri is going through that for real.

My ribs feel tighter than a corset, like they're squishing something, and the house has a clammy ache to it, the kind that comes at two a.m. when I'm the only one awake. If somebody else gets up, it might dissipate, or possibly spread.

I've put it off, but I have to Google him: I try "cop fired Manhattan KS." I try "police officer suspension Manhattan Kansas." I guess at his possible transgressions: murder, theft, brutality.

Finally I find a sliver of an article in the Kansas City Star: "Partner of slain Manhattan officer takes leave." It's him. His partner was run over by a suspect fleeing arrest, mowed down as he tried to stop the car, and three days later, my cop said, "I don't think I can do this anymore." He was placed on voluntary, indefinite leave.

That's it. That's his story, two short paragraphs and one direct quote.

When I Google his name, his Facebook page comes up first and then just generic sites: Yellowpages.com, background checks. He's not that cop in Missouri. He's probably never killed anyone. Neither have I. Well, I've killed a bird or two with my car. And I've killed chickens before. I didn't shed a tear. People think a folksinger must be tenderhearted, but my heart's not tender at all. That's why none of my songs are in commercials. That's why I get on people's bad side, even people I don't know.

I look at two photos of the cop, the photos that anyone with an Internet connection can see on his Facebook profile: He's somber in one, laughing in the other. The dour one was taken around Christmastime: either that or they left the marshmallow snowman on the mantel way too long.

I imagine that he's up, awake, somewhere in Kansas, doing what I'm doing, killing these hard minutes on the Internet. I hope he's petting a dog. I hope he's drinking bourbon.

I send him a Facebook message: "You might not believe it, but I'm sorry. I really am." It will probably go to Facebook's junk-mail purgatory. He might not see it at all.

Then I check Lacey's Twitter.

Then I Google myself.

Then I get a message back from him, just two words: "Me too."

THINGS BURIED

Toni Judnitch

CY HAD THIS HORSE, you know, and it was a sick old thing, and so he invited me over to his house to watch him shoot it. He said it like a joke, like hey Virginia what are you doing how's that kid and boyfriend of yours I got this horse with bad feet and this growth and I need some help taking care of it. That's how Cy operates—I swear the guy can't do anything without someone watching him do it, like when he butchered chickens in his yard drunk and nearly took his thumb off. Half the neighbors were there for that one, everyone running around every which way slipping in feathers and chicken blood and Cy blood and all that. I would think that it's annoying, him asking for spectators, and it is, but then he invites me over and there's this whole thing—the guy's all about ceremony. It's an event, and I had made a promise to myself to do things while I still could, you know? Hell, I'd shoot a horse once just to say I had. Feel my muscles moving. So, I drove up to his place, and the guy's sunburned as all hell and wearing a suit, the kind you can get at the Salvation Army for ten bucks, and he's standing outside in the dirt with this horse waiting there, his hand rested on its side, and Peggy his girlfriend keeps sticking her nose on the screen on her door asking me if I want to see the pigs.

"Leave her alone, Peggy," Cy kept calling out to her, and then he would turn to me and shrug, like he was going to say women, even though I am a woman, though not as done up as Peggy, I suppose, with her blonde hair pulled back and her pink lipstick on even though she's frying bacon in a trailer when it's ninety degrees.

"How you doing, Old Fella?" I patted the horse on the ribs, kind of rested my fingers between the bones. He flicked his tail. The guy had a tumor on his cheek almost as big as a baseball, just hanging there. I'd seen this horse before. Before he stopped drinking, Cy would throw parties and all of us, we'd go and try to wrangle up a couple horses from the field. You could always catch this one, and we'd say it was because he was the stupidest, but Cy wouldn't have that. He'd help us up onto the horse's brown back and start listing off the smart things this horse could do. Steve always knows when you've got a treat for him in your pocket, he'd say. Once Peggy and me had a fight and he unlatched himself out of the damn barn and came to find me, I swear.

Cy walked over then and starts pulling on this horse's front leg so he could look at the hoof. "So, his feet are bad," he said, picking some crud out from under there and dropping it on the ground. "Knew it for a while, I guess, but now he's standing funny." He kicked at the dirt with his feet, and I see that he's wearing some grass-stained tennis shoes with his suit. "But this horse is a saint," he said, all serious. "He deserves the best there is."

"You can tell by looking at him that he's something special." I nodded my head as I said that and made my voice real low, like I use when my kid brings me a piece of art or something, and I look at it and say, why yes, that is a raccoon, look at that, like I'm evaluating a Picasso or something when really it's just a blob of black and gray. Cy did this kind of thing with the chickens too, carried them around and told us their names, made us touch their warm feathers before he butchered them. Cy just smiled so I could see the gap between his teeth, and I knew he was glad it was me he called. Someone who got it.

"I'll be right back," he said, and he rushed up to his door, tripping over the shitty wooden steps he probably made himself. I stood there holding the lead rope, and I moved so I could look into the animal's eyes, like, what's in there, what could a horse possibly be thinking about on the day it's going to die, and what did he have for breakfast that morning, and what does all that mean? I could hear Cy yelling at Peggy about something, and then I heard him trip over a chair and then he came back out holding up a bottle of bottom-shelf vodka and a gun.

"Jesus Christ, Cy," I said, almost not even surprised. He started drinking straight out of the bottle and then handed it over to me. "Here you go, Virginia," he said, "let's have fun like old times." But he said it like he was urgent, his voice kind of heavy like he'd been crying.

"I'm underdressed," I said, gesturing at his suit, and then Cy walked over to his old truck and pulled out this big old sunhat out of the passenger seat, like something a real lady would have worn to the races or something fifty years ago. It's got these drooping sunflowers all across the front with hot glue dew drops resting on them.

"Here." He handed me the hat and the bottle, and he was looking at me like I was still nineteen and pretty, not like someone who's left a cane in her car at nearly thirty, and he's got this smile on his face I almost never see anywhere else, and I wasn't supposed to be drinking anymore either, but I did it. I took the hat and the bottle, and almost spit it up when he started laughing at me.

"Who says a funeral has to be sad?" he asked, and then Peggy stuck her nose to the screen again to see what we were doing, only I didn't care and neither did Cy because he went in for a hug right then in front of her. He smelled like he did at nineteen, I swear, and that got something going in me, and so I was trying to picture Raymond back home and Hank standing there in pajamas calling out for me and how all of me was getting looser instead of imagining Cy's arms tightening around me, of him sticking his thumbs through the belt loops on my jeans, pressing his mouth onto my neck.

"We should get started," I told Cy. "Where are we going to do it?"

"Follow me," he said then, and I did. I kept on leading the horse, and we went down this trail near the edge of the field where Cy's dad used to grow soybeans, and I swear I could hear the horse's bones creaking as he walked. It was almost painful hearing that, like the horse was going to fall apart before we even got him where he needed to be.

We walked single file for a long while, and even though the sun was setting, Cy was sweating like something else in that suit of his. He held onto the gun as he walked, and I could see that his hands weren't even wrapped that tight around it, like he might drop it in the dirt without even noticing. My hat flopped as I walked, and dragonflies kept acting like they were going to land on it. Sweat dripped down between my breasts, but my legs weren't trembling just yet. Cy kept looking back at us as we walked, only I couldn't tell if he was looking at me or Steve.

Cy had this pond on his land before it all dried up, and he invited me over to swim in it. It wasn't the kind of pond you could swim in, full of leeches and old Hamm's cans his dad used to toss in there, but with Cy stupid shit like that somehow made sense, and anyway it was something else, taking off all your clothes and running through the grass on the way down. We stood in the water together, and he starts telling me about leeches and how they help people with frostbite on their noses. Plop a couple of them right on, he told me, and you'll be good as new. I told him he was full of it even though I believed him, and later when we dragged ourselves out of the water, our bodies heavy from swimming, we checked each other for leeches that weren't there.

"Are we almost there?" I asked, but then Cy turned off the path and started walking across this fallow field. Grasshoppers jumped all around us as we walked, and the field was so folded over with weeds that I could see field mice running underneath our feet. He used to take me out in fields like this when it was starting to get cold, and we would roll out some old blankets he kept in the trunk of his car, and we would lie on them together. He would lift up my arms and even though dust and dirt stuck to the sweat, he would kiss them down from the shoulder.

"Here," Cy said, and he took another drink out of the bottle and passed it to me. There was a big hole dug into the middle of the field. The dirt was dark and rich, and I could see milky veins hanging along the sides. It was probably ten degrees colder down there.

"We should have brought sugar cubes or something," I said and took a drink. I passed the bottle back to Cy. He held it up to the horse's mouth.

"Horses are crazy drinkers when they get the chance," he said. "I read that somewhere."

"You're thinking of elephants," I told him, but Steve's old lips felt the bottle a little anyway. "You dug this yourself?" The hole was really deep. It looked like he had taken a Bobcat to it, but he said he had done it by hand, reached his hands over to show me the blisters between his thumb and index fingers on both hands, then turned them over to show me his palms. The welts were red and raw, and I ran my fingers over them. He didn't pull his hands away, just stood there watching me, and I almost wanted to lie down in that field with him there and his sunburned skin hot on top of me. The horse flicked his tail again, let out this low moan, maybe a yawn, and some dirt fell down into the hole.

Cy started talking really fast then, like he wanted to get everything out of him at once. "You should of seen the shit I was pulling out of this hole as I was digging, Virginia." He ran his fingers through his hair. Took another drink. "Old beer cans, this knife so rusted you couldn't even bend the blades back in, thrown shoes from way back before we were born. You should of seen it. I lined it all up along the fence when I got home to show it to Peggy, and you know what she told me? Told me to take that stuff down. And that's not right, I don't think. Those things mean something, I think. The things you pull outta somebody's grave." He looked up into the clouds when he said that, I imagined him dead then, and it was easy to do the way his eyes were all glassy and his suit was too big around his shoulders so he looked like something shrunken and unearthed.

He was holding on to more time, I could tell. His horse stood next to me with this tumor on his cheek and flies landing in his eyes, and that made me mad, I guess. I was tired. It felt like I wouldn't be able to make it back, even then. "No time like the present," I said, and I put my hands on my hips. Cy looked at me like I was Peggy, then. Like I was asking him to come in and do the dishes from last week.

He raised the gun. The wind picked up then, or maybe it had been blowing all along, but it blew through his hair so it lay flat across his forehead. That feeling, standing in a field with the wind blowing around you makes you feel present like other things can't. You're standing in the way of something, and it's all around you touching you and it amazes you that you're solid, then. My hat flew off and my hair was flying into my mouth and we still didn't move. Just stood there.

"I can't do it," Cy said. He held the gun away from him. "I can't do it, Virginia. I can kill pigs fine, I can kill chickens like nobody's business, but I can't do it. I don't know why, but I can't." He handed it over to me. Offered it to me and to nothing at the same time, like I knew he would. I could have let it drop. We could have walked back to his place and hired someone with a trailer to come load the horse up without ever having to see it.

I moved forward, and I thought I would hug Cy like I would my kid, tell him that it was all right, that it didn't matter, not really, but I didn't. I reached out my hand and took the gun from him.

"We should say a few words," Cy said, and I waited, but we just stood there. He started braiding Steve's mane, and it was almost unbearable, watching that kind of thing when you know what's going to happen next. When he finished, he patted the horse's side again. Led him over to the hole, so he was standing right on the edge. The horse turned his head and was looking right at me, that thing hanging off his face and his ribs showing on his sides.

I can't do it either, I could almost hear myself saying it, but I'm glad I didn't because it was a lie. I knew that I could, and I knew that it would be easy, even if the gun was heavy in my hands. Things get heavier, they tell you. You get tired more easily, they say, and everything gets loose. Your muscles start to go, they say, and they'll come to your house and wash your sheets and move your legs for you like they're worth moving. Eventually. But first things are heavy. Hell, even the sky over me felt like it was heavy with the clouds moving across it. I looked over my shoulder and saw that hat skimming along the field, and I looked at Cy, and the gun, and my hand shaking, and I can't tell you how mad it made me seeing my hand shaking when I wasn't afraid, and then the thing went off, I pulled the trigger, and there was blood on the ground and running down the animal's neck, and that shot was all through me, I swear, vibrating up my muscles and in my jaw. And how much longer was I going to feel something like that?

"Jesus," we said.

We waited for Steve to fall, but he didn't. He didn't even move. We checked to see if he was breathing, but he wasn't, and anyway I got him right in the head and all that blood and there was no question. Locked his knees. Go figure. A dead horse standing between us bleeding out of its head and its tongue hanging out. Cy's suit looked like it had blood on it, but it was just dirt. Maybe stained before he even got it. Coffee. Oil. Dirt from somewhere far away from the field where we were standing. We didn't move.

"Jesus," we said.

My hand still shook. I dropped the gun down into the hole, thought the thing would shoot up into the sky, but it didn't. Just landed quiet. I'd never killed anything before.

Cy got real pale. He said my name, once. "What now?" he said, but even as he said it, we both moved behind the animal and started pushing him on the ass, trying to get the knees to unlock. Our shoulders touched as we stood next to each other. We kept sweating. Our feet slipped back into the dirt as we pushed. Cy took off his suit jacket, and then gave it a running start, and the horse kind of tipped then and fell straight down into the hole, its face buried in dirt, but its legs still stiff and straight.

I got dizzy. I sat down and swung my legs into the hole. It would have been easy to roll myself down in there with the horse I was so tired. It was like everything got so I could hear the wind and the grasshoppers and the sound of silverware clinking together as Raymond pulled it down from the cupboard in our place ten miles away and water boiling and gas already building in the dead horse.

Like I was seeing how hawks see or something, little mice underneath all that grass. I was seeing everything all at once until blackness was coming in around the corners of my eyes like someone cracked an egg over my head.

Cy said my name. He said it again, poor guy. He was confused. He didn't know. I kind of twisted myself over and lowered myself into the dirt right next to where the horse's blood had fallen. Flies were already starting to land on it.

"I think this is how they do it at the high school when people faint at blood drives," Cy said, and held my legs in the air. That must have been something if someone had been around to see it, my feet up in the air resting on his stomach like that. I had never fainted before, didn't even have a hard time when it came to Hank. He was born lickety-split, and the nurse had looked at me like I was a real champ compared to the ladies who come in and scream their heads off about it. Raymond would have been the one to faint, if he had been there. I was there in the dirt looking at Cy the way he patted my legs and I started wondering what it would be like if he was in Raymond's place. It would have been better if he was in Raymond's place, maybe, but the way he was looking at me and saying my name and patting my knees, I knew I was already something else to him entirely.

"We should probably fill it in," I said, and he dropped my legs. I was tired, but I'm no lightweight. He invited me to have his help, and that's what was going to happen.

"Virginia," he said. He pulled me up. "Just leave it." But he saw me pick up the shovel off to the side of the hole, and he started kicking dirt in himself. Steve was down there dead, and he was twitching, we could see, even as we tossed dirt down. But we kept filling it in, over ribs and hooves and tail until Cy said he would do the rest himself, saw that I couldn't lift the shovel too well anymore, probably.

I took a step. Limped, and before anything else, and even though Cy's not that big of a man, he picked me up and carried me through that field. I didn't say anything. I rested my cheek against his chest, tried to hear his heartbeat and couldn't feel it.

"I won't tell anyone about this," he said. "I'll call Ray when we get back, and he'll come pick you up." In his voice, I could hear how easy it would be for him to watch Ray come up and lead me to his truck. How easy to go back to Peggy and the farm and the half-buried horse in his fields the next day, and the day after that.

"You're dead, Cy," I said. "Nothing's going on in there." I hoped he would laugh, but he didn't. He just kept carrying me across the field. I closed my eyes. I felt his footsteps hitting the ground, and wondered if things buried felt the weight of us under all that dirt.

NOTHING PRETTIER THAN THIS

Keith Lesmeister

I'D BEEN FARM-SITTING OUT AT LYLE'S for less than a day. This was
late October, an Indian summer worth remembering. I'd brought
along knitting supplies and a girl I used to know named Katharine.
She was married to this guy, Ted, who had no clue she was there.
She leaned against a fence post with the sun on her face, lighting
her up like some ancient piece of liturgical artwork.

"Those bitches are never coming back," Katharine said. She was
referring to the cows. She was younger than me, maybe twenty-nine.

"Have hope," I said. I put the emphasis on hope in a knowing
way, and I got the response I was looking for. She smirked, shook
her head.

Katharine and I had never been an actual couple, but we shared
a mutual distaste for the same things: corporate ambition, fast food,
oversized cars, reality TV, politics, and optimistic people. We
tended to find each other at just the right moments—when we both
needed someone to justify our misery.

The two dairy cows I was supposed to keep track of had gone
rogue. I'd milked them in the barn, and when I was leading them
back to their pen, they trotted off. Katharine had witnessed the
entire episode. At the time, she stood in the middle of the gravel
driveway wearing her signature outfit: a purple-and-gray flannel
and sweatpants. She sipped coffee. The autumn sun felt like a quilt.
When I managed to lose the cows, she told me I was worthless. A
few seconds later she clarified: "A worthless farmer."

"Since when did you start explaining yourself?" I said.

"Vincent," she said. She stepped toward me, set a delicate hand on my face. "I hope you don't love me, sweetheart."

"Why would I?" I said. "When have I ever?"

The dairy cows stood at the edge of the driveway, thirty-some feet away, gnawing on tufts of grass. Katharine continued to lean against the wooden fence with a piece of grass in her mouth like it was the most natural thing. I jogged around, swung wide, hoping to flank from the rear and herd the cows back. I got close, but they just hopped off the gravel and into the dull-green pasture that wasn't meant for their grazing. Started chewing on more grass.

"C'mon you motherfuckers," I said. Frustration rose up through my chest. I stuck my hand in my pocket and pulled out the shiny brown buckeye Katharine had given to me as a gift last fall. I meant to return the favor but never got around to it. I pressed into the groove, just big enough for my thumb. The cows gawked at me with those velvety dark eyes. They didn't have names. Lyle's wife, Leslie, referred to them as Number Eleven and Number Twelve—those classic looking dairy cows with patches of black and white and the tail that whips back and forth. Leslie took excellent care of the cows—raised them on good grass—and their coats shined in the morning sun.

"Here we go, girls," I said. I made a clicking sound with my mouth similar to how Leslie called them. Didn't work. I sprinted in their direction with hope to scare them back. Didn't work. I sparked firecrackers I'd found in Lyle's junk drawer—tossed them in the grass behind the cows. Katharine held her hands over her ears. Pop-pop-pop. The cows scampered away, but in the wrong direction—hauling ass toward the Catholic Church that sat on the blacktop road two miles away. Lyle's driveway was two miles long with nothing in between. That church was the closest thing to the farm. Otherwise it was just limestone bluffs and steep ravines. This was the Driftless region of northeast Iowa. The land looks alarmingly different than the rest of the state, which isn't possessed by dramatic hills and valleys. Millions of years ago the glacial drifts settled and leveled most of the Midwest flat as a concrete slab but spared this region and left it full of mysteries.

I'd started knitting two months ago at the recommendation of Katharine, who said it would calm my nerves while I tried to stay sober and contemplate ways of getting my wife and kids back. At home in my apartment, I'd knit with earplugs in so I wouldn't have to hear people yelling in the halls or fucking next door. Knitting wasn't so bad. I planned on making my kids' Christmas presents—hats, blankets, basic stuff.

"What should I do?" I said to Katharine. Her dark hair was cut short so it showed her neckline.

"Come sit by me." She sat down, crossed her legs. She unraveled a plastic grocery bag that held our knitting supplies. She handed me the blanket I was working on. It was her answer to almost everything.

There are things about our time here I'll never understand. Technology, for one. Fucking with food supplies, for another. All those chemicals and made-up ingredients destroying our physical and mental health so corporations can make ungodly profits and cloak it under the veil of feeding the world. Lyle taught me all that. And I think he's right. I lost my mother, dead at age fifty-four, and I'll never understand that either. She'd been sober for ten years. A healthy person. Smiled a lot. Cared for people. Cancer consumed her spinal cord, her brain. Died in a hospital bed. I never knew her like I wanted.

I've dreamt of her every six weeks since she's been gone. In the dreams, I hug her like she's still alive, and then I wake up and cry all day. I tell myself I'm a grown-ass man, that I shouldn't be sobbing like that. But I miss her. She hardly knew my kids.

The first dream I had, she was there in the dining room. I said to her, "Mom, where have you been? I've been looking all over for you." She didn't reply, just smiled. I looked behind me in the kitchen where all my family stood, and I said, "You guys, there she is, she's right there." They all gave me that look that people have been giving me since I was in middle school, like I don't know what the fuck I'm talking about, and then I turned around to prove she was there, and she was, but right away, she started shrinking. I stood up from the dining room chair. "Mom," I said. "Don't do that, Mom." I stood over her, looking down, pleading with her: "Don't do that." But then she was gone. I woke up after that, agitated. All day, it was like being hung over, only worse. My eyes were practically swollen shut, like a ten-round prize fighter. All day long, my shoulders would shake up and down, and I'd squeeze out tears between my swollen eyes.

Katharine was the only one in the world I trusted with this. She never betrayed me or what I shared about my mother. And a person who sits and listens to you—I mean really listens—is there anything in this world more valuable?

"Don't rush through it," Katharine told me about my dreams, my mother. I was standing next her, watching the cows. Our knitting supplies lay in clumps at our feet. Katharine rolled a joint on top of the fence post, smoked some, and passed it. I took a small amount and passed it back.

"Your kids doing well?" she said.

"I've got them next weekend." I reached into my pocket for the buckeye and held it in my hand, rubbed it. "They're getting big, you know, sassy and shit."

"What're you reading these days, Vincent?" It was the kind of question only Katharine would ask.

"Knitting for Dummies," I said. She managed a chuckle. I wanted to tell her about the books I'd been reading about building a yurt, but for now, I was gonna keep that to myself. Every time I shared one of my dreams, they'd seem to instantly dissolve.

We stood there for a while, not saying anything. Katharine slipped into one of those satisfying stares. I looked into the distance—the bluffs and trees and pasture that barricaded the land. I refocused on Katharine, who squinted into the horizon, eyelashes meshed together.

"This is the freshest air in the world," I said.

"Nothing prettier than this," she said.

*

I could see the cows standing in the driveway, like art models, or statues. I held the knitted blanket up against a fall-blue sky. One side appeared longer than the other.

"Your work is good," Katharine said.

I leaned in, and she let me kiss her on the mouth. But she was somewhere else.

I set the blanket down and drank some of the raw milk—the stuff I'd milked out of Eleven and Twelve before they cantered away from me. It tasted thick and slightly sour at first, but then it was fine. Tasted like everything else from the store, but a little warm. Lyle suggested I drink the milk. He said there were enzymes in raw milk that aren't in store bought. "Gets eliminated with pasteurization," he said. I set the milk down and dug the buckeye out of my pocket, rolled it around my palm. Katharine took a sip of the milk and made no motion whether she liked it or not.

Mid-afternoon, Katharine and I strolled around to the backside of the barn, just for something to do. Asian beetles and boxelder bugs swarmed the doorways and window sills, and the air smelled of decaying leaves. Katharine folded her arms in front of her, looked down at her shoes.

"Vincent," she said. "I have a decision to make." She placed a hand over her navel. A lone, wispy cloud angled its way across the northern sky.

"Wait," I said. "You're—"

She nodded.

I looked at her stomach, which gave no indication. The world temporarily fogged over. I went to her, held her.

"I can drive you anywhere you need to go," I said.

"I don't need your advice," she said.

"I would never—"

"I know what you meant," she said.

"Does he know?"

"Most likely not."

"Is it his?"

"God you're an asshole." She turned away from me. This new information suddenly changed everything about the last eighteen hours we'd been together.

"We're gonna be OK," I said.

"Don't say 'we,'" she said.

"I'm trying to help."

"Help by not saying anything."

I kissed her temple, her forehead. She felt cold. She had nothing to give. She needed her own time to figure things out. Katharine pulled away from me, slouched over to the barn, head down, arms folded. She looked small, and I wanted to protect her.

But maybe that's not how I really felt. Maybe I wanted her insomuch as she needed me—for her to ask of me, to rely on me, to depend on our being together. The truth is, neither of us knew what we wanted anymore, and up until then, I always felt like she had my best interests in mind. But now she had other concerns. I know now that she wanted some kind of permission from me to keep it. For me to show any amount of surprised joy. But that moment is gone.

I refocused on the cows.

On the gravel driveway, I spotted them still grazing nearby, near a toolshed. "Hi sweeties," I said, waving to them. "Just want you to know I'm still here." I stood there and took in the sights. Lyle's mutts found me, and their tails slapped my jeans. I petted them both. They sat down. It was that time of day when everything's quiet. Even the birds had stopped singing. They just fluttered around from evergreen to evergreen, silent as an empty confessional. The apartment was never like this. People milling around outside at all hours of the day, begging and screaming for someone or something.

I found a lawn chair and sat down. I rubbed my temples, thought about Katharine's baby—a little creature I would never meet. I thought about my own kids, how well they would like it out here, chasing the mutts and running around the pasture with the cows. I also thought of my ex-wife. I looked at the trees that lined the ravine, day dreaming an entire conversation with her—thinking about what I might say if I ever got a third chance at things. The gray-brown branches of the trees below started to form into shapes. They lilted together in the wind, and I watched Lyle's grass-grazing cattle herd—the ones he'd eventually butcher—work their way up the ravine. Lyle assured me that grass-grazing cattle could change the world. "Swap out grain for grass, Vincent," he'd said. "You know how much carbon we could harness in the roots of that grass? How much cleaner our water would be? How much healthier our meat would be?" I was never good with these kinds of questions, but his confidence made me feel like there might be something better out there.

The dairy cows slipped away without my noticing. They were nowhere to be seen. They say animals move toward food, but they're also prone to take the easiest path. It made sense to me that I should try walking the gravel driveway. It wasn't loose gravel. It was packed down and easy to navigate.

I sauntered down the driveway, calling for the cows. I turned back to see about Katharine, but she must've been huddling inside, collecting herself. The mutts joined up and quartered in front of me, working the edge of the driveway, sniffing at everything. I walked at a good clip, working up a sweat. The land, shades of autumn, stretched and rolled out like a wrinkled sheet. I peered into the ravine, thinking Eleven and Twelve might be grazing below, or drinking water from the creek. They weren't.

Near the end of the driveway, when I emerged from around the bend, under a canopy of bare tree limbs, I spotted gray-haired couples stepping out of Buicks and Oldsmobiles, wearing jeans and light fall jackets. I stood next to where the driveway and the parking lot of the church intersected and watched all those senior citizens going to Saturday evening service. Seeing them at that moment filled me with something close to hope. I waved, flapping my hand back and forth. Some waved back. They moved like snails, slow-stepping over the gravel parking lot. I could've hugged every one of them, given them a little pat on the ass. I loved them all.

Turkey vultures soared above the trees. I shoved a hand in my pocket and found my buckeye. I rubbed it vigorously. More cars and trucks pulled in. This was a country church, no houses nearby. Just an open grass field that butted up against a stretch of woods. An old, beat-up basketball hoop was connected to a shed behind the church, but there was no concrete to dribble on, just rocks and weeds.

Other vehicles pulled in and parked at the edge of the lot where the grass and gravel came together. I waved at more folks and tried to look friendly. There were some young couples holding hands, strolling toward the church. Still, it was mostly elderly couples, slightly slumped over. I heard something scuff the gravel behind me. Katharine was there, about twenty feet away, looking small and frail against the backdrop of hundred-year-old oak trees, a few rust-colored leaves still clinging to their crooked branches. I held my hand out for her to take, and she did. She rested her head against me, and I put my arm around her and brought her closer. She smelled like someone who'd been walking into the wind, with a hint of lavender.

A minivan rolled up, and a family hopped out. Mom and Dad and two boys wearing jeans and flannels. I let go of Katharine. The last boy out forgot to close the sliding door. I walked over. They noticed me right away.

"We're just farm-sitting down the driveway, here," I said, pointing in that direction. "We were just out for a stroll. You left your door open."

"How's that going for you?" the man said.

"What's that?" I said.

"The farm-sitting," he said. He walked around the van and slid the door shut.

"We're missing the milk cows, but I have an idea they might come back by morning so I can pump out all that milk." Lyle said if their teats engorge it can be painful as hell. I grabbed my chest, said to the stranger, "You know how they engorge." The man looked at his wife and kids then back at me. He kind of chuckled. Then they started for the church.

I wasn't ready to let them go. I looked back at Katharine, but she was paying attention to something off in the distance. Her hands were folded out front. The mutts sat at her side. The lowlight softened her face. She looked young and sad and helpless. Beautiful, really. Maybe the most beautiful I've ever met. I turned back to the family strolling away from me.

"I've got two kids," I said. The family stopped, glanced back. "I'm a good enough dad, just not a good farmer." Some people at the church entrance halted and looked at us. I didn't know what else to say.

The man—long-limbed and tall, but not skinny—pulled off his hat, which said, Allamakee County Co-op. He patted the top of his head. His jeans were dark blue. The woman wore a fitted canvas coat with a tie around the waist. The coat hung to mid-thigh. The man took a step closer to me. I thought he might be inspecting my hair, which was shaggier than usual, growing over my ears. "Well," he said, "church starts here in just a few minutes, so we better keep moving. You're both more than welcome to join us."

"Oh, thanks," I said. "I think we'll just make our way back. We've got dinner waiting on the counter," I lied. I stuck my hands in my back pockets and realized that I'd brought along both knitting needles. I pulled my hands out and rested them at my sides.

"You'll need to go looking for those milk cows, you hear me?" he said. "They won't come back on their own."

"Man, we're new at all this," I said.

"You'll be fine," he said. "Just keep looking—they usually don't wander too far."

"I don't know," I said. I wanted him to help us. I wanted him to relay some instruction, some sure-fire way to get them back.

"All right, then," he said. "Good luck." He waved and turned his back and strolled off to catch up with his family.

When the parking lot emptied of people, I left Katharine where she was, still staring off at the clear white horizon, and snuck up to the church and put an ear to the tall wooden door. The organ droned, people sang hymns. I moved to a window and watched the backs of their heads. I imagined their eyes sad and sincere, their mouths moving in funny ways.

Another minivan pulled in. I slipped away from the window and acted nonchalant. I stepped off the wooden stoop and greeted the family. I saluted the kids, which was something I'd never done. They saluted back and smiled, marching to the church, holding hands with their parents.

I had a family once. My son looked like those kids at the church— engaged and full of love. We hugged a lot. He smiled. We played catch. We'd fish off the side of a dock with night crawlers four inches long. We never caught anything, but we didn't mind. I told him jokes while my daughter sat in a lawn chair and read a book. She only tolerated me, but I think we were improving. And my wife, she was always there, doing her own thing. We'd catch each other, eyeing one another, and smirk at our dumb luck, our beautiful family. "We're so lucky," she said. "How'd we get so lucky?" The sun would set happy on those days. We were all trying. But as they say, sometimes trying just isn't enough.

Katharine and I stood in the church parking lot and watched the sun nestle itself behind the tree-lined bluffs. We started the two mile walk home. Darkness settled. A slight chill in the air. The dogs moved in front of us, their paws kicking up gravel. I patted my pocket and felt for the buckeye. I thumbed it while I searched for the cows. I called their names. I made that clicking sound, but it didn't travel far, absorbed into my blind spots. We walked for another minute before Katharine latched onto my elbow, burrowed in close. It was then that I offered her the buckeye. It lay in the middle of my palm. "For luck," I said. "I know you gave it to me, but you might need it more than myself."

She didn't say anything. Just folded my fingers over it and squeezed my hand.

We hiked off the driveway and into a field, still hollering for the cows. The field was uneven, and we were having a difficult time traversing the tufts of grass and mounds of dirt. It was that time of evening when the western sky turns a clear pale white, and everything else casts shotgun blue. The air felt crisp, dry. There was nothing around us, just a rolling field and a faraway tree line, its skinny limbs tall and silhouetted. But off in the distance an orange glow started to form. It wasn't uncommon to burn leaves or brush this time of year. Maybe it was a barn burning. Or maybe a house. We couldn't have known either way. The blaze stayed shallow, never amounted to much. We trekked toward it anyway, just for something to do, and after a while we could smell the faint odor of smoke. Katharine clutched my arm tighter now, like she'd never let go.

That night, farm-sitting, we hiked together for a long time, Katharine by my side. We'd been walking for so long that if we'd tried to stop, even for a moment, it might've felt strange. You see, we had a rhythm going, and it felt good, necessary. And for a while it felt like we were getting closer to the fire, but after we cut across a few fields trying to find its exact location, we understood finally that it was further away than we had originally thought. I didn't mind walking with Katharine by my side, though, so I didn't say anything. Just kept moving into that deep country darkness. Sometime later—I don't remember at which point in the night— she said something to me that, at the time, didn't seem as important as her holding on to my arm. She said, "It's becoming clear to me, Vincent, that we need a more convincing strategy." We kept walking for a while, and I tried to think of something satisfying to say to her, which ultimately never came to me. But here's the thing: until now, I thought she had been referring to the cows.

NOBODY UNDERSTANDS YOU LIKE YOU

Kelly Magee

We encouraged her to get the dog. Not that we take responsibility, because we don't, and the word we used was *puppy*, by which we meant a retriever for the kids or a terrier she could train to wave bye-bye, but she's one of those sanctimonious types hell bent on salvaging wrecks, so of course she went to the pound, and of course she started with Death Row, and of course she chose an animal no one else wanted. That no one wanted *for good reason* is our point, but she didn't ask our advice. Never mind that we shared twenty feet of chain link in the back. Never mind the howling. We'd have told her to avoid anything high-pitched or hairy, no googly eyes or missing legs, nothing elderly or special needs, and OK, pick an ugly one if you have to, but for god's sake, don't bring home the animal that belongs in the woods.

We might not have thought to say, specifically, don't bring home a wolf.

What she did was she brought home a wolf.

Claimed it was a mixed-breed husky, but no amount of paperwork could convince us it was domesticated at all. It didn't walk, it slunk. Army-crawled across the sidewalk. Patchy fur and beady eyes, silver tuft between its shoulders that stood up like a dorsal fin. The leash like an insult around its neck.

The day she brought it home, one of us—was it me?—whispered, *That thing has definitely eaten Grandma.*

Swear to god, right then every bird in the neighborhood went silent.

We didn't confront her right away. Poor thing was a divorced mom, no family or friends, and if she'd made a single good decision in her life, we didn't know about it. Her ex was a real condescending type who once stole a snow shovel off our porch and replaced it with an inferior snow shovel. We were glad she'd gotten rid of him. We wanted her to heal and be the good neighbor we knew she could be, inviting us over for dinner and whatnot, the kids clinging to our legs when we walked in . . . we didn't have children, but we thought we'd be good godparents, though we weren't entirely sure what the job entailed, and anyway, we weren't trying to jump the gun on the relationship, just that she was exactly the kind of lost soul we liked to befriend. We had a whole bevy of lost souls in our rotating potluck, and they always brought the best cocktails.

We hoped if she ever stopped moping she'd see how she didn't need anyone else because we could mow her grass in the summer, and bring chicken soup if the kids were sick, and give her a cup of sugar if she was—well, she wasn't the cookie-making type, but you know what we mean—and that's the kind of neighborhood we wanted to live in. We could've taught the puppy to balance a biscuit on its nose, or—we're not opposed to thinking big—to do magic tricks like in that video that went viral. We could've been famous, and not in the way we are here, now, talking to you.

She was suffering. You hear stories about mothers who crack, and you always wonder about the bystanders, the family, the *neighbors*, and there we were, watching her unravel and telling ourselves we had to do something. We're not heartless. We worried about the children and also our property values. There had been a number of car prowls and a problem with graffiti, and we're not saying her oldest son was responsible, but we'd caught him in the alley more than once. So yes, we called Child Services. And yes, they did a home visit. And when she asked if we knew who'd narked on her, and when she explained how *that little curve ball* was going to affect her custody battle, and when her tone got too snippy for us, we suggested she get a puppy.

But she brought home the wolf, and then instead of buying dog biscuits, we were stocking up on pepper spray to keep the thing from lunging at us every time we returned the gym balls her kids whiffed over the fence.

But now we're getting ahead of ourselves.

Those kids were trouble, it's true, but we admit to not entirely thinking through the whole Child Services thing.

The day she brought home the wolf, we were at her door within the hour, holding the gift we'd made, a mug for her and a matching water dish for the puppy. Her eyes slid from one of us to the other.

"Greg," she said. "Linda."

"Hi, Jamie," we said.

She smiled. Well, smirked. Difference between laughing at and laughing with, as Mr. Fletcher, our high school band director, used to say. Band kids get picked on, which was why we stuck together. *You should get married*, he told us. *Nobody understands you two like you do.*

The wedding was perfect. We said our vows in unison.

That was almost thirty years ago. Sometimes, when the rotating potluck lands at our house, we break out the clarinets and play our wedding march from memory. We can also do the fight song and national anthem, and we take requests when our friends remember to bring sheet music. Jamie came once, but she drank too fast and clogged the toilet, and when this one guy, Clark, who always said what everybody else was thinking, asked her what she did in her free time, she pounced. "Time is always free," she said, raising a shaky glass. "When we stop believing that, we cease to be human." The glass tipped, and the wine went everywhere.

She declined all invitations after that, even though we told her the stain came right up.

We appreciated that she thought about what it meant to be human. When we got philosophical, our friends told us to lighten up, and that was disappointing because of the unexamined life not being worth it or whatever.

The day she brought home the wolf, Jamie stood in her doorway waiting for us to say what we wanted, so we started in, volleying back and forth and interrupting each other how we do: *congrats on the new pet, is it really a husky? big enough to be a guard dog, must be some kind of zoo reject, not going to lie, looks like a flipping wolf!*

"A wolf?" she said. "I guess a little."

Not judging! Not criticizing! But what's the return policy because it seems dangerous, frankly, and we're worried about you and the kids, which, where are the little hellions by the way, hellions in a good way of course, they upstairs?

"With their father." She slumped against the doorframe. "He gutted me in court."

We gasped. She frowned.

"It wasn't because of you," she said. "He dragged in my whole personal life."

We knew what that meant. A visit from Child Services was nothing compared to her personal life, which, truthfully, we didn't approve of either. Her new friends were worse than her ex. We say friends, but they were her lovers or whatever you call it. They didn't make polite company or have real names. We called the last one the witch doctor because she carried this old-fashioned medical bag for a purse and wore a fur coat—we're put off by the whole business, so we don't even want to speculate—mink?—and once we asked our friends what everyone thought was in that huge bag, if it was herbs or spells or body parts on ice, but Clark just said it was probably booze, and where was the fun in that?

The witch doctor is the one you heard about, but there were others. One had a yappy dog she kept in her car all night, parked on the street in front of our house, so we left a note on her windshield that we didn't appreciate the dog's noise, and the next day our lawnmower got stolen.

Another one kept knives in her glove compartment. Don't ask how we know. Not pocket knives, either; more in the category of weaponry. *Deadly weapons*, as Kip Clipson, the host of *America's*

Likeliest Criminals, says, and if we're being honest, there were striking similarities between Jamie's new friends and America's likeliest criminals.

It was like Jamie needed to love things that were hard to love. Maybe that was her talent. Maybe that was her downfall. It was definitely her downfall, but maybe it was what she needed to do to survive. Like she dealt with pain by summoning it. If not pain, then danger. Maybe she thought she was being proactive, inoculating herself against real tragedy.

She wasn't. But we admire her for the thought, if that was her thought.

Is it wrong to say we expected better because she was a mother? We'll put it this way: Jamie was no victim. We're not saying she got what she deserved, but we want you to know it's not like it sounds. She took unnecessary risks. She fostered tendencies in herself she would've done well to suppress. We thought a puppy might convince her to act less like a sex-crazed lunatic. We hope you don't mind if we're blunt about that. It's not like we want to say these things. We liked Jamie. She was good people, as Mr. Fletcher used to say. She was solid.

But she left her windows open when she and her lovers were going at it—they called it *fucking*, if you want to know, and we didn't think that was appropriate in a house with children—and we don't think she even owned curtains.

Sometimes, listening to them, we'd kiss each other and promise never to be mad. Sometimes we got a little frisky ourselves and wondered what would happen if we let loose like that. We didn't really want to find out, just that they seemed so grateful to be alive and young and naked, and don't get us wrong, we love each other, but we're not young anymore, and we certainly never walked around naked. We've also never had to call the cops on each other, so there you go. It was like living next door to this great movie. Maybe it makes your life seem smaller, but once it's over, you're grateful to be back in your car and headed somewhere familiar.

Jamie never knew where she was going. She needed stability. We thought that even if a puppy didn't help, it couldn't hurt. Boy were we wrong about that.

To be fair, she didn't get a puppy. We want to be very clear about that. We never suggested she get a wolf.

We told Jamie we were sorry about the custody thing, and she invited us in for tea, and we would've gone in, we absolutely would've, if the wolf hadn't right then skulked up behind her. Fixed us in its evil gaze, tongue lolling. It looked at our necks and salivated. She'd tied a red bandana around its neck, which she took in one hand while she stroked its back with the other. Its expression didn't change or soften. Just meeting its eyes rearranged your soul.

We told her we didn't want to intrude, that we'd talk another time about the wolf.

She smirked again. It was hard not to take offense. "You really think my dog is a wolf." Like she was making note of it.

We backed off the porch, calling our goodbyes from the sidewalk. Jamie pet the wolf hypnotically, muttering, "Goodbye, neighbors."

We tried to talk to her about the wolf on three other documented occasions, but she refused to listen. We've been asked why we didn't call Animal Control, but you have to understand that the thing *came from Animal Control*. It's not like vigilante justice is in our natures. We were band kids. We preferred dinner parties to stakeouts.

We even called our realtor, Sue Singleton, and she did a walk-through but advised us to hold out until spring. "I'd call someone about that dog next door," she said when she left. "It's real off-putting."

We started unlatching Jamie's gate. That's our confession. Maybe it wasn't right, but we felt trapped. We wanted the wolf gone, and we didn't care how it happened.

Meanwhile the thing with Jamie got worse. The witch doctor was there whenever the kids were not, and we'd seen Jamie throw clothes on the lawn, and we'd seen her lie in the snow while the witch doctor tried to convince her to come inside, and we'd seen her drink a whole bottle of vodka and then vomit off the porch, and we knew she was falling apart. Domestic violence is wrong, and we were pretty sure Jamie was getting the brunt of it. It made us jumpy and exhausted. We never knew when they might have an outburst. Once the witch doctor pounded on our door, and when we didn't answer, she waved her hands around like she was either casting a spell or swatting bugs, but we were pretty sure it wasn't bugs.

"Perverts," she yelled. "Stay off our property." Which was a weird thing to say since it wasn't her property, and all we'd done was politely knock and inform Jamie that we'd seen the wolf stalking somebody's cat across from the Dairy Queen two blocks over.

Before she left, the witch doctor kicked a pot of our begonias off the porch. Jamie was over sweeping terra cotta shards before we could call the police, so we didn't call them, though in retrospect, we should have.

"Sorry about that." Jamie wore the red bandana around her head. "It's been hard."

We kept it short: *You deserve better.*

"I know," she said, nodding, but we could tell she didn't.

Later, Jamie and the witch doctor walked to the ravine at the end of our street and stayed down there a long time. Hours. When they returned, Jamie was wearing the fur coat and the wolf was back on its leash. Her ex dropped the kids off that evening, and the witch doctor made a huge meal that they all ate in the dining room like a regular family. Jamie set out a bowl of dog food, but the wolf looked like it'd just as soon eat her face.

Something bad is going to happen, we said to each other. Jamie's problems had become our problems. We talked about what we needed to do. We agreed that nobody was going to help us, but we were in this together.

You pulled out one of those weekly sales fliers, folded around an ad for a tent sale at Gun World.

I thought that was your idea.

Anyway, we went together.

*

We know how this sounds. It sounds fake, right? The wolf, the witch doctor? It sounds like we're making this up to get on TV.

We'll take a lie detector, if you have one.

The marquee outside Gun World advertised training classes and party rentals. We browsed the pink and orange Swiss Army pens in the tent out front before heading inside. The place was packed. A guy in a white button-down swiped our driver's licenses at the door and directed us to a waiting area, where a girl in an identical button-down shook our hands. "I'm Brittany," she said. "Is this your first visit?"

We nodded. Brittany wore a lot of mascara. She told us she was a psych major at Eastern and had four older sisters, which explained the mascara. She listened attentively to our story, frowning like she was used to hearing bad news.

"Nuisance animals compose a large chunk of our business," she said. "We know the value of a peaceful home." She folded her hands at her chest. "I'm a yoga instructor here, too."

Here? we said. *How wonderful and surprising!* We asked what we should do about the wolf, although we called it a dog. We didn't want to alarm her.

"I can't advise any particular course of action," she said. "But I can show you some options."

We told her that options were exactly what we needed her to show us.

She led us to a roped-off section where demo weapons hung on the wall like athletic shoes. They had names: Happy Ending, Last Resort, Old-Fashioned. One of us modeled the First Timer in a three-way mirror while the other compared Hustler Pro to Hustler Comfort. We eliminated anything too complicated or cheap. Brittany was encouraging but discerning, talking us out of the flashy Rorshach and the nostalgic Western. She recommended the Problem Solver for our needs, and we appreciated the ease of its point-and-shoot operation, as well as the hand-crafted holster. Brittany guaranteed our satisfaction and signed us up for a marksmanship class on Mondays and her own Yoga for Stress Reduction class on Wednesdays.

"It's for every body type," she said as we left.

On Mondays we learned how to aim and fire, and on Wednesdays, we meditated on a world where our problem no longer existed. Brittany wore a headset and asked us to imagine how it would feel to live in a stress-free world. She asked us to consider what we could do to eliminate the stressors in our lives. We peeked at each other and the cross-legged people around us, an older woman in sweats, a lanky man breathing loudly. We pictured them solving problem after problem like superheroes.

We appreciated how the class increased our ability to empathize.

At first, the presence of the Problem Solver really did seem to magically solve our problem. Jamie bought a padlock for the gate, and the witch doctor built this elaborate doghouse in the backyard. She had the kids out there hammering and painting and putting little candy-striped curtains in the windows. Jamie put down mulch in the front yard, even planted a couple of hot pink Gerber daisies. We would've picked something less ostentatious, but we were glad she was finally trying to fix the place up.

We felt OK and even went ahead with our night of the rotating potluck. That was when we brought out the Problem Solver for the first time.

No, that was you. I never would've done that.

Clark said, "That's frightening," but everyone else seemed impressed. You pointed it out the window at Jamie's house, where the wolf was standing in the window, staring at us as usual. The rest of us laughed nervously until you pulled back the hammer. "Play dead," you said.

The beast stared, unmoved.

"It's not loaded," I said, and you said, "Yes, it is."

You dropped your arm, the Problem Solver by your thigh. Said you needed to take a shower.

I said, "Right now? In the middle of the party?"

You raised the gun and pointed it at me.

Our friends tuttered around, *come on now* and *that's not funny* and they poured more wine and made jokes—*tough guy, eh?*—but they could tell I was shaken. You cracked a smile, finally, and said, "Just teasing."

But you sort of said it to the room, not to me.

Then you went upstairs and took a shower.

Later that night, you climbed on top of me, and I could've sworn your eyes glowed. We did it every night that week. Can we say that? It's true. You smacked my behind once. You'd never done that before.

I thought you said you liked it.

I never said I didn't like it.

We were so caught up in each other, we ignored what was going on next door, which is a shame because the next week was when all hell broke loose.

We've traced it to the doctor's bag. Seemed that Jamie, like the rest of us, was curious about what was in it. So she snooped, and whatever she found upset her. We heard them before we saw them. We were walking back from the Dairy Queen, where you'd put my hand in your pocket, and I'd felt the Problem Solver there. I hadn't known you'd brought it, but I kissed you right there on the sidewalk.

"You guys are so cute," a girl watering her lawn told us.

My hand was still in your pocket when we heard the yelling. We knew right away who it was.

"That's private property," the witch doctor barked.

"You lied to me," Jamie yelled.

And so on.

We weren't sure what Jamie had found, but there was a skirmish on the lawn, and at one point Jamie dumped the bag. We got a glimpse of ripped envelopes and tiny liquor bottles before the witch doctor scooped everything back up.

"You bitch," the witch doctor yelled.

Something was going to happen. We could feel it in the air, even before Jamie's son came outside with the wolf. Jamie told him to go back in the house, but he picked up a handful of mulch and threw it at her. Hard as he could, right at her head. The wolf jumped around like it was delighted, then it broke free of the leash and leapt right for Jamie's throat.

We could say we only meant to scare them. That's what people say about situations like this. But that would be a lie. We felt calm. Our blood pressure was normal. We didn't want to scare anybody. We wanted to save Jamie.

You took the gun from my pocket.

You were the one who'd brought it.

We'd always wondered what kind of people we'd be under pressure, and now we knew.

We were flipping amazing. The car prowls stopped after that.

We knew right what to do. Didn't we? Didn't we know exactly what to do?

We did.

And your aim! Blam: problem solved.

Shout out to Brittany at Gun World.

The poor kids, though. They were traumatized for a good long while, though we're sure they're OK by now, or at least we haven't heard otherwise. The thing we'll remember forever, though, is how Jamie held that damn wolf after it died. Everyone froze at the explosion of the gun, and it was like nobody wanted to move again to see what damage was done. The witch doctor held her bag like a shield to her chest. We never saw her again after that.

The wolf's head was blasted open, but Jamie, god bless her, crawled over and gathered that creature in her arms like he was her baby. Stroked its horrible side. Buried her face in its fur. That woman—she generated hope like a force field. Rejected the label *vicious dog* to the end, though that was the official verdict.

We never could explain to her that she didn't have to deal with all that transmutation of pain. We heard she moved into an apartment complex with a gated entry and no-pet policy.

Our new neighbors are a young couple in some buzzword science field we can never remember, bookish and waifish, the kind of people who reminded us of ourselves just starting out, before houses became things to stage, lists of interchangeable amenities and spin. Before we learned how to spray paint and spot clean. The day they moved in, the sun was setting behind the house in a way that covered the roof in light and made it seem holy, like the end of a movie. The trees were still as cardboard.

Welcome to the neighborhood, we said. *Let us know what we can do.*

THE MIRACLE YEARS OF LITTLE FORK

Rebecca Makkai

IN THE FOURTH WEEK OF DROUGHT, at the third and final performance of the Roundabout Traveling Circus, the elephant keeled over dead. Instead of stepping on the tasseled stool, she gave a thick, descending trumpet, lowered one knee, and fell sideways. The girl in the white, spangled leotard screamed and backed away. The trainer dropped his stick and dashed forward with a sound to match the elephant's. The show could not continue.

The young Reverend Hewlett was the first to stand, the first to signal toward the exits. As if he'd just sung the benediction, parents ushered their children out into the park. The Reverend stayed behind, thinking he'd be more useful here, in the thick of the panic and despair, than out at the duck pond with the dispersing families.

The trainer lifted his head from the elephant's haunch to stare at the Reverend. He said, "Your town has no water. That's why this happened." The elephant was a small one, an Asiatic one, but still the largest animal the Reverend had ever seen this close. Her skin seemed to move, and her leg, but the Reverend had watched enough deaths to know these were the shudders of a soulless body. The clowns and acrobats and musicians had circled around, but only Reverend Hewlett and the trainer were near enough to touch the leathery epidermis, the short, sharp hairs—which the Reverend did now, steadying one thin hand long enough to run it down the knobs of the creature's spine.

The Reverend said, "There's no water in the whole state." He wondered at his own defensiveness, until he saw the trainer's blue eyes, accusatory slits. He said, "I'm not in charge of the weather."

The trainer nodded and returned his cheek to the elephant's deflated leg. "But aren't you in charge of the praying?"

At home in the small study, surrounded by the books the previous Reverend had left behind two years prior, Hewlett began writing out the sermon. *Here we are*, he planned to say, *praying every week for the drought to end. And yet who among us brought an umbrella today?* He would let them absorb the silence. He'd say, *Who wore a raincoat?*

But no, that was too sharp, too much. He began again.

The Roundabout was meant to move on to Shearerville, but now there was the matter of elephant disposal. The trainer refused to leave town till she'd been buried, which was immaterial, since the rings and tent couldn't be properly disassembled around the elephant—and even if they could, their removal would leave her exposed to the scorching sun, the birds, the coyotes, and raccoons. The obvious solution was to dig a hole, a very large hole, quickly. A farmer offered his lettuce field, barren anyway. But the ground was baked hard by a month of ceaseless sun, horses couldn't pull the diggers without water, and although the men made a start with pickaxes and shovels, they calculated that at the rate they were digging, it would take five full weeks to get an elephant-size grave. These were the men who weren't away at war, the lame or too-old, the too-young or asthmatic.

The elephant was six days dead. Reverend Hewlett called a meeting in the sanctuary after Sunday services, which a few of the circus folk had attended—the bearded lady, the illustrated man, the trainer himself—and now more filed in, joining the congregation. A group of dwarfs who might have been a family, some lithe women who looked like acrobats. Reverend Hewlett removed his robe and stood at the pulpit to address the crowd. He was only thirty years old, still in love with the girl he'd left in Chicago, still anxious to toss a ball on Saturdays with whoever was willing.

He looked at them, his flock. Mayor Blunt sat in the second row—the farthest forward anyone sat, except, once a year, those taking first Communion—with his wife on one side, his daughter, Stella, on the other. The mayor had decided that the burial of the dead was more a religious matter than a governmental one, and had asked Reverend Hewlett to work things out.

The Reverend said, "I've been charged with funeral arrangements for the elephant. For—I understand her name was Belle. We ask today for ideas and able hands. And we extend our warmest welcome to the members of the Roundabout." In the days since the disaster, his parishioners had already opened their homes, providing food and beds. (The circus trailers were too hot, too waterless, too close to the dead elephant. And the people of Little Fork had big hearts.) The performers, in turn, had started helping in the gas station and the library and the dried-out gardens, even doing tricks for the children on the brown grass of the park. They were drinking a fair amount of alcohol, was the rumor by way of the ladies at the general store, more in this past week than the whole town of Little Fork consumed in a month.

Adolph Pitt, of Pitt's Funeral Home, stood. "I called on my fellow at the crematorium, and he says it's nothing doing. Not even piecemeal, even if the beast were—forgive me—even if it were dismembered."

"*She*," the elephant trainer said from the back. "Not *it*." The trainer still carried with him, at all times, the thin stick he'd used to guide the elephant, nudging it under her trunk, gently turning her head in the right direction. No one had yet seen him without it. Reverend Hewlett imagined he slept with it under his arm. The man slept alone in his scorching trailer, having refused all offers for a couch and plumbing. Hewlett was an expert now in grief—they hadn't told him, at seminary, the ways his life would be soaked in grief—and it wasn't the first time he'd seen a man cling to an object. Usually, he could talk to the bereaved about heaven, about the warm breast of God, about the promise of reunion. But what could he say about an elephant? The Lord loveth the beasts of the field? His eye is on the sparrow? Surely the burial would help.

Reverend Hewlett saw it as his duty to raise an unpopular option the men had been mulling over the past few days. The mayor couldn't bring it up, because he had an election to win in the fall. But Reverend Hewlett was not elected. And so he said it: "The swimming pool was never filled this summer. It's sitting empty."

Some of the men and women nodded, and a few of the children, catching his meaning, made sharp little noises and looked at their parents. The circus folks didn't much respond.

"It's an old pool," the Reverend said, "and we can't dig a hole this summer. We can dig a hole *next* summer, and that can be the new pool. This one's too small, I've heard everyone say since the day I got here."

"There's no dirt to bury him with!" Mrs. Pipsky called. "Maybe a tarp," someone said.

"Or cement. Pour cement in there."

"Cement's half water."

The mayor stood. "This town needs that pool," he said. The youngest Garrett boy clapped. "We'll find another solution."

And before the meeting could devolve into argument, Reverend Hewlett offered up a prayer for the elephant (the Lord loveth the beasts of the field) and a prayer that a solution could be found. He invited everyone to the narthex, where the women of the Welcoming Committee had laid out a sheet cake.

The Reverend made a point of greeting each visitor in turn, asking how they were enjoying their stay in Little Fork. "Not much," the illustrated man said.

The Reverend thought, with awe, how God had a plan for everyone. Some of these people were deformed—a man with ears like saucers, a boy with lobster-claw hands—and yet God had led them to the circus, to the place where they could find friendship and money and even love. And now He had led these people to Hewlett's flock, and there must be a purpose for this too.

In the corner, the fire eater chatted with the mayor's daughter.

Stella Blunt was sixteen and lovely, hair in brown waves, and he was not much older, with a small, dark beard that Hewlett figured was a liability for a fire eater. Stella leaned toward him, fascinated.

The following Sunday, most of them returned. They sang along with the hymns and closed their eyes to pray, and one of them put poker chips in the communion plate. The fire eater sat in the rear next to Stella. They looked down at something below the pew back, giggling, passing whatever it was back and forth.

Over the past week, the smell of the elephant had crept from the tent and over the center of town. It was a strangely sweet smell, at least at first, more like rotting strawberries than rotting meat. Reverend Hewlett had planned a sermon on the beatitudes, but when the time came for prayer requests, Larry Beedleman asked everyone to pray for enough food to last his guests (all five trapeze artists were living in the Beedlemans' attic), and Mrs. Thoms asked them to pray for the Lord to take away the stench of the elephant. Gwendolyn Lake wanted them all to beg forgiveness for the sins that had brought this trial upon them. So Reverend Hewlett preached instead about patience and forbearance.

After the service, he caught Mayor Blunt's arm. He said, "Isn't it time we used the pool?"

Blunt was a large man who tucked his chin into his neck when he spoke. He said, "I'll lose the vote of every child's mother."

"Have you seen," Hewlett said slowly, "the way your daughter looks at that boy?"

"We've taken him into our home," the mayor said. As if that were definitive and precluded the possibility of teenage love.

"Joe," the Reverend said. "You'll lose more votes to scandal than to a hole in the ground."

And so on Tuesday fifty men and women dragged the elephant to the town pool on waxed tarps and lowered her until she rolled in with a thud and a sudden release of the smell they'd all been gagging against to begin with. They covered her with cartloads of hay— everyone had a lot of hay that summer whether they wanted it or not—and they covered the hay with the gravel Tom Garrett had donated, and they covered that all with fresh tarps, held down by bricks.

Reverend Hewlett gave the funeral service right there, with the locals and circus folk in a ring around the pool. The elephant trainer sobbed into his small, calloused hands. He did not have the stick with him, for once.

Afterward, when the other circus workers went to take apart the tent, to fold up the benches and load things into their trailers, the elephant trainer stayed behind. He put his hand on Reverend Hewlett's arm, then drew it back. And, as if it choked him, he said, "I can't leave her here."

"Will you pray with me?"

"I'm saying I don't think I can leave this town."

"My son, I won't let anything happen to the grave."

"I'm saying that my parents were drifters, and I'm a drifter, and I've never had a part of myself in the soil of a place before. And now I do, and I think I ought to stay here for the rest of my life."

Hewlett marveled at the ways he'd misread this man. Perhaps it hadn't been grief he'd seen in the man's face, but thirst.

He said, "Then it must be God's will."

The tarp stayed put through the dry fall and the dry winter, and the smell subsided.

Before Christmas, Stella Blunt came to Reverend Hewlett for help. The fire eater was long gone, but her stomach had begun swelling and she was panicked.

The Reverend arranged, to her parents' naive delight, for Stella to spend the spring semester doing work at the VA hospital downstate. Only she didn't really go there; he set her up in the vestry with a bed and a little library. She wrote her parents postcards, which Reverend Hewlett would mail in an envelope to Reverend Adams down in Landry, just so Adams could drop them in the postbox and send them back to Little Fork.

Hewlett visited her three times a day, and Sheila Pipsky, who used to be a nurse and could keep a secret like a statue, stopped by twice a week. The Reverend would sit on the floor while Stella sat on the bed, legs folded. If he had time, he ate with her. They spoke French together, so she wouldn't grow rusty. When the church was locked up for the night, he'd turn out the lights and let her know she was safe—and she'd walk around and around the pews, up to the little choir loft, down the hall to the Sunday school classrooms. As she grew bigger, less steady on her feet, he'd hold her arm so she wouldn't trip in the dark. If he closed his eyes—which he let himself do only for a second at a time—he could believe he was walking down a Chicago street with Annette, the breeze on their chests, her hair in a clip.

"It's funny," Stella said to him once. They were standing in the nursery, the rocking horses and dollhouse lit with moonlight. "I thought I loved him. But if I loved him, I'd remember him better. Wouldn't I?"

Hewlett had the utterly inappropriate urge to touch Stella's cheek, the top of her white ear. He slowed his breath.

Stella giggled.

"What is it?" he said.

"Your shoes. They're untied, like a little kid's."

In May, the doctor came in the middle of the night and delivered a healthy baby girl, and Reverend Hewlett called the Millers, who had come to him praying for a child that fall, and they were given the baby and told she came from Shearerville. They named her Eloise. Hewlett had looked away when Stella said goodbye to the baby. He muttered a prayer, but it was a pretense—he couldn't absorb her pain just then. He chose, instead, to think of the Millers. He chose to thank the Lord. Stella stayed two more weeks in the vestry, and then she went home. Hewlett continued his nighttime circuits of the church, though. They'd become habit.

The elephant trainer worked on one of the farms, tending the cows and horses, until he decided to open a restaurant in the space left empty when Herman Burns had gone to war. He used to cook for the circus folk, after all, and he missed it. He served sandwiches and soup and meatloaf. Soon they were calling him by his name, Stanley Tack, and by June he had fallen in love with the Beedleman girl, and she with him.

It made Reverend Hewlett think, briefly, of writing home to Chicago, to Annette. He worried she was waiting for him, the way her girlfriends were waiting for their boys to return, battle-scarred and strong and ready to settle down. But the war abroad would eventually end; Hewlett's war never would. And Annette would not join him on this particular battlefield. She'd made that clear. She would stay in Chicago, in her brownstone, and type for a firm, until he came to his senses and moved home to teach history. That she never doubted this would happen broke his heart doubly: once for himself and once for her. She hadn't written in three months. And he did not write to her. To do so would be to punch a hole in his own armor.

As soon as summer hit, there was torrential rain—as if all the town's prayers from the previous year got to heaven at once, far too late. The bridge flooded out, and Stanley Tack's restaurant flooded, and nearly everyone you passed, if you asked how things were, would respond, "I'm building an ark!"

There were drowned sheep and missing fences at one farm, where the river now came to the barn door. An oak toppled in the park, roots exposed, like a loosened weed. Stella Blunt, lining up with the choir and looking through the stained glass, said, "It's like someone's trying to tear apart the world."

They sang "our shelter from the stormy blast" as thunder shook the roof. They sang "There Shall be Showers of Blessings," and some of them laughed.

Stanley Tack had come every Sunday that whole year, but always sat quizzical and silent through the prayers, the hymns. He never carried the stick anymore. He was always alone; the

Beedleman girl worked the Sunday shift at the hospital. He never put anything in the offertory and he never took Communion. Reverend Hewlett started to see this as a personal challenge: Someday, he would give the sermon that would bring Stanley to his feet, that would open his blue eyes to the light shining through above the altar, that would make him pause on his way out of church and say, "Do you have a minute to talk?"

They planned, as soon as the rain let up, to pour cement into the old pool and dig the hole for the new one. But the rain never let up. On the fortieth day of rain, folks stopped Reverend Hewlett at the pharmacy and the gas pump to joke: "Tomorrow we're due our rainbow, right? Tomorrow we get our dove?" At least no one much minded not having a pool that summer.

The Millers brought little Eloise to church, and she was baptized as Stella Blunt looked on from the choir. Reverend Hewlett poured water on the baby's head and marveled at her angry little eyes. The daughter of a fire eater, born into a land of water.

Despite the tarp, the pool had filled around the elephant and the hay and the gravel, and if you walked by and peered through the chain-link fence, you'd see how the tarp was now sort of floating on top, how the whole pool deck was covered in an inch of water that connected with the water in the pool. The children dared each other to reach through the fence and touch the dirty elephant juice. Mrs. Thoms wondered aloud if the elephant water would go through the pool drains and into the town supply.

One day, Reverend Hewlett braved the rain to visit Stanley Tack's restaurant. After the downstairs had flooded, Stanley had taken over the vacant apartment upstairs, cooking out of its small kitchen and serving food in what used to be the living room. On an average Saturday, you'd find three or four families huddled around the tables, eating soup and listening to the rain hit the windows, but today the Reverend was the only one in the place. It seemed people were leaving their houses less. The spokes of their umbrellas were broken, and their rain boots were moldy, and they realized there wasn't much they truly needed from out in the world. A lot of sweaters were knit that summer, a lot of books read.

The Reverend sat, and when Stanley brought his cheese sandwich and potato soup, he sat across from him. He said, "I believe this is my fault."

The only "this" anyone in town was talking about was the rain. Reverend Hewlett said, "My child. This weather is the will of God."

"You preached—you gave a sermon, right after I chose to stay. And I couldn't help thinking it was intended for me. The story of Jonah trying to sail away from Nineveh. Of God sending the storm and the whale."

The Reverend tried his potato soup and nodded at Stanley. The soup was good, as always. Never great, but always good. He said, "I was thinking of many things, but yes, one of them was you. The way the Lord sends us where we need to be, regardless of our plans. I was reflecting on my own life, as well. I ended up in Little Fork by chance, and in my first year, when I felt doubt, I'd think of Jonah in the belly of that fish. It was preaching, you know, that he was meant to do in Nineveh. That's what he was running from."

"Yes. But"—Stanley looked out the window, where the rain was slicing sideways—"what if this isn't my Nineveh? What if this is the place I've run away *to*, and all this, all the rain, is God trying to wash me out and send me on my way? Just as he sent that storm for Jonah."

This troubled the Reverend. He bought some time by biting into his sandwich, but then it troubled him even more. Stanley had reminded him of Annette, on the day he left Chicago, fixing him with dry eyes: "I don't see how you're so *sure*," she'd said. And he'd said, "There's no other way to be." And whether or not he was truly sure back then, he'd grown sure these past three years. Or at least he'd been too busy counseling others to foster his own concerns. He'd broken down in doubt a few times—not in God so much as in his plan—when he'd had to bury a child or when soldiers came home in boxes, but he'd always returned to a place of faith. Look at little Eloise, for instance, growing plump at the Millers' house. Exactly as it was meant to be. But somehow the elephant trainer's question had hit a sore spot in his own soul, a bruise he hadn't known was there.

He said, "All we can do is pray and ask that God make clear the path."

"And how, exactly, would He make it clear?"

"If you listen, God will speak."

Most always, when he said something like this, his parishioners smiled, as if assured they'd hear the voice of God that very night. Sometimes he even had to clarify: "This is not the age of miracles, you realize. His voice won't boom from the clouds. You'll have to listen. You'll have to look." And they'd leave to await the message.

What Stanley said was, "God doesn't talk." It wasn't something Reverend Hewlett was used to hearing in this town. And then, all seriousness, he said, "I think I've broken the universe."

Reverend Hewlett looked at his own hands, the veins and creases. He imagined they might crack open like the parched earth had last summer.

Or at least, he felt a small crack somewhere inside, one that didn't hurt but was letting in a bit of air. All he could think to say was, "It's raining in the next town over too. And in the next town beyond that."

Reverend Hewlett's name was Jack. This was increasingly easy for him to forget. He'd become John, and then—in the bulletins and on the sign outside the church—Rev. J. Hewlett, and since there was no one in Little Fork who didn't know him as the Reverend, since even the few Catholics who drove to services in Shearerville greeted him as "Rev" or sometimes, slipping, as "Father," he hadn't heard his own name in three years. Annette no longer wrote to him at all, no longer extended the tail of the J down like the first letter of a chapter.

And why had he left her? And why had he come here? Because he was needed. Because his mentor at seminary had said, "God is calling you there. God is calling me to send you there."

And that man, with his great beard, his walls of books, his faith in the hand of God, could not have been wrong.

That night there was a dance at the Garden Club, on the east end of town. It was Little Fork's version of a debutante ball, the same youngsters debuting themselves each year, in the same white dresses, until they were too old for these things, or married. Only tonight they were soaked through. Reverend Hewlett stood against the wall watching—his mere presence, everyone agreed, was salubrious—and observed the boys in their sopping bowties, hair plastered to their heads, and the girls wrapped against their will in their mothers' shawls. No boy would see through a wet dress tonight. Heaps of galoshes and umbrellas by the door.

They coupled and uncoupled in patterns that seemed casual, chaotic, but of course were not. Every move, every flick of the eyes, was finely orchestrated. There were hearts being broken tonight. You just couldn't tell whose.

Gordon Pipsky sidled up and offered a sip from his flask. Gordon's son was out there dancing, a girl on each arm. When Hewlett accepted, Gordon winked and grinned. "I'll never tell," he said. Even though he saw the Reverend take the Eucharist every Sunday. Perhaps what he meant was, "I'll never tell that you're just a man like me."

Was it a secret, really? He'd never been anything else.

He had felt like an impostor when he first put on his robe—but then everyone felt like an impostor, he'd learned in seminary. And now, after all this time, he rarely considered himself a fraud. But nothing had changed, really. Except that he had grown used to that robe, that second skin, just as he'd grown used to God's silent ways.

There was Stella Blunt, dancing in white. A debutante still.

The next morning, the rain stopped. Not the kind of pause that makes you worry the sky is just gathering more water, but a true, clear stop, the air bright and clean and dry.

And then the wind started.

For the first few hours, it just shook the windows and door hinges and made people sneeze—all that new mold now flying through the air—but by nightfall, it was bringing down tree branches and shingles. By morning, it had knocked down phone lines and garden fences and was tearing at the awnings on Center Street.

And worse: By late afternoon, with most of the surface water gone (blown to Shearerville, everyone said), the tarp blew off the old pool. No one was outside to see that part, but a fair number were witness to it flying smack up against the library, five blocks south, before continuing on its way. It took folks a while to realize what it was—and by that point, there was gravel skittering down the streets nearest the pool. There was moldy hay in everyone's yard.

Gwendolyn Lake came banging on the parsonage door to tell Reverend Hewlett. His first thought was to run and see if the elephant was uncovered, but his second thought was of Stanley, who should be kept from the pool. Stanley, who would want to run there but would regret it later. Who might take it all as some sort of sign.

Hewlett told Gwendolyn to get her brothers. "Use sheets," he said, "and bricks." He himself ran in the opposite direction, toward Center Street. The wind wasn't constant but came in great lumps: Every three or four seconds, a pocket of air would hit him, would lift him from beneath. If he'd had an open umbrella, he'd have left the ground. Trees were down, garbage blew through the streets, the bench in front of the barbershop was overturned.

Sally Thoms ran crying down the other side of the road, blonde hair sucked straight up like a sail. "My cat blew away!" she cried. "He was in a tree, and he just blew away!"

"I'll pray for you!" the Reverend called, but the wind ate his words.

He pulled with his full weight on the door beside the one that read stanley's diner, the door that everyone knew led up to the real place. Stanley stood in the kitchen, peeling carrots. He said, "You're early for lunch, Rev."

For some reason—even later he couldn't figure out what had possessed him—the Reverend said, "I'd be happy if you called me Jack."

"Sure," Stanley said and laughed. "Jack. You want to peel me some carrots, Jack?"

They stood side by side at the counter, working. "What do you make of this apocalypse, Jack?"

He began to answer as he always did of late—something about God wanting to test us now and then, maybe something about Job—but instead he found himself telling a joke. "You hear about the man who couldn't see what the weather was like because it was too foggy?"

"Ha!" He wasn't sure he'd ever heard Stanley laugh before. It was more a word than a laugh. Stanley said, "I know an old circus one. Why'd the sword swallower swallow an umbrella?"

"I—I don't know."

"Wanted to put something away for a rainy day."

It was a terrible joke, but Hewlett started laughing and couldn't stop—perhaps because he was picturing Stella Blunt's bearded fire eater, an umbrella blossoming in his throat, just as the baby had stretched Stella's figure. This wasn't funny either, but the laughter came anyway.

He went to the sink for a glass of water, to cure his laugh and the cough that followed it. As he drank, he looked out the back window, over the yards behind Fifth Street and the abutting yards behind Sixth Street. Down below, on the other side of the block-long stockade fence, the Miller family had ventured out into the yard with baby Eloise. In the time between gusts, they were examining the damage to the old well, the top of which had tumbled into a pile of stones. A summer of baking and a summer of rain must have loosened everything, and all it took was a day of wind to knock things about. There was Ed Miller, peering down the hole, and there was Alice Miller, holding the baby, when a blast of wind—up here Jack Hewlett could see and hear but not feel it— tore limbs from trees and tore shutters from houses and tore Eloise from her mother's arms and into the air and across the yard. He must have made a noise, because Stanley rushed to peer over his shoulder just in time to see the baby, her pink face and her white dress, go flying over the garden and over the next yard and finally into the Blunts' yard, where, just as she arced down, there he was, Mayor Blunt, running toward the child. He caught her in his arms.

Hewlett heard Stanley inhale sharply. Neither man moved.

The mayor had been outside alone—presumably inspecting the maple that had fallen across his yard, the one that, were it still standing, the baby would have blown straight into—but now his wife ran out, and his son, and Stella. The two men watched from above as Stella leaned over the baby, covering her own mouth. Her mother's hand was on her back, and Hewlett wondered if she was crying, and—if she was—how she'd explain it. Well, who wouldn't cry at a baby landing in their yard?

The wind took a break, and Mayor Blunt handed the baby to Stella and wrapped his coat around her front, covering them both. Hewlett imagined what the man would have said: something about "You know I can never hold a baby right." Or "This should be good practice for you!" And the mayor led a procession around the front of the house and down the street to the Millers'. Hewlett hadn't thought to look back to the Millers for a while—they weren't in their yard. Ed Miller had scaled the fence to the lawn between his and the Blunts' and was running through the bushes, around the trees, behind the shed. Alice Miller stood out front, hands to her head, shouting for help. She ran toward the Blunts when she saw them, but she couldn't have known what was under Stella's coat until the mayor pulled it back, chest puffed out, proud of his miracle. He handed the baby back himself. Alice Miller covered the infant with kisses and raced her into the house, Mayor and Mrs. Blunt following. Stella stayed out on the walk a minute, looking at the sky. What she was thinking, Hewlett couldn't even guess.

"Well," Stanley said. "Pardon the expression, but Jesus Christ." The carrot and peeler, still in his hands, were shaking.

Hewlett wanted to run down, to see if Stella was all right, to make sure the baby wasn't hurt. But he wasn't a doctor. And he couldn't leave Stanley alone, couldn't let him think of checking on the pool. So he just said, "I think we've seen the hand of God." He wasn't at all sure this was true. Part of him wondered if he hadn't seen a miracle at all but its precise and brutal opposite—a failure of some kind, or the evidence of chaos. Whatever he'd just seen, it troubled him deeply. Was God in the wind, blowing that baby back to Stella where she belonged? Or was God in the catch, in the impossible coincidence of the mayor being in the right spot, in the return of the child to the Millers? Or—and this was the thing about a crack in faith, he knew, the way one small fissure could spread and crumble the whole thing into a pile of rocks—was God in neither place?

Stanley put his carrot down and turned. His face was soft and astonished, blue eyes open wider than Hewlett had ever seen them. He looked like a man who'd just survived an auto crash, a man who'd taken part in something bizarre and terrifying, not just witnessed it from above. "It's not true, is it?" Stanley spoke slowly, working something out. "What I said before, about Nineveh. We're—we're all where we're supposed to be. I was supposed to wind up here." He braced himself on the counter, as if he expected God to blow him across town next. "A beast brought Jonah to Nineveh, and a beast brought me here."

Hewlett said what he'd said so many times before. "The thing is to be listening when God speaks."

By the time Reverend Hewlett walked home that night by way of the old pool, Davis Thoms and Bernie Lake were down there mixing batch after batch of cement and pouring it into the hole. For the first time in more than a year, there was both enough water to mix the stuff and not so much water falling from the sky that it would turn to soup.

He continued toward the parsonage. The wind was done. It had simply left town.

It was so strange to be outside without the roar of wind or rain, without the feel of air or water ripping at his skin, that Reverend Hewlett stood awhile on his own porch feeling that he was floating in the midst of vast and empty space. Everywhere he turned, there was nothing. No baking sun, no drenching storm, no raging wind. There were people coming out of houses, and people going into houses, and people walking from one store to the next. And people picking up branches, and people sweeping up glass. As if they'd been directed to do these things.

All this happened a very long time ago. And it's hard now to argue that what happened so far back *wasn't* inevitable. If the elephant hadn't died, there wouldn't be, on top of the old swimming pool, the playground that originally had some other name but quickly became known as Elephant Park; and the Little Fork High School football team would not be the Mammoths; and Stanley Tack wouldn't have stayed in town, and the son he had with the Beedleman girl (she was expecting already that day of the windstorm, she just hadn't told him yet) wouldn't have married Eloise Miller, and today the town of Little Fork wouldn't be half full of Tacks of various generations, all descended (though none of them know it) from a fire eater.

Jack Hewlett might not have given up the cloth and returned home to be with his girl, with Annette, who'd waited for him even after her letters stopped—only to be drafted two months later, no longer clergy, no longer exempt from war. He might not have died in France, a bullet through his lung. But who's to say that the outcome of that battle—even of the entire war—hadn't hinged, in one way or another, on the bravery of one man? He was, after all, an exceptional soldier. He took orders well.

Or at least it can be said: this world is the one made by the death of that elephant.

The Sunday following the storm, Reverend Hewlett looked out from the pulpit at his battered congregation. There were black eyes and broken arms from the wind, and the women with husbands stationed overseas were exhausted from cleaning up their own yards and their elderly neighbors' besides. It was a good town that way. These people believed in things. Eloise Miller, unhurt and pink, slept in her mother's arms through the service. A green bonnet framed her face.

Hewlett, under his robe, was thin. He'd lost five pounds that week. His stomach felt empty even when it was full, so why bother to fill it?

Stanley Tack held hands with the Beedleman girl. For the first time, he joined the hymns. He opened the book of prayer.

Stella Blunt looked pale and tired. Hewlett tried to catch her eye. He felt he owed her at least a look, one she'd be able to interpret later, the next morning, or whenever it was that the citizens of Little Fork would find the parsonage deserted.

If he owed anything to Stanley Tack, he'd already given it. Hadn't he handed the man his own faith? It was in safer hands now than his own.

He said, "Let us read from Paul's letter to the Romans: *Whom he did predestinate, them he also called: and whom he called, them he also justified: and whom he justified, them he also glorified.*"

He said, "Let us lift up our hearts."

THE GO SEEKERS

Christian Moody

IN THE FINAL WEEKS OF SIXTH GRADE the world is abloom, the sunset is late, and the game is a daily after-school frenzy that lasts deep into dusk. George and Elise hide beneath a garden gazebo, in a broom closet under a staircase in the historical society, in a long-abandoned tree house littered with disintegrated nudie magazines, and in a tarpaulin-draped canoe afloat in a rickety lakeside boathouse. Once, George and Elise spend the afternoon hiding in the TV room of an elderly widow who suddenly claps her hands at five p.m., serves them milk and cookies, and tucks them into the bed of a dusty room filled with rabbit dolls and balls of yarn. They crouch behind chimneys on roofs. They dig holes overnight, cover them with grass, leaves, and branches, and hide in them with juice boxes and crackers the following day. They spend every morning for a week constructing what they call the Movable Bush Suit, a giant shrub they wear around their waists, inside of which they creep from yard to yard. They learn by heart the attics of their neighborhood, the crawlspaces, undersides of porches, hollowed-out trees, drainage culverts, and cobwebbed corners of backyard barns: a world-within-a-world where they learn to live in the quiet and shadow.

In each hiding place, George is aware of the discreet way Elise moves and breathes in the dark. Her elbow taps his ribs. It lasts a few minutes. He can't remember when it first started. It has built up slowly in the darkness, and now it's as much a part of their hiding as holding their breath when a seeker steps near.

*

On the first official day of summer vacation George and Elise lie side by side underneath the school stage trapdoor on an Unofficial Hide, and George realizes that Elise is touching herself. Above them, fairytale scenery from the year's final production sits on the stage: a gingerbread house, a castle, a troll bridge. The curtain is drawn, the auditorium dark. George feels the familiar light tap of Elise's elbow against him. *Touch yourself* is a new phrase to George, something he picked up from an older kid or song or movie, and until now he hasn't understood what it means and still doesn't entirely connect it to what he himself does at night.

"Why do we do Unofficials?" he whispers.

Elise's elbow pauses.

"Unofficials are my favorite," she says quietly.

Unofficials are what they call it when they hide without a game happening, without anyone looking for them. Hiding for the sake of hiding. Elise's elbow patters against him again. He wants to ask why she likes Unofficials so much, but instead he lies in the dark and listens to her breathe. He wonders if it has to do with her mom, who simply up and left when she was still a baby, but he knows the question is off limits. He's tried before. George sometimes thinks about death when they're lying together in the darkness. He also thinks about whether or not Elise will fall in love with him and marry him when they're older. He believes that she will, that maybe this is what the game is all about—about being with Elise.

"Is it because, you know, your mom?" he asks.

Her elbow pauses. "Unofficials are even quieter than a game," she whispers. "I like how some sounds are far off. Cars. People's voices. Wind. And other sounds are close. Like your stomach, or when the wood planks of the stage creak for no reason. The whole world feels small, like it's forgotten you."

They breathe quietly in the darkness. Her elbow tapping resumes. Eerily, the stage creaks. Elise stills herself: "Do you think maybe someone stepped on that plank days or years ago, and it's just now lifting up?"

"The creak?"

"Yes."

"Maybe."

Her elbow starts up again. George hears Elise's father, the custodian for the combined school buildings, buffing the floors in the far-off high school hallways. He wonders if Elise hears it too or if parent sounds are invisible, like the hum of your own refrigerator, or your heartbeat. George likes Elise's dad. He lets them roam the empty school and hide wherever they'd like while he works. Getting to know the classrooms and hallways in their quiet, empty state has made it easier for George to survive in them when they are full.

"Why do you hide with *me*?" he asks her. It's a long time before she answers. Their conversations while hiding are always like this; minutes and minutes can go by between sentences. It's George's favorite way of talking, as if there is all the time in the world.

"You've always been part of my hiding, from the very beginning. Do you remember the leaves?"

"I don't know, maybe."

She describes it to him, her first memory of hiding. Even though he doesn't remember it, he begins the process of turning it into his own memory: They huddle together under a heap of raked leaves on Elise's front lawn. They are three years old and next door neighbors. The pleasant smell of autumn decay reminds them of Elise's father's spice cabinet, of the pumpkins, squashes, and gourds on his kitchen counter. The crinkly pile scratches and tickles George's skin, and so do Elise's lips against his ears: "Shh," she whispers. Her dad dumps another wheelbarrow load on top of them. Their shoulders move up and down with laughter.

"Hey, what's under there?" jokes Elise's dad.

They laugh harder. George wants to burst up through the oranges and yellows. Elise holds him still, in a tight embrace, like she still does when a seeker steps near.

"I think I might remember," he tells her now in the under-stage darkness. Elise's breath quickens. She shivers. From now on, Elise's memory of the leaf pile will be as vivid to George as if it were his own. Years from now, after the tragedy, everyone will think back to Elise's mother's abrupt absence, to Elise's many hiding escapades, her vanishing acts, and it will all become portentous in retrospect, a series of foreboding omens. Only George will remember the pile of leaves, Elise's breath, the way her elbow moves in the dark.

A few weeks later, in June of summer break, the game surges, swells, and swarms through the neighborhood. George and Elise type up House Rules. All players must read, sign, date, and return a copy. Teams of hiders form, teams of seekers form. The Webelos Scouts are seekers, and when they seek they do so in full uniform, carrying their homemade felt flag with a flaming arrow on it. The flag's forked tongues of fire are always peeling off and getting glued back on. Seekers tend to be like this, with their emblems and badges. They like to be seen and heard. They like you to know they are coming.

The Webelos' younger counterparts, the Daisies and Bobcats, are hiders, and their mascot is the poison dart frog. With a marker, they draw their frog insignia in secret places: ankle, wrist, armpit, shoulder blade, bottom of the left foot. The older D&D kids are hiders too. They play in hooded Druidic robes. You can't tell them apart. They favor dark hiding places where they whisper to each other in Old Elvish. The D&D kids are the ones who develop the dice-rolling system that George and Elise include in the House Rules 2nd edition, the first illustrated edition. The dice—twelve-sided, twenty-sided, and the strangely triangular four-sided die—determine which teams will hide each round, which teams will seek, and what the count will be. The probability is not equal: seeking teams mostly seek, hiding teams mostly hide, and the count is usually around one hundred. But a little randomness in the universe is necessary, and so sometimes hiders seek, seekers hide, and the count is under ten. The way the rules are rigged, George and Elise almost never seek, and when they hide they always hide together. They are a team of two, no mascot, no name. Their motto is silence, their insignia invisibility.

College kids home for the summer form their own teams, roughly divided into state school kids (hiders) and private school kids (seekers). There is a team of seeker-parents who bring their six-year-olds, even though everyone can see the adults are in it for their own deep-seated reasons. There is a team of newly single forty-year-old women from a nearby suburb who just don't give a shit. Their mascot is the flask that they pass back and forth in the dark. The teams assemble near the elementary school playground at 11 a.m. Sometimes the games last until midnight, until all the kids in the neighborhood have missed curfew and are grounded. George and Elise ask Elise's dad to drive them to a copy shop to have the third edition of the rulebook printed and bound. By July a fourth edition is printed with new cover art and a password-protected website that includes stats: top hiders, top seekers, and play-by-play accounts of the most legendary and epic games. The House Rules offer extra Advancement Points to the team that finds George and Elise. It's called the Find the Founders Rule. They hide together high in trees and deep in the tool sheds of retired old men who look baffled by the temporary alliance of divorcees and young Druids trampling through yards in search of a place to hide.

Years later, in sophomore year of high school, they are The Go Seekers, an official club. At their inaugural meeting in the school library George reads the Tennyson poem "Ulysses" out loud by candlelight to the twenty or so members. "Come, my friends," he reads, his face flickering above the flame. "'Tis not too late to seek a newer world." Outside, dark clouds rumble. The club members whistle and hoot. George feels like a miniature rock star. He's not sure what his English teacher would say about the poem, or if it even applies to hiding and seeking, but George and Elise and the whole club like the sound of it, and that's enough. He raises and deepens his voice for the thunderous last line, their club motto: "To strive . . . to seek . . . to find . . . and not to yield!" The club cheers. He blows the candle out. A hush falls. Rain drums the roof. In the darkness, students scamper through the high school corridors to hide. Eugene, Second Vice President of the club and Captain of the Seekers, begins the official count to one hundred on the principal's intercom. His voice echoes through the begloomed hallways.

By the end of the year Eugene is George and Elise's best friend and third wheel. Hiders need good seekers, and Eugene is the most persistent seeker they can find. He's also good at recruiting his own kind. Athletes, they realize, have the drive to pursue; they will sweat and suffer to know where you are. Nerds, too, can be tenacious finders, especially those students who stay late after school to conduct lab projects or write research essays. Musicians are especially persistent; they are willing to fail at something over and over, to chase a sound until it is perfect, and chase it farther until it is art. Eugene has all three seeker qualities: pole vault, math, piano. Like George, Eugene is in love with Elise. He is George's best male friend, and George hates Eugene more than anyone, even if he likes him too.

At high school dances George sits up in the gymnasium bleachers where other kids slurp and suck while making out. He watches Eugene and Elise dance. Eugene will always ask Elise to school dances before George does. This is because Eugene is a seeker and George is not. Sometimes, from a hiding spot deep inside a swarm of anonymous dancers, George watches Eugene and Elise jumping and grinding. He sees how their bodies touch. Over the course of many songs, Eugene always steers Elise right into the middle of the dance floor, where the lights flash the brightest, where the dancers who love their own moves peacock and prance and hope to be seen, Eugene chief among them. George knows that Elise hates the lit-up center of the dance floor, but he can see that she doesn't hate it as much as she says she does: she's as thrilled as she is horrified.

The epic spring break meet of their senior year takes place in the high school and lasts for three days. Of the nine other clubs at the meet, seven are from out of state. They assemble in the gym and go over the rules. George sits next to Elise. She has her game face on. It reveals nothing. On her other side, Eugene is smiling his giant, goofy seeker's grin. Elise will eventually want someone quiet to hide with forever, George tells himself, someone to breathe with in the dark, a family of hiders unhidden only to each other. He tries to believe this. George needs to win this meet: the trophy is a scholarship good for a semester's books and tuition, without which he won't be a freshman in college with Elise come fall. Elise says losing isn't an option; they'll be freshmen together if they have to transfigure into invisible vapor to hide and win. Bringing the national meet to their school was Elise's work, her brainchild, for George. The private school kids are utterly silent as the rules are read. They have special hand signs for communicating. They sit in lotus position and control their breathing. Their uniforms are silky cat-burglar unitards and soft leather moccasins.

The game is on. An hour in, George and Elise sit together in a ventilation duct after crawling on their bellies for a short distance at an excruciating pace. George guesses that they have maybe twelve hours before seekers start to poke their heads up through the vents with flashlights. This hiding spot would be a good short-game strategy, but it's not a viable three-day strategy. They sit at a T in the ductwork. One of the arms of the T is a main tunnel that joins the labyrinth of other tunnels. The other arm of the T is a dead end that sits above the high ceiling of one of the more remote girls' restrooms, where the middle school joins the high school. Footsteps and voices echo through the halls below. A crew of intentionally loud seekers passes beneath them. Beaters, they call these groups. Minutes later they hear a ninja-like sweeper crew following the beaters. The beater-sweeper sequence is a common technique: when the beaters pass, hiders feel safe to shift position, sneak out, or whisper, and then the sweepers sweep them up. Only amateurs fall for it. However, this sweeper crew has three additional solo sweepers who follow minutes apart, after the initial sweep, which makes their initial sweeper group more like a decoy, quasi-beater sweep. This is a good trick. These private school kids from Chicago are smart. George can tell it's them by the whisper of their unitards, by the miasmic cloud of sweaty moccasin leather and feet.

Elise gives George a hand signal when the corridors below are quiet again, and they squirm their way slowly down the offshoot duct to the dead end. Here, a vent looks straight down over the girls' toilets. It smells faintly of cigarette smoke and pee. George wonders what they are doing here, and then Elise swings open a false wall at the dead-end, revealing another ten feet of ductwork. They inch inside. Elise swings the wall shut and carefully latches it at the top and bottom. She turns on a tiny, battery-operated nightlight with an underwater scene of fish and seashells. It glows faintly blue, then green, then red.

George knows Elise well enough to show no surprise at this hideout. When Elise reveals something you don't make a big deal, you don't mention it, you pretend not to notice. At the same time, George feels startled and hurt. It appears that Elise has had this secret hiding place for a long time. There is a collection of blankets. A pillow. Packs of cigarettes. Rum bottles, full and empty. A flashlight. There is a stack of *National Geographic* magazines stolen from the library. Elise has torn out maps and photos and taped them to the wall: a diagram of ocean currents, mossy boulders in a forest. The entire ceiling is covered in photographs of women's faces. Some are actually old photographs, stained, creased, and weathered by time. Others appear to have been torn out of magazines.

Elise has also taped up a drawing she made with George in eighth grade, a map of a fantasy world they invented for a novel that they never finished. The Forest of Echoes. The Sea of Sad Memories. The Grief Islands feature Elise's rendition of a humanogriff, a creature they invented after imagining the offspring of a centaur and a hippo-griff (both back ends are horses, so it's bound to happen). The humanogriff inherits two enormous, useless humanoid appendages from its father instead of its mother's giant eagle wings. It flaps and flaps its gigantic arm-wings, wiggling the huge hands and fingers, but can never lift itself up to fly away from the Grief Islands. The map makes George feel a little better. He has a small presence here. Elise hasn't been hiding from him entirely.

She turns off the nightlight. They share a cigarette in the dark. It's not a great idea, but the nicotine-stained girls' bathroom below might mask the smoke. Elise turns on a tiny book light with a red bulb and writes in a journal. She hands it to George. This is how they will communicate for the next three days.

"My dad helped me make this," it reads. "I've spent every fifth period since seventh grade in here."

"Are we cheating?" he writes.

"Home team advantage," she writes.

Before bed, they hear other hiders crawl through the ductwork. After they pass, Elise's elbow taps his ribs in that familiar way. She pauses. She takes his hand in hers and sets it on his own crotch, where he's hard. He twitches in surprise. She moves his hand on it, and then she lets go. He goes ahead. She holds his free hand with her free hand. It's never felt so good before as it does now, close to her. He's delirious with it and not thinking clearly when he turns his head and finds her mouth. This is George's first kiss. It's not as he imagined it would be, except that it's with Elise. A minute later she pulls two tissues from a box and hands them to him. None of this feels as weird as it should. George never feels more at home in his body than when he is close to Elise in the dark. Over the next three days, George's second through ninth kisses will be the same as his first.

On day two a team of beaters crawls noisily through the tunnels, followed shortly by another team coming from the opposite direction. Individual sweepers follow each group quietly. One of these is Eugene. They know him by his expensive deodorant and the swish of his exercise pants. He pauses at the T. He might smell them too, Elise's brand of cigarettes, her sweat mingled with George's. This is how it should be, George thinks: Eugene close by, but always with a wall between them. After a half hour he moves on.

When they have the book light on, George looks up at the ceiling, at all the women's faces looking down at him. A face in the very middle, in an old photograph, reminds him of Elise.

George writes, "Is this one your mom?" and points to it.

"My dad gave it to me," she replies.

"Why all of the other faces?" he writes back.

Elise turns off the book light. They lie side by side in the dark.

Later that evening they hear caught hiders, now seekers, in the girls' bathroom, peeing lengthy pees. Early in the morning, Elise exits their hideout to squat over the vent and tinkle down onto the floor of the girls' bathroom. She pours George's rum bottle of urine down through the vent for him. They both did a cleanse and a fast before the meet—all the hiders talked about it—but now, on the final day, George has to poop wildly. Eugene crawls by twice more but doesn't stop. As hiders are caught, they go straight to the bathroom, where they fart and moan and sigh with relief.

Elise begins drawing a map in the notebook, and they pass it back and forth, adding topography, naming the cities, lakes, and mountains. This must mean that she can tell he is suffering, and she's trying to take his mind off it. She takes the pencil from George and writes: "When I find a photograph that makes me think of her, I tape it up here."

They work on the map. George knows the best way to get Elise to divulge information is to not ask her, to let her take her own time. Midway through an inscription on a historical statue in the public square of Loomopolis, a city of weavers, cloth makers, and story-tellers who live just inland from the Sea of Fog, where the coast meets the Weeping Grasslands, she takes the pencil from him again: "I don't remember her," she writes, "but I like to look at the photographs and imagine what she's like. If I imagine long enough, then I might get one moment with her right."

"What is her name?" he writes back, even though he knows it's a mistake. "We could find her."

She closes the notebook, turns off the light.

Finally, at the end of day three, the first horn sounds. They haven't named their world yet. That's always last. The first horn means that the seekers have an hour left.

There's a commotion of activity in the hallways, through the ducts, as the seekers get desperate. Elise grips George in a tight hug, like she often does, to keep them both still and quiet. It's George's favorite feeling in the world.

The second horn sounds, and the game is over. After visiting separate bathrooms, George and Elise run out through the high school doors holding hands and smiling deliriously. There is a large crowd. A band starts up. This is all unexpected. Apparently the national meet made the local paper. George and Elise are the lone hiders remaining. Cheerleaders stand on each other's shoulders. Tailgaters hold up bratwursts and beer and whoop and yell. Elise's dad sits on the hood of his truck and gives them a shy wave. George sees Eugene's face in the crowd, smiling his big goofy smile with so much sadness behind it that George drops Elise's hand for a moment. She takes it up again and holds both their hands overhead. She turns to him: "I don't want to ever talk about my mom after this." George nods. "My dad says it wasn't enough for her to live here, married to a janitor. She needed more, a bigger world. I don't want to be like her, but I think maybe I need more too." Their hands are still raised, the crowd still cheering. George looks at Elise's father on the pickup hood, a quiet man with a kind smile. He taught George how to play chess, is the best cook and gardener in the neighborhood. This photo of George and Elise will be a full spread in the yearbook. They will sign it together for almost everyone.

The flagship state research university they all choose is a hider's fantasy with its monastic, forested campus, footbridges over streams, gazebos in secluded groves, and turreted academic castles creeping with ivy. There are forgotten nooks, crumbling crannies, cloistered corners, hidden corridors, secluded study towers, and remote reading rooms. This is all lucky for George and Elise, who don't have any other options financially. Eugene, who does have many options, is accepted into the university's famed School of Music on scholarship. He will also pole vault and double major in mathematics.

They don't have to start a campus club because they can resuscitate a dormant club still on the books that last met during the seventies. The advisor is Full Professor Frederick Bilgarius of the

History and Philosophy of Science Department, a scholar of the Second Age of Exploration, especially Darwin's voyage aboard the *Beagle*. He has a hider's face; you can't see much of it beyond the bedraggled gray-and-white beard, stained yellow around the mouth from pipe smoke. His office is high up in a turret with curved windows overlooking the campus hedge maze, which is dotted with statues of fauns, dryads, Silvanus, centaurs, and Bacchus. Students run through the twists and turns below, laughing. George, Elise, and Eugene wait in creaky chairs while Bilgarius digs through one of many tottering, yellowed stacks of paper strewn with nutshells and seeds, corners chewed by mice. Miraculously, he produces the club's original charter, with Bilgarius as founding advisor. The club is called The Society for Undergraduate Crypsis and Mimicry—or The Cryps 'n' Mims—which will have to do. After much pipe sucking and staring out the window onto the tangled puzzle below, he agrees to update and amend the rules to what George, Elise, and Eugene have proposed. With one condition: That the most points be awarded for finding Full Professor and Club Founding Advisor Frederick Bilgarius. He signs with a flourish and when he smiles they see that he is missing a canine tooth. He probes the hole with his tongue. Bilgarius provides an impromptu lesson about aggressive mimicry techniques used by advanced under-graduate seekers: The professor crouches on the floor and opens and closes his hands to imitate real and false firefly flashes; he draws a golden orb spider web in yellow whiteboard marker on his window, appearing to capture students in the maze below. Then they are dismissed.

After weeks of practice, during which Bilgarius shows the thirty or so club members slides of butterflies that look like leaves, they finally have their first major meet over fall break weekend. Elise and George have discovered the drinking of red wine, and Saturday afternoon they hide sloppily in a bell tower with several bottles and are promptly found by Eugene, who gets drunk with them. When they wake up in a pile it is dark and, according to a note taped to George's chest, everyone is still searching for Full Professor and Founding Club Advisor Frederick Bilgarius. Finally, as dawn breaks

Sunday morning, someone sees that a section of the maze is smoking a pipe, and Bilgarius steps forward in an emerald academic robe sewn with hedge clippings, his face and beard leafier than the face of The Green Man carved above the labyrinth's archway entrance.

* * *

On Christmas Eve George and Elise hide deep inside the Waltham Rare Manuscript Library. They've been here since the December 22nd Solstice Hide-and-Seek Meet, a twelve-hour meet, noon to midnight. No one should be looking for them now except for Elise's new boyfriend and George's new girlfriend. They have both been dating an almost-significant other for about a month now, and they've both been prematurely invited home for Christmas to meet the family. If George were going to make it to Christmas Eve at his girlfriend's, he needed to start driving four hours ago. If Elise were going to make it to her boyfriend's, she needed to have shown up for her flight the day before. Breaking up is new to George, but he's hidden with Elise through any number of her break-ups so he knows how it's done.

This is the most comfortable hiding ever. They have wine, snacks, several board games in progress, and the gas fireplace is set to its highest crackle in the Waltham Family Foundation Game Archive, a walnut-paneled room with leather sofas, multiple game tables, and rare games from the ancient and modern worlds under glass. The playable, less-rare games are in the walnut cupboards, which is where Elise and George hid themselves during the twelve hours of the Solstice Meet, and also during two hours of the librarians' annual Christmas Party, after which they squirreled away leftover wine and hors d'oeuvres before the custodian cleaned it up.

In the locked and alarm-protected rooms below them a Gutenberg Bible and Shakespeare folio reside behind glass. There is a main reading room, where on non-holidays visiting scholars wear white archival gloves to read the letters of the Romantic poets. There is also a book bindery, repair studio, administrative offices, a staff break room, and endless rows of subterranean, climate-controlled stacks, where Elise and George initially planned to hide before they found the elevator to the Waltham Family Foundation Game Archive.

They spread dozens of boxes throughout the room, shuffle cards, set up spinners and dice, unfold boards, and place pieces in starting positions. They amend rules, and all the games become part of one large drinking game. They rotate through standards: Clue, Risk, Scotland Yard. They also play a naval game they don't quite understand, although they adore the intricate wooden ships with names like *l'Astrolabe* and *La Boussole*, and the map is beautifully illustrated with leviathans and mermaids. When you land on one of these sea monsters you have to take a double drink and remove an article of clothing. Before long they are down to their underwear and a few odd, errant items—a belt, a sock, a mitten—and are almost aware of what they intend to get into when they push away sofas to unroll the giant map that is Twister: Mythological Edition. This version of Twister features a Minotaur in a labyrinth, along with Scylla, Charybdis, Circe, and Sirens. When Elise half-attempts to crabwalk herself from smoldering Troy to the Oracle at Delphi she bumps George in the mouth with her crotch. They laugh. George is in love again, still. They collapse together, laughing, and without thinking he grabs her hips and kisses his way slowly up her stomach to her mouth, sets himself between her legs. It's George's first time.

"I'm sure we're both very single by now anyway," Elise says hours later, before they have sex again, for the second time in George's life.

For their freshman year Spring Break Invitational, The Cryps 'n' Mims organize their biggest game yet. The far-flung members of their former high school club The Go Seekers forgo spring breaks on beaches in Florida and Mexico and instead arrive on the slowly thawing campus for a real rager of a hide-and-seek. They bring new friends from their new clubs at their new universities. Even the Druids show up, their robes a little high off the ground now and faded. They've been studying video game design at art school, or doing computer things at MIT and Stanford. When they converge for a group hug their robes appear to blend into a single brown tent supported by a dozen pale, sandaled stick feet.

The groups now all have their own House Rules, so some arguing and compromising ensues. Elise stands on the Speaking Rock in the middle of campus. The rock splits a little brook that flows to either side. She answers questions, and the Druids act as scribes, taking down the rules.

"Name the boundaries," someone says.

"It's the campus map. You can't step foot off campus. You have to be on university-owned property at all times."

"Including, like, by air? By like hot air balloon?" someone says.

"Some part of your body has to always be touching the campus," she says.

"What if you, like, leap off the ground or climb a tree?" someone says.

"I think I've been clear enough," she says. "If a tree is on campus then you're on campus. Is it clear enough?"

The crowd shouts, "Yes!"

A representative of the Druids hands the scroll up to Elise on the Speaking Rock, and she reads the rules out loud. Everyone has agreed that this most epic of games won't have a time limit. Instead, George and Elise, in a nod to the original game in the original neighborhood, are to be like the golden snitch in a quidditch match: the game will only end when they are caught, and they are worth 150 points while other hiders are worth 10. This special rule requires the agreement and signature of Full Professor and Founding Advisor Frederick Bilgarius, who consents to being worth 11 points so long as whoever finds him buys him an immediate eight pints of ale.

"If they find us first, we're coming for you, Professor," say the Druids, each holding a flagon.

The professor tongues his tooth gap. "I'll be waiting," he says, and dons the hood of his emerald robes.

The "golden snitch rule" makes George nervous, since there are so many expert seekers here, all of whom will be looking for them. On one hand, there's a collective desire in the crowd to honor the original neighborhood game, which is nice. At the same time, George senses an even bigger desire to take him and Elise down for good, to end the myth and legend of their hiding skills. As far as he knows Elise doesn't have a secret compartment in an air duct anywhere. And yet, when he looks up at Elise reading the scroll on the Speaking Rock, she is smiling. She's radiant. She lives for this. If George and Elise aren't found, read the rules, then the game continues, no matter how long it takes. Whoever is on campus will search for the week, and whoever can travel back weekends will search on weekends. The game only ends when both are found.

A silence falls while a Druid shakes the D&D dice in a cup. The Druid pours, and the dozens of colorful and variously shaped dice clink and clatter into a tray. There is a collective gasp. The nearly impossible has happened: George is named a seeker and Elise is not. The dice are checked and re-checked. There is less than a 1 in 10,000 chance of George and Elise ever being separated. Yet, here it is. To make matters worse Eugene is a hider, and Eugene can't hide his wide-eyed grin about it, the chance to tuck himself close to Elise for a full week or longer. The rules are amended, and a Druid reads the newly amended article out loud, naming Eugene and Elise as the golden snitch. There's an air of disappointment, since the opportunity to take down the original Dream Team is gone. And yet, everyone knows that the true hider is Elise. She's the one to get.

"Good luck, my friends," George tells Eugene and Elise on a footbridge over the stream near the Speaking Rock. The three hug each other. "I'll be looking for you."

They turn to leave—George to the statue of Odysseus on the seeker's side of the brook, for the count, and Eugene and Elise to the Lightning-Struck Oak on the other side of the brook, the point from which all hiders will depart. "Wait," says George. He knows he's making a mistake. He stands at his end of the bridge, they pause at their end. "Elise, I love you," he says. "I've always loved you." He looks her in the eyes, but she has her hider's face on and he can't tell what she's thinking. Eugene looks stung. George turns and runs to the statue of Odysseus, heart pounding. He considers forgoing the game altogether. In the twilight, wearing a seeker's blindfold, he stands on the statue's plinth: "To find, to seek, and not to yield!" he exclaims. He blows the candle out, followed by silence—the non-sound of expert hiders hiding, seekers listening. In unison, they chant out loud to one hundred and eleven.

George doesn't abandon the game. He's on a quest. The thought of Elise and Eugene together has made a true seeker of him. After a mere six hours, he discovers the Druids huddled in a hollowed-out tree in the campus forest. The next morning he finds the former Chicago prep school kids, the ones who are now at Princeton, in the guise of hairnet-clad recycling sorters in the dining hall. The ones who are now at Yale—never much for hiding—are in the Music Library playing cards, singing *a capella*, and eating cheese and crackers. By Wednesday of spring break, only Eugene, Elise, and Professor Bilgarius remain. On Thursday, a mud-caked professor Bilgarius emerges from the pond in the campus meadow with a reed in his mouth. He sits down on the grass and asks for an ambulance. He'll be on medical leave for the rest of the semester.

Friday night there is a party, and the mood has changed from one of seeking to one of getting drunk and waiting. "E & E" is what people are calling them for short. They've already achieved a new hiding record. George, who has barely slept, imagines them in the dark, touching each other. He leaves the party wildly drunk, wide-eyed with heartbreak. Late Saturday morning the campus police find him naked in the grotto of the campus hedge maze with an out-of-town seeker he doesn't know. "You called me Elise all night," she tells him. "But you better not call me Elise now." The campus cops issue him a first-warning citation. Still a little drunk, he searches the campus woods alone.

When the week is over, some visiting teams stay an extra few days, sleeping on dormitory floors and common room couches.

Professor Bilgarius emails from his recovery room to tell the club to cooperate with campus police. He's CC'd top administration. The campus police investigate, and it turns out that Eugene has mailed a postcard to his parents, telling them he is OK. He has also unenrolled for the semester. Elise has done neither of these things, but of course she wouldn't. They're shooting for two weeks, the club members speculate. They're going for a month, they speculate later.

Two weeks back into classes, George is surprised to see Professor Bilgarius—who is supposed to be on medical leave—cross the stage of George's History of Evolution lecture in his emerald robes. The original professor has suffered a full-on heart attack and will need bypass surgery, Bilgarius explains from the podium, whereas he, Bilgarius, has merely suffered some hypothermia, angina, and humiliation from wading in cattails for nearly a week while sucking air from a reed tube underwater. "Medical leave?" he says, and then sticks out his tongue and blows a raspberry. "Discussing crypsis with bright young minds is the best medicine there is."

After that first lecture George finds himself in Bilgarius's office hours several times a week. The professor is content to smoke his pipe up in his turret and mumble and mutter behind his beard and robes, so long as George brings him chocolate, cheese, and strong ale. George tells the old man, many times over, the whole story from the beginning: the pile of autumn leaves, Elise's little arms around him. The hiding place—the ceiling of possible-mothers—in the air ducts. Sex in the Waltham Family Rare Games Archive. The misguided declaration of love on the footbridge. The professor blows large smoke rings into the air and then sends small rings through the bigger ones. His missing canine has been fixed and his teeth gleam, something he must have had done while on medical leave. They hug at the end of every session, with nary a word from Professor Bilgarius. The old wizard's arms are surprisingly strong and sturdy under the emerald robes.

The more advanced students complain that Bilgarius's lectures are merely chapters read out loud from his books *Love Among the Mimetic Weeds*, *The Milk Snakes of Mexico and Me*, and *Fly Orchid, My Heart*, all best sellers in the '80s, but George doesn't mind at all. He enjoys the bearded lull of the professor's familiar voice, and because George is awake all night, searching his mind for Eugene and Elise, the professor's lectures are one of the few times he actually sleeps. Then, exactly one month to the day the seekers chanted to 111, Professor Bilgarius is in the middle of a digression about female hyena pseudo-penises in a lecture that started out as a treatise on Müllerian mimicry in monarch butterflies, when he abruptly stops speaking. There is a long pause. He scans the auditorium with piercing eyes from his podium. "Hiding," he whispers in the parched voice of someone adrift at sea. The students lean forward in their chairs. The hush in the auditorium wakes George up, and he leans forward with his peers to listen. "Hiding," says Professor Bilgarius again. He sighs deeply. "I'm too tired. I can't anymore." He closes his book with a thump. He leaves the stage and walks up the center aisle toward the doors at the back. He pulls his emerald robe up over his head and drops it on the floor, tears off his beard, and it is Eugene in a white T-shirt and blue boxer shorts who exits the auditorium.

Later, after the police and campus administration have questioned Eugene at length, George and Eugene have a beer in a pub frequented by the older professors. Eugene has been drinking here as Professor Bilgarius for a month. The bartender doesn't even ask for their fake IDs.

"She wouldn't hide with me," says Eugene. "Because I'm not you, I guess. When I asked her to marry me, she told me if I could last longer than her in the game she'd consider it."

George wants to punch him. "You proposed?"

"You declared your love first. You spoke the unspoken. We've both loved her forever. What was I to do?"

"I've loved her longer."

Eugene shrugs. "Now I've lost her. I failed. She knew I would fail."

"A proposal would only guarantee that she would never marry you," says George. "Do you know her at all? Telling her I love her was the dumbest thing I've ever done."

Eugene shrugs. "I wear my heart on my sleeve," he says. "Apparently, so do you."

They sip beer. George wants to fight him, considers fighting him. But Eugene also feels like his closest link to Elise, like the only friend George has, which is exactly what Eugene is.

Eugene's story is this: he hid in Bilgarius's office, prepared with an emerald robe and beard he'd procured way back at the fall meet, waiting for the moment the dice would choose him as a hider. He'd long suspected that if he proved he could be a hider to Elise, she might love him. He knew Bilgarius's turret wasn't ideal concealment, but then again no one would think to look for Bilgarius there, and if they "found" Eugene as "Professor Bilgarius," Eugene's plan was to join the seekers and technically still be hidden and unfound. He'd reveal himself the moment Elise was found, and then she'd love him, and so on. It seemed brilliant, to Eugene.

As it turned out, no one from the game looked in the turret. The cleaning crew treated Eugene like Bilgarius when they emptied the trash at night, and colleagues—perhaps getting news from the custodians—wound their way up the turret stairs to inquire about his health. Eugene answered them with mumbles and a thumbs up. When a colleague came down with a heart attack, the department head asked Bilgarius—since he was on campus already and seemed in good health—if he'd return from medical leave and fill in.

"It was so lonely," says Eugene. He sips a fresh pint. He reaches out a hand to touch George's shoulder, hesitates, pats George, then grips his shoulder like a miniature, one-handed hug. "Our talks together meant a lot to me. You saved me with your company, I think. And your cheese."

George thinks about fighting him again, but instead grips Eugene's shoulder back. "I was so jealous," says George.

"I know, you told me, told 'Bilgarius,'" says Eugene. "Elise said that if I didn't out-hide her, she'd marry you instead. She said it was what she'd always planned."

George drinks deeply from his mug and searches Eugene's eyes for the truth. Eugene's never been a liar, and doesn't look like a liar now. Eugene stands up and extends a hand. "Congratulations," he says.

George laughs, nearly spitting out beer, and waves away the handshake. "You're drunk," he says. "Elise was joking. She was fucking with you."

George believes what he's saying, but he also doesn't want to. Of course they would marry each other. The leaf pile, the darkness beneath the stage, the Games Archive: What else is marriage but ending up with the person you most want to hide with? He believes it, and he doesn't.

"We'll find her. You two will be together," says Eugene, a tear sliding down the side of his nose.

George smiles, squeezes Eugene's shoulder with another one-handed hug. "We won't be together anytime soon," says George. "Maybe when we're ancient, like forty years old. Elise isn't going to settle down for a while. She hides from one relationship by jumping into another one. She likes sex with a lot of different people. She could have been with any number of people since the countdown. Let's find her."

"Let's find her," says Eugene, lifting his beer. They knock their mugs together.

The two friends don't so much look for Elise as wander campus and wait for her to reveal herself in the way of her choosing. George stands on his Footbridge of Embarrassment in the middle of campus, the brook trickling beneath it, and he thinks of a home with Elise. On the beach, their children splash through foamy fingers of surf. On the deck of a mountain home, George and Elise drink coffee and watch mist weave through the evergreens. On a boat somewhere in Scandinavian waters, they peer at fjords through binoculars, Elise's belly pregnant with their first child. It is dusk and fireflies twinkle across campus when George realizes that Eugene has already said goodnight and left George alone on the bridge. Some of the firefly blinks are mating calls. Others are the false flashes of predators. His heart feels insane.

Dogs are brought in to sniff the campus when Elise is declared a real missing person. Her face is on posters, and police interview all the seekers and hiders at length, again and again. The search continues through summer, with seekers of a different sort volunteering from all across the country. They spread their arms, touching fingertips, and walk the campus, the town, and the neighborhood back home.

News of the disappearance spreads across the Internet and hide-and-seek takes on a new popularity among teens, who feel the twinkle of danger and sex when they read about it online. Elise is on T-shirts. Her face becomes an Internet meme that has her hiding in the most ridiculous places. George worries that Elise will see these things and never come out. Internet infamy is her worst nightmare, a life she couldn't live. It could be years before she emerges, or forever. He believes, in his heart, that she's still hiding, that she's a master, that this is what she does. He imagines her sipping wine in a secret room behind a painting in the university art museum. He imagines her attending classes under a new identity she's been building for years. He imagines her in a foreign city, starting over, gone, hiding forever. Maybe she's found her mother and reunited. When he walks the campus with Eugene at the start of their sophomore year he finds himself following the smell of decay through the woods. He follows it all the way to a dead fawn. He lifts it with a big branch and looks under it, just to be sure.

* * *

Throughout the year George searches for Elise. He lifts manhole covers at night and descends ladders beneath streets and sidewalks. He spelunks the university's sewers and underground conduits with a headlamp affixed to his forehead. He sleeps in late and dreams of her stuck in tight places. He wakes up in a sweat, fighting his covers. Eugene transfers schools. In his last email to George he writes, "Please don't contact me again. It's too painful, and I've moved on." Ignoring him, George writes and texts, asking for help with the search, certain that his messages aren't getting through. Eugene blocks him on Facebook, across all social media.

George visits Professor Bilgarius several times per week, like he did when Bilgarius was Eugene in disguise. Bilgarius listens, nods, and smokes his pipe, and when there is nothing more for George to say they stand at the turret windows, sip liquor, and stare down into the hedge maze. Bilgarius gives George study abroad brochures: "Leave," says Bilgarius. "Go see places. Free your mind." He also gives George articles and books on crypsis and mimicry, on the history of natural history, and on Darwin's voyage aboard the Beagle. George reads them carefully many times over, hoping Bilgarius has given them to him because hidden somewhere within is secret information about Elise. He knows this is fantasy and he won't find clues about Elise within the pages, but George has run out of physical places to look and combing through texts satisfies his drive to search. He sifts through data. He finds overlooked connections. He seeks the words and meanings hidden behind other words and meanings. This academic work calms his mind, like doing a puzzle. His GPA goes up. He finds a home here, in his homework, and he shies away from parties, from football games, from people. It feels like hiding and searching at the same time.

In the summer George stays in the college town and works on a lawn care crew. He peeks into sheds. He stomps on the grass for signs of a hidden trapdoor. He spits on basement windows to rub away grime and peer in. If Elise is captive somewhere, she knows George will look forever. The idea could be keeping her alive.

"I'm looking for you," he whispers to Elise before he sleeps.

"What?" says a temporary lover, next to him in bed.

Junior year, George calls Elise's dad and asks for evidence that Elise was once real and not just a mental construct, an imaginary friend. The first time he calls, Elise's dad gives him detailed lists of memories and reasons, and they laugh and cry together. The second and third times Elise's dad hangs up.

Professor Bilgarius insists that George not enroll in the graduate program in the history and philosophy of science. He encourages George to skip graduate school altogether and to head out into the world to make money, shake things up, and live a simple and happy life. George doesn't listen, and in the second year of graduate school he teaches his own discussion section, and in the third year he teaches his own lecture. George sometimes stops mid-sentence to examine the faces of his students, to see if she's there, hiding under his nose. The students don't understand it, but they like it. They find it dramatic and piercing. *Have I have found you, Elise?* he sometimes writes in the margins of term papers. There are rumors among his students that he's been seen in strange places: Astraddle steeply pitched rooftops with a drink in hand, up in tree branches smoking a cigarette, emerging from manholes covered in grime, lying beneath porches, asleep on a sofa in the Waltham Family Game Archive late at night. All the rumors are true. George gives up on Elise. She is lost. He gives up looking for her monthly. He gives up weekly. He stands in Bilgarius's office and promises to give up by the next quarter-hour chime of the campus clock, and with each new chime he promises again.

The day before the final exam for George's lecture class, George gets a phone call from Elise's father. George has been calling the house from time to time, but he always hangs up before Elise's dad can pick up the phone.

"I won't call you anymore. I won't," George answers.

"It's OK," the man says. "We need to meet."

"No, I promise I won't call anymore."

"Do you have a car?"

"Yes, but I usually take the bus home to save on gas. I could come this weekend."

"I'll see you tomorrow evening. I'll text when I'm on campus."

George tries to reply and confirm but nothing comes out. The man hangs up.

It's dark, past dinnertime, when Elise's dad pulls up in front of the student union. George gets in the pickup. They shake hands awkwardly. They start driving. A few turns later they have left the college town and are driving down a dark country road. Elise's dad has finally lost it, George thinks. He blames George for Elise's disappearance and is going to murder him on some back road.

"Look," says George. "I don't know anything."

"I know you don't."

They keep driving. The dark road is long and straight, empty cornfields and patches of woods to either side. George quietly unclicks his seatbelt and places his hand on the door latch, in case he has to roll out. A few miles further, and Elise's dad abruptly slows down, clicks on his right blinker, and turns into a dirt tractor lane between fields. They slowly bump down the lane about a hundred yards, and then he turns the truck off. It's quiet. Wind blows over the bare fields. The engine ticks and cools.

"Why are we here?" says George. He is ready to run out across the fresh-tilled dirt if he needs to.

Elise's dad takes a deep breath. "I didn't mean to drive this far. I couldn't decide if I should tell you what I know. It's the right thing, for you, but maybe not for me."

George looks at the man, but the man stares down the tractor lane, searching the darkness with his eyes. The moon appears from behind a cloud and bathes the field in its light. George looks out the window, imagines tiny seeds under the dirt, roots and shoots pushing their way out.

"Here," says Elise's dad, and he hands George a folded piece of paper.

George opens it, looks at it by moonlight. It's a photo of Elise printed in color on a cheap home printer. She's sitting close to a handsome man with salt-and-pepper hair, a baby on her lap. Two things feel wrong with the picture. One, Elise has aged. Of course she has. Two, she's smiling and looks happier than he's ever seen her.

Her dad snatches the photo, opens the truck door, and sets it on fire with a lighter. It warps and blackens. He closes the door. The smell of burning paper lingers.

"Now you know," he says.

"Was that a real photo?" says George.

Her dad smiles while looking ahead out the windshield. "I always thought of photos as hard evidence," he says. "But to you guys—your generation—there's nothing more suspicious."

"I guess so," says George. "She's alive?" He knows it's true. He sees it on her dad's face.

"We've emailed. Talked on the phone once. She's happy."

George nods. He feels numb and doesn't know what to think.

Elise's dad looks George hard in the eye now: "You're to say nothing. Not a thing to anyone. Is this understood?"

George nods.

"Say it's understood."

"I promise I'll never tell."

Her dad's face softens. He places a hand on George's shoulder. "You remind me of her," he says. "You two were always together. All this time I kept telling myself you must already know, probably knew before I did. I'm sorry."

"How long have you known?"

"It was a little over a year after she left, and then one morning she called. It was an answered prayer. She told me that if I told anyone she'd disappear again. I believed her of course. You're the only one who knows. She's traveled, had a whole life. Maybe found her mother, maybe not. She has a child now, and I think she needs me. She might be changing. Having a kid will do that to you. I might actually see her again." He pauses to roll down his window. A cold breeze blows through the cab. He looks at George. "Please keep quiet. Don't ruin it. Don't make her go away again."

"I won't."

They sit in silence for a long time, and then Elise's dad starts the engine and backs out of the field. They drive to campus in silence.

"Do you need dinner?" he asks George back at the student union, pulled up to the curb.

"I'm good," says George. It feels too weird, too tense, and he wants the encounter to be over so that he can sit alone somewhere and figure out how he feels. There's only shock now, a kind of numbness.

"OK," says her dad. "If you change your mind, if you need company, I'm staying here in town tonight." He smiles. "You really were always around," he says. "Always the two of you. It's nice to see you again."

They shake hands. George gets out of the car. He pauses before he shuts the door. "She looks happy," says George. "In the photo. I think she's happy."

"Now you know," says Elise's dad. "Go live your life."

George can't sleep that night. He drives back to the old neighborhood. It's three a.m. when he parks in the lot of the local grocery chain and walks a mile to Elise's house. His own childhood home next door is dark and quiet, his parents asleep within. He knows how to go from fence to tree to rooftop to upstairs bathroom window, but he doesn't need to. He doesn't even need the key kept in the planter where it's always been. The back door isn't locked.

It's easy to find what he's looking for. It's right there in the messy spare room her dad uses as an office, scattered across a desk, some of it in a manila folder, the rest of it on the computer desktop. She's in Spain. Her husband is Spanish. Elise didn't even take Spanish in high school. She took Latin and French and dabbled very poorly in Japanese. It was like she took everything available except Spanish, and now she's in Spain. George is careful not to disturb anything. He snaps photos with his phone, and he texts himself her address and information. He doesn't want her dad to know, doesn't want Elise to know he's coming. He imagines he'll make it look like an accident, like he happened upon her while on vacation. Or maybe he'll just watch her from a distance to make sure she's as happy as she looks in all the photos he's found. She looks happy in every one.

He stands in her bedroom and loses track of time. On the wall is the framed yearbook photo of the two of them, emerging from the high school halls hand in hand, victorious. Every edition of the House Rules, the maps of the fantasy world they invented together—it's all here. Different scenarios pass through George's mind. He could declare his love, even though it backfired once and he's not even sure he feels it anymore. She's obviously in love with her baby and Spanish husband. He could be angry and confront her, but he's not sure he feels that now either. He could say goodbye to her. He'd like that.

"George?" he hears from downstairs. "Are you here?"

Elise's father must've been sleepless too. His mind must've turned to what he would do in George's position. George gets down on the floor and squeezes under Elise's bed, much more slowly than he did as a child. Elise's dad walks through the house. George lies on his back and listens. Elise's dad is quiet now. He enters the bedroom and stands silently. George imagines Elise squeezing him tight, like she would have long ago. Her dad sits on the bed, and it's several minutes before George realizes the man is crying. George has two possible plans in mind. The crying becomes sobbing. George's first plan is to drive to the airport to see if his credit card can handle a flight to Spain. Her dad collapses onto the covers. His heaves shake the bed. The second plan is to do nothing, to let her be gone and happy. He's not sure which is better, which he has in him. For now, though, he lies still, listens to Elise's dad cry himself to sleep above him. It feels good to hide again. The man sleeps. George hides. He listens to his own breath, crouched under the leaf pile in his memory. He feels the dry tickle against his skin, smells the scent of autumn decay. Elise's lips whisper against his ear.

DICKY LUCY

Kim O'Neil

—Cambridge, 1967—

I WAS A GREEN-EYED, BEE-HIVED GORILLA. I was the wild girl of Brighton. Nobody knew. I had a nineteen-inch waist and a D cup; they called me the Shelf; I cannot account for you girls. After your Gramp broke my nose and my arm, I moved. I lived at the Y. By day I kept up at Girls' Latin. I kept up my grades, the scholarship— nobody knew. We had uniforms, white and navy. Kneesocks and ascot. I kept mine pressed and clean because I loved them. When I met your father, it was easy not to tell him things. He never told me things, too. About money he in effect lied. It takes one to know one, but that applied to me, not him. The year was '67. Men like that never saw themselves as prey.

When I met him, did I think *house*? Did I think *bedsheets, yard, breakfast nook*? Did I think *patio*? *That,* and *dog* and *guinea pig* and *cat* and *hamster* and *turtle* and *dwarf rabbit* and, with some luck, *horse.* I wanted animals. I wanted a brass knocker and a singing doorbell, the melody "Que Sera." A wreath of baby gourds for Thanksgiving, gooseberries for Christmas. There would be a mantel and on it seasonal elves. The Easter baskets would be excessive. I'd litter the house with fat foil eggs, each one oozing a gold sugar yolk. Underfoot for months they'd be. I did, yes, think so, very much. I thought ballet lessons like everyone else thought but also roller skating lessons and ice skating lessons and painting lessons, and a Formica bar in the basement where a person could paint—I don't know why I thought you paint at a bar—and naturally, then, my thoughts needed you.

You ask about your father. That is half what I thought when we met.

When we met I nursed Dicky Lucy. At nineteen Dicky Lucy rolled a Chevy going eighty. The break was C1, the highest vertebra. When his mother, Mrs. Lucy, hired me on, I didn't know I was the fifth. I was volunteering with quad vets then, answering phones at Doody Diapers. I wanted weekend work. I'm not a nurse, I said on the phone, I got through one term but then what happened—

Do you chatter? Mrs. Lucy said. His best topic is boxing. Dicky hates world affairs, and when you come wear three-inch heels if you're under five five, a Cross Your Heart brassiere if you've got it, and stockings with seams. Show your figure, but not tarty. Are you any good with a gun?

I fed Dicky Lucy deviled ham on white rolls and floretted his pickles. I maneuvered his straw. I got him from his chair to the tub with the aid of a board. I scrubbed him and shaved him with sting-free kiddie soap. He had such a lot of hair. He was like my father in that. I combed his duckbill with a greasy grab of Vaseline and held a hand mirror to him, combed it four, ten times, until he was well pleased. We played Chinese checkers. I moved his marbles, illegal moves at his word and his voice that drill. My job was to lose and bemoan the loss. My job was to cut pictures from magazines and paste them in an album with rubber cement and no wrinkles at all: muscle cars and Ursula Andress. If the picture bubbled anywhere, Dicky Lucy said burn it. My job was to shoot Dicky Lucy's pump gun out the window at squirrels in the oaks. How humanly they shrieked. How the cantilevered limbs groaned with their running and sometimes fell. I missed and I missed. What else could I do? Dicky Lucy's *get hims* and my aim so poor. My sympathy lay with anything furred.

Dicky Lucy stayed midweek at a hospital in Weymouth, but on weekends he got dropped at his mother's. She lived back-to-back to Idy Bridges. Their porches faced off across a shared plot of knotweed that Idy was hard-set and ill-equipped to kill. Ray, Idy's youngest, was the last at home, work-study at Northeastern. He had a cherry Ford he tinkered with, Dicky Lucy knew well. At four every Sunday, Dicky Lucy made me dial. I hated telephones then the way I now hate cameras. A liar piece, my voice coming at you and pitched all wrong. Like with a gun, I could never seem to aim straight. Even my breathing on the phone to me sounds like a lie.

Why, hello, Ray, I'd say. It's Jane, at Dicky's. We were just wondering if you happened to be heading out, if it was not too much out of your way—

Weymouth was on the way to nowhere and Dicky Lucy was a hardship.

Dicky Lucy was vain.

And always, yes, your father would come.

Studious Ray; student of how objects transfused power, one to the other, a particulate sharing, like the transfusions, one to the other, blood or germ, of the living.

(Ray would correct me on this. Electrical engineering isn't like that, he'd say.)

And the way Ray hefted Dicky Lucy from his chair at the door to his Ford at the curb, the way Dicky Lucy needled him—*someday, I'll let you work on my toaster, smart guy*—that worked on me too.

It was the other half of my thinking.

It began the way things begin for men, with cars.

Before cars it would have had to have been horses. Before that, what? What else can men own and strap on and make be fast?

They were neighbors, Dicky Lucy and Ray, and they had gone to grade school and high school together but were not friends. Dicky Lucy was two grades ahead. This was when Rindge and Latin was two schools. Latin trained kids for college. Rindge trained kids for typing and plumbing, woodwork and metalwork and engines and babies. Ray had won some fame in his grade school days as the local whiz kid TV repairman, but it was Dicky Lucy, not Ray, who went on to Rindge. Mrs. Lucy gossiped with the indiscretion of the long-term lonely.

Sundays Ray would say just *I'll be over.*

He was, and took Dicky, and I'd take the train home.

But that day, for no reason, he said my name. And how it feels to hear a person say your name is only one of two things—happy or sick. The body keeps its decisions streamlined like that.

He said, Jane. You feel like taking a ride?

Then as now a man of small economies.

I packed Dicky Lucy's Weymouth bag. Within a quarter hour out front the Ford idled. The engine cut out. The door slammed but after too many seconds, into which I read *qualm* or *duty* or possibly *cigarette.* I put down the paste pot. The cement fumes got to me, and Ursula, like every trapped thing in there, began to look complicit and paid. She looked professionally malevolent, like she was driving a sled. I held the album page out to Dicky to vet. Not like that, he said, closer. In the light, he said, here. Goddamn, Jane. Turn it this way.

But my technique was good. He seemed disappointed.

I listened for footsteps. Mrs. Lucy waved me over to her ironing board, where she chain played three staggered hands of Patience and offered me ten dollars plus mail-in coupon to dye my hair blonde. I told her I wouldn't. She pulled the coupon from the socket of her breasts. It was pressed to a pill.

I detoured Dicky Lucy for the window, paused by The Castle (a picture someone had painted on glass in reverse, a feat of perversity that Mrs. Lucy and I took time to puzzle at: they must have painted it outside in, highlights then outer stone then inner stone then black, and when I looked at the painting I heard the turning of a key), then made a stop at Robin Redbreast (from the nuns' same yard sale, sequins on cotton ticking—*hand sewn by girls of twelve in the Philippines!* Mrs. Lucy said, aghast and gratified by the human cost of art, and the key fell away to the bottom of a well), and I tried to look like someone wanting air, not escape. I listened for footsteps in the same way the Lucys listened for mine, I imagine. That apartment was tightly crammed with Lucys. They were just two in five rooms, but they expanded to fill them. The place overheated. It smelled of pet store. Mice by the pound and interbreeding, although Dicky Lucy kept no pet.

Mrs. Lucy, said Ray—not, *how've you been, Dick.*

What I noticed usually when Ray entered was the disquieting size of his head. It was big. Blockish. Cowlicks feathered it. Yet that day there was something nicely transparent to the structure of it all: Cro-Magnon brows making caves for eyes, which were also big and set on the outer reaches of the face, like eyes of the hunted, optimized to see what's coming, field of view not depth, retiring and appraising but not afraid. They recalled to me the eyes of goats. Below those were the cliff-drop cheeks. Caliper legs. The neat and outsized hands of the handy. Ray looked like he would be good with a bow and arrow. My people earned as lookalikes and gamblers, and by habit I asked myself, *Who does he look like?* The answer you know from the movies I fed you—Tony Curtis minus the dandy, plus Steve McQueen's straight shooting minus the smartass—is less right than the answer you can't know, Eddy.

I could smell it on him. *Smoke* not *duty.*

Mrs. Lucy (*Queen for a Day* fan and aspirant) said, Ray, before you and Dicky head out, be a doll and fix the set? The picture isn't right. I keep getting fuzz.

Mrs. Lucy spoke always of heading *out*, not *back*: like they were two pals, rogues, out to paint the town red. In Ray's pocket she tucked an envelope she thought I didn't see.

While Ray folded himself down to the RCA, Mrs. Lucy told the legend of TV Ray. How when Ray was four, the Bridges were the first on the block to get a television set. Ray's father was a natural fixer. He had been promoted from subway driver to subway inspector and wore a badge like a policeman that he let Ray hold. When the TV broke, the repairman was stealthy. Trade secrets—he didn't want Ray's father to watch him working. So Ray's father and brothers left the room and Ray stayed, the youngest, playing one-man conkers with chestnuts on the floor. When the work was done and paid for, Ray's father showed that repairman out. Ray, his father said to him then. What have we got? Ray pocketed his winning chestnut (a two-er). Then he asked for a Phillips head screwdriver, removed the TV's backing, and indicated the new capacitor.

(Mrs. Lucy didn't say it then but later how that same week was when Ray's father died. One morning he was inspecting subways. The next he said to Idy, his wife and alarm clock, give me five minutes. He pulled the covers over his head and never woke.)

Ray, like his father, liked to fix things. You enjoyed watching him work the way you enjoyed watching him spoon up chowder. You begged tastes from his bowl, though you hated clams. If I fixed you your own, you wouldn't touch it.

Ray tried to show you about fixing. That it takes not talent but willingness to break what you hoped to fix. He knew defeat as disinterested, a condition of life and not of people. You hated to hear it. The way some stake all on the existence of the divine, you staked all on the existence of talent, and found, in its absence as in its presence, proof. Ray has less interest in failure than anyone I know. I think failure must be the bad hobby of narcissists, as the devil is the bad hobby of the devout.

What I'm saying is that your father was no baby. Ray had this easy rectitude he didn't know about. Mine was a forgery. Not to say fake. But those of us who must forge it admire that not knowing.

This all made Ray maddening to would-be bullies. I could see that.

And I could see it in Ray's back how he hated this story of Mrs. Lucy's. What he would not say lodged low on his spine. Where quite suddenly I wanted to touch.

Dicky Lucy watched me watch Ray at the TV and snapped his gum. His tongue was strong; he liked to body build what he could. He enjoyed toothpicks. He opened wide for me to lay them in. He spat them out in his can. He was always working something around in his mouth.

Goddamn, Ma, he said. We don't have time to goose around. TV Ray, what say we split?

Ray fiddled the tuner and rose. That should do it, he said to Mrs. Lucy. (*After* and not *before* it was true. The allergy to exaggeration. I say in twenty years you never took me to a movie. Well, Ray says. I thought we saw three.)

Jane will join us, Ray informed The Castle.

Dicky spat in his can. He flashed big gums. A date for TV Ray, he said as if to himself. He looked for me, but I was not there. I was halfway down the stairs with the bag.

Sure she will, I heard him say.

I always left before Ray lifted Dicky. When I lifted him for baths, we played the match on the radio. It was important to have near us the loud and comfortable sounds of regulated hitting. Dicky couldn't even compose an arm. They were arms once given to showboating (the first day Mrs. Lucy put me in a chair with a shoebox of photos, smiling pimpishly or maternally or both, and did not budge until I'd thumbed through all, and I learned that mobile Dicky had been stocky, procamera, pro-Elvis, pro-prom, and a wrestler, never without well-placed sidekicks; that Dicky Lucy favored the stranglehold). Now those sleeves waggled, light nearly as sleeves.

I know nothing about cars. Sometimes I walk to the wrong one and wonder for a minute why my key won't work. I suppose Ray's was beautiful. It shined in that street in a way that seemed to please him. As he brought Dicky Lucy out, he kept his eyes down as if in modesty. Maybe he had just washed it. I don't know how to desire a car. What nonpeople earn that check box, beauty? For men like Ray and Dicky Lucy, it's what they can put their hands on and ride: cars, horses, girls, boats, and motorbikes. They would never speak of beauty in a table or a fish or another man's baby. For women it's what they can put in a room, and their body is another kind of room. We learn to desire pearls, not oysters. Husbands, not men. We learn to want what we can affix to ourselves. For men, we practice a weird rehearsal, desiring ourselves as if we were men in order to learn how to be desired.

Dicky said, You kids take front.

We already had.

Ray took Mass. Ave to Fresh Pond Parkway to 2. I had been passenger on this route in all brands of jalopies, with all brands of unfitness to operate vehicles. It was a losing experience that had made me duller, not sharper. In car passenger seats I had to right the urge to be luggage. My job as Lucy's nurse and Ray's date was to be a person. I hoped to find a hawk so I could point it out. *Look.*

Dicky Lucy said: The radio's broke?

The window's broke?

Your foot broke?

Ray found a station Dicky did not fault. He took the Ford to seventy. The hood hiccupped and the dashboard too.

Don't stay mad, Ace, said Dicky Lucy.

Dicky Lucy said: Ace, tell us a story. We had us some good times in high school, tell her. TV Ray, my only friend. God we were tight. You don't love me no more like you used to, Ace. At night I cry. Tell her how you used to hang around the woodshop hoping to see me. Dicky, you used to say, Dicky, teach me how to live, teach me what it means to—

Knock it off, said Ray.

Dicky went quiet back there. The Ford jittered on to some dated music. I dated it to their high school years—maybe. I could only pretend to know, as I could only pretend to musical taste. It took me time to figure it out: music is what you find in high school, and where you find it is, my hunch, at friends' houses. My high school years lacked a house, so they lacked friends' houses, since you did not accept what you couldn't return. So they lacked music. How little I knew had a way of offending people.

Ray would pick it up, Dicky Lucy said louder than necessary, but we're flat maxed out. Fifth gear's shot to hell, a real pisser.

Dicky shouted: We'd like to open her up, Jane, but we can't do it. Cannot. Want to and can't. The clutch is a bitch.

There's nothing wrong with it, said Ray, and pushed it to ninety.

Dicky said: Easy, Ace. You'll muss my hair.

We now had the left lane all to ourselves. The car had assumed a syncopated rolling motion that seemed not exactly bad and at least rhythmic. It rolled along to Chuck Berry, and I tried to think of something I heard someone say about Berry to repeat. Berry is the best, I imagined myself saying, but I'd have had to shout it and possibly defend it. I looked for any bird of prey at all.

Did I mention that being driven in cars, when car or driver is off, makes me want to disappear? To be a glove of myself? To stow away in the glove compartment? Every bit of blood in me gunned for my feet, slammed there, flip-turned, gunned for my heart. It's a terrible thing to feel your blood doing laps inside you. If they could induce it, they would torture with it. They'd make nonbelievers pray. I found myself praying to Franny, *help*.

Dicky said: Having fun yet, Jane?

Ray held steady to Yankee Division Highway when up from the floor came the thick and dire smell of burnt hair. Ray sat up straight. He set the Ford south. My silence seemed a bad agent, a bad hand on the wheel. Berry was out on parole, I thought to say, or was it the other, and then Berry was gone and it was Cline strung out wailing "So Wrong" and I had nothing on Patsy Cline.

Dicky said, Let's vote. Can we? Who thinks this date's a pisser? Can we speak our hearts? At this juncture, I feel that I can. I say this date's a pisser and I say you're not speaking your hearts and I love you kids like I love myself. That's what hurts. Ray, let's turn it around. Let's go the long way, show Janie a good time.

Yankee Division was the newish beltway, the first of its kind. It had a residual hick feel then. For stretches there was nothing but state-owned trees. The road's shoulder banked sharply down to softwoods.

The car floor palpitated. In relief I saw it down there near me. Mrs. Lucy's envelope.

Is that yours? I could say to Ray at last.

As I reached for it Ray said leave it but I said I had it and Ray took a hand off the wheel to beat me to it and Dicky crooned, *I've seen the light, darlin', I'll make it right.*

The car pulled right, jumped the shoulder, and nose-dived the bank. Each rut in the bank telegraphed itself to our spines as pine needles rushed to enfold us. Dicky's voice vibratoed. The last thing I heard was a high-pitched hooting from the rear, a sound I could not place until later at Mass General as Dicky Lucy's laughter.

We all survived this, no one unchanged.

The dashboard snapped two of my ribs, my collarbone, and rebroke my broken nose.

Dicky regained sensation in his feet. A medical anomaly, unwelcome both to the doctors, who could not explain it, and to Dicky, who could not scratch the toes that itched him.

Ray, protected in the enclave of the floor space, came out of it intact, all eight points of his cranium accounted for, but carless and amorous. I was in rehab two weeks. On each day he visited, Ray sat sweating on a green shell chair at my bedside in the same navy suit and navy-striped tie, elbows propped on knees. He suffered to converse with me. He brought me maple candies molded in the shape of maple leaves. Somehow, in his romantic detective work, he had hit upon the bad information that I loved seahorses, and each day brought me a different seahorse token—statuettes, jewelry boxes, pendants, pins. I had been much in hospitals throughout my childhood, and his solicitude, and his mistake, touched me with its excess. It was a brand of excess I craved. I asked him to remove that suit. I asked him to roll up his sleeves and side part his hair like Eddy. We weren't much for talk, and shared a distaste for ceremony. The day I left Mass General, I conceived Ruth. The Brighton courthouse was our second date.

When Mrs. Lucy advised a week after my discharge that I find a husband, since care for Dicky in my fragile state was impractical, I was not quite truthful. I said that I would try.

HOW WE LEAVE HOME

Leslie Pietrzyk

I.

A STORY WANTS TO START AT THE BEGINNING.

Here could be the beginning, that summer in Iowa when we longed for adventure. We sprawled on towels on the glittering concrete of the pool deck at Mercer Park and sighed, arching our necks, flexing our toes, bemoaning how boring Iowa was, how bored, bored, bored we were—how we needed—no, deserved—adventure. We glopped handfuls of baby oil over each other's shoulders, desperate for any zinc-nosed lifeguard to swivel his head our way.

It was 1981.

The adventure on my horizon was that I would leave for college in Chicago in three weeks. I hadn't told my friends. They saw me on the path we all followed: state school in our town, living at home in my childhood bedroom, working a mall job. The only thing different would be nothing. Same people at the same parties at the Reservoir in their same rundown cars, same brand of beer bought from the same place that sold to minors, Dirty John's on Market Street.

I felt sorry for my friends, the dull blur of them, and they sensed my pity. All summer they'd been avoiding me, or cutting me with the slightest of slights—like not acknowledging my new haircut. It was OK. I floated a stratosphere or two above them. I was leaving. I was out. I was so out, and the poor things didn't even know.

At the same time, I missed them already, their clattering gossip about people we'd known since third grade. I was the one insisting on this afternoon at the pool. I wanted to bawl. I loved them so much. I wanted to tell them that adventure was stupid and all wrong.

My stomach curled and flip-flopped, so I pushed my salted nut roll to the edge of my towel. It seemed accusatory. Usually it was my favorite choice from the pool vending machine. I could smell peanuts over the chlorine lacing the air, so I concentrated on the lifeguard scanning the blue pool, the screeching kids, the chubby moms clustered in the semi-shady corner.

"Well, I'm going in," Janey said, as she rose, all six-feet-one-inch of her. She wore a pink, glittery headband, too narrow for her crazy wad of dark hair—"that girl needs to learn control," my mother said about Janey; my mother worshipped control—and Janey tugged off the band, letting it drop to the concrete as she shook free her hair. Her coppery skin glistened with baby oil; she tanned the best and showed off with white tank tops deep into autumn. Though she and I had been friends since seventh grade, it was an uneasy friendship, each of us certain we were better than the other without evidence backing us up.

She was too tall for our school, with too much hair, and just always too much something. After my new haircut, with five inches chopped off and bangs, she stared at my face with intensity and said, "God, please wear mascara."

Now, she glanced down at me sitting cross-legged on my towel and demanded, "Come with me." I scrambled up, startled to be noticed, grateful, nervous—so nervous that my bare foot crunched the discarded hairband as I followed her; I heard it snap. We moved fast over the stovetop-like cement, and the pain scorching my feet felt distant.

We sat on the lip of the pool, dangled our legs in the water. "I wish the water was blue," I babbled, "not clear."

"There's islands in the world where it is," she said hazily.

The lifeguard whistled at some boys dunking each other—"no roughhousing," he yelled. Whistle Nazi, we called that one, even as we flipped our hair when his gaze skimmed us.

"Our last summer together." More babbling.

"Look," Janey interrupted. "I know you're pregnant. I already know that."

That hot sun was frying me. I half-jumped, half-fell into the cool, colorless water that should have been the cheerful turquoise of the painted walls and floor—I disappeared into the cold, scraping my hands back and forth against the rough cement to make them bleed.

What my mother said: "That girl needs to learn control."

I could drown myself, never emerge, but I wasn't good even at holding my breath, and when my head bobbed up to the surface, there was Janey, sitting very still, staring over the water with the same abstract gaze as the Whistle Nazi. She said, "What are we going to do?"

"How do you know?" I asked.

"You're too quiet," she said. "That candy bar's been there all afternoon. And honestly, you know you're an unlucky person. You barely did it with Brad, like once or twice?"

That was fine. Let her think it was Brad. That was better.

"I can't tell anyone," I said. "Not anyone. Not even one person."

We glanced at the clutch of girls, at my former friends, sun glare flashing off their oiled shoulders. One of them rolled over, and then another and another. I felt suddenly invisible.

"I won't," she said.

I had to trust her. So I asked, "How much money do you have?" She waitressed the late shift at Country Kitchen when drunks and frat boys stumbled in for scrambled eggs and fried potatoes, and she said that either they gave her excessive, drunk-guy tips or else she got stiffed, no in-between.

She hugged her knees to her chest. "Aren't you afraid?" she asked.

"No," I lied.

"Were you going to tell me?" she asked.

So easy to lie. "When it was the right time."

She shook her head, hair flailing. I thought about the white puff of a dandelion gone to seed, blowing at it with one huge breath to make a wish. How little girls ran around yards all summer blowing the tops off dandelions. I taught my little sister to do that. This little girl could too. Like me, she'd catch fireflies and yell, "I'm telling," and crook her eyes in her elbow at the parts of movies where animals might get hurt, and write her name across the dark with a lit sparkler and eat her hot dogs burned black. All those things little girls did, things I did, that I taught my little sister. So I shoved that little girl out of my head. I pushed her away, like pushing a swing on a playground and watching the body on it sail off into a pure blue sky. I would never think about her again. All I needed was Janey's tip money.

"What about him?" Janey asked.

"What about him?"

"You have to tell him," she said. "Don't you?"

"I don't have to do anything," I said.

"Wow," she said.

The moment fell heavily between us, separating us irrevocably but neatly, like a guillotine severing the head from the body. Every single person in the pool was screaming, yet I couldn't distinguish a word. Janey wouldn't meet my eyes, so I looked down at my wavy, water-distorted legs.

"OK. I'll drive you," Janey said. "I can get the car." She and her older brother shared a crappy Pinto, the kind that might blow up if it got rear-ended. Her brother was a pothead and definitely mellow. There was nothing he cared about except pot and pizza. Janey and I talked about whether that might be a good life, pot and pizza, and sometimes we agreed that it would be, and other times one of us argued it would be boring.

"I can take the bus," I said. "I figured out the transfer and the route."

She shook her head. "You can't take the bus."

Exactly why I didn't want to tell Janey, because I didn't need her being nice. I only needed her money. But I didn't know how to say that. So she would drive me there and call up afterwards and watch me with shiny, sad eyes and hug me for no reason, hanging on until I squirmed away. I had to hate her, I had to. And she would tell: I handed over every dime of my summer tip money to my best friend for her abortion and then she left town for college without saying goodbye. When I would have done anything for her. I wondered how I would tell the story, until I remembered that I would never tell the story. That was the only bright spot: that all this could happen and no one would know.

"I hear it's not a big deal," Janey said.

"That's what I hear too," I said.

She got up into a crouch and reached out her hand to me, wanting to help me out of the pool, but what I did when I took her hand was yank really hard and dodge aside, wrenching her headfirst into the water. She shrieked, and the Whistle Nazi about broke his whistle on us, and I watched Janey's big body lash and twist underwater, her limbs reorganize into standing, until her head emerged, her hair tamped and streaming rivulets, water beading her oily shoulders. She tugged both suit straps straight, then fixed me with her eyes. As the lifeguard yammered about roughhousing, I waited for Janey to tell me to take the bus and pay for it myself besides, to call me a slut. But she smiled at me, a too-wide, circus-clown, sad, sad, sad smile. Now she would always see me like this: pitiful.

II.

Maybe this story starts before that day at the pool. Maybe it starts when we were fifteen, sixteen, too old for the slumber parties we still organized, any excuse to flee our houses, dart free of our mothers' watchful eyes. Too young for dating, we tried anyway, none of us landing with the cute, crush-boys of our giggles and chatter, each of us compromising, so it was Homecoming Dance with whoever asked, always yes-thank-you, playing at gratitude to pimply-faced boys. We didn't talk about that boy passing us in the hall after school, that boy, the one raking his long hair back with both hands before slouching over the drinking fountain, that boy whose sudden presence in any doorway set loose a smolder of longing we knew to keep secret. Each of us kissed Janey's pothead brother who was surprisingly tender, bestowing secret nicknames we pressed close to our hearts. We whispered them in our dark bedrooms during icy winters and sweaty summers; I was Desi after confessing that I wanted Desiree for my French class name, hating the teacher who assigned me Claudette and called me arrogant. But he didn't count, just Janey's brother, just a pothead drifting through the fringes of the back parking lot smoking dope in tricked-out vans. Though he was an excellent kisser; though he never pushed for more, recognizing his exact but limited role of First Big Kiss; though Janey didn't mind and we suspected he kissed her too; and though we would never break tradition and not kiss him when our turn came, it was understood that kissing Janey's pothead brother was not enough. Understood that there had to be more, and some of us needed whatever that more was, or told ourselves we did.

Desiree, desired, desire. . .the clutch of the words, their pinch. Bearing down like a marble rolling through my brain, the echo of each syllable merging with the thump of my heart, aligning to the push and pull of my breath, melding with the drumbeat of my being, until I couldn't speak what the word itself meant to me: it was a throb I was never without, that was all.

My mother's baby brother was being divorced, which didn't happen to people in Iowa back then, especially not twice. He landed on the battered couch in the unfinished basement, T-shirts and denim spilling from a Hefty bag after his wife kicked him out of their cheap apartment because, he said, now she was a hot-shit secretary on the university payroll. Before, she spooned up lunches at Southeast Junior High, a hairnet lady no better than the others. Now, every morning she looped a paisley polyester scarf from Younkers around her neck and wore pantyhose. She kept the dog, which pissed him the most, he said, because she fed it table scraps so's it would get fat and lazy. "I only just grabbed up my guitars," he said, "before she was fixed to hurl them into the alley."

My uncle was a musician who slept all day and woke up about when my parents got home from their jobs. He'd trudge barefoot up the basement stairs, eyes watery and red-rimmed, his hair stiff with leftover sleep, a crunchy sheen to his skin, then saunter over for a mug-to-the-brim of black coffee from the fresh pot my mother put on for him right after she walked through the door. According to him, she always loved him best of her brothers, even with him being the black sheep of the family till kingdom come, no matter what he did, or how he proved himself, no matter if he got a gold record or if The Man in Black, Mr. Johnny Cash himself, recorded one of his songs; "people need someone to blame for how their stinking life turned out," he said, "and for a shitload of them, I'm it." That's how he explained it to me, when I sat up late at night, reading at the kitchen table and he dragged in, the tang of cigarette smoke and butts coiled round him, shadows of rough brown liquor on his breath and smelling of something more, something leathery and sweaty that made me think of the secret pleasure of working a hunk of gristle: this essence later what I sought in every man.

He'd drop into the chair opposite me, ask what I was reading and half-listen, his eyes scattered beyond me, beyond this kitchen where the stripes on the wallpaper mismatched by a quarter-inch; my mother complained but wouldn't rip it down to put it up right. I'd go on about my book—as long as I wanted because he didn't stop me—so I theorized about who the murderer might be in whichever Agatha Christie I was dug into. When I was done talking, he'd take a turn, telling me about the band and the bar, who hit it good, who was trash, who played stoned or drunk or strung out, something he scorned as "disrespecting the groove"; he played guitar with a bunch of bands, his name bannering posters tacked up all around downtown; he was locally famous for his guitar-playing, he told me, and I was oddly proud, as if scraps of that glory might blow my way if people at school connected him with me. When I asked why he wouldn't stick with one band, his own band maybe named after him, he said that was going to be forever the million dollar question and if he had the answer he'd know why he couldn't stick with one woman or one anything. We'd talk for an hour, maybe longer, and he'd suck down a mug of cold, leftover coffee and a juice glass of Wild Turkey, and sing lines from songs noodling in his head—"that's where the shit is, writing songs"—and once I was brave enough to ask him to write a song about me. "You betcha," he said, and did I want happy or sad, and "sad" was the right answer, and he said, "Good girl, it's in the works," and tapped his forehead with two fingers, but I never heard any lines. He wasn't allowed to drink or smoke in the house, but he did anyway on these nights. Mornings after, I'd catch my mother dumping the ashtray and rinsing the brown circle of bourbon ringing the juice glass, hurrying before my father was awake.

I watched his head tilt when he drank, my eyes tracking the path of the bourbon rolling from the glass on down through his throat, tiny, delicate muscles rippling all along his neck as brown liquid tumbled its way down. He didn't mind when I snuck sips, and I felt—or I imagined I felt—his eyes watching the delicate muscles shift along my throat, too.

Some nights he didn't come home. I'd wait as long as I could stand, my face swallowed up in yawns, then tiptoe upstairs to my bedroom, intending to lie awake until the back door rasped open, instead dropping into immediate, dreamless sleep.

Then there were three nights in a row when he didn't come home and the ashtray stayed clean. I craved the ache and burn of his Wild Turkey, so maybe now I was an alcoholic, which is what my father called my uncle when he was out of the house, spitting the word at my mother because he thought no one else was listening.

Janey's pothead brother called me wanting to go to a movie, but I said no-thank-you. When I hung up the phone, my mother didn't set aside *Family Circle*, but she said, "Not like you're collecting phone calls from boys every day, you know. Wouldn't want you to think you're too good for everyone. Be more like your sister, why don't you?" My sister was at the table drawing on the back of used worksheets, picking colors from a coffee can of old, dull crayons, sitting in the chair where I would wait for my uncle. The rims of her ears flushed seashell pink. She was only seven or eight, and terribly quiet, the kind of little girl who sat where she was told to sit, making it easy to forget about her. Somewhere in my heart I understood I was responsible for her, but I had to not think about that. She was so quiet that I could convince myself things would work out OK for her. I wanted her to say something, to talk or cry or shriek or pound fists on the table or fling crayons to the floor. To stop drawing happy-family figures. The last thing on earth that could be true was that I thought I was too good for everyone—though possibly I thought I was too good for Janey's pothead brother, and yet it was possible that maybe, actually, probably I wasn't. But I had to tell myself that yes, I was. No-thank-you, I had said, I had said that.

I marched upstairs to my bedroom and tried on shorts in front of the dresser mirror until I figured out the shortest pair, the Levi's cut-offs I made at the last slumber party. Then I yanked off my T-shirt and bra and slid on the bright red tube top no one but me had seen. In the mirror, my boobs looked like tomatoes, which wasn't a good thing, but this was the sexiest shirt I owned. Maybe not buy red next time. Later, with everyone in bed, I crept downstairs and sat at the table in my outfit, barely able to focus on *The Murder of Roger Ackroyd*. I knew who had done it because I peeked at the last page. I could have been reading harder, better books, but I liked Agatha Christie because the problem always got solved. Plus, with so many books, nearly a hundred, I could never read them all or if I did, it might be a thrilling accomplishment. I longed for the tickle of bourbon skimming my tongue, the abrupt burn and razor slice of it, neck muscles tightening and loosening. I wanted the bourbon. I was an alcoholic. He had to come tonight. My thoughts mishmashed on top of themselves.

I must have set my head down and fallen asleep on top of my paperback because I was startled to see my uncle in the doorway, a smile screwed sideways across his face. "Look at you," he said, ambiguously. He tossed his jean jacket onto the back of a chair with a soft thump, an even drape, like of course it would land that way.

Gravity had shifted my tube top, and I wanted to tug it higher, to my chin, wanted to run upstairs for a real shirt, for jeans that weren't chopped apart, but I kept my hands still.

"Look at you," I said straight back. He stretched his black V-neck T-shirt to sniff the armpits, one then the other. "I'll get glasses," I said. I stood tall in front of him, sweeping in a swift, giant breath that lifted my boobs, a trick we learned at slumber parties. My shorts bit tight at my crotch, and some of the cut-off fringe felt feathery against my leg. I idly scratched a slow, teeny spiral with one thumb.

"Glass," he said. "Singular. I'm not taking the heat for my niece turning up drunk." He looked away, stared at the misaligned wallpaper and rested one hand up against a seam as if noticing it for the first time.

I got two anyway, jelly glasses with Scooby-Doo characters, because the real juice glasses were dirty in the dishwasher, making sure to reach up to the very top shelf of the cupboard, to the way back, balancing precariously on my tippy-toes. I plunked the glasses on the table and said, "I promise I won't get drunk." I trailed a finger in a lazy cross-my-heart that intersected the edge of my tube top, my finger flaring off the slope of my breast, as if launched from my nipple. I let it point directly at him. His hand on the wallpaper crunched into a fist that he dropped at his side.

"Probably should get myself some sleep," he said, sinking into his usual chair. I understood: certain words must be spoken and dispensed with. Like lines in a play, people were assigned specific roles for right now. "One drink," he said, reaching for his jean jacket, for the bottle tucked into the inside pocket. "Only one."

"One drink," I mirrored. "Only one."

He poured a half-inch into my Scooby glass, an inch into Shaggy, and said, "Bottoms up." He lifted the glass to his lips, locked my gaze onto his as he watched me over the rim. A flick sent the brown liquid cascading down his throat, through those undulating muscles. His eyes pinned mine, and the rush of liquor tightened his face, almost imperceptibly, like something suddenly coated with frost, and finally a quick buzz of good sense made me afraid.

"The narrator did it," I said, grabbing *The Murder of Roger Ackroyd*. "The guy telling the story. He's lying the whole time." With both hands, I pressed the book to my chest, against the crack between my two boobs. Cleavage, it was called, though I had never dared call it that. The book was slightly sticky, or it was that patch of naked skin that was sticky. My heart hammered into the layers of paper.

"Shoot," he said. "Most about anyone lies when they're telling stories. That's what a story is, just a long, fearless lie unwinding." He extended a hand for the book, which I reluctantly gave him. He glanced at the front cover then flipped to the back, his eyes skipping the words. With one thumb he riffled the pages. Then he let the book drop upside-down onto the table. It looked stupid sitting there, just as I looked stupid sitting there in my tomato-red tube top and my cut-offs, my ragged-edged fingernails, bitten and torn, that wouldn't hold polish more than a day without chipping. "You don't have to drink it," he said, nodding at my glass. Automatically, I curled my fingers, covering Scooby with my palm.

I'd been thinking about this bourbon for three days. I'd been thinking about Janey's pothead brother and Janey and the rest of them whispering in the dark at slumber parties and my mall job scooping warm Karmel Korn into cardboard boxes and plastic tubs. I wanted more than this forgettable college town in Iowa, more than what I had. I didn't know what I wanted, only that: more.

I drank. Wild Turkey plunged into the pit of my body, into that hollow emptiness that I didn't like to think about, filling it with an explosion of blistering flame. It was bourbon I wanted, another inch.

Talk about *Roger Ackroyd*. Talk about the gig, a good one with a cranking crowd and a decent take. Two glasses of bourbon for me, bigger, taller. Five for him. We found the bottom of the bottle. When he grabbed my shoulders and jammed his lips onto mine, when his tongue scooped through my mouth, when he moaned my name, my real name, no childish nickname, and muttered, "Oh shit-shit-shit-shit," when his hand snaked down through my tube top and I straddled him right where he sat in my father's chair, when these things happened and then more things happened, more, I kept my eyes open. I saw everything. It was my own life arriving—finally—and there I was, watching it all spool loose.

The next day, my uncle told my mother from then on he was crashing in a friend's basement, on a friend's battered couch. But also he scribbled that address across a scrap of paper that he slipped to me, and the address after that, and the address after that so I would always know exactly where to find him.

III.

Maybe the story starts on another day, the day I understood that I was smart enough to escape to a college in another city, that all I would have to do was convince them that my dream was to be a doctor or scientist, that they would want me if I doled out some heartbreak in an essay, that I could fill out and sign financial forms myself, that I needed a teacher—who was a man, who drank bourbon when he wasn't at school or when he was—a teacher who had gone to any college in any city who could send someone a letter recommending me. That's all: problem solved. Maybe that's the day the story starts, when that silver gleam of light winked from across the other side.

Or maybe the story starts at night, on the night I listened to my father's gentle shuffle on the hall's shag carpet, my little sister's bedroom door yielding to his hand, his murmur—heard or imagined—that she should stay quiet. The bed's squeak. The squeak. That squeak. Maybe the story starts that night or the nights I sat up late in the kitchen, flipping through English murder mysteries, pretending I cared whodunit, the overhead light blaring at its brightest, listening. Maybe this story starts on the night my grandfather's footsteps traveled a different hall, to my father's little-boy bedroom, my father told to stay quiet, and no one sitting silent guard in the kitchen. Maybe there is nowhere for this story to start.

IV.

I didn't want to travel back home for Thanksgiving, so I expected my friend Jess to invite me to her parents' house with her. Her parents told her I was "polite" and "well-mannered." They liked me. But she didn't ask. Every freshman on campus was chattering about Thanksgiving break, dying to get home. Maybe Jess thought I was like them. If I mentioned Thanksgiving, Jess jumped in with, "That will be great for you to be back, won't that be great?"

There were some reasons to go home: Dorm cafeteria closed, starting Wednesday. Library closed, starting Wednesday. If I stayed, I'd be eating pork-flavor ramen noodles out of my roommate's hotpot for five days because they were seventeen cents a package. My roommate hated me using her hotpot, claiming the water she boiled for tea tasted like meat. She hid it in a shoebox the back of her closet. We loathed each other. If I stayed, people would feel sorry for me, even my roommate, whose parents booked her on a plane home to Fort Lauderdale.

For my Greyhound fare, I borrowed money from my roommate's purse and skulked around the laundry room pocketing stacks of people's dryer quarters, and I snagged the tip jar at the campus Cone Zone. Someday I would pay all of this back, everything. That refrain circled in my brain like a bird trapped in a room.

My bus left Chicago at four a.m. Thursday, the cheapest fare, meaning I would pull into Iowa City around nine a.m., about when my mother started the stuffing. She loved stuffing, and Thanksgiving was the only time she allowed herself to eat it, so she would be in her best mood, listening to the Frank Sinatra records she took from the farm after my grandfather died. There was one he taught her to dance to. That one she played the most. With no one else awake, she'd keep the stereo low and she'd possibly be singing. I imagined pushing open the back door—a surprise, since I hadn't told anyone I was coming, because that's how expensive long distance was—my mother's startled smile (I hoped), a tight hug (I hoped). She'd hand me an apron, and I'd start chopping onions right alongside her. We wouldn't talk; we were better off with a task, when we had something to think about that wasn't conversation, so we'd dice onions and celery, and there'd be the sizzle of real butter in the frying pan, and she'd sing, "I've Got the World on a String." She knew each word exactly how Frank sang it.

My little sister would be next awake and she'd wrap her arms around my waist and squeeze. She wouldn't talk either, but she'd be happy. Maybe she'd sit at the table and read. Or she might draw. She loved to draw. Her lips moved when she read, but maybe she finally broke that habit while I was away. She'd tuck her bare feet up on the chair rung to get them off the cold floor. She'd draw a picture of me.

That's what I imagined. That's as far as I got.

The reality was, I had to get to the house from the bus station. Usually I would expect to wait for a city bus, but none ran on Thanksgiving. If I called for a ride, the surprise would be wrecked. There would be talking. I couldn't stop at hello.

I stood at the pay phone, nickels scraping together in my fist. The huddle of people exiting the bus with me had dispersed immediately, collapsed into noisy, sloppy hugs, everyone exclaiming how great it was to see everyone, how great everyone looked, then dashing outside to waiting cars with running engines billowing white clouds that lingered like mist after the parking lot emptied. A single hovering taxi got snapped up, not that I had cash for a taxi, and not that that would work, Chicago-me pulling up like a queen. "You come from Chicago in that thing?" my mother would say, "well la-di-da to you."

The rain nailing the window looked vicious and cold, ready to jump the line over to sleet. I only had a backpack to carry, but our house was across town, two long miles, maybe three.

Still. I didn't call. I couldn't. I imagined onions and celery sputtering in that pool of real butter, my thumb and two fingers crackling leaves of sage into powdery bits: the bottomless scent of sage and thyme and butter and my mother's Chanel No. 5, her only everyday indulgence. The turkey resting on the counter, now a heap of pale flab, pocked with goose pimples, but we would knead handfuls of soft butter onto it, up and underneath each fold of skin, raining a shower of salt and pepper and paprika: our day together a fervent vigil of basting and peeking and worrying, aromas rolling in waves, our stomachs pleasantly anxious with hunger. Throughout, Frank Sinatra crooning and the slight clickety of the record reaching its end, my sister hopping up to drop the needle back at the beginning, sending Frank's orchestra on another round. The warm kitchen. The plates with the yellow roses from my mother's dead mother who I never knew, the dishes we weren't allowed to use unless it was a holiday because one might chip or break. Ironing the tablecloth, stiffening it with starch and chunky squirts of steam. The quiet morning. The morning like everyone else's morning: the people who had gotten off the bus, Jess with her parents in Oak Lawn, my roommate in Fort Lauderdale. A TV commercial morning. "What are you thankful for?" people asked on TV Thanksgivings, and right now, until I dialed, it was possible someone would speak those words today at my house.

The nickels were warm in my hand, and solid.

It would be my father who would drive to get me. My father would be there. Of course.

Finally I picked up the phone and pressed the coins into the slot, listening to their jangle and then the dial tone. I went through the seven numbers. I expected the bark of my father's sleep-rage: "Wha—?" or my mother, a rough sigh, impatient as she eyed pans simmering on the stove. But the phone simply rang. And rang. Ten times, fifteen, twenty. I stopped counting. What a lonely sound, an embarrassing sound: a phone echoing across an empty house because no one was home. Not even a dog or cat listening; "pets eat," my mother said, "who can afford that?" She said something like that about everything. I hung up, my money spitting back out at me.

You told us you were leaving. I could hear my mother's words as if she stood next to me, whispering them. You left. You left us. You left US. Only she wouldn't be bold enough to say "us" though I understood the "us" was there and, now, always would be.

The bus station wasn't a place where anyone would want to wait: two short lines of bolted-to-the-ground bucket seats in blue leatherette made it impossible to lie down, and the vending machine was stripped, except for one slot of flamboyantly orange peanut butter crackers. The drinking fountain dribbled water and out-buzzed the fluorescent lights overhead. I smelled little kid vomit when I turned my head left.

The red-headed man at the ticket counter perched on a stool, looking my way, though it was possible he was merely staring into space, which is what I hoped. His eyes looked ironed flat, like his IQ might be in the double-digits, like sitting here might be the only job he would have in his life. I hoped he wasn't watching me, worrying I might cry, wondering what to say. He wouldn't have missed the empty clang of the coins rattling down the chute. I suspected he saw countless sad stories unfold in the bus station, and I suddenly understood that mine wasn't even the saddest. Thinking that made me more pitiful, more embarrassed, and then he dipped his head and flipped over a page of comics in his newspaper with a soft rustle.

I didn't blame him. I looked like a loser. I had abandoned them, all of them—my sister, my mother, Janey, Janey's pothead brother who smashed up the Pinto two days before I went to Chicago, the teachers who wanted to help me, my uncle, even this dumb ticket man staring blankly at his paper—and how dare I think that after leaving them as I had, that I could return anytime I wanted. There was no one to call. There was no one here.

The ticket man said, "Next bus heading to Chicago pulls in at twelve-oh-seven roundabouts." He spoke loudly, as if making a scheduled announcement to the room, eyes directed upwards, at the wall clock.

I nodded, appreciative of this sliver of kindness, and slumped deep into a bucket seat, backpack on the floor, straps tangled in my feet. I wanted to kick it hard across the room. Maybe I misdialed, or maybe they were in the bathroom or down in the basement where there was no extension. Maybe the phone company had an outage for a minute. I thought about trying again. Because where would they be? We always had Thanksgiving at home; there were out-of-town aunts and uncles and cousins who came, but they came to us, not the other way. I jumped up, hurried back to the phone, the man's eyes tracking me.

The coins were poised at the slot, and I let them go. Chink, clink, and that catch of the dial tone. I punched each number deliberately, pausing after the confirming beep, the random pattern of these numbers carved into my memory. I closed my eyes and listened to the ring.

There were two phones in that house, one mounted on the kitchen wall, crossing over the seam where the stripes didn't match. That phone was dull yellow, with a short cord, so you had to sit at the close chair of the kitchen table. Anyone heard what you said when you talked on this phone. The other phone was upstairs in my parents' bedroom; it was no-nonsense black and heavy and sat in the middle of my father's nightstand. A coil of thin cord attached it to the wall, and when you were feeling brave, you could grab that phone and let the cord snake behind as you walked into the bathroom, where you could balance on the edge of the tub for a halfway-private conversation, until he or my mother hollered to hang up already, or someone needed the bathroom, or you imagined you heard the slow creep of footsteps edging the door. That phone gave the illusion of privacy, but it wasn't private. That was the phone my father called my uncle on, threatening to sic his old high school buddy the cop if he ever came around again. "Or maybe I'll kill you myself," he said with slow, practiced calm, "depending on the mood you catch me in." That was the phone my mother used to call my uncle and arrange to meet at First National Bank downtown so she could withdraw money from my little sister's savings account so he could make rent. The day before I ran off to Chicago, I called my uncle on that phone, needing to tell him I was fine, that I was fine, that they said everything worked out fine, though he had no idea why I wouldn't be fine, but some girl named Sandy said my uncle had hitched to New York or New Orleans or somewhere last week and skipped out on rent again and could I— which is when I hung up.

Those were the two phones in my family's three-bedroom, one-and-a-half bath house with its unfinished basement and the lilac bushes in the back yard and roses in the front and a tree with acorns by the old blue swingset. But what color were my bedroom walls and was it apples or lemons on the kitchen floor mat in front of the sink and what brand of soap in the shower? My heartbeat zoomed fast, faster, and ragged breath tore out of my lungs. I thought I would know those things forever.

They had left me, and so I was alone now, away and free, and yes, that was what I wanted, yes, yes—that was what I spent my whole life wanting, the one thing. But not like this. Not this.

In a rush I remembered: mint green, apples, Ivory. I remembered it all, and how dare it feel beautiful: the frayed buttonholes of my uncle's jean jacket; the blonde fuzz fringing Janey's pothead brother's chin; the effervescent blue of water lapping across Mercer pool; Janey's glittery pink headband; and my little sister drawing pages of pointy-roofed houses flanked by four figures holding hands and a spotted dog, a dandelion-yellow sun shining down from the upper left corner, pictures my father stacked in a pile on his nightstand.

I opened my eyes. I hung up the phone.

I took my coins, dug out the last few from my backpack, and plunked them down the vending machine and ate six packages of peanut-butter crackers for Thanksgiving dinner, and waited for the bus to Chicago. The man at the ticket counter dozed over his newspaper, chin bobbing above his chest, a light snore now and again. The sleet storm clawed at the large windows overlooking the empty bus bay. I thought about telling this to my friend Jess, my mother's stuffing recipe, Frank Sinatra, the four of us linking hands around the table covered with the embroidered cloth my great-grandmother brought from Luxemburg, each of us listing three things we were thankful for, the buttery crackle of turkey skin, letting my little sister win the wishbone battle, my mother dropping one of the yellow rose saucers on the floor but it miraculously not breaking, seconds and thirds on pumpkin pie, and sprawling on the living room carpet rubbing our bellies, all of us laughing at the same nothing.

I thought about my story all morning, waiting for the storm-delayed bus to drag in, and later, slumped in an aisle seat at the back next to a tattered man sniffle-shooting the snot back up his nose every two seconds, and on the el from the bus station while watching a mother half-heartedly joggle an ugly, cow-eyed baby against her shoulder as it squalled, and trudging from the el to the dorm under burned-out streetlights, kicking a dented RC can along the sidewalk; I thought about my story so hard that it became real, and I couldn't wait to tell Jess, who loved best that we were all laughing on the floor even though no one knew what was so funny.

Then Jess told me her story. It sounded about as good as mine. A great Thanksgiving, we agreed, great.

V.

And now here we are, at the end of our story. Which is where every story truly begins.

THE GENESEE TOWERS

Kelsey Ronan

IN THE MICHAEL MOORE EXHIBIT of the city history museum, Leann bit into the sandwich her mother had packed for her, watching, again, the boarded shop fronts of Downtown Flint roll across the screen. The Beach Boys sang "Wouldn't It Be Nice," flashes of *Flint Journal* headlines announced the rising lay-off numbers from General Motors, and Leann licked a smear of organic mayonnaise from her finger. She and her sister Esther weren't volunteering out of civic pride but to sidestep their father's moralizing. He was readying for re-election (Sheldon Williams, City Council, 8th Ward), and they knew that when he found them on the Adirondack chairs flipping through *Seventeen* he'd lecture endlessly about gratitude and privilege and remind them that he intended to run for mayor after this term and that they were the potential first daughters of Flint. So Esther manned the gift shop cash register and Leann roamed the exhibits, making sure the nonexistent patrons weren't touching anything. Their boss, Mrs. Nichols, stayed in her office "archiving" until someone was willing to fork over the extra bucks for a guided tour.

Leann balled up the empty Ziplock bag and left the dark room where *Roger and Me* played in a constant loop. She passed the 1913 Chevy Classic, the '47 Fleetmaster, the '57 Riviera coupe, the '77 Phantom. She passed the wheels from the first carriage factories, picket signs from the 1937 Sit-Down Strike, pictures of the tanks that rolled off the assembly lines during WWII. She passed empty Paramount Potato Chip canisters and Vernors bottles spilling out of Hamady Brothers sacks like a Thanksgiving cornucopia. She found Esther frowning at the computer behind a spinning rack of postcards. *Greetings from the Vehicle City.*

"Excuse me, Miss," Leann said in her white lady impersonation, her voice flattened to a nasal honk. "I think someone drove off with the Centurion."

"I'll alert my superior," Esther murmured. On her computer screen, a white girl and an Asian girl walked over a leaf-strewn yard in matching sweatshirts. In the fall Esther was beginning her senior year, and she was preoccupied with imagining herself at college among various columns and leaf piles and diversity statistics.

"Where is the boss anyway? Seen her?" Leann propped her elbows onto the counter.

Esther shook her head. At the dinner table their parents had been lamenting a recent statistic claiming Flint had the country's highest per capita murder rate, and Leann had a theory Mrs. Nichols was in the basement "archiving" a collection of firearms for the *Flint 2010* exhibition.

"You're the most boring person on Earth, by the way," Leann informed her sister, watching her scroll. "There must be a scholarship you can get for that."

Esther sighed. "*C'mon*, LeeLee, can't you go learn something?"

"Nerd," Leann muttered under her breath and returned to *Roger & Me* just as the evicted family, circa 1988, hauled out a Christmas tree, tinsel sagging toward the snow. Her father believed Moore was a shameless opportunist, cashing in on vulnerable people, and would have been furious to find her watching it. She thought of this with satisfaction as she kicked off her sandals and unwrapped a chocolate bar she'd stashed behind the television to soften it in the electronic heat.

Lost in the eternal *Roger & Me* noise, she failed to hear the click of Mrs. Nichols' loafers. When she did hear the sharp "What are you doing, Leann?" she knew it was all over: mouthful of contraband, bare toes flexing on the floor. She blinked back at Mrs. Nichols, whose eyes were narrowed to slits behind her chunky glasses.

Leann walked back to the gift shop, where Esther was still considering mascots and steepled buildings.

"I need a ride," she announced. "I got voluntold to leave."

Their mother called them down to the kitchen. Esther had broken the news of Leann's firing while her mom ran on the treadmill. "Maybe it won't be a big deal," Esther said. "She didn't even stop jogging." Now, back out of her spandex, their mother was sitting at the kitchen table with her hands clasped. Their father was beside her, arms crossed over his chest. He was still in his suit, the collar pinching into his puffy neck, his bald pate shining in the kitchen light.

"Sit down," he commanded. From years of Take Your Daughter to Work Days and public access clips, the girls knew when their father was ready to lacerate someone, the way his words were issued slow and precise.

"Tell me, Leann, how useless do you have to be to make a person turn down your free labor? And do you recognize how poorly this reflects on your mother and me? Or your sister, for that matter?"

Leann gave him the same apathetic shrug she'd given Mrs. Nichols. Behind her, Esther shrank into the doorframe.

"Well?" he said.

Leann held his gaze, her chin slightly stuck out. They stared at each other a few seconds more before their father dismissed them. "Let me know when you have an answer, Leann."

"We look fat as hell," Leann said.

Sheldon Williams had draped his daughters in baggy Re-Elect Williams 2010 T-shirts and forced them out to walk the blocks of the 8th Ward. They curled flyers into storm doors and under wiper blades. Like Jehovah's Witness kids set on the streets to win souls, they skirted sprinklers, confronted angry dogs, and called greetings into screen doors. "Vote Williams for Flint's future!" they called in unison. Leann twisted and knotted the excess fabric to hold the shirt tighter to her body. She wore nail polish the exact Williams 2010 maroon and reapplied lip gloss every few blocks.

"We look fat as hell and it's like a million degrees."

"We have four more blocks," Esther said. "Dad said we just had to make it to the park."

Leann dropped to the curb and pressed her back against a stop sign pole. The houses here were pressed closer together, the yards littered with dog shit and abandoned toys. A gaggle of ten-year-olds were playing basketball on a hoop they'd dragged to the street. An old woman watering her flowers yelled back, "Do your mothers know you're out on the street with that dirty talk?"

"Thank Jesus," Leann said, catching the rising chimes of "Camptown Races" as an ice cream truck crept around the block.

"Can't we just get this over with?" Esther groaned.

"Union break," Leann said and stepped forward to order, leaning into the cool of the van.

Esther peeled the top off her push-up. "So I was looking at schools in Chicago. Wouldn't that be cool, to live in Chicago?"

Leann shrugged. Branded with their grandmothers' old lady names in a sea of Shakishas and Jasmines, she and her sister had formed a collective, an *us*. They dropped a double negative here and there, left the Gs off verbs, tried out the *N* word that launched their father into Malcolm X-inspired tirades, but they always sounded too self-conscious, unnatural. They cowered with embarrassment when their parents showed up for conferences and spelling bees—too well-dressed, too old. They fought hard through a cultivated indifference not to be called *stuck-up* or *bougie*, and suspected they resisted torment because God had spared them glasses, braces, and chubbiness—but they relied solely on each other. Now that Esther was applying to colleges, she expected her sister would join her the following year. She approached the applications like a negotiation. Leann, though, couldn't bring herself to care.

"Go where you want," Leann shrugged, nipping off some of the nuts studding her Choco Taco.

"I wish you hadn't screwed up the thing at the museum. Colleges look at community service and that sort of thing."

"Community service," Leann repeated, gnawing into the waffle shell, "Is what they give convicts."

They finished their ice cream in silence. Leann stood and stuffed a wad of pamphlets into the sewer grates. "Vote Williams for Flint's Future, raccoons!"

The boys howled behind them, the basketball thudding off the backboard. "Shit!" one of them yelled. The sisters rounded the corner as the old woman with the hose demanded he go get his mother. "I want to tell her myself you're ruining this neighborhood!"

Esther asked their father if she could spend the rest of the summer interning at City Hall. She followed him through the rounds of neighborhood association meetings, press interviews, and Saturday morning community clean-ups. Leann was unmoved by Esther's new business attire and smug looks, but felt vaguely betrayed by her shift in allegiances and was bored with her new solitude.

"We'll find you something else to do," their mother consoled Leann as she dropped her off at the mall again.

Opportunity presented itself when a boy in a hat and apron was walking through the Macy's wing with a tray of orange chicken samples. "Wanna try?" he offered. He was older than her, and a tattoo star on his bicep rippled slightly when he held the tray out between them. Leann ate three pieces, collecting the toothpicks in her palm. When he said, "I think we're looking for somebody. You need a job?" she shrugged and followed him up the escalator. She went home with a new pair of pink flats, an apron draped over her arm, and Ajay's number dialed into her phone.

At dinner, their father announced that Esther's first assignment at City Hall was to review the Genesee Towers case. It was a nineteen-story block of concrete, half parking garage, half office building, the tallest building in Genesee County. Pieces of it had begun to fall to the sidewalk below and the streets around it were blocked off. A legal battle had escalated between the city and the owner, until the landlord won and the city was left with a $2 million bill.

"The City's appealing the case to the Michigan Supreme Court," he said, angrily spearing a piece of goat cheese in his salad. "The criminal left for New York City and insists the building shouldn't have been condemned. Meanwhile the thing's a giant hazard. The bus station's just across the street, for God's sake. Seniors and children walking under it all day."

"We're going to have to fight him," Esther agreed. No one noticed or cared when Leann fluttered a hand to her heart and theatrically mimed her "*we*."

"It's absurd what people think they can get away with," her father continued. "People just think there'll always be someone else to come along and clean up the mess."

Leann thought it was an opportune time to announce that, as of tomorrow, she would be serving the good citizens of Flint at the Golden Wok.

"So now I'm working too," she added and ignored her sister's glare.

"Honey," her mother said, eyebrows arched. "The food court? You're sure this is what you want to do?"

Their father said nothing, and Leann stared at him, waiting for him to acknowledge that she, too, was a *productive member of the community*.

"You'll be so cute in an apron," Esther said. "You get a name tag, too?" She was wearing one of her new collared shirts and a black pencil skirt that Leann had already guffawed at, telling her sister she looked like a flight attendant.

"Shut up, American Airlines." Leann returned smugly to her meal.

When she got her name tag, she requested it say LeeLee rather than Leann. Her hoop earrings swung beneath a baseball hat with an embroidered panda pulling bamboo from a wok. Ajay grinned at her over steaming trays of white rice and sweet and sour chicken. "Quit playing," she said when he rotated the bill of her hat or pulled the bow of her apron she'd tied as tightly as she could to carve a waist out of the baggy uniform. She watched over her shoulder as he went out on lunch break, slumped in a booth with a plate of crab Rangoon, pulling apart the stars of fried dough. Isabel, who worked the counter with her, scowled and asked, "You know he's like twenty-two, right?"

Ajay kissed her for the first time after the restaurant closed, cleaning out the deep fryer. On a break, they sat out on the loading dock by the dumpsters. It was chilly—a storm had blown in during the afternoon, sweeping out a spell of ninety-degree days—and when she hugged herself, Ajay wrapped an arm around her. Leann had not been kissed since ninth grade when Trevor Mitchell pressed her against the gym wall at homecoming and stuck his Tahitian Treat-sugared tongue in her mouth. "It was terrible," she'd reported back to Esther, swearing off fruit drinks for a year. Now Ajay bent his head and Leann offered up her lips. His tongue flicked into her mouth. The birds that lived off cold French fries and half-eaten pizza slices slept in their nests in the gutters above. The security guard turned slow circles in the parking lot.

The next day the manager was gone and Ajay had the key to the supply closet. Grabbing her purse to leave on break, he waved her inside with a quick security check over his shoulder. The door bolted behind him.

They waltzed clumsily into a makeshift bed Ajay had assembled from Golden Wok polos and napkin bundles, too accustomed to their mutual spring roll smell to mind it on each other's bodies. The pain startled her, and she gripped fistfuls of his shirt until it subsided.

Through the rest of her shift she imagined how she'd describe it to Esther. Ajay's tattoo that marked him as rebellious and desirable. The muscles flexing under his shirt. Not how the back of her head knocked against an open box of fortune cookies, but how he had groaned "You know I wanted you," with his mouth hot against her ear. Not how she'd spent the rest of her shift uncomfortably wet and worrying that Isobel, side-eyeing her from the soda fountain, knew exactly what had happened, but how Ajay smirked at her conspiratorially with each superfluous check if they had enough napkins and fortune cookies at the counter, and how, probably, he was in love with her.

Leann had her chance as soon as she came home: their parents were at a charity dinner and Esther was in her bedroom with her laptop and stacks of binder-clipped documents detailing the saga of Genesee Towers. Leann sat cross-legged on the rug and gave her sister the details precisely as she'd rehearsed them while she ladled lo mein. She stressed how cute Ajay was. How cool. How much older.

But Esther was not surprised or impressed, did not gasp for more details or emit any sisterly squeals. She screwed up her face and said, "A cook? You lost it to a *cook*?"

Leann's heartbeat accelerated, quick and heavy. "What's wrong with that?" she snapped. "You too good for food now, too?"

Esther held her grimace. "God, Lee, how old *is* he?"

"Have fun at City Hall," Leann said and heaved herself from the rug. "Jealous-ass virgin." She locked herself in the bathroom and stood trembling in the shower until Esther rapped on the door and yelled that she had to brush her teeth.

While Leann was slopping fried rice onto plastic plates and having sex in storage closets, the Supreme Court dismissed the case, meaning Flint would have to pay for Genesee Towers as well as the owner's court costs and ten years of interest. The final number neared $8 million. An emergency property tax would be necessary to gather the money, a percentage of the building paid for by each Flint home-owner. Sheldon and Esther stayed at City Hall later and came home with twin scowls. People were angry. Letters and emails flooded the *Flint Journal* and the mayor's office. Councilman Williams's daughter helped take the endless calls from constituents demanding to know what they were going to pay and how they were supposed to afford it.

"It's a hell of a time for an election," he said, over and over, shaking his head. "Here's a big goddamn tax grab. Vote Williams."

Esther followed her father to UAW halls and church basements, where he explained to his constituents that they would see an additional percentage on their fall property taxes. In the worst neighborhoods, $20, $50 maybe. In the last struggling middle class neighborhoods, a few hundred dollars. In the Williams's own neighborhood along the golf course, several hundred.

Most of Esther's and Leann's communications consisted of barbed insults in passing. "How's your new boyfriend?" Esther would say. "What's it like kissing Dad's ass as a full time job?" Leann would respond. But she couldn't help noticing how wilted Esther looked coming home behind their father, kicking her heels off at the front door.

There were rumors, Leann's mother told her as she dropped her off at the mall, that the state would be appointing an Emergency Financial Manager to the city. "Your father might be kept on as an advisor," she said, "But there would be no power in the council anymore. If he decides to run for mayor, it wouldn't look good that he was part of this administration."

Leann nodded. She sat there for a moment with her mother's worry, watching cars pull in and out of spaces. More and more she felt cast off from the family by her inability to see their father as a crusader battling to right all the wrongs. As Leann saw it, her father's dream was to turn Flint into one big dinner table that he could sit at the head of, forcing flavorless food on them and telling them why they should be grateful to be choking it down. "I gotta go," she said finally and hurried up to the Golden Wok.

In the storage closet that afternoon, watching Ajay step back into his jeans, Leann had asked why he never took her anywhere. He'd smirked and asked where she wanted to go.

"I don't know." She had shrugged self-consciously and applied a few more coats of lip gloss than were necessary, smacking her lips until she could taste the chemical peach.

"Wait for me when you get off," he'd said, walking out with a case of fortune cookies under his arm.

Ajay took her to see his friend Israel, who lived downtown in a duplex a few blocks from the bus station. "Israel's an artist," Ajay told her in the car. "You like people like that?" She said she guessed so. Ajay parked at the curb and told her to carry the Styrofoam containers of sesame chicken and fried rice.

Israel had glasses he kept pushing up the slope of his nose. "This is LeeLee," Ajay said as he moved past Israel into the small kitchen, dropping the bags onto a table scattered over with papers and dirty paper plates. Israel nodded. They followed him to a couch, a particle board coffee table with rolling papers and a baggie of weed.

"I got some sweet new pictures," Israel said. His head was tilted back, his short braids spilling over the upholstery.

"Don't show her, man, her dad's on City Council," Ajay grinned. "Get your stupid ass arrested."

"No shit." Israel looked at her.

"It's fine," she waved a dismissive hand. "I'm not like that."

Israel laughed at her and stood. "Good to know," he said. "You wouldn't want to be like *that*."

"Israel's a fucking criminal," Ajay said to Leann, and Israel's laughter echoed back to them from another room. He returned, handing her an open laptop. "Better promise not to tell your dad," he said.

She scrolled through images of naked elevator shafts, spilling open into art deco ballrooms with peeling gold wallpaper. "The Durant Hotel," Israel said, jabbing the screen as it filled with a portrait of a dead rat bloated on the filthy tiles. "And that's the Capitol Theater," he said when they got to the photographs of chandeliers and gilded ceilings, velvet upholstery worn threadbare. Lowell Elementary, where the doors had been ripped off the hinges, ceramic fountains broken to shards. All the empty buildings her father fretted over at the dinner table.

"I like your aesthetic," Leann said. Israel snickered.

She thought of the museum, how she and Esther had joked about the *Flint 2010* exhibit. She imagined Israel's pictures lining the walls of the museum, the exhibition lights reflecting off the polished grills of all those old cars and casting ghostly shadows onto Israel's pictures.

"What's this?" she asked, pointing to a picture of a wall of frosted glass, tattooed in bubble-lettered nicknames and fuck yous.

"The Genesee Towers," Israel said. "I got in there a couple weeks ago but the light was too shitty to do much. I need to go back."

Ajay nuzzled into her. She could feel his lips spreading into a smile against her neck, the prickle of stubble above his lip. "You wanna picnic in the Genesee Towers, boo?" he asked her.

Israel knew the way to get in; a busted window in the alley clear enough to crawl through. Ajay helped lift her in. The bottom floors were a parking garage, the dark magnifying their emptiness. They walked up the ramps, past gang tags and spray-painted faces with watching eyes. She sought Ajay's hand and he laughed at her. "We playing boyfriend-girlfriend?" he asked.

Her hand fell loose and sweaty at her side. She thought of her father at the dinner table, her sister in her career outfits. The statistics they rattled off, her father's angry face rising above all the salad bowls and dinner plates. A city of incompetent, foolish people. Everything in need of fixing, tearing down, making right again.

They made it up to the office floors and looked out at the city below: the neon bar signs, the buses weaving in and out of the station. Then she heard the zoom on the camera. "Look at me," Israel said. It took her a moment to realize he was talking to her. She turned to face the dark eye of his lens, the flare of the flash. He followed her across empty rooms, snapping photos at her back. LeeLee climbing the stairs. LeeLee among the ruins. "You're not going to show these to anyone, right?" she asked. She was relieved when he grew bored with her and wandered off.

Ajay came up behind her, his hands sliding over her stomach, slipping down to the crotch of her jeans. Israel had gone downstairs to shoot more of the parking garage, he told her. She turned, full of the things she was going to say to him, like what did he mean about playing boyfriend-girlfriend, and didn't he like her, but he pressed his mouth to hers before she could, and his hands were sliding up her Golden Wok polo.

"Not on this floor," she said, turning from him.

"We can stand," he murmured into her neck, and she let him. Already she was thinking that this was the last time, that she would tell him to take her home and that she would never step foot into the mall again, not even with her mother, not even with Esther, and then she heard Israel hiss, "Jay. Cop's downstairs."

Israel bolted, Ajay following. Leann called after him, hooking her bra. Unsure where to go, she stayed in the room, breathing quietly against the window until she could see the policeman swing back into the patrol car at the curb. Ajay and Israel, she knew, were long gone; she didn't bother looking for them as she moved back down the stairs and found her way back out of the building.

Across the street at the bus station, men were gathered in front of the statue of Rosa Parks, laughing. On the benches in the middle of the concourse women sat with their shopping bags, or half-watching their children, half-watching Dr. Oz. The buses were nosed up to the sliding doors.

"Which of these buses go down Miller Road?" she asked the woman at the information desk. Behind the thick pane of glass, with her chunky gold earrings and sour mouth, the woman looked regally bored. A calendar behind her showed a tropical beach scene, a palm tree leaning over an endless expanse of golden sand.

Whatever the woman answered was lost in the noise, the PA system announcing that buses would be departing in five minutes.

"Can you repeat that?" Leann strained toward the glass.

The woman sighed and held up three fingers. Leann turned and found the crowd waiting outside the terminal.

"Where you trying to go?" a man asked her. He was holding an empty pop bottle and watching her with loose, swimming eyes.

"Home," she said stiffly, and looked away. She watched a mother resituate the toddler on her hip, watched the child look around the concourse and screw its face up to cry.

"Where you stay at?" the man wanted to know. He twisted his hands around and around the bottle.

"At my house."

The man laughed and grinned at her. "You got a man?" he asked. She wished it was so much earlier, that she could have walked up Saginaw Street to City Hall and asked the secretary to call her father. She hadn't been in the office since she was a little girl when on half-days her mother would sometimes take Leann and Esther to see him on his lunch hour. A break from his important world of memo-bearing secretaries and phone calls from constituents wanting to know why their city wasn't better. Leann turned her back on the man, staring hard at the cardboard advertisements for pop and cigarettes at the station convenience store, trying not to cry

"Stuck up bitch," the man sneered, his face veering close to spit the words in her ear before he walked away. The terminal door hissed open and the PA system announced that buses were now loading.

Leann sat alone in the back, her head tilted against the window. A girl in a fast food uniform stared moodily out the window, her hair stuffed into her cap. She could've been a hundred teenage girls Leann had sat in classes with, or had met on the other side of storm doors while she held up her father's propaganda.

Unsure where to get off, Leann pressed the button once the houses were familiar, bigger and farther apart. She walked down the road while the streetlights came on around her. She turned into her parents' subdivision, twisting around the wide lawns and long driveways. Dogs barked at her behind invisible fences. Across the golf course the truck plant, one of the city's last factories, exhaled smoke from its hundred white smokestacks.

When she came in Esther glanced up at her. "Tell me if this sounds right," she said. "Dad said I should write a letter to the editor about the Genesee Towers. The building represents the failures of the mayor's inept administration. Is that too much?"

Leann dropped to the couch, curling fetal. She watched Esther hunch over her laptop.

"I'm quitting that job," she said. She felt Esther's gaze swing toward her, and she closed her eyes.

*

Leann went with Esther to the Mott Park Neighborhood Association meeting. She wore a pretty top and a skirt she borrowed from her sister. They distributed pamphlets to the concerned citizens settling into the collapsible chairs in the basement of a Baptist church, clutching their Styrofoam coffee cups and snickerdoodles brought by an old woman who introduced herself as Bev from Cartier. "How nice of you girls to come," she said and watched with satisfaction while they bit into the cookies. "These are wonderful, ma'am," Esther said, and Leann marveled at the voice that came out of her sister. How much older it sounded.

They sat in the back and watched their father in his suit. Esther took notes on a yellow legal pad. Leann picked at the excess material of her sister's skirt, a size too big. Their father explained how the emergency tax would be calculated. "I know how hard you work to pay your bills," their father said. "I know this is asking a lot. But believe that this is a step toward progress."

He stopped to survey the room. He drew a deep breath and said he'd be happy to take questions.

Their father gestured to an older man at the back in a baseball cap. He stood and introduced himself as Jim from Monteith Street. "What plans does the city have for the structure?" Jim wanted to know.

Their father paused a moment. "Well," he sighed wearily. "I guess everyone will get a room that they can decorate however they want."

The people of the Mott Park Neighborhood Association laughed. But Leann knew he didn't mean to be funny, that he was seething, furious at the ineptitude of virtually everyone he knew. "Is Dad joking?" Esther whispered.

Leann shrugged. Her father looked small and defeated. His shiny brown scalp ringed by grey hair. His shirt rumpled. He collected himself and began to discuss the options. The lot could be bulldozed, he said, a park put in its place. An offer could be made to attract developers. "This could be a pivotal moment in the revitalization of downtown. Together we'll reclaim the tallest building in the county, redefine Flint's skyline—what greater symbol of all we've striven to achieve?"

Esther returned to her notes. While her father spoke, Leann imagined a room on the nineteenth floor of the Genesee Towers, at the top of the stairwell with all its dead pigeons and broken glass. A window overlooking the sprawl of the city. She imagined herself on her knees, scrubbing away the graffiti and the grime until she could look out and see her father's city clearly.

THE LAST DAYS OF PEACE AND LOVE

Valerie Sayers

THE FIRST TIME I SAW this chick in a skin-tight micro-mini, I knew
her. She was everything my mother had spent a lifetime warning
me not to be: fishnet stockings, skirt barely covering her crotch, so
much dark eyeshadow she looked like her boyfriend had popped
her in one eye and then the other. The other typists wouldn't have
dreamed of showing that much flesh—they wanted to get home on
the subway without getting groped—but maybe this one hadn't
heard that the Sixties were over. She was on her way to the ladies'
room, thrusting her pelvis out in a kind of runway walk crossed
with a keep on truckin' slouch. When she spotted me, she gave a
little wave, as if she'd figured out who I was too.

I was an actor—I guess in those days I said actress—so I knew
how to look like I hadn't been staring. This was only a three-week
gig, at a structural engineering firm: I was the receptionist at the
front desk, answering the phone in my best Judy Holiday voice. The
typists were hidden away in back, and once I saw her, I knew why.

The Seventies were just the Sixties dribbling away: the war was
finally over, but Jean-Paul and I were still nostalgic for
demonstrations and street theatre. We spent so much time in acting
class, or posing for glossy eight-by-tens, that we hardly knew who
we were in real life. Married? What was that? Our apartment was
so small we had to wedge ourselves into the single bed Jean-Paul
brought from his parents' place.

So the next morning, when the Sixties chick stopped at the

front desk on her way in, my nerves tingled all over again. She took her sweet time and leaned over my phone console in such a seductive slouch that I wasn't even surprised when she batted her eyelashes at me. "Didn't you used to go to the Fillmore?"

"Sure," I said, "sometimes." She was certainly alarming. Now she was wearing a floral scarf in a gauzy material tied tight to form a halter. Jeez: nobody wore a halter to work in an office like this, much less a scarf pretending to be a halter. Where'd she think she was, Altamont?

"I think maybe I danced with you one time."

I gave her a noncommittal smile. Her nipples were tight little corkscrews poking through her gauzy top.

"Wanna go to lunch later?"

I couldn't afford to go to lunch—I always brought a yogurt and passed myself off as a starving artist—and I didn't know where to look when I looked at her. "Sure." I was mesmerized and besides, she was as sweet as a puppy. Her name was Lorraine Straveski. Sweet Lorraine.

When we walked out on Broad Street that noontime, Sweet Lorraine Straveski linked her arm through mine so that all the men ogling her perky breasts, bouncing along under her yellow daisy scarf, had to glance at me too. I thought I was playing a grown-up— I had on a thrift-store Christian Dior jacket—but next to her I probably looked like a nun. Her crazy ringlets were streaked with gaudy yellow, and my mother would have pointed to her dark roots as the definitive evidence: she was a slut, all right.

Somehow Sweet Lorraine picked up the mother-vibes right away. At lunch the first thing she said was, "What's the worst way your mother ever humiliated you?" and I was so freaked by her mind-reading that I drew a blank. I wasn't a big confider, the kind of instant-girlfriend who could tell the story of my life to someone I'd just met. She had mossy green eyes, lined with brilliant blue, and teeth that protruded ever so slightly. When she took out her aviator glasses to read the menu, I could see her at forty, ruling the typing roost in a peekaboo blouse. If I really wanted to tell her the worst thing my mother did, I'd tell how she wouldn't let me visit when my father was diagnosed with lung cancer because I was living in sin.

"Let's see. She used to come tearing down the driveway when my boyfriends brought me home late." I heard myself giggle.

"Ha," she said, just like that: ha. "Mine took my favorite bikini and shredded it with her toenail scissors. Her toenail scissors."

I liked her. My family tensed at touch—my brother was ten years older and tried not to touch me at all—but when Lorraine came up behind me to knead my shoulders, I felt us both melt away. "I've got tits," she said the first time we hugged, "but you've got boobs."

When the job was over and I scored a bit part in a domestic comedy working itself out at the Playwrights Workshop, Lorraine made sure we got together on Mondays, when the theatres were dark. We went to happy hour at one Wall Street bar or the other. My girlfriends had drifted away since college—well, maybe even before then, maybe since I got married—and I liked hearing Lorraine chatter, liked the sample bottles of perfume she got from who-knows-where, liked sitting under the gaze of so many eyes, even if they were gazing at her and not at me.

She told me she didn't speak to her mother in Dayton anymore, not at all, and maybe I liked the sound of that too. Once Jean-Paul married me, my mother forgave me, but now my father was dead and I was nineteen-and-married and I wasn't so sure I forgave her. Lorraine said Oscar, her shrink, advised her to cut her mother off cold. What kind of shrink would advise such a thing? She said Oscar was SAI, for Self-Actualizing Interpersonalist, and all her roommates were too. They all lived in single-sex apartments and slept with each other as often and variously as possible so they didn't get "y'know, all hung up on somebody." We were in a smoky bar when she told me about sleeping with as many guys as possible and then blew Marlboro rings, wondering whether she'd shocked me.

I put on my Jeanne Moreau face and aimed for unshockable. "SAI guys?"

"Mostly. Once I had, like, three dates in one night? And I put in my spare diaphragm by accident? I mean, on top of the other one. Six months later I go to the E.R. and they tell me it's like a petri dish in there."

"Oh man." I probably blanched. OK, so I was no Jeanne Moreau. No matter how much sex talk you heard back then, somebody was always upping the ante: I mean, the whole concept of a Sexual Revolution was still pretty new to me. I'd slept with a few too many boys before Jean-Paul, but how many guys could you fit in by nineteen? This talk of back-to-back men was like news from an exotic country I'd never get the chance to visit now.

"So what do you think?"

I thought this SAI thing was like Amway or Scientology, and Lorraine needed to find new members. I smiled mysteriously. I had about twenty-five smiles in my repertoire: this one was my Jeanne Moreau special.

After a while, Lorraine started slipping complaints about the Self-Actualizing Interpersonalists into our Monday nights. They made her feel like shit for skipping out on college. They were always telling her how much she didn't know. They picked on her at their weekly critiques. She made life among the SAIs sound like Vietnamese re-education camp.

One night, she lowered her voice as if there might be self-actualizing spies all around us. "I have to get out of that apartment. It's just, like, where do I go?" She looked as miserable as I'd ever seen her. Jean-Paul and I had just rented one of those huge apartments off West End Avenue and the only way we could afford it was to get roommates, but I hadn't mentioned the move to Lorraine—I could imagine doing all kinds of things with Lorraine, but living with her wasn't one of them.

She drummed her fingers on the table hard enough to make my ice clink. "Oscar says yeah, move out, but that's only cause he wants to get his hands on me."

How did a typist pay for a shrink, anyway? And how about Oscar getting his hands on her? Was that literal? It was enough to bring out my own maternal side, and the Kahlúa—Lorraine's drink—brought out my bad judgment. I told her about our apartment after all.

"Yeah?" She did her best not to look too eager. "A commune? Is it gonna be, like, political?"

"I guess we're mostly looking for company." It finally occurred to me—I can be a little slow in the insight department—that I hadn't mentioned it before because of course Jean-Paul would look at her the way every other man did.

"I can't believe it! It's like the answer to my prayers."

Somehow I couldn't imagine Lorraine praying among her interpersonalists, and I had a bad feeling. How could Jean-Paul help looking at her the way every other man did?

I hadn't lied to Lorraine: Our ersatz commune wasn't political in the least. We had a freelance (meaning unemployed) journalist, a snarky MFA poet back in the maid's room, and an Oh wow sociology grad student we called Sosh in the dining room. You had to pass in and out of his room to get to the kitchen, but Sosh said: "Hey now, good people, I sincerely enjoy interacting with you on a regular basis."

Anyway, aside from disturbing Sosh's studying on our way to make a cup of tea, there wasn't any interacting. Lorraine asked about house meetings, like the ones the Self-Actualizing Interpersonalists had, but we weren't the meeting type of commune, either. We had three bedrooms on the other side of the dining room: us, the journalist, and now Lorraine. We could go for days without laying eyes on anyone but Sosh.

The first week she moved in, Lorraine knocked on everybody's door and offered up a joint. Nights, a string of boyfriends came to see her. If the guy went home early she stood in our doorway, semi-clothed and reeking of sex, asking us in that bouncy Midwestern way if we'd gone on any auditions. "Meet any famous people today, guys?" She thrust out her bony pelvis while she looked at Jean-Paul with a Here I am in the next bedroom look. Once she actually stroked her own nipple, right through her camisole, and we both stared in fascination.

When I pointed out that she was trying to seduce him, Jean-Paul said: "No more than she's trying to seduce you." Well, yeah, I told him, I knew what she was doing with the shoulder-kneading—even Ethel Feeney would have known what that meant.

Sweet Lorraine professed awe at my married state: "I never thought I could be OK with, you know? One person? But Jean-Paul . . . ."

I tried not to bristle. By then Jean-Paul had the lead in a new translation of *The Lower Depths* at the Desperado Theatre Cooperative (no, really), and even if Lorraine hadn't been doing her best to get him into her bed, his dubious triumph on Avenue C already had me plenty jealous. I hadn't scored a single bit part since that crappy comedy, but Jean-Paul had landed two off-off leads, in plays I loved. He was a great actor, brooding but not too, fearless about blazing away with his dark eyes. And maybe he was on the short side, but that didn't stop avant-garde directors from casting him, or women from coming on to him. It sure didn't stop Lorraine.

Jean-Paul smoked dope with her late into the night, listening the way he listened to other actors. He specialized in rescues: he'd rescued me from my mother's fury, hadn't he? Lorraine told him she'd always wanted to go college, so every few days he gave her a new book, Castaneda or Wittgenstein or Stanislavsky, and she curled up with it for a good three minutes before she abandoned it for a High Times. I lay awake till two, three, four in the morning, listening to his good deep voice in the next room, explaining Wittgenstein, rescuing her.

"Why doesn't she just take a class at the New School?"

"She needs to build up some confidence. She's got some good ideas."

"Oh yeah? Such as?"

He grinned at me in his raffish avant-garde actorly way. My mother said Jean-Paul was naïve, but I didn't think he was, not for a minute. "Anyway," he said, "maybe I can give her some good ideas."

*

One night she stood in our doorway and made an alarming screeching sound. I followed her to the bathroom, where she sat herself down on the cold tile, gestured to her closing throat, and suggested that maybe she was losing her mind. I was terrified, but I played it as if she were just being melodramatic. "Want me to call Oscar?"

She drew a finger across the throat, meaning, I guessed, that she would rather slit it than speak to Oscar. So I sat there on the edge of the tub, panicking right along with her. I hadn't understood that she was on the brink. She was always so smiley at work, so touchy-feely.

"Oscar said professional standards were guidelines." She rolled her head in an alarming way. "Do you hear that buzzing? Oh God. Is the floor tipping?"

"Does this guy even have a license?"

And she launched in again. "License! Oh, man. I'm having some trouble swallowing." She sobbed and hiccupped for a while, then slowed down and became very formal. "When I was a little kid, I couldn't ever like sit still, so my mother would strap me to the kitchen chair with belts. And like the more I struggled, the tighter she tied. Sometimes she left me in the kitchen for hours." I wasn't entirely sure whether this was a factual history—she was pretty spacey by then—or some kind of control-and-punish metaphor, but I let her talk and talk, and when she finally fell asleep on the cold tile, it was almost midnight. I tucked a towel-pillow under her head and was covering her with another towel when Sosh showed up.

"Never mind," he said, blushing. "I can hold it."

In the morning she was in her own bed, but that afternoon she waltzed into the kitchen, naked, singing "Honky Tonk Women" so slowly she sounded like a dying turntable. I stood there transfixed: her hips curved as neatly as a nice cheap bottle of Mateus. By then Sosh, who'd been reading when Lorraine passed through—that must have been a vision—stood in the doorway. Even he could see what was going on this time.

"We've got to call her people," he whispered, but we were her people now—her ersatz people—and I hadn't guessed what it would cost her to leave her other people, or what it would cost us to nurse her through this. I walked her back to her room, feeling like a hospital orderly, and got her to confess that she'd taken a whole lot of pills since she got up off the bathroom floor.

"You mean your Valium?" She didn't appear to understand the question. "Reds?" She finally settled dreamily on ludes, but that was just to make the questions stop, and anyway she didn't have a clue how many. I walked her up and down to keep her from passing out. Jean-Paul was due home any minute, so I pulled one of her silky nightgowns over her head, and that was what she was wearing under Jean-Paul's camouflage jacket when the two of us coaxed her all the way to the E.R.

We waited up all night, praying they'd check her in. But she wanted to go home, so they pumped her stomach and released her to us, her ersatz people leading her from St. Luke's through the Upper West Side in a negligee and cowboy boots, Jean-Paul's jacket barely keeping her decent.

She liked to leave her door open, so sometimes I could see her staring out, grinning in an eerie way. It unnerved me that Lorraine and I both spent so much time alone, time I spent running lines with myself for the roles I fantasized playing when I was a grande dame of the theatre: Winnie, Mother Courage, Sabina. What was I thinking? I couldn't even get a walk-on. Most of the roles I had played, even back in college, were dumb new comedies that required me to take my shirt off. Jean-Paul was out discussing inflectionless readings with avant-garde directors and I was reading Backstage as a bedtime story.

My torpor grew in inverse proportion to my sense of my future as an actor. I could make them sit up if they let me play the whole scene, but lately their eyes glazed over before I even started to read. Once I'd seen Lorraine's slinky body naked, I found my own boobs maternal, though up till then I'd kind of believed they were the assets Jean-Paul joked about. I couldn't even afford classes anymore. The temp jobs were drying up.

The air on W. 100th Street started to smell rancid, fetid. Inside, it was Lorraine's smells that got to me: Kahlúa and dope and Marlboros, Shalimar and damp rayon panties. She'd quit typing and found a gig hostessing downtown: the way she went off to work now, in lowcut black, I figured it was a dicey lounge, maybe a strip joint. She stumbled into the living room with strange guys, mostly just business guys out tomcatting, but every once in a while a biker or a hardcore stoner. We all started locking up our possessions. Finally, when the last stoner stayed for three days and poked around the whole apartment, we convened an official ersatz commune meeting.

We all sat in Sosh's room on crates, bummed and silent. After a long while the journalist said: "We don't want to, uhm, interfere with your private life but we really don't like so many strangers coming in." He didn't even look at her. Lorraine was smoking a fat joint, blitzed out of her mind for a meeting she knew was called on her account, but after the journalist her head hung low.

"We just want to make sure you're all right," Sosh said in his gentle unironic way. "We're worried about you." Lorraine looked up—she made eye contact with me first, then Jean-Paul—and beamed a betrayed smile around the room before she rose.

In a while we heard the shower running and the sound of her singing "Gimme Shelter." I pictured her in there slitting her wrists, but she came out wearing lowcut black and smelling of Shalimar, and off she went off to work, same as always. We heard her coming in, alone, sometime before dawn.

I developed such an aversion to the sound of Lorraine's singing, the sight of her stroking herself, that I began scurrying away whenever she was home, but one morning she showed up in my doorway, wearing a man's unbuttoned dress shirt. I gave her my fake friendly Judy Garland smile. It was hard to believe we'd ever been friends, but she was still running her hands down her hips as if to say, Well, if you won't give me a hug I'll just have to do it myself.

"Guess what? I'm dating a record producer," she breathed. Did she think we were still two hippie chicks sharing boyfriend stories?

"That's great." Even I could hear the chill in my I-do-not-want-to-be-having-this-conversation voice, and Lorraine heard it for sure. Before I slipped past her, she got even.

"I just hope Jean-Paul doesn't get upset when he hears about it."

What else could she mean? It was what I'd been suspecting for months, but for the first time I gave her a hint of my fury: I slammed our door as hard as I could, and then I turned the lock we had installed against her stoners. It gave a cold click, but I could still smell her standing there, warm from her bed. Did they meet after curtain and get a room? Have hot and heavy quickies in the kitchen? Through the door I heard her say, in a voice from some bad trip: "It's not like he pays me."

THE SLUT. Jean-Paul and I had never once discussed fidelity. It seemed, I don't know, uncool: his folks were French. We were children of the sexual revolution. Love the one you're with! We'd always treated marriage as a big fat joke: a joke like living in an ersatz commune to cut down on the rent, to cut down on the strange loneliness of living with another person. I thought about it all the time, didn't I, what it would be like to give off available vibes to directors who saw me walk into the room with my cheap wedding band and stopped listening then and there. I could hardly breathe. Oh sweet Jesus. Had she been turning tricks in this apartment? Were all those skeevy men johns?

I did my deep-breathing warm-ups for as long as I could focus—about twelve seconds—and then I fell face-down on the bed. After a beat, I crawled up and grabbed a jacket. Let her come after me if she dared. In the elevator, I pounded the panel till the whole car jumped. Outside, I had no idea where I was going, but I turned south on scuzzy Broadway. Every panhandler and junkie and crazy I met set off my mother's voice: The city! Believe me, the filth and degradation will get old fast. And in the other ear, Lorraine: I hope Jean-Paul doesn't get. . . .

I tramped my filthy degraded city all afternoon long. By the time I turned west, I was nursing a blister and the winter sun was setting over the Hudson. My fury wasn't spent, exactly, but it had transformed itself into the same kind of detachment I could work myself into before a performance. On the elevator I recited the lines I would say to Lorraine, because even after all my hours of walking I still hadn't worked out what I would say to Jean-Paul.

But when I let myself in, the apartment had a weird empty vibe: no perfume or dope or incense, no light above Sosh's desk. I retreated to our room and lay on our bed, practicing how calmly we would work out who got stuck with the ersatz commune and who had to move out—we'd both signed the lease. In a terrifying flash I saw myself back in my old bedroom, my mother's holy cards tucked into every mirror. I must have drifted off finally.

I woke to the weight of Jean-Paul's hand on my back and the thick sweet smell of his breath floating toward me: Kahlúa. "Feeney, you awake?"

I didn't know whether I was awake, or where I was, or why Jean-Paul was giving me a blow-by-blow of some adventure he'd had with Sosh: a baseball bat, a doorman, a sprint from East Village to West. "Where've you been?"

He laughed into my ear. "Decking Lorraine's pimp."

The strangeness of that, or maybe the sweet puff of his laughter fluttering in my eardrum, had a curious effect: I fell back into a skittering sleep, and dreamed of Lorraine, that slut my mother had always warned me I might become. She paraded past me in tattered fishnet stockings, in red satin bustiers, in nothing but her corkscrew nipples. Sweet Lorraine: not just a slut but a whore, and not a metaphorical whore but a real live whore, the only whore I was likely to ever meet. She lived with me! She was my friend! Or once upon a time she had been my friend. I could feel her hand on my shoulder, where Jean-Paul's rested.

"Sosh said he'd get her money. . . . just riding shotgun. . . ." He still sounded euphoric.

Jean-Paul rode shotgun in a mobster's sedan. It was a lucid dream: I must have drifted off again, which made its own kind of sense. I'd been drifting off for the last six months, hadn't I, floating along on the little-enough money Jean-Paul made loading trucks, not sure how much he resented carrying me, or being married to me for that matter. I'd locked my dreamy self into a lonely bedroom in a lonely apartment in a dirty degraded city where your last girlfriend turned tricks.

In the morning I didn't even know if I'd dreamed the story or Jean-Paul had told it in voiceover, but in my sleep I'd learned it by heart. The pimp was only a kid from Brooklyn with a braid down his back. He'd sized up Jean-Paul and Sosh and laughed in their faces. When Sosh demanded Lorraine's money and the guy came at them, Jean-Paul summoned his stage fight training and landed a sucker punch. Then, having destroyed Lorraine's livelihood, they hightailed it out of there and ran all the way to the Lion's Head, where they drank themselves silly on her sweet drink.

That was the story. It could have happened, or parts of it could have happened. And I could have dreamed it, and Jean-Paul could have made it up. In the early light he drooled onto his pillow. I remembered one of his lines for sure: She'd show up at the Hilton and let some accountant from Cleveland handcuff her to the bed. I stared down at my husband—husband—and imagined asking him the true story. I'd watched her stroke her nipple. I knew I'd never ask.

He sensed me and stirred miserably in his own dreams. The Rescuer. The Defender. I whispered: "What's she going to do?"

He groaned like a man in the clutches of a head-splitting hangover, or maybe a serious case of guilt. "You mean," he said, "what are we gonna do." It was an uninflected reading.

We don't even know who told us to look in Brooklyn: we only knew it was as far away from the Upper West Side as we could imagine. We took a couple of long subway rides, checked out signs in brownstone windows. Give me a month, the landlord said.

I found I could worry about Lorraine again, now that we were leaving, and she gave me plenty to worry about: one morning I found her passed out on the kitchen floor. They let me ride in the ambulance with her, and after another stomach-pumping, she let me talk her into a week on the locked ward. I was her only visitor. I had so many questions. I don't mean the Jean-Paul question—the only way I was going to get out of the ersatz commune was to forget there even was a Jean-Paul question—but the kind of questions Ethel Feeney's daughter would never breathe: Handcuffs? What if they took too long? What if you couldn't get, you know. . . .

Lorraine came home from the hospital a whipped puppy. I could already see the blank wide-eyed look she would give me through her aviator glasses when I told her we were moving. Even Sosh was looking for a new place.

Face it, we were leaving her, just sprung from the psych ward, to fend for herself. This was serious bad karma. If Ethel Feeney had known, she either would have said we were well out of there, or she would have said we were committing a grievous mortal sin, and I didn't even know anymore which one she would pick.

On moving day, bouncing along the Brooklyn Bridge, Jean-Paul pointed out the Statue of Liberty as if he were a sightseer, not someone who'd spent his whole life in this city. "She'll be OK." He veered along the decrepit roadway in our rented truck, grinning obscenely at our liberation. What a tidy story he'd told me, complete with sucker punch. He made soothing sounds as I wept, his cheerful new patience as suspicious as the cheap new Brooklyn rent. I could see whatever happened between them looming over us as we tried to hang on: to acting, to the city, to a marriage made too young.

And I could see an afternoon when the sun was just going down over the Hudson and Lorraine, wearing a shrunken Sticky Fingers t-shirt and her pointy tooled cowboy boots, curled up in the bathroom one last time. The hairballs blew around her like tumbleweeds, and I sat on the closed toilet lid, helpless, looking down on her as she alternated full-body trembling and sweet giggling. Was I supposed to take care of her? I couldn't even take care of getting myself one good role, much less take care of Sweet Lorraine Straveski.

I can't believe I could get so freaked out with you guys around. She started to choke. I wanted to get down and give her a good shoulder squeeze like the squeezes she'd given me, but I couldn't figure out how to get close to her on the floor. I stood up, sat back down, prayed we wouldn't have to go to the hospital again, seriously considered running away: from her, from Jean-Paul, from New York and all its sorrows. She looked up at me with those crazy green eyes.

It's OK, she said, as if I were the one in trouble, as if I were just like her: an angry mother's daughter, lost in the city she thought would save her.

BUYING THE FARM

Arlaina Tibensky

MY MOTHER IS MAKING AN OMELET AGAIN. She has a special hammer. There is a feather sticking to her bare heel. One egg can feed my family for one week straight, but not me. No way am I gonna shovel forkfuls of ostrich embryo in my mouth. They are nothing but stupid, dirty chickens from hell.

My father, the entrepreneur, plucked us from our green, suburban home in the western Chicago suburbs, and dropped us down in Southern Illinois to get rich quick. "Mark me," he said. "Within five years, people will be begging for ostrich meat, lowest ratio of sat fat to meat going." And here we are. Giant birds and farmer neighbors and omelets every day for the rest of my life.

The shell of an ostrich egg is about an inch thick, like a bone water balloon. Mom makes the hole, squats, and lifts with her scrawny knees to empty the shell like a jug into a big aluminum bowl like Wilma Flintstone. "Dammit Marion, I've done it again." She's getting better at choosing the unfertilized eggs but occasionally she slips. I can't help myself, I look in the bowl and there it is, half-formed, a sprinkle of beak, of eye and the beginning of wings like a baby's nipples. A Tabasco splash of blood and I almost want to heave myself. It's her own fault. She agreed to this life.

"Gotta go," and I'm out.

While I'm at school my parents tend the farm. There is constant care to be taken with the birds. They are not easy like cows. They forget to eat. If they do remember, it is usually because they accidentally see their own poop and want to gorge themselves on it, as if it's some delicacy my father purposefully hides from them. With their long lashes they will rob us blind.

It doesn't help that my father's idea of marketing is praying for a nation-wide heart attack increase and painting THE OSTRICH KINGDOM on an abandoned billboard off Route 10 in front of the house. The billboard's only real purpose is to let my bus driver know where to stop. If I don't stand directly in front of it, he zooms right past me and so I stand there, Princess of the Ostriches, running a lint brush over my sweater and cords until every fleck of gosling down is removed.

I told my dad we don't have a chance. I offered proof. He used to have this ostrich farmer email pal in Australia. Even though Aussies will eat anything—puffin, crocodile, llamas, dingoes, porpoises, kangaroos—this farmer lost all his investors.

"And Americans are picky," I said, "they like their meat between bread, with mayonnaise and a pickle."

"Ostrich burgers," my Dad answered. "Now you're thinking."

The Australian farmer had to let his birds loose in the bush. Butchering was too expensive, but would have been less cruel. These birds are afraid of everything.

Buying lunch at the cafeteria is my one luxury in life. And what do they offer me? Grits with an oil slick on top of them. Sloppy Joes. Rubber chicken fillets with food coloring painted on them to look like grill marks. In my old school at least we had a choice of entrees. We had a salad bar and pizza every day. Still, I smile and say yes to each item the ladies behind the line slide toward me. It is all delicious because it is not ostrich.

There is this guy, Carl. He always sits alone. He is the school's only vegetarian. Greasy hair, polyester fleece, gray eyes sunk way deep in his face. His Adam's apple waves at me while he takes swallow after swallow of iced tea. I smile at him on accident when I toss the paper from my tray into the garbage can.

"Hey," he says. "Wanna carrot?" He pulls a baby from the orange swarm on the table.

"No thanks," I say, and turn away quickly, my face all red. If you think carrots are not romantic, you have never met Veggie Carl.

I don't have time for extra curricular activities. I'm on the swing shift on the farm. In that way I'm not much different from the other high school kids here. They need to fertilize and mow and bale and grow things with their parents. I need to feed a herd of big birds and keep myself from screaming when I think about the life we left behind.

At our new house, I grab a bag of Fritos off the kitchen counter and turn on the TV. I like to watch shows about teenagers whose parents are lawyers, psychiatrists and ministers. City teenagers, suburban teenagers, teenaged witches and vampires, reminding me that the rest of the world is out there. In five minutes I'm out there too, with all this farm business behind me.

"You should be hatching, Marion." My mother has become an Amazon since buying the farm. Her arms are hard and tan. They hang from her sleeveless shirts and end in bony hands with chipped nails, square as tiny TV sets. The babies need help with the birthing. They are inbred and weak and aren't strong enough to get past their shell without breaking their necks or suffocating to death.

"Where's the Ostrich King?" I ask.

"He's at the slaughterhouse. He was last on the list again. You should be in the hatchery. Now." I wait for one more hit of canned laughter before I listen to her and head out to the Quonset hut.

The eggs sit on piles of hay in large troughs of galvanized steel. I've been rotating them for a month and a half and some are almost ready to come out. All I have to do is wait till they poke a hole big enough for my finger to fit through and then pull the thick shards from the wet body. The hut is close and warm and smells like dry hay and baby vomit. There are a dozen of them waiting to go. They don't all come out at once. They start tapping quietly at their own pace. The eggs are so large that when I put my hand on them to check I might as well be feeling a pregnant woman's stomach.

When Mom and Dad first bought the farm they had to start from scratch. Dad bought three-dozen fertilized eggs from an ostrich vendor. They sat up all night together, then in shifts. Mom made thermoses of coffee and they made plans in the hatchery among the heavy white eggs trembling with their future. My parents probably did it in here for all I know. They're weird like that.

An egg in the corner is ready for me. I approach it from the side, and like Dad taught me, hook my finger down and around and gently pull up and out. I take another chunk and another until the gosling is exposed, a hairy coconut with a beak, new and long-lashed.

Another one has a hole and then another one. I can only work so fast and start feeling anxious. I picture them all struggling to get out and breathe, their tiny hearts ticking like crazy. I run down back and forth the length of the hut, the arch of corrugated metal above me like the ribcage of a whale. If these goslings die, my parents will kill me.

"Need some help?" My father is calm and sure, opening holes like flicking switches. "You take the left side. Come on now, hustle." He doesn't see the ostriches. He sees hides, feathers, and moon steaks. But there he is, saving them with violent tugs and practiced authority. I finish my side—and there. They're out, all of them, wet and sharp-toothed and hungry.

"How's it goin'?" He smiles and wipes sweat off his face with a blue bandanna. "Now what?" He's quizzing me.

"Bring them to the brooder to dry." Yes, I know the answer.

"That's my girl." He hands me a stack of blankets and we quickly make small hammocks between our arms and carry the birds over to a pen at the far end of the hut. I'm slow. They're tiny. Just out of their little spaceships and I don't want to bruise them or hurt their rubbery bones. Dad turns on a heat lamp over the pen and sits on a feed drum. He's starting to look like a farmer. There are pale untanned creases around his eyes that make him seem twinkly and robust.

"How was school?" he says. We're well into October now and the sun is sinking big and orange. The goslings are drying off and some are starting to squawk. It's like the dawn of time in here.

"Fine," I answer. It will never be fine.

"I can watch these little burgers for a while," he says.

"Dad," I say. "How can you be the way you are?" I stand up and head toward the house. When I look back, he's standing in the center of the newborns as they raise their scrawny necks and stare at him. If they could talk, they'd call him Daddy.

The next morning, Veggie Carl is waiting for me at my homeroom door. He's tall, standing up, leaning against the corner locker. He has covered his books in brown paper bags so no one on the street can tell he is still in high school. I smile at him before I go in and join the homeroom prayer. I think to thank God that Veggie Carl is at my school. I sneak a look at him through the window in the door. He is staring at me so deadly serious he could melt the glass.

So we eat lunch together. Big deal.

"What's your story?" I ask him. I can't help staring at his vinyl cowboy boots. His feet look like adult feet, like he could have his own farm, a wife and three kids just up the road a piece.

"No story. Got held back last year after I was suspended. Bad attitude," he says. He leans toward me. "I have a truck. You wanna ride home?"

I will meet him in the senior parking lot. I will carry my books in the crook of my arm. I will wait for him like a regular teenager in a movie.

In Chicago I could walk for twenty minutes and get anywhere I wanted. At least I could get to a train station. Here, I could walk until my legs fall off and I'd be in practically the same place I started. The corn and soybeans are hypnotizing. All that green stretches out around you and it seems as if you're traveling over things, smooth like a people mover at the airport. It's still like that in Veggie Carl's truck, but we are definitely getting somewhere. His truck is big, old, rusty, and green but it is the most exciting place I've been in months.

"Half the people here don't even know that tofu's made from soybeans. And they're growing the crap," he says. For a vegetarian, he's pretty surly. I realize it could be an act to get girls. He lights a cigarette and is inhaling hard. He looks like he is twenty years old.

"My parents have an ostrich farm," I say. It's easier this way, getting it all out. If he can't take it I better know now.

"Yeah. Everyone knows. It's cool." This is the stupidest thing he has said. Who is everyone, I think. Everyone knows? And then he says, "I'll drive you home a lot, if you want." He flicks his ash out the window. He doesn't smile.

"If you want to," I say. I can hardly breathe.

"Where do I turn?" he says.

"There's a big sign. Can't miss it." We approach the billboard, which is floodlit and obscene as a cheap strip club. He parks behind the sign and we sit there while the engine pings. The ride is over faster than I expected and he's sitting there resting his thumbs in the finger grooves of the steering wheel. The light is on in the Quonset hut. Brightness is spilling from the cracks at its base so it looks like a spaceship about to take off.

"Take me to your leader," I say, and immediately regret it. But Veggie Carl must think it is the sexiest thing he has ever heard because he leans over with no warning and is on my mouth. His stubble pricks my face. Just when I start getting into it the door of the hut opens, blinding us both with hatching light.

My dad looks into the cab of the truck. He is the Ostrich King and this is his kingdom. He walks right up to Carl's side window. He sticks his hand in and demands Carl shake it. I wipe my mouth off and open it to speak. My lips are numb from making out.

"Carl, this is my dad, Dennis."

"Nice to meet you, Dennis," Carl says. My own mother doesn't call him Dennis. She calls him Den, like the room. Dad just keeps shaking Carl's hand.

"Same here," Dad says, giving Carl a hard squint like he's going to punch his lights out. But my father just stands there, trapping us, like he's in control when actually this is Carl's truck, and I want to be in it.

"Mom just made supper. Why doesn't your friend join us? Plenty to go around."

"Cool," Carl says. There is lip gloss on his mouth.

My mother looks pretty tonight. She steamed some zucchini and the kitchen is warm and damp like a clean dog mouth. Her cheeks are pink and her hair's gone curly from the heat. I see her eyes blink when Carl walks up to her table set for three.

"One more, hun. This is Carl," Dad says and sits down.

"Hi," she says. "Take a seat." I help pull another plate from the cabinet. She looks at me. She silently mouths the word "Cute" and I am glad.

"Cute and vegetarian," I whisper.

"Does he eat eggs?"

"We'll see. I don't."

Then we're all sitting there, passing plates, and it starts.

"There's more to an ostrich than meat, Carl. There's the eggs, of course. You've got your bone meal, dog food ingredients, and feathers. What they call drab feathers are a pet industry favorite."

I feel sorry for my parents then. My mom in her hoop earrings holding one of my father's hands as he makes the ketchup fart all over his ostrich omelet. Carl smirks like a prisoner at the warden. He eats the potatoes and the zucchini and sips water from a glass with cherries painted on it that Mom and I got together at Marshall Fields, back when we were normal.

"Put it however you want, Dennis," Carl says. "Meat is murder." He holds a fork with zucchini speared onto it while talking, like he's going to jab someone in the throat with it.

"It's hard to eat animals when they're alive, Carl," my mother counters, chewing beneath her smile.

"It's a living," my father says and reaches for another hunk of omelet.

"Give me a break." That's me talking and I toss my paper napkin onto my plate. Suddenly I need to get out of that yellow kitchen with its dark seam of grease and ostrich down between the linoleum and cabinets so I tell my parents Carl has to get home. I am outside before Carl knows what's happening and he takes almost five minutes to join me.

When he finally does I don't know what to do. We start walking on the dirt footpath Dad made between the sections of the farm. I watch Carl's boots push through the dust. He grabs my hand and it seems almost natural. "Wanna see the ostriches?" I ask. It's something to do.

"Yeah," he says. The birds are sleeping outside, standing up. There is feather rumbling and that sinister quack talk they do. Their rumps are bright white like bustles in the dark. Carl stops walking and stands in front of the biggest one, sizing it up. He puts his hand out like he's feeding something trained at a zoo. And surprise surprise, the stupid thing hisses and spits.

"Whoa," he says and the bird takes off running in circles, awkward and ridiculous, a woman in spiked heels running from a mugger.

"Yeah, well," he says. "There you have it." I don't know what exactly it is that he has, but he is beautiful and entirely hipless. I am the one that's starting, pulling him close to me and getting on tiptoe so he can reach me better. I just want this to feel normal. A boy, a girl, kissing, even though deep down we are not like that at all.

We fumble with coat zippers and his height for a few minutes but then we're fine. The ostriches watch as he pushes his tongue in my mouth. They chortle and hiccup when I break for a second to come up for air. I'm glad of them for once, glad there is someone to witness this. I'm sweating and shaken up from it all, as if I've been plotting a murder.

"You'd better go," I say, not because I mean it, but because I feel it's what I'm supposed to say.

When I get back into the house, my parents are sitting on the couch and I'm sure they've been making out. My mother sits up, her shirt mussed and my Dad crosses his legs.

"Goodnight. Carl said thanks for dinner." Which he didn't, but I'm sure he would have if he thought of it. In my room, door shut, button lock pushed, I take off my clothes and stand in front of the full-length mirror in my underwear. I have tacked ostrich feathers around the frame. When the feathers are off the birds, they are exotic and pretty and look like they fluttered off a Mae West costume. The feminas are my favorite. They're the kind people stick onto pens for signing guest books at weddings.

I throw a red bandanna over my lamp and un-tack the feathers and arrange them into a fan in each hand. I'm fan dancing, teasing my invisible audience. My hair has grown and I make it dangle far down my back, femina feathers hiding and exposing my skin. There's a knock on my door.

"Can I come in?" My mother. I throw on a T-shirt, pull the bandanna off the lamp and open the door. "Have tea with me." She hands me a mug, peppermint, and just walks right in and sits on my bed.

"So. Tell me about Carl." She folds her legs underneath her, planning to stay awhile. If I had friends, I'd be telling them all these things.

"He's a senior. He thinks he's subversive. He gave me a ride home. That's about it." She smiles and picks a feather up off the floor and runs it through her fingers so it looks like a trained caterpillar.

"Good kisser?" If she weren't my mother I'd tell all. But she is my mother, so I shrug, take a sip of tea. She leans back and stretches out on my bed. The soles of her feet are dirty, her toenail polish is chipped. I am exhausted from the dinner, the kissing, the beasts running willy-nilly in the backyard. She sighs and closes her eyes. "Mar?" she says.

"Yeah?" On my bed in my teenaged room she looks like one of us, tough and small. Her left ear is pierced three times. Thin lines have surfaced at the corners of her mouth but from a few feet away she looks the same to me as she did in third grade.

"You don't still hate it here. Right?" she says. It's not even a question. There she goes, my only possible ally.

"It's growing on me," she says. Like a fungus, I think but she's not done. "Your Dad's really happy here and when he's happy, I'm happy, you know? We might turn a profit next month. How crazy is that?"

"Very." I'm as surprised as she is. She is actually liking it here. Everything about her is pissing me off, even while she's being completely nice.

"And if that happens, Den and I have decided to stick it out, go in for another three years."

"Get out of my room." Am I screaming? I can't tell. I think so because she jumps up and closes the door tight behind her.

The room is quiet once she goes. It deadens my anger and I remember that I had questions for her, important life questions. "Thanks for the tea," I say to the door. I'm getting pretty good at ruining things.

I finish the test first. I make sure to push my paper enough toward Carl so he won't fail English again. I turn it in and sit back down and try to amuse myself for fifteen minutes by staring out the window. If I sit on my legs I can see far past the skinny track team running laps. Beyond the fence, there's acres of soybeans, Heineken bottle green, low to the ground and shining in the sun.

Carl turns his test in after me. He walks up and back, his jeans making creases like smiles as he moves. I look down at my lap and there is a note, a folded up paper triangle: Ditch Homecoming with me Saturday. Carl is a rock star among farmers. I am sweating and the bell rings.

Homecoming is a test run for prom and all the girls are talking about dresses. They dog-ear pages of magazines that feature taffeta. They meet after school to try hairdos, set up elaborate dates—who's picking up who, where they're going after. It's called homecoming because people who went to school here years ago are also invited. Most of them still live three blocks away. They haven't gone anywhere.

"Sure, pick me up," I tell him. He opens his mouth to talk and his teeth are shiny.

"OK," he says. "The truck's not far. I got a good spot this morning." We walk to the senior lot and we are officially a couple. We eat lunch together. I got a note today. He drives me home after school. He holds the passenger door open for me and I wish someone had a camera. Carl uses one hand to hold mine and drives and smokes with the other.

"I like driving you around." These are the words he has just said. Not so far from "I love you" and we have only been going out for two weeks. I am not surprised. This is real. This is happening right now. I am not looking back on it wistfully. It is not teaching me anything. I am living it as we speak.

When I finish saying goodbye to Carl and get into the house, my father is sitting at the kitchen table, reading Ostrich Health and Upkeep, drinking a glass of buttermilk. He's developed an ulcer and some local guy suggested he drink it to relieve the burn.

"Hi Dad." I'm feeling good and he looks solid sitting there. I want to hug him hard like when I was a kid, but after forty-five minutes of Carl daring me to put my hands down his pants it would creep me out.

"Mom tell you about the figures?" He's smiling, then takes a gulp of milk.

"She mentioned it." I grab a Coke from the fridge. "I guess that's good." I imagine mixing Coke and buttermilk together.

"Yes it is. How's the boy?"

"He's not a boy."

Dad ignores me. "We got a young bird with a pussed eye. The vet dropped off these eye drops for it. She's trouble." I know the one he means. She is a bitch of an ostrich. "I need some help. Mom's gone off to Kroger's."

"Fine." And we go.

Why would someone take such good care of birds he is going to drive to the slaughterhouse? If the other ostriches find out that one of them is sick or weak, they pick on it. Like a pack of bullies, they take little swipes whenever possible. Then the bird stops growing. It doesn't lay eggs. Money down the drain.

By the time we get out to the pen, the sky's gone red. Dad and I corner the bird and her dark feathers look maroon, tail feathers pink. A circle of white goo is over her right eye like she's wearing a monocle.

The other birds are screaming and chortling and running in circles. They seem terrified. I take a rope and corral them away from the sick one. "Tell me what I need to do." This seems like a job for a doctor or at least a very large Hell's Angel. The bird is taller than my father. Her slim neck looks velvet-flocked and stretches with muscle. Her legs are rock hard beneath the soft feathers on her rump. She is unearthly as Godzilla.

"Listen," Dad is whispering. He is holding a broomstick. Now I'm scared. "When I say, gently, yet firmly place your hands around her collarbone and push down." He is quoting from the guidebook. He has no idea what he's doing.

"Be careful," I say, but it's all going to go wrong. I feel it. We are in way over our heads but my parents refuse to see it. He slings an arm over the ostrich's back and simultaneously pushes the broomstick behind its knees with his foot.

"Now!" We are not ready for this but I shut up and listen, suddenly pushing with all my weight on its collarbone with both hands. She's down. She smells. Her feathers are damp with fear sweat. The birds behind the rope crane their necks like they are watching a wrestling match. Dad whips an eyedropper big as a baby's bottle from his shirt pocket and aims for the milky eye. The bird is mute with terror. She blinks a couple times and with a last gasp at survival, breaks free from my grasp and pauses a second before her head is hot up into my face and she bites my neck.

"We're trying to help you, you stupid smelly thing!" I push her away from me. I'm bleeding. Dad lets her go and she takes off around the pen, shaking her head and blinking so much she looks like she's flirting. Dad seems a little dazed but he's already got a bandanna pressed to my neck and is holding me up as we walk back to the house.

"Their teeth are quite tiny. You're OK. Sit down. Let me take a look." Of all the things I ever thought would happen to me in my life, getting bit by an ostrich was nowhere on the list. Dad bends down close to the wound. "It's nothing," he says. "It's a big ostrich hickey."

But it isn't nothing. I want him to say something bad about the birds but he can't. This is all part of the great adventure. Now he's spraying an antiseptic on my neck in breathy spurts, shh shh shh, like he's trying to keep me quiet about the whole thing. "Sorry about that kiddo." He looks shaken up and I want to tell him that it's not the birds I hate so much as him.

I go to my room and check out the damage. Reddish pinpricks of blood near the edge of my bra strap. Fingerprint-sized bruises are beginning to darken. I imagine headlines in the Streetor Record: GIRL DIES OF OSTRICH BITE. My heart is thumping away. I have never been that close to any of the adult birds. The skin on her feet and legs was like snake skin dipped in wax. She was helpless when we held her down.

I wear a turtleneck. Simple. Mom has baked something with apples in it. My parents know about homecoming but don't know we're ditching it. Carl assured me that lying would make it more fun. The house smells good. Mom ran a rag over surfaces so the place looks halfway decent. The bell rings and Dad answers it. I hear the hellos and imagine hand shaking. Carl comes into the front room and catches me biting my cuticles to the bone. He's got a plastic carryout container with a wrist corsage in it.

"Here," he says.

"Thanks." Mom has wrapped up some apple stuff in Tupperware.

"Here, sweetheart," she says to Carl, "this is for you. You might get hungry later. It's meat-free."

"Don't do anything crazy," Dad says. Carl nods.

"Ready?" Carl asks.

Am I ever.

"What do you wanna do?" he asks. But I think he has a secret plan. I shrug. We go out back and lean against the gate of the ostrich pen. It's cold enough to see my breath. The stars are out and seem like they are right on top of us, lower than they ever were back home. The birds are huddled together for warmth.

"Let's go casual driving," he says.

"Great," I say. I have no idea what he is talking about. We drive past school first and look at our classmates all dressed up, tripping in heels to the gymnasium door. We park in back by the dumpsters and make out for an hour. I do my best to keep him away from parts I'm not ready to show him.

"Let's go." He pulls onto a back road where there are few lights and fewer cars. We're on the shoulder now with the engine running and the radio off. I hear his belt buckle clink, fly unzip.

"What are you doing?" He is taking his pants off.

"Casual driving. You know, naked. Clothes free." He seems nervous, his eyebrows lifted as if he's begging me to say it's OK.

"Maybe you don't remember but I'm not from around here." I grab onto the door handle but I know already that I'm not going anywhere, that this is a test.

"Look, I'm doing it." He angrily pushes his pants down and takes his shoes off, seething on his dusty truck seat in his boxers. He seems vulnerable, half-clothed, like I've caught him in the bathroom. I get that he's doing this for me, even if he has done it before, that he is raising the stakes for us. I want him to know that he has not underestimated me.

"Fine. Don't look." I take off my wrist corsage so I don't hurt it when I pull my turtleneck over my head. Then my skirt, shoes. I hear him tossing his sweater and pants in the back seat, then his boxers. My bra is easier to get off than my underwear. The final movement of it gives me trouble because the elastic waistband seems tight as a rubber band. For a minute I wonder at what I am doing, sliding my underwear past my knees and kicking them onto the carpeted hump beneath the consul of Carl's truck. Once everything's off, I put the corsage back on my wrist. I look at Carl quick as he pulls out onto the road and we are moving along. Two snails in a shell.

It's cold. I sense in the corner of my eye that he's turning up the heat. It blasts from the vents onto my skin, all my fine hairs vibrate in the hot air. I lean back and let myself feel what it is like to be naked, next to a naked man, driving 80 miles an hour in this town where everyone else is playing it safe. I swallow hard and really get an eyeful of him. Even his hands seem exposed. He's white and thin. Hair on his chest and dark vines of hair all over his legs, all the way up to his hips. It looks like he's half man, half goat.

I open the window halfway and stick my arm out, trying to grab at the darkness, the gallons of crisp air that rush in. I open it further and stick my head out, opening my mouth and letting my chest smash against the glass until my teeth are chattering and my hair twirls into knots. I feel like I could live in the woods, fly as easily as yawning. Carl just keeps on driving, whooping and pounding on the roof with his fist.

We stop at an abandoned cul-de-sac, breathing hard as if we've been running. I hear a weird noise, like a gosling warble, and realize it's me, giggling like a crazy person. I don't know what's supposed to happen now. My corsage is wilting and the car smells like apples and cinnamon.

Carl's hand is creeping toward me. It clamps over my bare thigh and once he touches me, he is on me, pinning me to the seat cushion with all his weight. I think of my Dad quoting the guidebook gently, yet firmly. He is using the armrest in the door for leverage. I try to control the whole thing, until I give up and grit my teeth.

Doing it is nothing like it was supposed to be, but it is done. I stare at telephone wires through the driver's side window as the wind ruffles the trees like prom dresses. We lay there in the quiet, my legs dangling off the seat. There is nothing to say. We quickly put our clothes back on. We eat my mom's baked goods as the truck tires pull the road underneath us. It's over. I just want to go home.

When we get to my parent's driveway, something fast blurs past the headlights.

"What the hell was that?" Carl says, the first thing he's said to me in the past forty-five minutes. There's a high-pitched shrieking in the air that could be the wind. It is not the wind. I know what it is. What else could it be? There's my mother in unlaced boots creeping along hedges between sections of the farm, holding a flowered sheet in her hands to make a trap.

"Damn!" Carl sees them before I do, ostriches, about twenty of them, loping in frantic circles across the yard and through miles of open fields. Somehow they have escaped from their pens. They're running fast with their lopsided gait, pushing their toenails into the ground for speed.

"Get out of the car!" My father yells and pulls on my door handle like he's drowning. He is in pajamas under his coat and baseball cap. Emergency floodlights bleach the farm black and white like a silent movie. Carl gets out and rushes toward the Quonset hut then back to me. He was naked and powerful in the dark. Now running after birds, clothed, he is as dumb as a box of hair. The ostriches are scattered, on their own, flouncing their tail feathers and useless wings as they head for the woods, the highway, anywhere. Their eyes are high, reflecting the moon. Go go go I whisper as they tear across the ground, trying to fly.

Winner of the 2018
Jay Prefontaine Fiction Prize

GIRLS GIRLS GIRLS

Cady Vishniac

ELKIE TRUSTS DON ABSOLUTELY. He's a cross between a boyfriend and a father, though Elkie knows boyfriends and fathers aren't supposed to be the same thing, and he's not at all like a regular client. But then one Sunday he doesn't show up. She knocks on the door of his usual room at the Radisson by John Glenn International and doesn't hear the familiar plodding of Don's feet, his gravelly voice telling her to hold her horses. She texts him, *Are you here? I have that spring break thing at seven.* She counts to ten, then twenty. She is sweating in a bustier-and-panties set by Agent Provocateur. Don fails to appear.

Elkie tries his cell, which rings four times before going to voicemail. She looks up and down the beige hallway. No maids, no bellhops. She leaves a message. "Hello? It's Crystal. Are you OK?" Crystal is what Don calls her, even though he—alone among the men with whom she spends her afternoons and evenings—knows her real name.

She examines the door. A *Do Not Disturb* sign is tucked into the keycard slot, which could mean Don doesn't want to be disturbed and could mean he hasn't checked in yet. Maybe his wife has discovered Elkie and Don's emails, their texts, and is listening to Elkie's voicemail right now. She could threaten divorce, threaten to take the kids. Don always tells Elkie his wife is the worst kind of gold digger.

She checks her phone. After five. She really does have to meet with the Ohio State Spring Break Service Club at seven tonight, at her apartment with her mother and grandmother, her friend Brianna, who is the club's secretary, and the other members—young people looking to pad their CVs before applying to med school or law school. They're going to South Dakota's Pine Ridge Reservation this March to build straw bale homes for indigent Oglala Lakota. Elkie is the club president.

She knocks again, then she presses her ear against the door, over the peephole. She closes her mascaraed eyes and wrinkles her nose and concentrates, not sure what she expects to hear. Don may or may not be on the other side, snoring in one of the cozy Radisson armchairs. He may or may not have his face planted in the red Radisson rug, his body twisted in some freak fall. Don has young children, but he's no longer a young man. He's sexy the way George Clooney is sexy, with graying temples. Sexy, but when she's riding him he's been known to growl, "Try not to blow out my hip," in a way that's both playful and serious.

She pulls back from the peephole, then she texts Brianna because she texts Brianna after each appointment to make it known that she's fine. Only this time, instead of texting, *I'm fine*, Elkie writes, *Don's a no-show*, and Brianna writes back right away: *Men*.

Elkie's phone says it's 5:10. She'll call Don. She'll get in touch later.

Brianna sends a second text, *Come home early? I made cookies.* Brianna is forever plying Elkie with carbs, which Elkie can't have because she's watching her weight. Her clients always tell her how skinny she is, how sexy and skinny.

She walks back down the hallway. The heels of her new Blahniks drop with each step, the leather straps chafing. A pair of identical blisters have sprouted up on the inside of each arch, which is a problem. She has an appointment tomorrow with a man who likes to lick her feet. She stops at the elevators and presses the down button, and just as the button lights up, her phone vibrates again. This is normal because Brianna is one of those people who sends a bunch of short texts in row. Because Elkie receives an awful lot of texts from an awful lot of men.

She looks down at the screen and sees a message that is not from Brianna, not from a horny stranger, but from Don. Maybe he's stuck in traffic or forgot his son had a Little League game.

Only it isn't Don. It can't be. Someone else must have his phone, someone with a bad sense of humor. Someone who has texted, *My husband passed this weekend.*

Don's wife is named Monica or Mona or maybe even Mandy. She and Don haven't made love since their daughter was born, and to add insult to that injury, she's had affairs. She won't let him get a divorce because she likes his money. Don told Elkie a month in. He took her to dinner at a TGI Fridays a block from the Radisson, an impossibly slow walk for Elkie, who insisted on wearing her regulation heels from the Pussycat Club. Over dinner, he handed her a black box containing a Tiffany watch, then he burst into tears.

Elkie is certain the message about Don's death is fake, but she's still worried about how someone has accessed Don's phone. She walks to the hotel parking garage and finds her car and drives it home. She needs advice, but she has to wait until she's in her cramped apartment, until she's kicked off the Blahniks and kissed her grandmother's tissue-paper cheeks and greeted Brianna with the words, "Hey loser, what are you doing on my couch?" Until she's entered the kitchen and made her mother promise not to go overboard making food for the Service Club members, since Brianna already brought cookies and most of the girls are on diets anyways.

"Five kinds of hors d'oeuvres, max, and remember we're underage. No Dom Perignon, none of your finest aged Glenlivet. I mean it." Elkie puts her hands on her hips and wags a finger at her mother.

"You sure know booze, considering how underage you are," her mother says. She pulls a bag of popcorn from the microwave. "How about this and a veggie platter with ranch? And how was your day?"

Don—that's how Elkie knows booze. Don bought a bottle of Perignon and a lap dance from Elkie when they met at the Pussycat, with its rusted billboard advertising *GIRLS GIRLS GIRLS*. Don's the one who poured Glenlivet into a bulb-shaped glass on her last birthday. But Elkie's mother doesn't know about Don, and Elkie herself is reciting a pack of lies. She stands by the counter and says she's getting good at espresso art, the customers tip well, and she's learned to enjoy the smell of coffee grounds at the campus cafe where she's a barista. Then she goes back to the living room and plops down on the couch next to Brianna, who's watching *Bob's Burgers*. Elkie's grandmother croaks from her easy chair in the corner,

דו וואָקסט אַזוי שיין, קיין עין הרע.

"I love you too, Grandma," says Elkie. One of the underwires on her bustier is pinching. She tries to adjust it through her shirt.

"You don't even know that's what she means," says Brianna. "You need help with that thing?" She's eating one of the cookies, smiling with her cheeks full. In moments like this one, Elkie is intensely jealous of her friend's uncomplicated relationship with food. "These came out so great." Brianna's tank top is cut low, her shorts so short that her thighs make sticky sounds against the imitation leather of the couch.

"Can you tell me what this is?" Elkie hands her the phone, open to the message from Don's wife. Brianna looks, then she launches herself across the couch, looping her strong arms around Elkie's back. "I'm so sorry."

קענסטו מיך העלפֿן?

asks Elkie's grandmother, then she whispers,

איך דאַרף פּישן.

She's leaning forward in her chair, as if she wants to get up and hug Elkie too.

"Don't worry, Grandma. Brianna's overreacting."

Brianna pulls back with her hands still gripping Elkie's arms. "You're always talking about this guy. You're not like the tiniest bit sad?"

"She's just making it up. She must have caught him." Elkie's stomach growls, and she decides she's earned a cookie. She reaches over to grab one, which has the added bonus of forcing Brianna to release her.

Brianna gives Elkie her serious look. "Most people don't make up dead husbands."

"She's not most people. Don't make that face." Elkie recalls all the crying Don has done over his wife when he's with Elkie, how many times his wife has threatened suicide. She's manipulative.

אָט איז אַן אמתע נויטפֿאַל

says Elkie's grandmother.

"It's wild how your grandma can only speak German now," says Brianna.

"Don't try to change the subject. Should I wait for him to call me?" Elkie says this with her mouth full. The cookie is so good. Brianna put in M&Ms instead of chocolate chips.

"Just write like, 'Sorry for your loss,'" Brianna says. "Because her husband is dead."

This is when Elkie's mother speaks up. "Who's dead?" she asks. Both girls jump out of their skins for an instant, but just as quickly force themselves to relax. On the TV, Bob is having an allergic reaction to lobster.

"All the characters on this show. I read about it online." Brianna's a film studies major, so internet forums about random cartoons are her homework. "Hi, Miss Clark. Didn't see you there."

"You mean like a fan conspiracy theory?" Elkie's mother sniffs. "I was just poking my head in. I made you girls some chicken for after your meeting." She sniffs again. "Mom?" And this is when Elkie notices her grandmother is hanging her head and panting. Elkie's mother, all business, pats down her own mother's moist lap.

"Christ, Miss Clark. We didn't understand she had to pee," says Brianna. "We can like help you clean up."

איך האָב פֿינט ווערן אַן אַלטע. איך בין עקלדיק

says Elkie's grandmother.

"It's not a big deal," says Elkie's mother. This is the example she's set Elkie's whole life, that of a woman who barely notices the world on her shoulders, a woman who never gets angry, who is proud of Elkie without asking questions, no questions at all, not even the sort of questions that might prove she's paying attention.

Brianna fidgets on the couch. "You sure, Miss Clark?" Brianna's not trying to be invasive, Elkie knows. She's just bad at watching other people handle things. She'd rather help.

Before Elkie's mother can answer, the phone vibrates again, long and insistent. "Pick up. That might be your friends," she says. She drapes Elkie's grandmother over her shoulder like a wet dishrag and staggers toward the bathroom.

Elkie watches them go then shuts off her phone. It's no one she knows.

"You OK?" Brianna asks. "Like would you be OK if it turned out he really did die?" She is using another face Elkie can't stand: a deep frown of concern.

Don did not die. Elkie's conviction has grown in the last two hours. He might be hurt. He might have had an accident, or his wife might have thrown a fit, locked him in the basement. But he wouldn't go and die on her. Each Sunday they meet at the Radisson, but in between, they text. They have to. She does text Brianna when her appointments are done, but she also texts Don. It's Don who would check on her if anything went wrong, who would run to the Radisson or the Sheraton or wherever else in his tight jeans, shoulder down the door without caring if the maids or bellhops saw, loom tall over any threat in her hotel room, tell a violent man to hold his horses.

Don can't just drop dead.

She's about to explain this to Brianna, but then they hear knocking at the door. The Service Club. The conversation is tabled for later, for a whisper session on the green of the Oval, between classes. Or maybe tonight, after the shuffling noise of Elkie's mother lifting Elkie's grandmother into the bedroom. Sometime when they're alone.

Elkie dreams, except the dream is something that really happened. The one time she and Don spent a whole night together. She had a cold with a sore throat and runny nose but came to see Don anyway. He took one look at her and said, "Honey, why?" Then he swaddled her in the hotel bed. He had her call her mother to say she was spending the night in Brianna's dorm.

He didn't ask for sex, though Elkie wouldn't have minded. Instead, they lay down together, breathing into each other's faces. Elkie said, "But you'll get sick too," and Don said, "Worth it." He could be cute like that. He even went out later that night and got her cough drops and Vicks.

Her dream flashes forward to last winter break. She spent most of her days holed up in the hotel with Don, who told his wife he had to travel for a work thing. Elkie was studying to place out of 100-level chem and bio. Don would ask her for a definition of Dalton's Law or a chemical equation for methane, and when she got these wrong, he'd toss all her cards up in the air and tell her to take off her shirt. Sometimes she'd forget an answer on purpose.

They did not mention his wife once, not all week. They did go down to the hotel's pool, the hot tub, the sauna, where the tan skin of Don's legs turned a brick red. Where he called her his sweetheart, his darling girl.

Elkie dreams about Don because he's fun, because she loves him in an uncomplicated way. She doesn't dream about her mother because supporting an adult human being is not fun, because it's not uncomplicated loving someone who can't bring herself to tell you you're making way too much money for a barista, dressing way too nice to make coffee. She doesn't dream about her grandmother because her grandmother has always been so boring. Ever since Elkie was born, all her grandmother has done is read the newspaper front to back, then a magazine from the supermarket, *Time* or tawdry celebrity stuff or a specialist publication for builders of model cars, then another, then another. Toward the end of the month, she'd run out and read things over again.

After Elkie's grandmother stopped speaking English, Elkie's mother ordered some magazines in German. But Elkie's grandmother didn't like these. She summoned the last of her strength to throw them across the room.

איך וועל ניט קיינמאָל לייענען דייטש

she said.

Elkie can't think about this too hard, about her grandmother stranded in her chair with no reading material. She certainly can't dream about it; she won't let herself.

She wakes up with her milk-white toes pressed to Brianna's chin. She feels the same discomfort she gets when they try to take photos together on Elkie's phone—Brianna looks like a real person but Elkie is washed out, an eraser streak on the world. She brought this up once, but Brianna didn't get it. "You're not an eraser, Elkie, like Jesus Christ," she said. "Your phone camera can't handle contrast. I'll check out a Nikon and we can shoot better pictures." Brianna does her work study in the photo lab.

They fell asleep like this last night after Brianna looked up from her laptop and said, "Fuck me, is it really midnight?" Elkie looked up from her epigenetics homework, a review of histone modifications, and said Brianna could just crash here. It's weird, but they never got around to talking about Don again. Elkie was waiting for it, but Brianna just stared at her computer. Elkie figured she had a paper due soon. Brianna writes most of her papers the night before they're due, but she gets As anyway.

Elkie disentangles herself from Brianna, making as little noise as possible. Her Blahnik blisters are so red she might have to lance them, but the meeting with the Service Club members went well— one of the pre-law guys has a cousin who works for Greyhound, so maybe they can get a discount on a charter bus to South Dakota. She's going to build homes, build her resume, and build her leadership skills with a documented history of community service. In under four years, she's going to be a medical student, then someday a resident, then a doctor. Don is going to call her soon. He might have already.

Elkie reaches for her phone, which she always leaves on the shelf next to her bed, in front of the vampire novel Brianna got her. She slips out and pads toward the bathroom, where she flicks on the light and the vent, and pushes in the lock on the door. She yanks up the rusted shower valve, then runs hot water. She won't step in just yet. Instead, she turns the phone on.

Three voicemails. A client rescheduling from three to four next week. Two calls from men who want to set up first meetings. The emails are six new appointments, almost thirty inquiries, and a dozen missives she deletes after reading. Bored kids, men with no intention of following through, obvious serial killers or cops.

They write things like *titties aren't even that big* and *can i hide near while u fk another man* and *its a dangerous world out there, if you worked for me id protect you* and *I Hope someone Jams a Samurai Sword up your Pussy* and Elkie's personal favorite: *Is your fridge running?* An e-newsletter from the pre-med office at school. Still nothing from Don. His wife must have him in a real bind. In the peace and privacy of her bathroom, Elkie tells herself she can wait for him.

Even with the vent on, the running shower steams up the whole room so that a fog rises between her eyes and the screen. She goes to texts, expecting at least a dozen, but there are no new ones. This is so odd as to be unthinkable. Is her phone broken? Hacked? She checks deleted messages because maybe a hacker would delete all her messages as some sort of prank, and that's when she spots it: Brianna's betrayal.

Don: *My husband passed away last weekend.*
Crystal: *I know this is weird but my friend thinks you're faking.*
            Like you're faking your dead husband.
            She's in denial.
Don: *Who is this?*
Crystal: *Sorry for your loss.*
Don: *WHO*
            Tell your friend she should be ashamed of herself.

Elkie does not read the rest of her messages. She does not take her shower. She turns the water off, leaves the vent on, unlocks the door, and thuds back down the hall. She doesn't care about making noise, waking her mother and grandmother. She doesn't care. She opens the door to her bedroom and yells, "You're so fucking nosy! What's your problem?"

Brianna doesn't get up, but her eyes snap open. She wasn't really asleep in the first place. "You're gullible. Some dude tells you his wife is a bitch and you're like all over it."

How unfair, how stupid. Brianna's life is ordinary: dorm, class, friends her own age, out-of-state parents mailing giant checks. She's never understood Elkie's adult existence, the adult relationship with Don.

"You think you're so much smarter than me," Elkie says, "but you'd be broke if your dad wasn't a lawyer. You'll probably go broke anyway. Film studies."

"At least I'm not a hooker."

"Get out. Go find a bus back to your stupid dorm. Don't even talk to me."

"Fine." Brianna puts on her socks and shoes and bra in the early morning stillness of Elkie's room, sunlight streaking in the window. There are no sounds but Elkie's mother and grandmother waking up, making their slow breakfast-time procession to the kitchen.

Elkie and Brianna have only been mad at each other once before. One of Elkie's clients wanted to watch porn so Elkie put some on, only the woman in the first scene was black and the client made a face and told Elkie to fast-forward. "I'm just not into that sort of thing," he said, and Elkie was confused because the woman was pretty, and anyway, the client himself was black. Did he hate himself? Later, she tried to tell Brianna, but Brianna said she didn't want to have a conversation about whether black women are pretty or black men hate themselves or race in general. She sulked for a week after that, pouting whenever she thought Elkie wasn't looking.

But this morning, Brianna is beyond sulking. She throws her laptop in her book bag and looks Elkie in the eye and says, "Fuck you. I don't even know why I hang out with you." Elkie keeps her face straight. She pretends that's not the most hurtful thing she's ever heard.

*

When Brianna is gone, Elkie's mother shouts, "What's with the yelling? Grandma's upset." Elkie meets them in the kitchen. Her grandmother is strapped into the special old-person highchair and her mother is flipping pancakes over the stove.

איך פֿאַרשטיי אַז מיידלעך שלאָגן זיך, אָבער

דו זאָלסט דיין באָבע לאָזן שלאָפֿן, נו?

asks her grandmother. A drop of maple syrup dots the corner of her mouth. Elkie wipes it away with the sleeve of her nightshirt, and her grandmother smiles.

"What happened?" says her mother. She points the spatula at Elkie. "You want a pancake?"

"Brianna hates my boyfriend," Elkie says. "Just one. Butter, no syrup."

"The butter's in the fridge." Elkie's mother scrapes the pancake from the bottom of the pan and plates it. "You have a boyfriend? I haven't met a boyfriend."

"He works at the cafe. But he didn't call me yesterday because he's so busy." Elkie takes her plate to the table, then she remembers the butter and gets back up again. Then she decides she doesn't need butter after all, sits back down, and takes a bite of plain pancake. The truth is she's never dated in her life, not unless spending time with Don counts as dating.

"Well, if this boyfriend is too busy for you, I don't want to meet him. He's a shit." Her mother pours one last dollop of pancake batter onto the pan. It hisses and steams because she's got the heat too high, as always. She's been burning breakfast Elkie's whole life.

דיין מאַמע איז ריכטיק, אַלע די מענער זיינען קאַק.

Grandma cackles.

Not using butter was a mistake. There is a dry ball of dough in Elkie's mouth, and when she swallows, it lodges in her throat.

It was stupid to talk down about film studies. Elkie met Brianna because she used to also be a film studies major. They went to the same freshman seminar and had the same work study job in the photo lab, and neither of them were in the Spring Break Service

Club because it didn't exist yet. Brianna founded the Friday Night Documentary Club—it still has twice as many members as the Service Club, and Brianna is still its president. Each Friday the club would max out its budget on popcorn, which Elkie would pop and bag. After the documentary was over, the one about legal marijuana for people with chronic pain or the one about the death of American manufacturing or the one about those bubbly drag queens from Texas, they would talk about how they would have done it better. Brianna wouldn't have taken the chronic pain angle, because she thinks marijuana should be legal for everybody, for any reason. Elkie wouldn't have made the documentary about manufacturing in the first place because who cares about manufacturing? The government should just pay people to learn new jobs.

They don't have these sorts of conversations anymore, not in the several months since Elkie officially switched her major, and she worries that she and Brianna are slowly growing apart. It's not that Elkie hates the couch, the Bob's Burgers marathons, not that she doesn't want to talk about documentaries anymore.

"I have to be realistic," she told Brianna when she announced she was quitting the film club. "My mom's plan is to sit in that apartment with Grandma until we run out of money, and then, I guess, she'll act surprised the money's gone." Meaning Elkie needed to take control. Meaning she could not, cannot, follow her heart, find her path, explore possibilities for the future, whatever it is people are supposed to do in college. Following the heart is for children, and Elkie cannot be a child anymore. She has dependents. She has to work hard for the next decade, and maybe then she can catch a movie.

Mondays are her slowest days at the college, not that days matter for Elkie as much as nights. Each period is just another step toward becoming Doctor Clark. Each class exists only in the sense that she can wrest an A and a letter of recommendation from the instructor. She didn't move from Miami or Beijing to go here and she doesn't live in a residence hall. She can drive away whenever she wants. She hasn't noticed how she's any different from the person who majored in film—or if she is different, that's Don's influence. She has not been transformed by spending time in labs, but her whole way of thinking has been rearranged by the way Don emails her his favorite articles—a profile of an MIT mathematician who also plays pro football, essays explaining deep time or slow food.

This morning she has bio lab, a calm two hours during which she streaks eight yeast strains across eight plates using eight sterile toothpicks. Then it's off to epigenetics, her favorite elective. Don sends her articles about epigenetics from time to time. Most people don't understand how it works, that a human being's genetic code is a list of potentialities rearranged by their lived experience, that a person can pass on that experience in their DNA to children and grandchildren. A Holocaust survivor or a slave, for instance, might have a grandchild with a flat affect, someone who makes reckless decisions. It wouldn't be the grandchild's fault. It's also true that not everybody likes to talk about this. Brianna, especially, would be livid at the implication that people who look like her, black people whose ancestors were maybe slaves, have crazy DNA.

Elkie talked with Don about the famous examples, the topic of the lecture her professor gave on the first day of class. For now she's stuck on eukaryotic methylation, chromatin remodeling. She doesn't even pay attention to today's lecture because she's busy moping. Should she text Brianna? But who goes into a friend's private stuff like that?

Something has to give, so she digs out the phone and opens up her messages and ignores the several dozen men who are trying to get in touch with Crystal from the ad on BigDoggie. She undeletes the conversation with Don's wife, moves it back to her inbox. Writes a response.

Crystal: *I'm not ashamed. Just don't take the kids away.*
Don: *What kids?*
Who is this?
Do I want to know who this is?

Crystal: *You cheated on him first.*
Don: *I never cheated on my husband.*
             Who is this?
Crystal: *Just please don't take his kids. He loves them so much.*
Don: *We have no children.*
             Who is this?
             Why don't you understand Joe is dead?

That throws Elkie, the name Joe. Maybe this is all a misunderstanding and Don had to get a new phone number. Maybe she is texting Joe's widow while Don rides out the aftereffects of some catastrophe. This sort of thing happens to people if they forget to pay their bills for too long.

Crystal: *I don't know a Joe.*
             Maybe this is all a mistake? Did your husband just get this phone?
Don: *No mistake. He had this thing for years. You're in it.*
             It says your name is C.
             This is him.
             Was.

The picture she sends is one Elkie has seen before. In it, Don wears a leather jacket and holds a little boy with blond curls. His son. They took this photo at the harvest fest in Stowe.

Crystal: *I thought you said no kids?*
Don: *That's my nephew's son.*

Mona or Monica or Mandy has fully committed to the dead husband thing. Elkie is not fooled, not even by the twist of the fake name. She turns her phone back off again. She has to stop by the Recreational Activities Office to fill out a request form for a faculty chaperone to Pine Ridge. And she works this afternoon, this evening, one to six: she's scheduled four men back-to-back with fifteen-minute intervals. A Sheraton three blocks from the bus station. She's panicked, at first, about her safety. Don is missing and Brianna is pissed, and two of these appointments are with new clients; she'll be seeing strange men with nobody to check up on her.

*

What would happen if she let the wrong man in at one o'clock? Would the next man circle the hotel for hours, waiting for her to pick up the phone? When she failed to do so, would he call the police, or go home? Elkie doesn't believe her clients are bad men, not most of them, but she can't see them ensuring her safety either. Not at the cost of getting arrested themselves. Elkie has never had a client try to hurt her, but Don was always making her promise to be safe.

She settles herself in the hotel room. She showers, hides her book bag under the bed, puts on wet eyeliner and CK One and a new white bustier set, this one from Va Bien. It came with a matching white kimono. She gargles with the hotel's mouthwash. She's got an hour to kill and she might as well book herself out to the end of the month.

She has to turn the phone back on to do this, which means a half-hour responding to texts and emails and voicemails. All men, all calling for Crystal. Still no Brianna, which is horrible but fair, and no Don, which is not fair at all.

When she's done booking, there's still half an hour left. Too little time for homework, too much time to just sit there. Nobody to talk to. So she texts the wife again.

Crystal: *You win.*
              Why are you doing this?
              Can you at least let me know he's OK?
Don: *No, I can't do that. He is dead.*
              Who is this?
Crystal: *Don is my friend.*
Don: *How close were you?*

Elkie's phone vibrates, a call this time. Her first appointment is ten minutes away from the Sheraton, and he wants to know where to find her. She gives him the room number. Then she hits the power button.

Her first appointment is one of the new clients, so she makes him show her his ID. He says no way, but then he stops and says, "Fuck it," and reaches into his pocket.

He pulls off his belt and lets his pants fall to the floor and holds his surprisingly long dick in his fist. He asks her what a nice girl like her is doing in a place like this, and she says, "I like to pay bills for my mom. She can't work since my grandma had a stroke. Plus, I'm in school."

He ejaculates immediately. She gets him some water from the hotel room's kitchenette and talks more about college because that's clearly what he's into.

"I'm pre-med," she says. "I'm an honors student."

The second time around is more successful, with Elkie on top. The man grits his teeth to keep from coming again. Elkie makes up a story about sleeping with one of her TAs, a lesbian tryst, in exchange for an A. The man calls her his little slut.

"Was your mom a little slut, too?" he asks. "I bet you come from a long line of nymphos."

Elkie keeps moving up and down on him in steady rhythm. Her thighs are cramping, so she leans forward to grab the headboard. She doesn't want to talk about her mother this way, so she says, "Could be. I could inherit a vulnerability for addiction in general, which could be expressed as sex addiction. If my mom acted on a sex addiction, then a theoretical addiction gene, or really it's genes, would be more likely expressed in her, and therefore more likely passed on to me. That would fall under environmental impact, I think. I'm taking a class that's sort of about this."

At first she feels like she's blown it with the mini-lecture, but the guy pumps his hips faster. Without warning, he reaches up an arm and wraps his hand around her neck. Tighter and tighter. He makes eye contact the whole time, the way Don would when Elkie was on top. Only Don never strangled her. Only Don's eyes were a piercing green, and this man's eyes are a boring gray. Elkie doesn't let herself cough or gasp or even look surprised.

"Smart girl," he groans as he comes again, "teaching me like this."

He leaves five minutes early. She uses the extra time to hop in the shower, then she turns her phone back on. Her next appointment has already texted asking for the room number, so she texts it back to him. Then she goes back to her conversation with Don's wife:

Don:	*Were you having an affair with my husband?*
Crystal:	*It's more like he was helping me. He found me in a bad situation and he showed me how to do something else.*
Don:	*What was the situation?*
Crystal:	*I had a job but I didn't like it. He showed me how to find a better job.*

This part is true. Don found her at the Pussycat and watched her writhe uncomfortably under the gazes of dozens of men. He took her to the champagne room and told her she seemed like a nice girl, a shy girl, the sort of girl who does better one-on-one.

Don:	*Why didn't you like your job?*
Crystal:	*Long story.*
Don:	*Did you sleep with him?*
	What sort of person sleeps with a married man?

Elkie doesn't like how this is all coming back on her. Don's wife made him disappear, and now she's scolding Elkie. As if she has a leg to stand on. As if she weren't cheating on Don first, as if she weren't the real whore.

Crystal:	*I am the best sort of person.*
	You're a hag.
	I'm pre-med and honors. I do charity work.

She turns the phone off again, just in time. Her next appointment, one of her regulars, is knocking at the door. She lets him in, and right away, because she knows he doesn't like small talk, she opens up her kimono.

"Nice," he says. He proceeds to use every minute of his hour, bending Elkie over the bed, the hotel's desk, bathroom sink. He takes her standing in the shower and reverse cowgirl on the bed and pulls her hair and tries at one point to go Greek, but Elkie clenches so tight he can't fit, a trick Don suggested for precisely this situation, if a man ever tried Greek with her.

This man always feels to her like she's standing in a tornado, the way he tosses her body around. Some days she hates it, but today she wants to be battered.

He leaves and she turns her phone back on. Don's wife is taking a new tack.

Don: *Pre-med?*
         How old are you?
         Nobody's hurting you, are they?
Crystal: *Where is Don?*

Her next client is the foot man, but he's running late. She runs her feet under the hot water in the bathtub, pats them clean with a towel, and puts scented lotion on her knees, close enough for him to smell, but far up enough that he won't lick it.

When the foot man finally shows up, he's nicer, somehow, than Elkie remembered. He shakes her hand and kisses her cheek and tells her to keep her underwear on. Then, yes, he masturbates while sucking on her toes, but he's done quick and it doesn't tickle too much.

"Those blisters are huge," he says. "It's good you didn't try to pop them." He buckles his pants without bothering to zip his fly, then he reaches for a briefcase by the nightstand. "I have a couple things." He pulls out a first-aid kit with a tiny bottle of yellow liquid, which he explains is castor oil, and cotton balls. He pours the castor oil on the cotton and wipes Elkie's arches.

"Do you lift heavy objects?" he asks her. "Maybe carry them around the room? You have interesting callouses."

"I lift my grandma when my mom needs help." Elkie is surprised at how much she likes the cold feeling of the oil on her feet. It soothes her blisters almost instantly. She wonders whether the foot man carries around his first-aid kit all the time, how he got so helpful, if he inherited helpfulness genes. If he comes from a long line of podiatrists.

"Your grandmother can't walk?" the foot man asks. He is circling her blisters, playfully, with the cotton.

"Or talk to us. She had a stroke, an embolism. Now she can only speak German."

"Is she from Germany?" The foot man is squeezing her toes again, breathing hard.

Elkie figures if he's asking questions, he wants her to keep talking. "She's never told us." Elkie tries to sound untroubled and sexy for the foot man, but her grandmother's past is a sore subject. Before the stroke, if anybody ever asked Elkie's grandmother about her childhood, she'd stare off into space and mouth something to herself for maybe a half-hour, ignoring the people around her. A person could pull the chair out from under her when she got like this, and she wouldn't notice.

The foot man is looking at Elkie expectantly, like he wants more of an explanation, so she says, "Grandma used to get weird when we asked where she was from. Even Grandpa had no idea. But she didn't even have an accent before the stroke."

"Maybe she practiced to get rid of it." He throws the cotton swabs in the trash bin and pulls a pack of moleskins from his first-aid kit, placing one over each of Elkie's blisters. His fly is still open, and his penis sticks out erect in front of him.

"My mom says I should take German next semester," Elkie says.

"Das ist eine gute Idee," says the foot man. He masturbates again, then he packs up his first-aid kit and briefcase and tips her a full hundred on his way out. Even Don never gave her this big a tip, not even that first night at the Pussycat, though he did spend freely on champagne.

Elkie turns on her phone one last time and is relieved to see no new messages from Don's wife. She lounges around the room waiting for the next client, the second new client, but he never gets in touch. Elkie's been stood up. She blocks his email and his phone number, grabs her book bag from under the bed, and then heads to her car.

When she gets home, Brianna's on the couch again, and worse, Elkie's mom is sitting on the couch with her. They're watching *Crooklyn* and shoveling microwave popcorn into their mouths. Even Elkie's grandmother is rapt, staring at the television.

"They should make more movies about girls," Elkie's mother says. "Eleanor, did you have fun at work?"

Brianna makes eye contact. "Elkie always has fun at work. I used to make fun of her for brewing all that coffee but I was just being an asshole."

עס זאָל מער קינאָ וועגן שוואַרצע מיידלעך זייַן.

דייַן חברטע, למשל, איז אן אמת מענטש.

אפשר, בסוד, טשיקאַווער פון דיר, קיין העט בדעה.

She dissolves into incomprehensible laughter.

"What Grandma said." Elkie's mother pats Brianna on the back. "You kids almost gave me a heart attack this morning." She sidles out to the kitchen wearing the smile of a woman who knows she's done excellent parenting. Elkie hates seeing her this smug, loves seeing her leave.

Brianna says, "Not my fault. She called me."

Elkie sits on the couch next to Brianna, in the space her mother just vacated. "If I say you might be right about Don, will you please still be my friend?"

"I'm still your friend. I know you're just going through a hard time." Brianna leans in to hug her, and the couch squeaks. "You need to hang out with guys our age." She says this like any guy their age would want a prostitute girlfriend.

"You could do so much better than me." Elkie hugs her back. "You're so normal."

"I'm pushy. I know it's annoying, but I can't stop myself. My parents are the same way, but I thought maybe if I didn't also become a lawyer . . . "

Elkie's shocked to think Brianna has her own insecurities, her own problems, and then she feels like an idiot for being shocked. Everybody has their own problems, right? At least Brianna's problems are working out for Elkie. She comes from a long line of people-fixers.

"I'm glad you care enough to push," Elkie says, and then, "His name was really Joe. I feel so stupid."

"You're not stupid. That's not your issue."

They hug and then stay there with their arms around each other. Neither girl moves for a minute, three minutes, ten. Even Elkie's grandmother has nothing to say. Elkie's chest is sinking into Brianna, into the couch, into the floor, through the ceiling, and into the apartment downstairs. Don helped her study and he made her the account on BigDoggie and he told her about his kids. She believed every word. But Elkie could be wrong. She could always be wrong.

Elkie isn't used to crying, hasn't cried about anything in years, but over dinner her eyes are red-rimmed and her bones might be made of jelly. Her mother, who still thinks she's going through a breakup, tells her no boy is worth this kind of pain. She says, "You don't need men, honey. You can make a life without any men around."

Elkie knows. Every woman in her family has made a manless life, at one point or another, and now it's her turn. They have cursed her with their manless genes.

Her grandmother shakes her head.

סיאיז ניט ריכטיק פאַר מיר. איך קען

דיין האַרצוייטיק, איך בענק נאָך מייַן מאַן, טאַקע.

She spits three times, neatly, into her palm.

"That's kind of gross," says Brianna.

"She did it when I was a girl, too," says Elkie's mom. "Ice cream?" She goes to the freezer. Brianna offers to put on more *Bob's Burgers*, and that feels like a good idea. Everybody watches cartoons in the living room, handing a box of Breyers back and forth until Elkie's mother and grandmother both shut their eyes.

Brianna whispers, so as not to wake the older women. "Your mom is right. You should forget you ever met Don. I can tell his wife to leave you alone." Elkie turns her phone on and hands it over, and Brianna says, "Huh." She shows the screen to Elkie.

Don: *Look. I'm Maria.*

 Are you some sort of sex worker?

Elkie takes the phone.

Crystal: *Yes.*

I'm with my friend again. She texted you the first time.
I shouldn't have called you a hag.

"You could also meet her, if you need like closure. I'd go with you to meet her. Just in case she turns out to be an axe murderer." Brianna scratches her chin. She's considering her price. "But you have to go to my dorm with me and watch *Alien vs. Ninja,* and you have to pay attention even if you think it's like the corniest thing you've ever seen because I'm writing about it for class. And you can't just stare at my popcorn. You have to eat like three handfuls and tell me how good it tastes."

Elkie doesn't say yes and doesn't say no. She takes the phone back. Weighs her options. Turns it off.

"Whatever you want," Brianna says. "Either way."

"I want to relax." It's a tall order, Elkie knows.

"It wouldn't be the end of the world if you took out a loan. You're going to be a doctor, right?" Brianna peers around as if she's scared, as if Elkie's mother is only pretending to rest and will open an eye any second to ask who they're texting so late. "I'm not saying this because I have a problem with what you do, I swear, but nobody works their way through school anymore, not since your grandma was our age. Like when do you sleep?"

It's a good question.

"How about now?" Elkie says. "Let's sleep now."

"You're so withholding." Brianna gets up off the couch and crosses her arms. "Here I thought I was getting through, like maybe this was your come-to-Jesus moment."

"I promise to come to Jesus in the morning." Elkie gets up, too, and creeps with Brianna back to the bedroom. They sleep there, again, head-to-toe, their homework untouched. It doesn't matter. Brianna skips her homework sometimes without getting in too much trouble, and Elkie can take the day off tomorrow. She's never been absent before; her teachers will believe her if she says she got sick.

The last thing she sees before she goes down is the ghostly underside of Brianna's foot, the skin wrinkled as the surface of the ocean, as wrinkled as hotel bedsheets, and then Elkie is dreaming of bedsheets, of Don. She can't help dreaming of Don one last time, but this time the dream isn't about something that really happened. They're naked, holding hands in an endless ocean of bedsheets, and he's pudgier than she remembers, with skin that is not tan but mottled. His eyes are still green, but cloudy, his temples not graying but white, wiry white hair springing from his crotch. Not Don then, but Joe. It is Joe who makes no move to comfort Elkie, Joe who opens his mouth—but no apology comes out. He just blows black smoke until it fills Elkie's field of vision, and then the dream is over. Joe has no children. There is nobody to inherit his lie, and nobody to carry it on. He will never exist again.

THE WOODCUTTER

Rachel Yoder

His name was Hunter Jim. Actually it was Jim Hunter, but once I got it in my head, that's what stuck. I bought a half cord of firewood from him, and he brought along this big guy in his navy blue pickup to unload it.

Hunter Jim didn't stay to help, just dropped off the big guy in overalls, then introduced me to a woman who had followed him to my house in her beat-up car. He referred to her as his *lady friend*, Jean or Marie or something, one of those meek, hippie types with long ashy hair and a macrobiotic diet, who looks like she might blow over if you say boo. She held her hands as though she were praying, except with her fingers pointed down.

"I need to see about some business dealings while I'm here in town. I'll be back in a while," he said, folding into the car, Jean/Marie at the wheel, and like that, they were gone.

The guy in overalls—Casey, he said his name was—I felt bad for him. He was out there all by himself unloading, and it was obvious Hunter Jim was taking advantage of his nature, shy and simple, with a thick tongue that stumbled through his sentences. I went out and asked did he want some water or something, and he said sure. After he drank, he threw me the pieces of juniper from the bed, and I stacked them in straight rows, one on top of each other, at the head of the driveway.

He didn't understand why I knew how to stack wood the way I did, and I told him I had done it for years back in Ohio with my dad, rode beside him on the tractor to the clearing at the edge of our property, helped him haul wood back to the house. We got the work done fast and he thanked me, then asked for another glass of water, which I got him, and then he waited there for a good forty-five minutes, sitting on the tailgate, swinging his big man legs until the woman and Hunter Jim came back.

"If you could just leave the payee line blank I'd be much obliged," Hunter Jim said as I wrote him a check, leaning close to watch. I could smell him, white soap. The skin on his cheeks was tanned and soft-looking. "It's easier to make it payable to one of my many creditors this way," he explained, folding the check and putting it in his shirt pocket.

Hunter Jim made me uneasy with his *much obliged* and *creditors* and the worked-over fisherman's cap and deck shoes he was wearing, even though we were in Arizona high desert, nowhere close to any place where you'd need his sort of coastal clothing. He was in his late forties or early fifties, with a moustache like a thick caterpillar that crawled when he talked, outdated eyeglasses with dark plastic rims and thick lenses. He reminded me of someone in a bad disguise.

"If you ever have a need of any kindling, you just give me a call. I've got plenty up at my place," he said, easing himself into the truck. I assured him I'd be fine on kindling, pointing at the ponderosa forest surrounding us.

"Pine doesn't start very well, and besides, it might get wet. I'd hardly depend on this stuff to get you through," he said as Casey slammed the passenger door. I glared at Hunter Jim, and he straight-stared back at me, the smile of his mouth pulling his face apart into expressions shaded and volatile. I looked at him openly and wouldn't stop.

I told him I owned this cabin. I knew how to build a fire. I'd be just fine. He looked at me through the open window, his face finally organizing itself into something familiar and human.

"Give me a call. Anytime," he said as he gunned the engine. The woman took off in her little beat-up car, then Casey and Hunter Jim. I was glad to see him go.

*

It was the first fall alone I'd ever had. I was twenty-four and far away from the religious upbringing I had been looking to leave behind. You might know this one: young and dumb with the story of myself. The last time I'd touched my parents had been years ago, when I left. I stood on the porch beneath a trellis wrapped thick with white moonflowers. The blooms blew in the breeze like clean laundry on the line. My mother's thin shoulders. My father's open palm.

It was about work. That's what I said. I had an unimportant job in a high-desert town. I thought I knew how to do it, head west toward nothing I knew, a big dry barren, full of threat of death or some ecstatic vision blowing up out of the dust.

But of course I was angry. I enumerated the amorphous wrongs: Raised Mennonite with outdated ways. Cursed female crossed with smart.

"At the very least, I wish I'd been dumb," I raged at my father. "Dumb and ugly."

"I am what I am," he said. "And you. You."

He'd been raised Amish and carried his childhood with him like a donor heart in a small white cooler that one day he might use to save his own life. As families do, his had aged into more moderate theologies, turned Mennonite. And this he had given to me. But I didn't want it and tried to give it back.

Before I left, I had only loved Ruth. This was my father's sister, a middle-aged Mennonite virgin who took her coffee black and tilled the garden each spring in a long skirt. She had tended house for a living at the residence of an old woman who was known for her proclivities toward verbal abuse, then worked for a time at the local day care, but finally settled on a job at the meat locker where she wore a thick navy coat regardless of the season. She spent her days hefting bloody sides of meat around the walk-in freezer and butchering with a big knife.

It was not normal for a Mennonite woman to live like this, and always the talk turned toward getting her married. My father knew so-and-so who is said to have a brother who's a good, godly man.

While doing missionary work, my uncle met a man in Kentucky who built his own house and lived off the land and wasn't picky. Men arrived at her house unannounced, sent by one of her brothers. She was obliged to smile and serve them coffee and cakes and talk about the harvest that season or the lesson of last Sunday's service.

But she never married. This I gripped across two thousand miles of highway, windows down, speeding through the flat grasslands, under skies painted with pink clouds, past a vast crater pitted from a long-ago collision. That Ruth existed meant I might exist, too.

I needed space. I wanted to be scared and strong. Instead I wound up living in a double-wide on a washed-out dirt road with an older man named Ezra. I tried not to think about this, how I wasn't on my own even though that's what I'd wanted, how my life had become a series of sad ironies. He wore a handlebar moustache and had a giant eye tattooed on the back of his neck. When I asked what the eye tattoo meant, he said it was personal and not to ask again.

I told myself I would only stay with him until I got on my feet, but I wound up living in the double-wide for three years. That last year with Ezra he fell asleep as soon as his head hit the pillow, and then I lay on my side staring at him for hours as he snored. Before he got in bed, I would lay there tucked in and watch him undress, watch him deliberately fold his pants and shirt, watch him look in the mirror and twirl the ends of his moustache between his fingers, watch him sit down on the edge of the bed with his back to me, watch him snap off the lamp, watch him slide his legs beneath the sheets, watch him arrange himself there and close his eyes. He'd do all this without looking at me. *Good night*, I'd say. *Good night*, he'd say, then turn on his side and be gone. This was the game we played as things fell apart, me staring at him and him pretending I wasn't there.

He collected books about dreams and reality, how one could provide insight about the other. He wanted to find a way to dream while waking and was convinced he could resolve the problems of his daily life while asleep. He believed the boundary between these worlds was fluid or perhaps didn't even exist at all. He spent weekends poring over his books in the makeshift study, a population of small clay men that he'd sculpted sitting on the windowsill and table beside him. As a hobby, he liked to photograph these men in tiny postapocalyptic settings he constructed. We had a number of these images framed on our trailer's walls.

Sober, he was one way. Drunk, the man was quite another, able to be manipulated into certain affections, but only after especially heavy drinking, a long afternoon and even longer night spent at The Birdcage downing two-for-ones and smoking rollies. He liked me best when I'd been drinking and had become simpleminded, hopping up and down and clapping my hands to Tom Petty on the jukebox, missing the dartboard entirely and driving steel-tipped spikes into the wooden wall. He laughed, self-satisfied. *My baby*, he said.

One night my high heel got stuck between the slats on the deck out back, and I had to slip my foot out and then pry the shoe from between the beer-soaked boards. When I pulled it free I knocked myself ass over teakettle and just sat there cursing and making little kitten noises and saying how I was all dirty and messed up and needed another drink. He pulled me up and wrapped his arm around my waist as I stood there lopsided with a shoe in my hand. I rested my head on his shoulder and sighed, then nuzzled my nose into his neck. We danced between the pool tables, and he kissed me on the lips, these little kisses, over and over again. When we went out, I always felt like we were performing for someone, but I didn't really care. I wanted him to love me even if it really was just cheap theater. That's how my whole life felt anyway, a big act.

We walked home from the bar since we'd been driving drunk too much. That night in the darkness, he became agitated with me for walking too fast or too slow. I hadn't listened. I wasn't nice enough. I hadn't waited for him while he took a piss in a bush. I didn't care. I slept on the couch that night and woke up feeling sick. He was in the kitchen brewing coffee with tobacco strewn all over the counter, rolling a crooked cigarette.

He moved away to Tucson, and I bought a cabin on Cherokee Lane with a couple thousand down. For the most part I was successful in avoiding happy hour and instead stayed home to paint a kitchen wall Christmas-ornament red and sew striped curtains for the screen porch. In the mornings, I smoked long brown cigarettes on the porch and stared out at the steaming pines, the blackbirds moving among them and up into the clear sky.

Soon enough the season grew colder and I started building fires with the juniper from Hunter Jim, blazing infernos that licked up the inside of the chimney pipe and heated the whole house like a sweat lodge. The house was so hot I wore tank tops inside, then opened the windows and kept loading on the firewood. At night, I closed the orange eyes of the stove and, lying in bed, listened to the metal tick and ping as it cooled. In the morning, I dug through the gray ashes in the bottom of the stove, uncovered the neon-orange coals, and started the fire all over again.

That same September, this guy named Chas, who lived in Colorado, was back in Prescott for an extended visit, working on a photo series, black and whites I knew had something to do with nudity. My friend Kate called me up one morning and asked did I want to pose for one. He'd asked her, but she didn't want to do it alone. He remembered my name and wondered would I be interested. Sure, I said. Of course.

Chas and I had met only once before, at his going-away party a year earlier. He was also older, a friend of Ezra's.

"It's a binge, my dear," he had said in a fake British accent. Chas tipped back a bottle of dark beer, and the veins in his neck raised. He wasn't a big man, but his body was all muscle, the human incarnation of a fist. He wore a finely trimmed, faintly red goatee. He seemed sanitized, as if he'd taken many showers that day.

I was drunk myself, in the living room staring at these huge photos he'd taken: Thumb Butte black against nuclear sunsets, a long panorama of this place called the Dells where smooth volcanic rocks bulbed up and out of the earth like mushrooms. Ezra was somewhere outside. I didn't know where, and I didn't care.

Chas was most notorious for being in lingering love with Beth Cantrell, wholesomely blonde, with perfect posture and a year-round tan from camping and rock-climbing and kayaking. She was eleven years younger than he was. They'd dated a number of years before, but now she stayed away from him for the most part since it was commonly held he was still a little obsessed. From the talk, I also gathered his general mental stability was questionable, as was his heterosexuality, and that most considered him a savant of some sort.

He drove me and Kate into the national forest, and we got undressed in a big drainage pipe that ran under the road. He had a gym bag full of tall patent boots and latex garments and dressed us up in them, then posed our bodies at unnatural angles and told us not to move as he stared through the camera, adjusting things. He took one shot and then the rain started and that was that.

On the way back to town, as water washed across the windshield, Chas looked at me and I looked at him and he said, "Movie?" and I said, "Movie at my cabin," and Kate, sitting between us, rolled her eyes. We dropped her off and then went to Cherokee Lane, watched a movie as a matter of formality, and crawled under my big down comforter out on the futon on the porch. It was still raining, and he started kissing me.

"I haven't been with a woman for three years," he said. This meant Beth had been his last. I liked that.

He bought bags of groceries at the health food store, spinach and tortillas and black beans and strawberries, food with whole grains and omega-3 and flaxseed, this tea called maté that smelled like freshly cut hay, which he drank through a metal straw from a gourd. He was very concerned with staying alive and wouldn't drink my coffee or cream.

"Poison," he said in the morning, boiling water for his tea. "I need to keep a clean system."

He left during the days to do whatever, and I went to work, and in the evenings he was there or he wasn't. I didn't keep tabs. It was come-and-go as we pleased, meet up whenever, no pressure. It was about sex and that was it. I only wanted to sink into someone.

"I love these thighs," he'd say, running his hands over the curves I would have rather not had. "Sexy." All I could think about though was Beth Cantrell and her flatness and straightness and how he actually loved her. I wouldn't have minded him falling in love with me, even though I knew that wasn't really what I wanted.

His birthday was in early October, and the week before, he propped himself on his elbows in my bed. He'd just done all these things to me.

"Do you think you'd have a threesome with me for my birthday?" he asked. "That's what I want."

I thought about it, and Chas looked at me sweetly, smiling his best underjawed smile. Thinking about being in bed with two other people made me feel as though I were full of punched-out windows. I wanted to be OK, wanted to be strong and unhurtable, but I lay there and could only breathe and stare at the ceiling as pairs of blackbirds flew in and out of me, their wings making the noise of skirts swishing together on a slow dance floor.

"I'll think about it," I said. The next day I told him no. Soon after that, I didn't want to sleep with him anymore. I didn't want him even to touch me. "Time to go," I said one morning, but he already knew. He packed his gym bags with the boots and latex and baby powder and masks. He gave me a hug. "It was fun," I said, even though right then, standing by the open door, the whole thing was poised to tip over into something else. I could feel it teetering inside of me.

"Cheerio, then," he said, patting my arm. He loaded his truck and drove up Cherokee Lane and over the hill.

There was this game I liked to play when I was a kid where I'd make the square-jawed neighbor girl pretend to be a man and then kidnap me and lock me in a tower, which was really the hall closet full of coats and flannel shirts that smelled of my father's sweet cigars and green hay perspiration. I made her hold my wrists behind my back, push me into the darkness, and tell me I could never leave. After she slammed the door and turned a key, a rush of dark, glittering heat moved up my legs and into my stomach. It felt like a thousand points of shorted electricity, a sky full of stars blinking into being and then dying in explosions. And that's what I had wanted, for Chas to take me away, to have me whole, to lock me up. I wanted the sky to fall into me and then split open. There were too many people in the world was the problem. For just one of them to want me all for himself—why was that so hard? Just one. That's it.

It started raining in earnest in late October, and rivulets of water slid down the slanted wood ceiling in the mudroom. I climbed up on the metal roof and fixed the holes with layers of thick black tar and wire mesh. I'd been diligent in collecting kindling from across the road in a cardboard box I kept on the porch, but once a constant drizzle set in and the kindling dwindled to nothing, I was shit out of luck. I tried using cardboard and scraps of lumber I had around the house, but eventually I didn't have what I needed to start a fire. I dug up Hunter Jim's brown business card and contemplated it. Easy, I thought, and free. I wouldn't have to pay a dime for what he'd give me, and I could get him to deliver it.

I called him and he answered the phone with, "Howdy." Just from the sound of my voice he recalled my name, first and last, and that I lived on Cherokee Lane, and yes, certainly, he had some kindling for me.

"When could you bring it by?" I asked.

"Oh, no," he said. "You'd need to come up here to collect it. I've got plenty at my house." I imagined it piled next to his woodshed, which would be flush with evenly cut logs. That's how my father kept things in Ohio, long rows of wood with pretty round ends that dwindled the further it wore into winter. Brown morning after brown morning, my father split wood out back. For the big logs, he drove a red metal wedge into the middle of the wood, then jimmied it out and sank the ax-head into the gash. After he loaded the hot orange mouth of the stove, he sat in an easy chair and read the Bible. As a child, once I learned about death, I cried thinking about how he'd be gone. Heaven didn't comfort me. I couldn't think beyond his body and its warmth, his thick-fingered hands.

The stack of juniper at the head of my driveway, the swaying pines with shaggy bark that smelled miraculously of vanilla, the cabin door I'd painted purple, the screen porch, the woodstove in my living room, the Sears Roebuck sewing machine heavy as an anvil on my kitchen table, the curtains I'd sewn and hung, the tulip bulbs I'd already buried in the flower beds, the mulch I'd covered them with—all of it was an attempt to return to goodness. But I was in the desert. I didn't believe in God anymore. I believed in myself, and this felt safe, like an armor. I could handle anything. I actually said this to people: I can handle anything. And Hunter Jim—what a joke, I thought. We made arrangements for me to stop by early the next week. I could get what I wanted by my own means and in my own way.

What I'm trying to get at is a sickness of the soul. I was ill that fall. The season was turning. I had no kindling, and the bar was warm. I went and I stayed. Ezra showed up, too. He'd ridden his motorcycle from Tucson, and I wanted him to come home with me but he wouldn't. He just sat on a stool, shoulders hunched, sipping whiskey from a short glass. I would have done anything for him, would have kissed the palms of his hands. He didn't know this, or maybe he did and that was the problem. He stared at himself in the mirror behind the rows of liquor bottles. I drank too much and laughed when I was near him. I assume I drove home later because that's where I wound up.

I don't know what time it was or how long I'd been home but someone came into my room at some point, and when I saw his silhouette I couldn't remember who I was or where I'd come from.

"Hey," he said. He kicked off his shoes at the foot of the bed. My brain was doing that thing, turning over like a dying engine.

"You," I said. I remember deciding the man was Josh, an ex of mine who did not even live in Arizona but had to go on antidepressants back when I dumped him. He was nice. I wanted it to be Josh in particular so I could just lie back down and not worry and go to sleep. I was so tired. He left the room and I blacked back into the bed and then he was there and slid beside me with his cool legs.

It was only after he began kissing me and I tasted his tobacco, I realized it was Ezra. It could have been anyone up to that point.

We started having sex, but once he really got going, it felt as if I wasn't even there anymore. I cried and told him to stop, please stop, and he rolled off.

The next morning we squinted at each other across the kitchen, him leaning on the counter sipping a cup of coffee, me standing next to the kitchen table in my robe with my arms crossed and all my hair piled on top of my head. Whenever Ezra and I had sex, I burned down there and swelled shut. I was actually allergic to him. I'd forgotten about this. In the driveway, as he left, he looked like a toy in his helmet and leather coat. He revved the motorcycle and peeled out. It was still early.

I was cold. I tried starting a fire with cereal boxes and balls of newspaper but the logs were too big. I got black soot all over my robe cuffs and burned my fingers with the matches. My head hurt, and I was searing between my legs, and my nose was stuffed up from too many cigarettes.

I went to the grocery store and bought a package of hot dogs and some buns, went home and ate three of them, ate two more, buried them in the trash, then pulled them out an hour later and ate the rest. I put on two sweaters and a pair of gloves. I watched as the day closed itself up like a box. I was waiting for something, a sign of kindness, relief. I smoked cigarettes on the porch, wrapped in a blanket, watching as the black bodies of the birds moved through the air.

Sitting out there, I thought about things, thought about quitting drinking, but then it was Halloween and there was a party at Beth Cantrell's house, and cheap red wine, and of course I had to. I saw Chas there, dressed in heels, black stockings, tiny shorts, and a shiny red corset. He was wearing eyeliner, which accentuated his high eyes. It was a binge.

"Chas," I said when he walked by. He turned his head but couldn't see me. He followed Beth out of the room. You could tell she didn't care about him from the way she walked, from her certainty he would follow her wherever she went. I pushed past a glitter fairy and a hairy man wearing a long blonde wig and drove home mostly sober, then lay in bed, lips stained purple from party wine, and stared at the ceiling, wondering when something would start to matter.

Hunter Jim looked the same as he had before, the deck shoes, the ratty jeans and plaid shirt rolled up at the sleeves, the caterpillar moustache, the thick dirty glasses, the fisherman's cap. I parked my car by his house, and when he came out, the way he smiled at me, I could tell he thought he was handsome. He liked the way his face looked when he shaved in the morning. I couldn't stand him.

"Well hello there, friend," he said. I searched behind him for the kindling pile, the neat lines of chopped wood, and saw neither. There was just a little shed back there with a padlock on the door, something wrapped in a blue tarp at the side. He lived next to the national forest in a rough-sided log cabin. I wondered if Jean/Marie was inside. It seemed she wasn't.

"Do you have four-wheel drive?" he asked, eying my car, a rusted wagon.

"Yeah," I said.

"It'd be better if I drove it up," he said, pointing toward the road. "It's rough going. You don't want to get stuck. Get out." His truck was in the drive. I wondered why we couldn't use that but didn't ask. I watched myself open the door and hand him the keys, watched our hands move next to one another and then away. I opened the passenger door and for exactly one second had a question in my mind, but it passed through before I could understand.

"I knew you'd come over," he said as he drove.

"I thought you'd have kindling at your house," I said. "That's the way you made it sound."

"Did I?" he asked. "Now why would I do that?" His question twirled and untwirled in the air as he drove us far into the woods.

The ruts in the road were worn deep from the rains. He finally turned on an old forest service road that cut steeply through the top of a wooded hill. When he pulled to a stop, the car was buried between the high earthen walls strewn with chunks of sandstone and clay and broken sticks. Hunter Jim pulled the emergency brake and smiled. A button on his shirt had come open, and I could see his chest and the hair.

"Oh," he said, following my eyes down to his shirt. "Believe me, I know."

I got out and started picking sticks off the ground and tossing them in the box I had in the back of the car. Hunter Jim meandered from stick to stick, as if sorting and selecting only the best ones. As he bent, I saw he was wearing a length of baling twine around his waist, threaded through the belt loops.

"I wanted to spend some time with you," he said, smiling again, and I smiled back politely. "You seem like you're a fascinating young woman." I laughed, politely again. Humor him. Be agreeable, kind. I had been taught from an early age to listen to men, to nod, to smile and answer them.

He started asking me questions, felt this was really the time to try and get to know me. Where I was originally from and all that.

"Ohio," I said.

"Whereabouts?" he asked.

"Oh, the eastern part," I said, trying to be unspecific.

"So you must have grown up on a farm," he said.

"Just a big garden," I said.

"And were you religious?" he asked.

"What?" I said. A fat little bird kicked up dirt under a bush. It seemed peculiar.

"Religious," he repeated.

"I was raised Mennonite, yeah," I said. He put his hands on his hips and leaned back, stretching.

"I knew it," he said, "but I was thinking Mormon, perhaps."

I didn't know what to say. I pressed a smile on my face. I wanted him to think that I didn't think anything was strange. This seemed important.

"You know, we met before I brought you that wood," he said. I squinted at him, and he nodded.

"Oh, right," I said. "Right." The box was half full. He was slowing down, collecting sticks neatly in his hands.

"I've been thinking a lot about you since I dropped off the wood," he said. I kept picking up sticks. He had stopped and was standing in the middle of the road, rubbing his hand back and forth against his stomach. My muscles pulled tight to my bones. "Your father," he said. He fidgeted with the knot of baling twine at the top of his pants. He fondled the frayed ends with his fingertips. "He was either a physician, a minister, or a politician. Am I right?"

Every grain of dust was coming into view. Rocks tumbled down the hill when my feet touched them, and I could smell car oil and creosote. A dark shimmer moved through me. I used to have this dream, of a jester chasing after me as I drove a jeep down a dirt road. The bells hanging from the points of his red and yellow hat jingled as he ran.

"He paints houses," I said. This was true. Hunter Jim was staring at me, leaning forward on his toes. I could see myself tossing him words like bits of raw meat and him plucking them from midair with his mouth. "He used to be a minister," I said. "And he's run in a couple of local races. Not a doctor, though."

"I knew it," Hunter Jim said. He went back on his heels and then took off his hat and felt his hair. He patted it down and whistled back at a bird, then laughed. "What a great day!" he said. "Don't you think it's beautiful out here?"

"That's plenty," I said. The box wasn't full, but I wanted to leave. He brought a handful of sticks to the car, and I moved away.

"Oh, no. Let's fill it," he said, looking in the box. "You want it good and full."

"OK," I said. I looked at his hands. They were pink and clean and without callus—the hands of a man who didn't know outdoor work. I missed my mother. She had a red birthmark on the pretty curve of her foot, and I hadn't seen it in years.

"You're so obedient," he commented.

The sky was flat with gray clouds. A bird sang. I was up there, far away from everyone, on a hidden road with Hunter Jim, who had my car keys squirreled in the warmth of his pocket. I had this feeling of having suddenly come to, as if I'd been gone for a very long time and was only now just opening my eyes behind the wheel of a soundless, speeding car on a dark highway.

This is it, I said to the girl bending to collect sticks from the dusty road. This is when it finally happens.

I was so calm, with red barns and castles and entire glittering cities, every place I'd ever seen or imagined or hoped to be, collapsing inside me.

I kept picking up sticks. They were crooked and had mint green fungus growing on them. He asked me something, did I like living in Prescott, something like that. I said yeah. He asked something else. I said yeah again. I stopped talking after that. It's that I couldn't.

"All good," he said when the box was full. I told myself to make him give me the keys, but instead got back in the passenger side without saying anything. This is when he drives you somewhere else, I told the girl in the car. She was so beautiful, so beautiful and stupid. I saw what Hunter Jim saw in her, and it was heartbreaking.

He drove, and we came to a drooping chain slung across the road.

"You're going to have to get out and get that," he said. I did. I got out and unhooked it, let him through, and got back in. I didn't know why I was the way I was. The windows were open as we drove. I looked at my hands. My cuticles were all torn up. We curved through the woods, down a hill, and then I saw his house. He pulled to the side of the road, turned off the engine, and handed me the keys.

"You can get more kindling any time you want," he said.

"OK," I said.

The driver's seat was still warm when I got in. I closed the door and stared at the road, feeling for the ignition. He stood beside the car, next to my open window. That's when he started clapping, slow, spreading his hands wide in between. The claps popped from his force.

"Bravo," he said. "Really, really well done." I got the car started, put it in gear, and undid the emergency brake. He laughed. "Ha!" he said, bucking his head up to the sky. "Ha!" I looked at him, and he had this smile on his face, not happy or hungry but something altogether different. He pushed his clapping hands toward the window. "Bravo," he said again. "Good job for making it through that."

The world outside was a photograph of itself, exactly the same but different. I let out the clutch and pushed on the gas. I could hear him clapping as I drove away.

I went to work and came home. I made fires. I listened to men and their guitars on the stereo long into the night. I thought about Ezra and what was so tied up inside of him he couldn't undo it. "Like a hard, black rock," he used to say of his heart, balling his hand into a fist. I thought about Chas and how, after a certain point, it was all I could do not to turn and try to hurt him when he touched me. One minute, we were sleeping together. The next, I couldn't stomach him, not even a little. I wondered, was this what normal people, walking around in the world, were these the things they felt and, if so, what did they do when they felt them? I mean, where did they put the feelings?

I had wanted to be alone and now I was, but it didn't feel like an accomplishment. It was the darkest part of the night, when even the wild, dirty pigs that liked to root up my tulip bulbs were somewhere with their dirty pig families rubbing noses against each other's hairy skin while sleeping. Inside my head, inside that cabin, I couldn't, so I walked.

I walked out the door to the bleached asphalt of Cherokee Lane and, farther, over the crooked roads in our pine-thick neighborhood, past the quiet-as-dead sleepers in their cabins, up and over and out onto the bigger streets, past the Safeway glowing cold with twenty-four-hour light, past the lifeless Mexican place that served cactus tacos, through town square where even the boot-scuffed doors of Whiskey Row were locked tight. I walked until I rubbed my heels raw inside my shoes and stopped in front of a low, ugly building where the Unitarians met on Sundays. It was a Thursday. I tried the door. It opened and I went in.

Dark shapes filled the dark sanctuary. I sat in a pew right in the middle of the room and watched the earliest light illuminate the windows like a candle. Modern items of worship—electric guitars, a retractable screen on which to project holy words, poorly painted ivy framing stenciled letters: "The way and the truth and the light"— slowly appeared at the front of the room. It was all so futile.

I closed my eyes to feel the heat of a faraway star on my cheek. When I was a small girl, twice a year in the empty Mennonite church at the end of the gravel lane, the men adjourned to one hallway, the women to another. I went with my mother, a young, dark beauty with slender ankles. In the clean hall, some of the women sat on a long backless bench with tubs of water at their feet, and the others knelt before them. The women on the benches lifted the hems of their skirts and raised one foot, then the other, above the basins. The women kneeling on the floor cupped their hands and spooned water over the feet, some bare and pale, others still in tan hosiery. No one spoke. Pairs of shoes were strewn about. It smelled of the dirt and creases of unknown bodies, of yeast and sweat and bathroom powder, balms made of beeswax, even of the summer garden, a whiff of a tomato plant, the ground they walked on, the freshly turned earth. It was an act of humility, my mother told me as she knelt and held a naked foot in her hands. It was an act of human grace.

A door creaked and I opened my eyes to find the room lit up like a greenhouse or newly painted nursery.

"Oh, hi," the woman said as if she'd been expecting me. She looked like she'd been crumpled into a tiny ball by a big hand and then flattened back out. She went to the back of the room where three coffee makers and stacks of cups sat on a long table and started making pot after pot. Soon a young, hunched couple with unwashed hair appeared and sat a few rows in front of me, touching shoulders but not saying a thing. A few more people milled at the back of the room where the coffee makers made dove noises. Men shaped like trash bags full of trash, skinny women with tight muscles wrapping their arms, insane boys with bright eyes, girls trying to make themselves disappear—one by one they filed in as if saints at the end of a hard pilgrimage.

Soon, a meeting commenced. They started talking about powerlessness—step one, they said, step one—and about getting fucked up, about God and surrender. They were talking about choices, how they'd made bad ones, talking about trying harder and then messing up again, apologizing, forgiveness. They were laughing and cussing, checking their palms when they didn't know the words. They were drinking coffee and Big Gulps, twitching, missing fingers, brains fried and scratching themselves, wrinkled, tired, homeless, thick men preaching humility in loud voices, cracking jokes, telling stories about diners and stashed bottles and empty wallets. They were broken down but not all the way. They were trying to wake up, five o'clock in the morning drinking coffee, so many cups of coffee, talking, saying how it was, how it is, how it will be.

"The Devil Has No Shadow" by Brigitte Leschhorn. First appeared in *Boulevard*.

"X" by Michael Martone. First appeared in *Always Crashing*.

"My Mother Was a Beauty Queen" by Michele Morano. First appeared in *Ninth Letter*.

"The Creeping End (a triptych)" by John McNally. First published in *Beloit Fiction*.

"Some of Us Are Gone" by Ander Monson. First appeared in *Ploughshares*.

"Stop 'n' Go" by Michael Parker. First appeared in *New England Review*.

"Preservation" by Casey Pycior. First appeared in *Crab Orchard Review*.

"How to Survive a Non-Funeral" by S. A. Rivkin. First appeared in *Glimmer Train*.

"Hello Kitty Head" by Lee Ann Roripaugh. First appeared in *Sou'wester*.

"Why Guineas Fly" by Mark Sanders. First appeared in *A Sandhills Reader*.

"Shelter" by Sara Schaff. First appeared in *Southern Humanities Review*.

"The Junk Drawer" by Christine Sneed. First appeared in *Literary Review*.

"Older Sister" by Christine Sneed. First appeared in *New England Review*.

"King of the Big Ticket" by Evelyn Somers. First appeared in *Copper Nickel*.

"The Mistake" by Evelyn Somers. First appeared in *Moon City Review*.

"House Ghosts" by Maura Stanton. First appeared in *Ghost Story*.

"Far Be It for Me to Say" by Maggie Su. First appeared in *Mid-American Review*.

"The Wall" by Emma Törzs. First appeared in *Missouri Review*.

"Go" by Mary Troy. First appeared in *Boulevard*.

"A Story's End" by Lee Upton. First appeared in *Notre Dame Review*.

"How Will You Not Drown?" by Shubha Venugopal. First appeared in *Nimrod*.

"Move" by Cady Vishniac. First appeared in *Mid-American Review*.

"Museum of Menarche" by Laura Maylene Walter. First appeared in *Ninth Letter*.

"Violate the Leaves" by Theodore Wheeler. First appeared in *Boulevard*.

"Ocean Bound" by Kelsey Yoder. First appeared in *Five Points*.

BIOGRAPHIES

Mike Alberti grew up in Albuquerque, New Mexico and received his MFA from the University of Minnesota. His fiction has appeared in *Colorado Review*, *Crazyhorse*, *Gulf Coast*, *Indiana Review*, *One Story*, and elsewhere. His work has been supported by fellowships from the James Merrill House, the Jerome Foundation, the MacDowell Colony, the Minnesota State Arts Board, the Ucross Foundation, the Vermont Studio Center, and the Virginia Center for the Creative Arts. He lives in Minneapolis, where he serves as the Managing Director of Minnesota Prison Writing Workshop.

Ron A. Austin holds an MFA from the University of Missouri–St. Louis and is a 2016 Regional Arts Commission Fellow. *Avery Colt Is a Snake, a Thief, a Liar*, his first collection of linked stories, won the 2017 Nilsen Prize. The book will be released in fall of 2019. Austin's short stories have been placed in *Pleiades*, *Story Quarterly*, *Ninth Letter*, *Black Warrior Review*, *Midwestern Gothic*, *Juked* and other journals. He, his partner Jennie, and son Elijah live in St. Louis with a whippet named Carmen.

Abby Bardi is the author of the novels *The Book of Fred*, *The Secret Letters*, and *Double Take*. Her short fiction has appeared in *Bellingham Review*, *Monkeybicycle*, *Quarterly West*, and several anthologies. She was born and raised in Chicago and has lived in Japan, England, and currently, Ellicott City, Maryland.

Jason Lee Brown is the author of the forthcoming story collection *Midwest Everyman*, the novel *Prowler: The Mad Gasser of Mattoon*, the novella *Championship Run*, and the poetry chapbook *Blue Collar Fathers*. He is the editor-in-chief of *River Styx* literary magazine and co-editor of the poetry anthology *The Book of Donuts*.

Michael Byers has taught creative writing at the MFA program of the University of Michigan since 2006. He is the author of *The Coast of Good Intentions* (stories) and two novels, *Long for This World and Percival's Planet*. His stories have been anthologized in *Best American Short Stories* and *The O. Henry Awards* and elsewhere, and his work has received awards from the Henfield Foundation, the American Academy of Arts and Letters, and the Whiting Foundation. His novella *The Broken Man* (PS Publishing, UK) was a finalist for the World Fantasy Award.

Alison Clement has published two novels, *Twenty Questions* and *Pretty is As Pretty Does*. *Twenty Questions* won the Oregon Book Award for Best Novel. *Pretty* was a Barnes and Noble Discover Great New Writers and BookSense selection. Her short stories and essays have appeared in *The Sun, Salon, Alaska Quarterly Review, Calyx* and *High Country News*. One of her stories was chosen as a notable in *Best American Short Stories* 2007. Another was nominated for a Pushcart Prize. She recently earned her MFA at Oregon State University and now teaches writing at a community college.

Robert Day's short fiction has received *Best American Short Stories* and *Pushcart Prize* citations. Among his awards and fellowships are National Endowment of the Arts, Yaddo and McDowell Fellowships, and a Maryland Arts Council Award. His fiction has appeared in such places as *TriQuarterly, North Dakota Quarterly,* and *New Letters*, and his nonfiction has appeared in *American Scholar, Washington Post Magazine, Smithsonian,* and elsewhere. He is the author of the novel *The Last Cattle Drive*, a Book-of-the-Month Club selection; two novellas, *In My Stead* and *The Four Wheel Drive Quartet*; and two short story collections, *Speaking French in Kansas* and *where i am now*. He has taught at the Iowa

Writers Workshop; University of Kansas; and Montaigne College, University of Bordeaux. He is past president of the Associated Writing Programs; the founder and former director of the Rose O'Neill Literary House; and founder and publisher of the Literary House Press at Washington College where he is an adjunct professor of English literature.

Steve De Jarnatt had a long career in film and television as a writer, director, and producer. Some of his '80s cult oeuvre—*Miracle Mile* and *Cherry 2000*—have been having a nice revival in recent years with Blu Rays in the US through Kino Lorber Classics, as well as in France, Germany, and the UK. He got off the show biz train a few years ago to learn the craft of fiction, and his writing has since appeared in *Cincinnati Review*, *New England Review*, *Fifth Wednesday*, *Joyland*, *Santa Monica Review*, *Meridian*, and others. His story "Eggtooth" won the *Missouri Review* Audio Contest in 2014, and he had stories selected for *The Best American Short Stories* 2009 and *New Stories from the Midwest* 2013. He currently teaches at Ohio University School of Media Arts and the Dodge College of Film and Media Arts at Chapman University. He is thinking about starting a band.

Daniel A. Hoyt's books are *This Book is Not for You*, a novel, and *Then We Saw the Flames*, a story collection. His work has appeared in *Iowa Review*, *Missouri Review*, *Cincinnati Review*, and other cool midwestern literary magazines. Dan teaches at Kansas State University and lives in Manhattan, Kansas, where he listens to rock and roll in basements and co-parents his son.

Toni Judnitch earned her MFA in fiction from Southern Illinois University in Carbondale. Her work has appeared or is forthcoming in *Sycamore Review*, *Nashville Review*, *Ninth Letter*, *Third Coast*, and *AGNI*. She was the winner of *New South*'s 2018 prose contest. Currently, she is a PhD candidate studying fiction at University of Cincinnati, where she is at work on her first novel.

Shanie Latham is managing editor of *River Styx* magazine and does proofreading and page layout for *Boulevard* and *Story* magazines. She is an associate professor of English at Jefferson College in Missouri and co-edited *The Book of Donuts*, a tasty poetry anthology. Her own poems have appeared in *Big Muddy* and *Slant*.

Keith Lesmeister is the author of the story collection *We Could've Been Happy Here* (MG Press, 2017). His fiction has appeared in *American Short Fiction*, *Gettysburg* Review, *North American Review*, *Redivider*, *Slice Magazine*, and many others. His nonfiction has appeared in *River Teeth*, *Sycamore Review*, *The Good Men Project*, *Tin House Open Bar*, *Water~Stone Review*, and elsewhere. He earned his MFA from the Bennington Writing Seminars. He lives in the Driftless region of northeast Iowa.

Kelly Magee is the author of *Body Language*, winner of the Katherine Anne Porter Prize, and *The Neighborhood*, as well as several collaborative works, including *With Animal*, co-written with Carol Guess. Her work has appeared in *Nimrod*, *Granta*, *Gulf Coast*, *Kenyon Review*, *Crazyhorse*, *Hobart*, and others. She teaches creative writing and queer studies at Western Washington University.

Rebecca Makkai is the Chicago-based author of the novels *The Great Believers*, *The Hundred-Year House*, and *The Borrower*, as well as the short story collection *Music for Wartime*. Her short fiction won a 2017 Pushcart Prize, and was chosen for The Best American Short Stories for four consecutive years (2008 to 2011). The recipient of a 2014 NEA fellowship, Makkai is on the MFA faculties of Sierra Nevada College and Northwestern University, and she is the Artistic Director of StoryStudio Chicago.

Christian Moody's publications include stories in *Esquire*, *Alaska Quarterly Review*, *Cincinnati Review*, *Best New American Voices*, and *Best American Fantasy*, among others. He holds an MFA in Creative Writing from Syracuse University and a PhD in English (fiction focus) from the University of Cincinnati. Currently, he is an Assistant Professor of English at the Cleveland Institute of Art and lives with his family in Indianapolis.

Antonya Nelson teaches creative writing at the University of Houston and is the award-winning author of three novels and four short story collections. Her stories have appeared in *The New Yorker*, *Harper's*, and *The Best American Short Stories*. She divides her time among Texas, Colorado, and New Mexico.

Kim O'Neil is author of the linked story collection *Fever Dogs* (Northwestern University Press, 2017), which was a finalist for the Balcones Prize and from which "Dicky Lucy" comes. Her work has been published in *Electric Literature*, *Juked*, *Packingtown Review*, *Faultline*, and elsewhere. She lives in Chicago, where she is Senior Lecturer in English at the University of Illinois at Chicago, Assistant Director of the UIC Writing Center, and at work on a second book.

Raised in Iowa City, Iowa, **Leslie Pietrzyk** is the author of three novels, most recently *Silver Girl*, released in February 2018 by Unnamed Press. Her collection of unconventionally linked short stories, *This Angel on My Chest*, won the 2015 Drue Heinz Literature Prize and was published by the University of Pittsburgh Press. Her previous novels are *Pears on a Willow Tree* and *A Year and a Day*. Short fiction and essays have appeared/are forthcoming in *Washington Post Magazine*, *Southern Review*, *Ploughshares*, *Gettysburg Review*, *Hudson Review*, *The Sun*, *Arts & Letters*, *River Styx*, *Iowa Review*, *The Collagist*, and *Cincinnati Review*. Pietrzyk is a member of the core fiction faculty at the Converse low-residency MFA program.

Kelsey Ronan grew up in Flint, Michigan, and lives in Detroit. Her stories and essays have appeared in many magazines and literary journals, including *Michigan Quarterly Review*, *Utne Reader*, *Kenyon Review*, *Belt Magazine*, *Indiana Review*, and others. Her essay on the Flint Water Crisis, "Blood and Water," was honored as a notable essay in *Best American Essays 2017*, and she was the winner of *New Ohio Review*'s 2018 Nonfiction Contest, judged by Roxane Gay.

Valerie Sayers is the author of six novels, including *The Powers and Brain Fever*, as well as scores of stories, essays, and reviews. Her literary honors include an NEA fellowship in fiction and two Pushcart Prizes for stories. She teaches at the University of Notre Dame.

Arlaina Tibensky is a Chicagoland native and the author of the young adult novel, *And Then Things Fall Apart*, a Junior Library Guild Selection, and an ALA/YALSA Reader's Choice nominee for realistic fiction. Other work can be found in *One Teen Story*, *One Story*, *Inkwell*, *McSweeney's Internet Tendency*, *Madison Review*, and once on *The Dinner Party Download* on NPR. She's taught workshops throughout New York City, has an MFA from Columbia University, and has been recognized by the Sustainable Arts Foundation, the New York Foundation for the Arts, and The Northern Manhattan Arts Alliance.

Cady Vishniac earned her MFA from Ohio State and is now an Endelman/Gitelman Fellow at the University of Michigan. Her work has appeared in several magazines, including *New England Review* and *Glimmer Train*. The story in this collection appeared first as the winner of the 2017 Fiction Prize at *Salamander* and was also the recipient of the 2018 Editor's Reprint Award at *Sequestrum*.

Rachel Yoder is a founding editor of *draft: the journal of process*, which publishes first and final drafts of stories, essays, and poems along with author interviews about the creative process. She also is the creator and host of The Fail Safe, an interview podcast that focuses on writing, failure, and process. In 2017, she was selected as one of five Iowa Arts Fellows for her work in publishing, arts programming, and writing. Her stories and essays have been published in *New York Times*, *Chicago Tribune*, *Paris Review Daily*, and *The Rumpus* among many other online and print publications, and her writing has been awarded with The Missouri Review Editors' Prize in Fiction. She works as a literary programmer for the Mission Creek Festival and Witching Hour Festival in Iowa City, where she lives with her husband and son.